THE
PASSIONATE
FRIENDS

A NOVEL

BY

H. G. WELLS

AUTHOR OF
"ANN VERONICA" ETC.

"There are at least two sorts of women"
—OTTO LIMBURGER

ILLUSTRATED

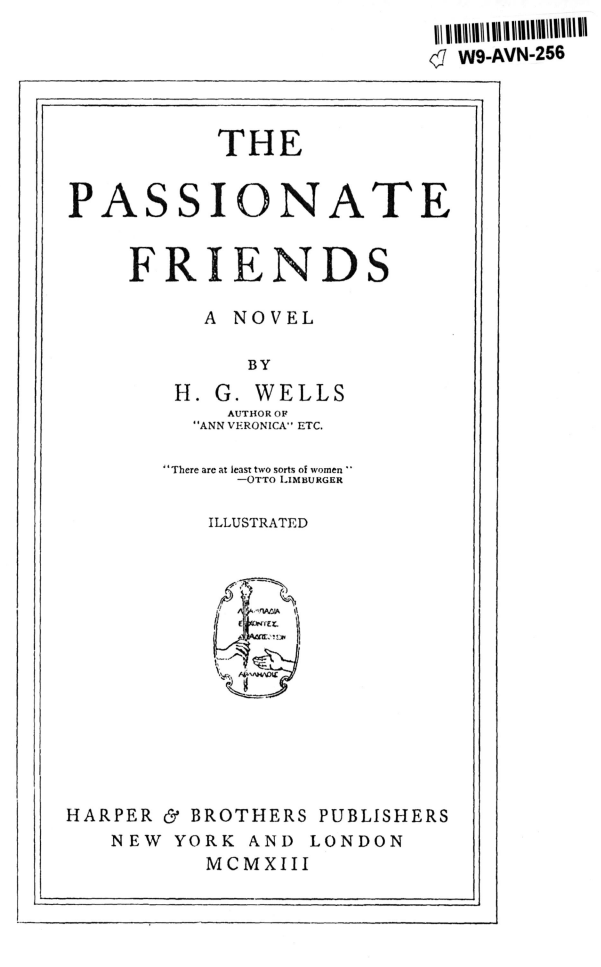

HARPER & BROTHERS PUBLISHERS
NEW YORK AND LONDON
MCMXIII

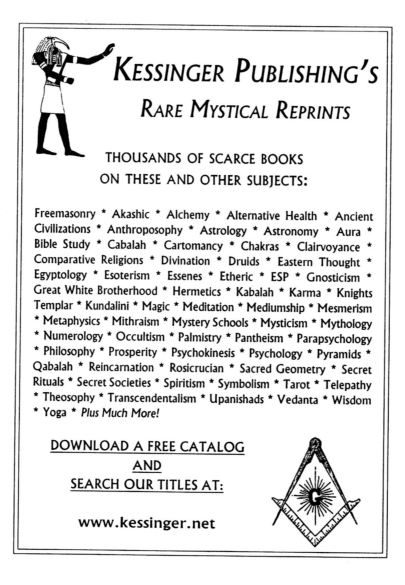

H-N

[See p. 435

"SOME MOMENTS ARE ETERNAL"

TO

L. E. N. S.

CONTENTS

THE PASSIONATE FRIENDS

THE PASSIONATE FRIENDS

CHAPTER THE FIRST

MR. STRATTON TO HIS SON

§ 1

I WANT very much to set down my thoughts and my experiences of life. I want to do so now that I have come to middle age and now that my attitudes are all defined and my personal drama worked out I feel that the toil of writing and reconsideration may help to clear and fix many things that remain a little uncertain in my thoughts because they have never been fully stated, and I want to discover any lurking inconsistencies and unsuspected gaps. And I have a story. I have lived through things that have searched me. I want to tell that story as well as I can while I am still a clear-headed and active man, and while many details that may presently become blurred and altered are still rawly fresh in my mind. And to one person in particular do I wish to think I am writing, and that is to you, my only son. I want to write my story not indeed to the child you are now, but to the man you are going to be. You are half my blood and temperamentally altogether mine. A day will come when you will realize this, and want to know how life has gone with me, and then it may be altogether too late for me to answer your enquiries. I may have become inaccessible as old people are sometimes inaccessible. And so I think of leaving this book for you— at any rate, I shall write it as if I meant to leave it for you. Afterwards I can consider whether I will indeed leave it. . . .

The idea of writing such a book as this came to me first as I sat by the dead body of your grandfather— my father. It was because I wanted so greatly such a book from him that I am now writing this. He died, you must know, only a few months ago, and I went to his house to bury him and settle all his affairs.

At one time he had been my greatest friend. He had never indeed talked to me about himself or his youth, but he had always showed an extraordinary sympathy and helpfulness for me in all the confusion and perplexities into which I fell. This did not last to the end of his life. I was the child of his middle years, and suddenly, in a year or less, the curtains of age and infirmity fell between us. There came an illness, an operation, and he rose from it ailing, suffering, dwarfed and altogether changed. Of all the dark shadows upon life I think that change through illness and organic decay in the thoughts and spirits of those who are dear and close to us is the most evil and distressing and inexplicable. Suddenly he was a changeling, a being querulous and pitiful, needing indulgence and sacrifices.

In a little while a new state of affairs was established. I ceased to consider him as a man to whom one told things, of whom one could expect help or advice. We all ceased to consider him at all in that way. We humored him, put pleasant things before him, concealed whatever was disagreeable. A poor old man he was indeed in those concluding years, weakly rebellious against the firm kindliness of my cousin, his housekeeper and nurse. He who had once been so alert was now at times astonishingly apathetic. At times an impish malice I had never known in him before gleamed in little acts and speeches. His talk rambled, and for the most part was concerned with small, long-forgotten contentions. It was indistinct and difficult to follow because of a recent loss of teeth, and he craved for brandy, to restore even for a moment the sense of strength and well-being that ebbed and ebbed away from him. So that when I came to look at his dead face at last, it was with something like amazement I perceived him grave and beautiful—more grave and beautiful than he had been even in the fullness of life.

All the estrangement of the final years was wiped in an instant from my mind as I looked upon his face. There came back a rush of memories, of kind, strong, patient, human aspects of his fatherhood. And I remembered as every son must remember—even you, my dear, will some day remember because it is in the very nature of sonship—insubordinations, struggles, ingratitudes, great benefits taken unthankfully, slights and disregards. It was not remorse I felt, nor repentance, but a tremendous regret that so things had happened and that life should be so. Why is it, I thought, that when a son has come to manhood he cannot take his father for a friend? I had a curious sense of unprece-

3

dented communion as I stood beside him now. I felt that he understood my thoughts; his face seemed to answer with an expression of still and sympathetic patience.

I was sensible of amazing gaps. We had never talked together of love, never of religion.

All sorts of things that a man of twenty-eight would not dream of hiding from a coeval he had hidden from me. For some days I had to remain in his house, I had to go through his papers, handle all those intimate personal things that accumulate around a human being year by year—letters, yellowing scraps of newspaper, tokens, relics kept, accidental vestiges, significant litter. I learnt many things I had never dreamt of. At times I doubted whether I was not prying, whether I ought not to risk the loss of those necessary legal facts I sought, and burn these papers unread. There were love letters, and many such touching things.

My memories of him did not change because of these new lights, but they became wonderfully illuminated. I realized him as a young man, I began to see him as a boy. I found a little half-bound botanical book with stencil-tinted illustrations, a good-conduct prize my father had won at his preparatory school; a rolled-up sheet of paper, carbonized and dry and brittle, revealed itself as a piece of specimen writing, stiff with boyish effort, decorated in ambitious and faltering flourishes and still betraying the pencil rulings his rubber should have erased. Already your writing is better than that. And I found a daguerreotype portrait of him in knickerbockers against a photographer's stile. His face then was not unlike yours. I stood with that in my hand at the little bureau in his bedroom, and looked at his dead face.

MR. STRATTON TO HIS SON

The flatly painted portrait of his father, my grand-father, hanging there in the stillness above the coffin, looking out on the world he had left with steady, humorous blue eyes that followed one about the room,—that, too, was revivified, touched into reality and participation by this and that, became a living presence at a conference of lives. Things of his were there also in that life's accumulation. . . .

There we were, three Strattons together, and down in the dining-room were steel engravings to take us back two generations further, and we had all lived full lives, suffered, attempted, signified. I had a glimpse of the long successions of mankind. What a huge inaccessible lumber-room of thought and experience we amounted to, I thought; how much we are, how little we transmit. Each one of us was but a variation, an experiment upon the Stratton theme. All that I had now under my hands was but the merest hints and vestiges, moving and surprising indeed, but casual and fragmentary, of those obliterated repetitions. Man is a creature becoming articulate, and why should those men have left so much of the tale untold—to be lost and forgotten? Why must we all repeat things done, and come again very bitterly to wisdom our fathers have achieved before us? My grandfather there should have left me something better than the still enigma of his watching face. All my life so far has gone in learning very painfully what many men have learnt before me; I have spent the greater part of forty years in finding a sort of purpose for the uncertain and declining decades that remain. Is it not time the generations drew together and helped one another? Cannot we begin now to make a better use of the experiences of life so that our sons may not waste themselves so much, cannot we gather into books that men may read in an hour or so the gist of these confused and multitudinous realities of the individual career? Surely the time is coming for that, when a new private literature will exist, and fathers and mothers behind their rôles of rulers, protectors, and supporters, will prepare frank and intimate records of their thought and their feeling, told as one tells things to equals, without authority or reserves or discretions, so that, they being dead, their children may rediscover them as contemporaries and friends.

That desire for self-expression is indeed already almost an instinct with many of us. Man is disposed to create a traditional wisdom. For me this book I contemplate is a need. I am just a year and a half from a bitter tragedy and the loss of a friend as dear as life to me. It is very constantly in my mind. She opened her mind to me as few people open their minds to anyone. In a way, little Stephen, she died for you. And I am so placed that I have no one to talk to quite freely about her. The one other person to whom I talk, I cannot talk to about her; it is strange, seeing how we love and trust one another, but so it is; you will understand that the better as this story unfolds. For eight long years before the crisis that culminated in her tragic death I never saw her; yet, quite apart from the shock and distresses of that time, it has left me extraordinarily lonely and desolate.

And there was a kind of dreadful splendor in that last act of hers, which has taken a great hold upon my imagination; it has interwoven with everything else in my mind, it bears now upon every question. I cannot get away from it, while it is thus pent from utterance. . . . Perhaps having written this to you I may never show it you or leave it for you to see. But yet I must write it. Of all conceivable persons you, when you have grown to manhood, are the most likely to understand.

§ 2

You did not come to see your dead grandfather, nor did you know very much about the funeral. Nowadays we do not bring the sweet egotisms, the vivid beautiful personal intensities of childhood, into the cold, vast presence of death. I would as soon, my dear, have sent your busy little limbs toiling up the Matterhorn. I have put by a photograph of my father for you as he lay in that last stillness of his, that you will see at a properer time.

Your mother and I wore black only at his funeral and came back colored again into your colored world, and in a very little while your interest in this event that had taken us away for a time turned to other, more assimilable things. But there happened a little incident that laid hold upon me; you forgot it, perhaps, in a week or less, but I shall never forget it; and this incident it was that gathered up the fruits of those moments beside my father's body and set me to write this book. It had the effect of a little bright light held up against the vague dark immensities of thought and feeling that filled my mind because of my father's death.

Now that I come to set it down I see that it is altogether trivial, and I cannot explain how it is that it is to me so piercingly significant. I had to whip you. Your respect for the admirable and patient Mademoiselle Potin, the protectress and companion of your public expeditions, did in some slight crisis suddenly fail you. In the extreme publicity of Kensington Gardens, in the presence of your two little sisters, before a startled world, you expressed an opinion of her, in two languages and a loud voice, that was not only very unjust, but extremely offensive and improper. It reflected upon her intelligence and goodness; it impeached her personal appearance; it was the kind of outcry no little gentleman should ever permit himself, however deeply he may be aggrieved. You then, so far as I was able to disentangle the evidence, assaulted her violently, hurled a stone at her, and fled her company. You came home alone by a route chosen by yourself, flushed and wrathful, braving the dangers of Kensington High Street. This, after my stern and deliberate edict that, upon pain of corporal punishment, respect and obedience must be paid to Mademoiselle Potin. The logic of the position was relentless.

But where your behavior was remarkable, where the affair begins to touch my imagination, was that you yourself presently put the whole business before me. Alone in the schoolroom, you seem to have come to some realization of the extraordinary dreadfulness of your behavior. Such moments happen in the lives of all small boys; they happened to me times enough, to my dead father, to that grandfather of the portrait which is now in my study, to his father and his, and so on through long series of Strattons, back to inarticulate, shock-haired little sinners slinking fearfully away from the awful wrath, the bellowings and limitless violence of the hairy Old Man of the herd. The bottom goes out of your

8

heart then, you are full of a conviction of sin. So far you did but carry on the experience of the race. But to ask audience of me, to come and look me in the eye, to say you wanted my advice on a pressing matter, that I think marks almost a new phase in the long developing history of father and son. And your account of the fracas struck me as quite reasonably frank and honest. "I didn't seem able," you observed, "not to go on being badder and badder."

We discussed the difficulties of our situation, and you passed sentence upon yourself. I saw to it that the outraged dignity of Mademoiselle Potin was mocked by no mere formality of infliction. You did your best to be stoical, I remember, but at last you yelped and wept. Then, justice being done, you rearranged your costume. The situation was a little difficult until you, still sobbing and buttoning—you are really a shocking bad hand at buttons—and looking a very small, tender, ruffled, rueful thing indeed, strolled towards my study window. "The pear tree is out next door," you remarked, without a trace of animosity, and sobbing as one might hiccough.

I suppose there are moments in the lives of all grown men when they come near to weeping aloud. In some secret place within myself I must have been a wild river of tears. I answered, however, with the same admirable detachment from the smarting past that you had achieved, that my study window was particularly adapted to the appreciation of our neighbor's pear tree, because of its height from the ground. We fell into a conversation about blossom and the setting of fruit, kneeling together upon my window-seat and looking up into the pear tree against the sky, and then down through its black branches into the gardens all quickening with spring. We were on so friendly a footing when presently Mademoiselle Potin returned and placed her dignity or her resignation in my hands, that I doubt if she believed a word of all my assurances until the unmistakable confirmation of your evening bath. Then, as I understood it, she was extremely remorseful to you and indignant against my violence. . . .

But when I knelt with you, little urchin, upon my window-seat, it came to me as a thing almost intolerably desirable that some day you should become my real and understanding friend. I loved you profoundly. I wanted to stretch forward into time and speak to you, man myself to the man you are yet to be. It seemed to me that between us there must needs be peculiar subtleties of sympathy. And I remembered that by the time you were a man fully grown and emerging from the passionately tumultuous openings of manhood, capable of forgiving me all my blundering parentage, capable of perceiving all the justifying fine intention of my ill-conceived disciplines and misdirections, I might be either an old man, shriveling again to an inexplicable egotism, or dead. I saw myself as I had seen my father—first enfeebled and then inaccessibly tranquil. When presently you had gone from my study, I went to my writing-desk and drew a paper pad towards me, and sat thinking and making idle marks upon it with my pen. I wanted to exceed the limits of those frozen silences that must come at last between us, write a book that should lie in your world like a seed, and at last, as your own being ripened, flower into living understanding by your side.

This book, which before had been only an idea for a book, competing against many other ideas and the demands of that toilsome work for peace and understanding to which I have devoted the daily energies of my life, had become, I felt, an imperative necessity between us.

§ 3

And then there happened one of those crises of dread and apprehension and pain that are like a ploughing of the heart. It was brought home to me that you might die even before the first pages of this book of yours were written. You became feverish, complained of that queer pain you had felt twice before, and for the third time you were ill with appendicitis. Your mother and I came and regarded your touzled head and flushed little face on the pillow as you slept uneasily, and decided that we must take no more risks with you. So soon as your temperature had fallen again we set about the business of an operation.

We told each other that nowadays these operations were as safe as going to sleep in your bed, but we knew better. Our own doctor had lost his son. "That," we said, "was different." But we knew well enough in our hearts that you were going very near to the edge of death, nearer than you had ever been since first you came clucking into the world.

The operation was done at home. A capable, fair-complexioned nurse took possession of us; and my study, because it has the best light, was transfigured into an admirable operating-room. All its furnishings were sent away, every cloth and curtain, and the walls and floor were covered with white sterilized sheets. The high little mechanical table they erected before the window seemed to me like an altar on which I had to offer up my son. There were basins of disinfectants and towels conveniently about, the operator came, took out his array of scalpels and forceps and little sponges from the black bag he carried, put them ready for his hand, and then covered them from your sight with a white cloth, and I brought you down in my arms, wrapped in a blanket, from your bedroom to the anæsthetist. You were beautifully trustful and submissive and unafraid. I stood by you until the chloroform had done its work, and then left you there, lest my presence should in the slightest degree embarrass the surgeon. The anæsthetic had taken all the color out of your face, and you looked pinched and shrunken and greenish and very small and pitiful. I went into the drawing-room and stood there with your mother and made conversation. I cannot recall what we said, I think it was about the moorland to which we were going for your convalescence. Indeed, we were but the ghosts of ourselves; all our substance seemed listening, listening to the little sounds that came to us from the study.

Then after long ages there was a going to and fro of feet, a bump, the opening of a door, and our own doctor came into the room rubbing his hands together and doing nothing to conceal his profound relief. "Admirable," he said, "altogether successful." I went up to you and saw a tumbled little person in the bed, still heavily insensible and moaning slightly. By the table were bloody towels, and in a shallow glass tray was a small object like a damaged piece of earthworm. "Not a bit too soon," said the surgeon, holding this up in his forceps for my inspection. "It's on the very verge of perforation." I affected a detached and scientific interest, but the prevailing impression in my mind was that this was a fragment from very nearly the centre of your being.

He took it away with him, I know not whither. Perhaps it is now in spirits in a specimen jar, an example to all medical students of what to avoid in an appendix; perhaps it was stained and frozen, and microtomized into transparent sections as they do such things, and mounted on glass slips and distributed about the world for curious histologists to wreak their eyes upon. For a time you lay uneasily still and then woke up to pain. Even then you got a fresh purchase on my heart. It has always been our custom to discourage weeping and outcries, and you did not forget your training. "I shan't mind so much, dadda," you remarked to me, "if I may yelp." So for a day, by special concession, you yelped, and then the sting of those fresh wounds departed.

Within a fortnight, so quickly does an aseptic wound heal up again, you were running about in the sun, and I had come back, as one comes back to a thing forgotten, to the first beginnings of this chapter on my desk. But for a time I could not go on working at it because of the fear I had felt, and it is only now in June, in this house in France to which we have come for the summer, with you more flagrantly healthy than I have ever known you before, that my heart creeps out of its hole again, and I can go on with my story.

2

CHAPTER THE SECOND

BOYHOOD

§ 1

I WAS a Harbury boy as my father and grandfather were before me and as you are presently to be. I went to Harbury at the age of fourteen. Until then I was educated at home, first by a governess and then by my father's curate, Mr. Siddons, who went from us to St. Philip's in Hampstead, and, succeeding marvellously there, is now Bishop of Exminster. My father became rector of Burnmore when I was nine; my mother had been dead four years, and my second cousin, Jane Stratton, was already his housekeeper. My father held the living until his resignation when I was nearly thirty. So that all the most impressionable years of my life centre upon the Burnmore rectory and the easy spaciousness of Burnmore Park. My boyhood and adolescence alternated between the ivied red-brick and ancient traditions of Harbury (and afterwards Christ-church) and that still untroubled countryside.

I was never a town dweller until I married and we took our present house in Holland Park. I went into London at last as one goes into an arena. It cramps me and wearies me and at times nearly overwhelms me, but there it is that the life of men centres and my work lies. But every summer we do as we have done this year and go to some house in the country, near to forests or moorland or suchlike open and uncultivated country, where one may have the refreshment of freedom among natural and unhurried things. This year we are in a walled garden upon the Seine, about four miles above Château Galliard, and with the forest reaching up to the paddock beyond the orchard close. . . .

You will understand better when I have told you my story why I saw Burnmore for the last time when I was one-and-twenty and why my memories of it shine so crystalline clear. I have a thousand vivid miniatures of it in my mind and all of them are beautiful to me, so that I could quite easily write a whole book of landscapes from the Park alone. I can still recall quite vividly the warm beauty-soaked sensation of going out into the morning sunshine of the Park, with my lunch in a little green Swiss tin under my arm and the vast interminable day all before me, the gigantic, divinely unconditional day that only boyhood knows, and the Park so great and various that it was more than two hours' going for me to reach its eastern fences. I was only a little older then than you are now. Sometimes I went right up through the woods to the house to companion with Philip and Guy Christian and their sister—I loved her then, and one day I was to love her with all my heart—but in those boyish times I liked most to go alone.

My memories of the Park are all under blue sky and sunshine, with just a thunderstorm or so; on wet days and cold days I was kept to closer limits; and it seems to me now rather an intellectual conviction than a positive memory that save for a few pine-clad patches in the extreme south-east, its soil was all thick clay. That meant for me only beautiful green marshes, a number of vividly interesting meres upon the course of its stream, and a wealth of gigantic oaks. The meres lay at various levels, and the hand of Lady Ladislaw had assisted nature in their enrichment with lilies and water plants. There were places of sedge and scented rush, amidst which were sapphire mists of forget-me-not for long stretches, skirmishing commandoes of yellow iris and wide wastes of floating water-lilies. The gardens passed insensibly into the Park, and beyond the house were broad stretches of grass, sun-lit, barred with the deep-green shadows of great trees, and animated with groups and lines of fallow deer. Near the house was an Italianate garden, with balustradings and statuary, and a great wealth of roses and flowering shrubs.

Then there were bracken wildernesses in which the does lurked with the young fawns, and a hollow, shallow and wide, with the turf greatly attacked by rabbits, and exceptionally threadbare, where a stricken oak, lightning-stripped, spread out its ghastly arms above contorted rotting branches and the mysterious skeletons of I should think five several deer. In the evening-time the woods behind this place of bones—they were woods of straight-growing, rather crowded trees and standing as it were a little aloof—became even under the warmest sunset grey and cold—and as if they waited. . . .

And in the distant corner where the sand was, rose suddenly a steep little hill, surmounted by a wild and splendid group of pines, through which one looked across a vale of cornfields at an ancient town that became strange and magical as the sun went down, so that I was held gazing at it, and afterwards had to flee the twilight across the windy spaces and under the dim and darkling trees. It is only now in the distant retrospect that I identify that far-off city of wonder, and luminous mist with the commonplace little town, through whose narrow streets we drove to the railway station. But, of course, that is what it must have been.

There are persons to be found mixed up in those childish memories,—Lady Ladislaw, tall and gracious, in dresses of floating blue or grey, or thin, subtly folding, flowering stuffs, Philip and his sister, Guy, the old butler, a multitude of fainter figures long become nameless and featureless; they are far less vivid in my memory than the fine solitudes of the Park itself—and the dreams I had there.

I wonder if you dream as I dreamt. I wonder whether indeed I dreamt as now I think I did. Have I, in these latter years, given form and substance and a name to things as vague in themselves as the urgencies of instinct? Did I really go into those woods and waving green places as one keeps a tryst, expectant of a fellowship more free and delicate and delightful than any I knew. Did I know in those days of nymphs and dryads and fauns and all those happy soulless beings with which the desire of man's heart has animated the wilderness. Once certainly I crawled slowly through the tall bracken and at last lay still for an interminable while, convinced that so I should see those shadows populous with fairies, with green little people. How patiently I lay! But the stems creaked and stirred, and my heart would keep on beating like a drum in my throat.

It is incredible that once a furry whispering half-human

creature with bright brown eyes came and for a time played with me near where the tall ferns foam in a broad torrent from between the big chestnuts down to the upper mere. That must have been real dreaming, and yet now, with all my sanities and scepticisms, I could half believe it real.

§ 2

You become reserved. Perhaps not exceptionally so, but as all children become reserved. Already you understand that your heart is very preciously your own. You keep it from me and everyone, so much so, so justifiably so, that when by virtue of our kindred and all that we have in common I get sudden glimpses right into your depths, there mixes with the swift spasm of love I feel, a dread—lest you should catch me, as it were, spying into you and that one of us, I know not which, should feel ashamed.

Every child passes into this secret stage; it closes in from its first frankness; it carries off the growing jewel of its consciousness to hide from all mankind. . . . I think I can see why this should be so, but I cannot tell why in so many cases no jewel is given back again at last, alight, ripened, wonderful, glowing with the deep fires of experience. I think that is what ought to happen; it is what does happen now with true poets and true artists. Someday I think it will be the life of all normal human souls. But usually it does not seem to happen at all. Children pass out of a stage—open, beautiful, exquisitely simple—into silences and discretions beneath an imposed and artificial life. And they are lost. Out of the finished, careful, watchful, restrained and limited man or woman, no child emerges again. . . .

I remember very distinctly how I myself came by imperceptible increments of reservation to withdraw those early delicacies of judgments, those original and personal standards and appreciations, from sight and expression. I can recall specific moments when I perceive now that my little childish figure stood, as it were, obstinately and with a sense of novelty in a doorway denying the self within.

It was partly, I think, a simple instinct that drew that curtain of silences and concealments, it was much more a realization that I had no power of lucidity to save the words and deeds I sought to make expressive from complete misunderstanding. But most of all it was the perception that I was under training and compulsion for ends that were all askew and irrelevant to the trend of my imaginations, the quality of my dreams. There was around me something unfriendly to this inner world—something very ready to pass from unfriendliness to acute hostility; and if, indeed, I succeeded in giving anything of my inner self to others, it was only, as people put it, to give myself away.

My nurses, my governess, my tutor, my father, the servants about me, seemed all bent upon imposing an artificial personality upon me. Only in a very limited sense did they want me. What they wanted was something that could be made out of me by extensive suppressions and additions. They ignored the fact that I had been born with a shape of my own; they were resolved I should be pressed into a mould and cast.

It was not that they wanted outer conformity to certain needs and standards—that, I think, would be a reasonable thing enough to demand—but they wanted me to subdue my most private thoughts to their ideals. My nurses and my governesses would rate me for my very feelings, would clamor for gratitude and reproach me bitterly for betraying that I did not at some particular moment—love.

(Only yesterday I heard Mademoiselle Potin doing that very same thing to you. "It is that you do not care, Master Steve. It is that you do not care. You do not want to care.")

They went too far in that invasion of my personal life, but I perceive quite clearly the present need for most of the process of moulding and subjugation that children must undergo. Human society is a new thing upon the earth, an invention of the last ten thousand years. Man is a creature as yet not freely and instinctively gregarious; in his more primordial state he must have been an animal of very small groups and limited associations, an animal rather self-centred and fierce, and he is still but imperfectly adapted either morally or physically to the wider social life his crowding interactions force upon him. He still learns speech and computation and civility and all the devices of this artificially extended and continually broadening tribal life with an extreme reluctance. He has to be shaped in the interests of the species, I admit, to the newer conditions; the growing social order must be protected from the keen edge of his still savage individuality, and he must be trained in his own interests to save himself from the destruction of impossible revolts. But how clumsily is the thing done! How we are caught and jammed and pressed and crippled into citizenship! How excessive and crushing is the suppression, and how inadequate!

Every child feels that, even if every child does not clearly know it. Every child presently begins to hide itself from the confused tyrannies of the social process, from the searching inspections and injunctions and interferences of parent and priest and teacher.

"I have got to be *so*," we all say deep down in ourselves and more or less distinctly according to the lucidities of our minds; "but in my heart I am *this*."

And in the outcome we all try to seem at least to be *so*, while an ineffectual rebel struggles passionately, like a beast caught in a trap, for ends altogether more deep and dangerous, for the rose and the star and the wildfire,—for beauty and beautiful things. These, we all know in our darkly vital recesses, are the real needs of life, the obediences imposed upon us by our crude necessities and jostling proximities, mere incidentals on our way to those profounder purposes. . . .

And when I write thus of our selves I mean our bodies quite as much as our imaginations; the two sides of us are covered up alike and put alike into disguises and unnatural shapes, we are taught and forced to hide them for the same reasons, from a fear of ourselves and a fear of the people about us. The sense of beauty, the sense of one's body, the freedom of thought and of desire and the wonder of life, are all interwoven strands. I remember that in the Park of Burnmore one great craving I had was to take off my clothes there altogether, and bathe in a clear place among loosestrife and meadowsweet, and afterwards lie wet and naked upon the soft green turf with the sun shining upon me. But I thought also that that was a very wicked and shameful craving to have, and I never dared give way to it.

§ 3

As I think of myself and all these glowing secrecies and hidden fancies within, walking along beside old Siddons, and half listening to his instructive discourse, I see myself as though I was an image of all humanity under tuition for the social life.

I write "old Siddons," for so he seemed to me then. In truth he was scarcely a dozen years older than I, and the other day when I exchanged salutations with his gaitered presence in the Haymarket, on his way I suppose to the Athenæum, it struck me that he it is who is now the younger man. But at Burnmore he was eighteen inches or more above my head and all the way of school and university beyond me; full of the world they had fitted him for and eager to impart its doctrines. He went along in his tweeds that were studiously untidy, a Norfolk jacket of one clerically-greyish stuff and trousers of another somewhat lighter pattern, in thick boots, the collar of his calling, and a broad-minded hat, bearing his face heavenward as he talked, and not so much aware of me as appreciating the things he was saying. And sometimes he was manifestly talking to himself and airing his outlook. He carried a walking-stick, a manly, homely, knobby, donnish walking-stick.

He forced the pace a little, for his legs were long and he had acquired the habit of strenuous pedestrianism at Oxford with all the other things; he obliged me to go at a kind of skipping trot, and he preferred the high roads towards Wickenham for our walks, because they were flatter and there was little traffic upon them in those days before the motor car, and we could keep abreast and go on talking uninterruptedly. That is to say, he could.

What talk it was!

Of all the virtues that the young should have. He spoke of courage and how splendid it was to accustom oneself not even to feel fear; of truth, and difficult cases when one might conceivably injure others by telling the truth and so perhaps, perhaps qualify the rigor of one's integrity, but how one should never hesitate to injure one's own self in that matter. Then in another phase he talked of belief—and the disagreeableness of dissenters. But here, I remember, there was a discussion. I have forgotten how I put the thing, but in some boyish phrasing or other I must have thrown out the idea that thought is free and beliefs uncontrollable. What of conformity, if the truth was that you doubted? "Not if you make an effort," I remember him saying, "not if you make an effort. I have had my struggles. But if you say firmly to yourself, the Church teaches this. If you dismiss mere carping and say that."

"But suppose you can't," I must have urged.

"You can if you will," he said with a note near enthusiasm. "I have been through all that. I did it. I dismissed doubts. I wouldn't listen. I felt, *This won't do. All this leads nowhere.*"

And he it was told me the classic story of that presumptuous schoolboy who went to his Head Master and declared himself an atheist. There were no dialectics but a prompt horse-whipping. "In after life," said Mr. Siddons, with unctuous gratification, "he came to recognize that thrashing as the very best thing that had ever happened to him. The kindest thing."

"Yes," urged the obstinate rebel within me, "but —the Truth, that fearless insistence on the Truth!"

I could, however, find nothing effective to say aloud, and Siddons prevailed over me. That story made my blood boil, it filled me with an anticipatory hatred of and hostility to Head Masters, and at the same time there was something in it, brutally truer to the conditions of human association than any argument.

I do not remember the various steps by which I came to be discussing doubts so early in my life. I could not have been much more than thirteen when that conversation occurred. I am I think perhaps exceptionally unconscious about myself. I find I can recall the sayings and even the gestures of other people far more distinctly than the things I said and did myself. Even my dreams and imaginings are more active than my positive thoughts and proceedings. But I was no doubt very much stimulated by the literature lying about my home and the gleans and echoes of controversies that played like summer lightning round and about the horizons of my world. Over my head and after I had gone to bed, my father and Siddons were talking, my cousin was listening with strained apprehensions, there was a new spirit in my father's sermons; it was the storm of Huxley-Darwin controversies that had at last reached Burnmore. I was an intelligent little listener, an eager reader of anything that came to hand, Mr. Siddons had a disposition to fight his battles over again in his monologues to me; and after all at thirteen one isn't a baby. The small boy of the lower classes used in those days to start life for himself long before then.

BOYHOOD

How dramatic a phase it was in the history of the human mind when science suddenly came into the vicarages, into all the studies and quiet places that had been the fastnesses of conviction and our ideals, and denied, with all the power of evidence it had been accumulating for so long, and so obscurely and inaggressively, with fossils and strata, with embryology and comparative anatomy, the doctrine of the historical Fall and all the current scheme of orthodoxy that was based on that! What a quickening shock it must have been in countless thousands of educated lives! And my father after a toughly honest resistance was won over to Darwinism, the idea of Evolution got hold of him, the idea that life itself was intolerant of vain repetitions; and he had had to "consider his position" in the church. To him as to innumerable other honest, middle-aged and comfortable men, Darwinism came as a dreadful invitation to go out into the wilderness. Over my head and just out of range of my ears he was debating that issue with Siddons as a foil and my cousin as a horrified antagonist. Slowly he was developing his conception of compromise. And meanwhile he wasn't going out into the wilderness at all, but punctually to and fro, along the edge of the lawn by the bed of hollyhocks and through the little green door in the garden wall, and across the corner of the churchyard to the vestry and the perennial services and sacraments of the church.

But he never talked to me privately of religion. He left that for my cousin and Mr. Siddons to do or not to do as they felt disposed, and in those silences of his I may have found another confirmation of my growing feeling that religion was from one point of view a thing

25

somehow remote and unreal, claiming unjustifiable interventions in the detailed conduct of my life, and from another a peculiar concern of my father's and Mr. Siddons', to which they went—through the vestry, changing into strange garments on the way.

§ 4

I do not want to leave the impression which my last section may have conveyed that at the age of thirteen or thereabouts I walked about with Mr. Siddons discussing doubt in a candid and intelligent manner and maintaining theological positions. That particular conversation, you must imagine with Mr. Siddons somewhat monologuing, addressing himself not only to my present self, but with an unaccustomed valiance to my absent father. What I may have said or not said, whether I did indeed dispute or merely and by a kind of accident implied objections, I have altogether forgotten long ago.

A boy far more than a man is mentally a discontinuous being. The drifting chaos of his mind makes its experimental beginnings at a hundred different points and in a hundred different spirits and directions; here he flashes into a concrete realization, here into a conviction unconsciously incompatible; here is something originally conceived, here something uncritically accepted. I know that I criticized Mr. Siddons quite acutely, and disbelieved in him. I know also that I accepted all sorts of suggestions from him quite unhesitatingly and that I did my utmost to satisfy his standards and realize his ideals of me.

BOYHOOD

Like an outer casing to that primordial creature of senses and dreams which came to the surface in the solitudes of the Park was my Siddonsesque self, a high-minded and clean and brave English boy, conscientiously loyal to queen and country, athletic and a good sportsman and acutely alive to good and bad "form." Mr. Siddons made me aware of my clothed self as a visible object, I surveyed my garmented being in mirrors and was trained to feel the "awfulness" of various other small boys who appeared transitorily in the smaller Park when Lady Ladislaw extended her wide hospitality to certain benevolent London associations. Their ill-fitting clothing, their undisciplined outcries, their slouching, their bad throwing and defective aspirates were made matters for detestation in my plastic mind. Those things, I was assured, placed them outside the pale of any common humanity.

"Very unfortunate and all that," said Mr. Siddons, "and uncommonly good of Lady Ladislaw to have them down. But dirty little cads, Stephen, dirty little cads; so don't go near 'em if you can help it."

They played an indecent sort of cricket with coats instead of a wicket!

Mr. Siddons was very grave about games and the strict ritual and proper apparatus for games. He believed that Waterloo was won by the indirect influence of public school cricket—disregarding many other contributory factors. We did not play very much, but we "practised" sedulously at a net in the paddock with the gardener and the doctor's almost grown-up sons. I thought missing a possible catch was an impropriety. I studiously maintained the correct attitude, alert and

27

elastic, while I was fielding. Moreover I had a shameful secret, that I did not really know where a ball ought to pitch. I wasn't clear about it and I did not dare to ask. Also until I was nearly thirteen I couldn't bowl overarm. Such is the enduring force of early suggestion, my dear son, that I feel a faint twinge of shame as I set this down for your humiliated eyes. But so it was. May you be more precocious!

Then I was induced to believe that I really liked hunting and killing things. In the depths of my being I was a gentle and primitive savage towards animals; I believed they were as subtle and wise as myself and full of a magic of their own, but Mr. Siddons nevertheless got me out into the south Warren, where I had often watched the rabbits setting their silly cock-eared sentinels and lolloping out to feed about sundown, and beguiled me into shooting a furry little fellow-creature—I can still see its eyelid quiver as it died—and carrying it home in triumph. On another occasion I remember I was worked up into a ferocious excitement about the rats in the old barn. We went ratting, just as though I was Tom Brown or Harry East or any other of the beastly little models of cant and cruelty we English boys were trained to imitate. It was great sport. It was a tremendous spree. The distracted movements, the scampering and pawing of the little pink forefeet of one squawking little fugitive, that I hit with a stick and then beat to a shapeless bag of fur, haunted my dreams for years, and then I saw the bowels of another still living victim that had been torn open by one of the terriers, and abruptly I fled out into the yard and was violently sick; the best of the fun was over so far as I was concerned.

My cousin saved me from the uttermost shame of my failure by saying that I had been excited too soon after my dinner. . . .

And also I collected stamps and birds' eggs.

Mr. Siddons hypnotized me into believing that I really wanted these things; he gave me an egg-cabinet for a birthday present and told me exemplary stories of the wonderful collections other boys had made. My own natural disposition to watch nests and establish heaven knows what friendly intimacy with the birds—perhaps I dreamt their mother might let me help to feed the young ones—gave place to a feverish artful hunting, a clutch, and then, detestable process, the blowing of the egg. Of course we were very humane; we never took the nest, but just frightened off the sitting bird and grabbed a warm egg or so. And the poor perforated, rather damaged little egg-shells accumulated in the drawers, against the wished-for but never actually realized day of glory when we should meet another collector who wouldn't have—something that we had. So far as it was for anything and not mere imbecile imitativeness, it was for that.

And writing thus of eggs reminds me that I got into a row with Mr. Siddons for cruelty.

I discovered there was the nest of a little tit in a hole between two stones in the rock bank that bordered the lawn. I found it out when I was sitting on the garden seat near by, learning Latin irregular verbs. I saw the minute preposterous round birds going and coming, and I found something so absurdly amiable and confiding about them—they sat balancing and oscillating on a standard rose and cheeped at me to go and then dived nestward and gave away their secret out of sheer impatience—that I could not bring myself to explore further, and kept the matter altogether secret from the enthusiasm of Mr. Siddons. And in a few days there were no more eggs and I could hear the hungry little nestlings making the minutest of fairy hullabaloos, the very finest spun silk of sound; a tremendous traffic in victual began and I was the trusted friend of the family.

Then one morning I was filled with amazement and anguish. There was a rock torn down and lying in the path; a paw had gone up to that little warm place. Across the gravel, shreds of the nest and a wisp or so of down were scattered. I could imagine the brief horrors of that night attack. I started off, picking up stones as I went, to murder that sandy devil, the stable cat. I got her once —alas! that I am still glad to think of it—and just missed her as she flashed, a ginger streak, through the gate into the paddock.

"*Now* Steve! Now!" came Mr. Siddons' voice behind me. . . .

How can one explain things of that sort to a man like Siddons? I took my lecture on the Utter Caddishness of Wanton Cruelty in a black rebellious silence. The affair and my own emotions were not only far beyond my powers of explanation, but far beyond my power of understanding. Just then my soul was in shapeless and aimless revolt against something greater and higher and deeper and darker than Siddons, and his reproaches were no more than the chattering of a squirrel while a storm uproots great trees. I wanted to kill the cat. I wanted to kill whatever had made that cat.

BOYHOOD

§ 5

Mr. Siddons it was who first planted the conception of Life as a Career in my mind.

In those talks that did so much towards shaping me into the likeness of a modest, reserved, sporting, seemly, clean and brave, patriotic and decently slangy young Englishman, he was constantly reverting to that view of existence. He spoke of failures and successes, talked of statesmen and administrators, peerages and Westminster Abbey. "Nelson," he said, "was once a clergyman's son like you."

"England has been made by the sons of the clergy."

He talked of the things that led to failure and the things that had made men prominent and famous.

"Discursiveness ruins a man," I remember him saying. "Choose your goal and press to it."

"Never do anything needlessly odd. It's a sort of impertinence to all the endless leaders of the past who created our traditions. Do not commit yourself hastily to opinions, but once you have done so, stick to them. The world would far rather have a firm man wrong, than a weak man hesitatingly right. Stick to them."

"One has to remember," I recall him meditating, far over my head with his face upturned, "that Institutions are more important than Views. Very often one adopts a View only to express one's belief in an Institution. . . . Men can do with almost all sorts of Views, but only with certain Institutions. All this Doubt doesn't touch a truth like that. One does not refuse to live in a house because of the old symbols one finds upon the door. . . . If they *are* old symbols. . . ."

Out of such private contemplations he would descend suddenly upon me.

"What are *you* going to do with your life, Steve?" he would ask.

"There is no happiness in life without some form of service. Where do you mean to serve? With your bent for science and natural history, it wouldn't be difficult for you to get into the I.C.S. I doubt if you'd do anything at the law; it's a rough game, Steve, though the prizes are big. Big prizes the lawyers get. I've known a man in the Privy Council under forty—and that without anything much in the way of a family. . . . But always one must concentrate. The one thing England will not stand is a loafer, a wool-gatherer, a man who goes about musing and half-awake. It's our energy. We're western. It's that has made us all we are."

I knew whither that pointed. Never so far as I can remember did Mr. Siddons criticize either myself or my father directly, but I understood with the utmost clearness that he found my father indolent and hesitating, and myself more than a little bit of a mollycoddle, and in urgent need of pulling together.

§ 6

Harbury went on with that process of suppressing, encrusting, hardening, and bracing-up which Mr. Siddons had begun. For a time I pulled myself together very thoroughly. I am not ungrateful nor unfaithful to Harbury; in your turn you will go there, you will have to live your life in this British world of ours and you must learn its language and manners, acquire its reserves and develop the approved toughness and patterning of cuticle. Afterwards if you please you may quarrel with it. But don't when the time comes quarrel with the present conditions of human association and think it is only with Harbury you quarrel. What man has become and may become beneath the masks and impositions of civilization, in his intimate texture and in the depths of his being, I begin now in my middle age to appreciate. No longer is he an instinctive savage but a creature of almost incredible variability and wonderful new possibilities. Marvels undreamt of, power still inconceivable, an empire beyond the uttermost stars; such is man's inheritance. But for the present, until we get a mastery of those vague and mighty intimations at once so perplexing and so reassuring, if we are to live at all in the multitudinousness of human society we must submit to some scheme of clumsy compromises and conventions or other,—and for us Strattons the Harbury system is the most convenient. You will have to go to the old school.

I went to Rendle's. I just missed getting into college; I was two places below the lowest successful boy. I was Maxton's fag to begin with, and my chief chum was Raymond, who is your friend also, and who comes so often to this house. I preferred water to land, boats to cricket, because of that difficulty about pitch I have already mentioned. But I was no great sportsman. Raymond and I shared a boat, and spent most of the time we gave to it under the big trees near Dartpool Lock, reading or talking. We would pull up to Sandy Hall perhaps once a week. I never rowed in any of the eights, though I was urged to do so. I swam fairly well, and got my colors on the strength of my diving.

On the whole I found Harbury a satisfactory and amusing place, I was neither bullied nor do I think I greatly bullied, and of all that furtive and puerile lasciviousness of which one hears so many hints nowadays— excitable people talk of it as though it was the most monstrous and singular of vices instead of a slightly debasing but almost unavoidable and very obvious result of heaping boys together under the inefficient control of a timid pretentious class of men—of such uncleanness as I say, scarcely more than a glimpse and a whisper and a vague tentative talk or so reached me. Little more will reach you, for that kind of thing, like the hells of Swedenborg, finds its own.

I had already developed my growing instinct for observance to a very considerable extent under Siddons, and at Harbury I remember myself, and people remember me, as an almost stiffly correct youth. I was pretty good at most of the work, and exceptionally so at history, geology, and the biological side of natural science. I had to restrain my interest in these latter subjects lest I should appear to be a "swat," and a modern-side swat at that. I was early in the sixth, and rather a favorite with old Latimer. He incited me to exercise what he called a wholesome influence on the younger boys, and I succeeded in doing this fairly well without any gross interventions. I implied rather than professed soundly orthodox views about things in general, and I was extremely careful to tilt my straw hat forward over my nose so as just not to expose the crown of my head behind, and to turn up my trousers with exactly that width of margin which the judgment of my fellow-creatures had decided was correct. My socks were spirited without being vulgar, and the ties I wore were tied with a studious avoidance of either slovenliness or priggish neatness. I wrote two articles in the Harburonian, became something of a debater in the Literary and Political, conducted many long conversations with my senior contemporaries upon religion, politics, sport and social life, and concealed my inmost thoughts from every human being. Indeed, so effective had been the training of Harbury and Mr. Siddons, that I think at that time I came very near concealing them from myself. I could suppress wonder, I could pass by beauty as if I did not see it, almost I think I did not see it for a time, and yet I remember it in those years too—a hundred beautiful things.

Harbury itself is a very beautiful place. The country about it has all the charm of river scenery in a settled and ancient land, and the great castle and piled town of Wetmore, cliffs of battlemented grey wall rising above a dense cluster of red roofs, form the background to innumerable gracious prospects of great stream-fed trees, level meadows of buttercups, sweeping curves of osier and rush-rimmed river, the playing fields and the sedgy, lily-spangled levels of Avonlea. The college itself is mostly late Tudor and Stuart brickwork, very ripe and mellow now, but the great grey chapel with its glorious east window floats over the whole like a voice singing in the evening. And the evening cloudscapes of Harbury are a perpetual succession of glorious effects, now serene, now mysteriously threatening and profound, now towering to incredible heights, now revealing undreamt-of distances of luminous color. Assuredly I must have delighted in all those aspects, or why should I remember them so well? But I recall, I mean, no confessed recognition of them; no deliberate going-out of my spirit, open and unashamed, to such things.

I suppose one's early adolescence is necessarily the period of maximum shyness in one's life. Even to Raymond I attempted no extremities of confidence. Even to myself I tried to be the thing that was expected of me. I professed a modest desire for temperate and tolerable achievement in life, though deep in my lost depths I wanted passionately to excel; I worked hard, much harder than I allowed to appear, and I said I did it for the credit of the school; I affected a dignified loyalty to queen and country and church; I pretended a stoical disdain for appetites and delights and all the arts, though now and then a chance fragment of poetry would light me like a fire, or a lovely picture stir unwonted urgencies, though visions of delight haunted the shadows of my imagination and did not always fly when I regarded them. But on the other hand I affected an interest in games that I was far from feeling. Of some boys I was violently jealous, and this also I masked beneath a generous appreciation. Certain popularities I applauded while I doubted. Whatever my intimate motives I became less and less disposed to obey them until I had translated them into a plausible rendering of the accepted code. If I could not so translate them I found it wise to control them. When I wanted urgently one summer to wander by night over the hills towards Kestering and lie upon heather and look up at the stars and wonder about them, I cast about and at last hit upon the well-known and approved sport of treacling for moths, as a cloak for so strange an indulgence.

I must have known even then what a mask and front

I was, because I knew quite well how things were with other people. I listened politely and respected and understood the admirable explanations of my friends. When some fellow got a scholarship unexpectedly and declared it was rotten bad luck on the other chap, seeing the papers he had done, and doubted whether he shouldn't resign, I had an intuitive knowledge that he wouldn't resign, and I do not remember any time in my career as the respectful listener to Mr. Siddons' aspirations for service and devotion, when I did not perceive quite clearly his undeviating eye upon a bishopric. He thought of gaiters though he talked of wings.

How firmly the bonds of an old relationship can hold one! I remember when a few years ago he reached that toiled-for goal, I wrote in a tone of gratified surprise that in this blatant age, such disinterested effort as his should receive even so belated a recognition. Yet what else was there for me to write? We all have our Siddonses, with whom there are no alternatives but insincerity or a disproportionate destructiveness. I am still largely Siddonsized, little son, and so, I fear, you will have to be.

§ 7

The clue to all the perplexities of law and custom lies in this, that human association is an artificiality. We do not run together naturally and easily as grazing deer do or feeding starlings or a shoal of fish. We are a sort of creature which is only resuming association after a long heredity of extreme separation. We are beings strongly individualized, we are dominated by that passion which is no more and no less than individuality in action,—jealousy. Jealousy is a fierce insistence on ourselves, an instinctive intolerance of our fellow-creatures, ranging between an insatiable aggression as its buoyant phase and a savage defensiveness when it is touched by fear. In our expansive moments we want to dominate and control everyone and destroy every unlikeness to ourselves; in our recessive phases our homes are our castles and we want to be let alone.

Now all law, all social order, all custom, is a patch-up and a concession to this separating passion of self-insistence. It is an evasion of conflict and social death. Human society is as yet only a truce and not an alliance.

When you understand that, you will begin to understand a thousand perplexing things in legislation and social life. You will understand the necessity of all those restrictions that are called "conventionality," and the inevitableness of the general hostility to singularity. To be exceptional is to assert a difference, to disregard the banked-up forces of jealousy and break the essential conditions of the social contract. It invites either resentment or aggression. So we all wear much the same clothing, affect modesty, use the same phrases, respect one another's "rights," and pretend a greater disinterestedness than we feel. . . .

You have to face this reality as you must face all reality. This is the reality of laws and government; this is the reality of customs and institutions; *a convention between jealousies*. This is reality, just as the cat's way with the nestlings was reality, and the squealing rat one smashed in a paroxysm of cruelty and disgust in the barn.

BOYHOOD

But it isn't the only reality. Equally real is the passionate revolt of my heart against cruelty, and the deep fluctuating impulse not to pretend, to set aside fear and jealousy, to come nakedly out of the compromises and secretive methods of every-day living into the light, into a wide impersonal love, into a new way of living for mankind. . . .

CHAPTER THE THIRD

INTENTIONS AND THE LADY MARY CHRISTIAN

§ 1

I KNOW that before the end of my Harbury days I was already dreaming of a Career, of some great and conspicuous usefulness in the world. That has always haunted my mind and haunts it now. I may be cured perhaps of the large and showy anticipations of youth, I may have learnt to drop the "great and conspicuous," but still I find it necessary to believe that I matter, that I play a part no one else can play in a progress, in a universal scheme moving towards triumphant ends.

Almost wholly I think I was dreaming of public service in those days. The Harbury tradition pointed steadfastly towards the state, and all my world was bare of allurements to any other type of ambition. Success in art or literature did not appeal to us, and a Harbury boy would as soon think of being a great tinker as a great philosopher. Science we called "stinks"; our three science masters were *ex officio* ridiculous and the practical laboratory a refuge for oddities. But a good half of our fathers at least were peers or members of parliament, and our sense of politics was close and keen. History, and particularly history as it came up through the eigh-

40

teenth century to our own times, supplied us with a gallery of intimate models, our great uncles and grandfathers and ancestors at large figured abundantly in the story and furnished the pattern to which we cut our anticipations of life. It was a season of Imperialism, the picturesque Imperialism of the earlier Kipling phase, and we were all of us enthusiasts for the Empire. It was the empire of the White Man's Burthen in those days; the sordid anti-climax of the Tariff Reform Movement was still some years ahead of us. It was easier for us at Harbury to believe then than it has become since, in our own racial and national and class supremacy. We were the Anglo-Saxons, the elect of the earth, leading the world in social organization, in science and economic method. In India and the east more particularly we were the apostles of even-handed justice, relentless veracity, personal clean-liness, and modern efficiency. In a spirit of adventurous benevolence we were spreading those blessings over a reluctant and occasionally recalcitrant world of people for the most part "colored." Our success in this had aroused the bitter envy and rivalry of various continental nations, and particularly of France, Russia, and Germany. But France had been diverted to North Africa, Russia to Eastern Asia, and Germany was already the most considered antagonist in our path towards an empire over the world.

This was the spacious and by no means ignoble project of the later nineties. Most of us Harbury boys, trained as I had been trained to be uncritical, saw the national outlook in those terms. We knew little or nothing, until the fierce wranglings of the Free Traders and Tariff Re-formers a few years later brought it home to us, of the commercial, financial and squalid side of our relations with the vast congeries of exploited new territories and subordinated and subjugated populations. We knew nothing of the social conditions of the mass of people in our own country. We were blankly ignorant of economics. We knew nothing of that process of expropriation and the exploitation of labor which is giving the world the Servile State. The very phrase was twenty years ahead of us. We believed that an Englishman was a better thing in every way than any other sort of man, that English literature, science and philosophy were a shining and unapproachable light to all other peoples, that our soldiers were better than all other soldiers and our sailors than all other sailors. Such civilization and enterprise as existed in Germany for instance we regarded as a shadow, an envious shadow, following our own; it was still generally believed in those days that German trade was concerned entirely with the dishonest imitation of our unapproachable English goods. And as for the United States, well, the United States though blessed with a strain of English blood, were nevertheless "out of it," marooned in a continent of their own and—we had to admit it—corrupt.

Given such ignorance, you know, it wasn't by any means ignoble to be patriotic, to dream of this propagandist Empire of ours spreading its great peace and culture, its virtue and its amazing and unprecedented honesty,—its honesty!—round the world.

§ 2

When I look and try to recover those early intentions of mine I am astonished at the way in which I took them ready-made from the world immediately about me. In some way I seem to have stopped looking—if ever I had begun looking—at the heights and depths above and below that immediate life. I seem to have regarded these profounder realities no more during this phase of concentration than a cow in a field regards the sky. My father's vestments, the Burnmore altar, the Harbury pulpit and Mr. Siddons, stood between me and the idea of God, so that it needed years and much bitter disillusionment before I discovered my need of it. And I was as wanting in subtlety as in depth. We did no logic nor philosophy at Harbury, and at Oxford it was not so much thought we came to deal with as a mistranslation and vulgarization of ancient and alien exercises in thinking. There is no such effective serum against philosophy as the scholarly decoction of a dead philosopher. The philosophical teaching of Oxford at the end of the last century was not so much teaching as a protective inoculation. The stuff was administered with a mysterious gilding of Greek and reverence, old Hegel's monstrous web was the ultimate modernity, and Plato, that intellectual journalist-artist, that bright, restless experimentalist in ideas, was as it were the God of Wisdom, only a little less omniscient (and on the whole more of a scholar and a gentleman) than the God of fact. . . .

So I fell back upon the empire in my first attempts to unify my life. I would serve the empire. That should be my total significance. There was a Roman touch, I perceive, in this devotion. Just how or where I should serve the empire I had not as yet determined. At times I thought of the civil service, in my more ambitious moments I turned my thoughts to politics. But it was doubtful whether my private expectations made the last a reasonable possibility.

I would serve the empire.

§ 3

And all the while that the first attempts to consolidate, to gather one's life together into a purpose and a plan of campaign, are going on upon the field of the young man's life, there come and go and come again in the sky above him the threatening clouds, the ethereal cirrus, the red dawns and glowing afternoons of that passion of love which is the source and renewal of being. There are times when that solicitude matters no more than a springtime sky to a runner who wins towards the post, there are times when its passionate urgency dominates every fact in his world.

§ 4

One must have children and love them passionately before one realizes the deep indignity of accident in life. It is not that I mind so much when unexpected and disconcerting things happen to you or your sisters, but that I mind before they happen. My dreams and anticipations of your lives are all marred by my sense of the huge importance mere chance encounters and incalculable necessities will play in them. And in friendship and still more here, in this central business of love, accident rules it seems to me almost altogether. What personalities you will encounter in life, and have for a chief interest in life, is nearly as much a matter of chance as the drift of a grain

44

of pollen in the pine forest. And once the light hazard has blown it has blown, never to drive again. In other schoolrooms and nurseries, in slum living-rooms perhaps or workhouse wards or palaces, round the other side of the earth, in Canada or Russia or China, other little creatures are trying their small limbs, clutching at things about them with infantile hands, who someday will come into your life with a power and magic monstrous and irrational and irresistible. They will break the limits of your concentrating self, call you out to the service of beauty and the service of the race, sound you to your highest and your lowest, give you your chance to be godlike or filthy, divine or utterly ignoble, react together with you upon the very core and essence of your being. These unknowns are the substance of your fate. You will in extreme intimacy love them, hate them, serve them, struggle with them, and in that interaction the vital force in you and the substance of your days will be spent.

And who they may chance to be and their peculiar quality and effect is haphazard, utterly beyond designing.

Law and custom conspire with the natural circumstances of man to exaggerate every consequence of this accumulating accident, and make it definite and fatal. . . .

I find it quite impossible now to recall the steps and stages by which this power of sex invaded my life. It seems to me now that it began very much as a gale begins, in catspaws upon the water and little rustlings among the leaves, and then stillness and then a distant soughing again and a pause, and then a wider and longer disturbance and so more and more, with a gathering continuity, until at last the stars were hidden, the heavens were hidden; all the heights and depths of life were obscured by stormy impulses and passionate desires. I suppose that quite at the first there were simple curiosities; no doubt they were vivid at the time but they have left scarcely a trace; there were vague first intimations of a peculiar excitement. I do remember more distinctly phases when there was a going-out from myself towards these things, these interests, and then a reaction of shame and concealment.

And these memories were mixed up with others not sexual at all, and particularly with the perception of beauty in things inanimate, with lights seen at twilight and the tender mysteriousness of the dusk and the confused disturbing scents of flowers in the evening and the enigmatical serene animation of stars in the summer sky. . . .

I think perhaps that my boyhood was exceptionally free from vulgarizing influences in this direction. There were few novels in my father's house and I neither saw nor read any plays until I was near manhood, so that I thought naturally about love and not rather artificially round and about love as so many imaginative young people are trained to do. I fell in love once or twice while I was still quite a boy. These earliest experiences rarely got beyond a sort of dumb awe, a vague, vast, ineffectual desire for self-immolation. For a time I remember I worshipped Lady Ladislaw with all my being. Then I talked to a girl in a train—I forget upon what journey—but I remember very vividly her quick color and a certain roguish smile. I spread my adoration at her feet, fresh and frank. I wanted to write to her. Indeed I wanted to devote all my being to her. I begged hard, but there was someone called Auntie who had to be considered, an Atropos for that thread of romance.

Then there was a photograph in my father's study of

the Delphic Sibyl from the Sistine Chapel, that for a time held my heart, and—Yes, there was a girl in a tobacconist's shop in the Harbury High Street. Drawn by an irresistible impulse I used to go and buy cigarettes—and sometimes converse about the weather. But afterwards in solitude I would meditate tremendous conversations and encounters with her. The cigarettes increased the natural melancholy of my state and led to a reproof from old Henson. Almost always I suppose there is that girl in the tobacconist's shop. . . .

I believe if I made an effort I could disinter some dozens of such memories, more and more faded until the marginal ones would be featureless and all but altogether effaced. As I look back at it now I am struck by an absurd image; it is as if a fish nibbled at this bait and then at that.

Given but the slightest aid from accidental circumstances and any of those slight attractions might have become a power to deflect all my life.

The day of decision arrived when the Lady Mary Christian came smiling out of the sunshine to me into the pavilion at Burnmore. With that the phase of stirrings and intimations was over for ever in my life. All those other impressions went then to the dusty lumber room from which I now so slightingly disinter them.

§ 5

We five had all been playmates together. There were Lord Maxton, who was killed at Paardeberg while I was in Ladysmith, he was my senior by nearly a year, Philip, who is now Earl Ladislaw and who was about eighteen months younger than I, Mary, my contemporary within eight days, and Guy, whom we regarded as a baby and who was called, apparently on account of some early linguistic efforts, "Brugglesmith." He did his best to avenge his juniority as time passed on by an enormous length of limb. I had more imagination than Maxton and was a good deal better read, so that Mary and I dominated most of the games of Indians and warfare and exploration in which we passed our long days together. When the Christians were at Burnmore, and they usually spent three or four months in the year there, I had a kind of standing invitation to be with them. Sometimes there would also be two Christian cousins to swell our party, and sometimes there would be a raid of the Fawney children with a detestable governess who was perpetually vociferating reproaches, but these latter were absent-minded, lax young persons, and we did not greatly love them.

It is curious how little I remember of Mary's childhood. All that has happened between us since lies between that and my present self like some luminous impenetrable mist. I know we liked each other, that I was taller than she was and thought her legs unreasonably thin, and that once when I knelt by accident on a dead stick she had brought into an Indian camp we had made near the end of the west shrubbery, she flew at me in a sudden fury, smacked my face, scratched me and had to be suppressed, and was suppressed with extreme difficulty by the united manhood of us three elder boys. Then it was I noted first the blazing blueness of her eyes. She was light and very plucky, so that none of us cared to climb against her, and she was as difficult to hold as an eel. But all these traits and characteristics vanished when she was transformed.

For what seems now a long space of time I had not seen her or any of the family except Philip; it was certainly a year or more, probably two; Maxton was at a crammer's and I think the others must have been in Canada with Lord Ladislaw. Then came some sort of estrangement between him and his wife, and she returned with Mary and Guy to Burnmore and stayed there all through the summer.

I was in a state of transition between the infinitely great and the infinitely little. I had just ceased to be that noble and potent being, that almost statesmanlike personage, a sixth form boy at Harbury, and I was going to be an Oxford undergraduate. Philip and I came down together by the same train from Harbury, I shared the Burnmore dog-cart and luggage cart, and he dropped me at the rectory. I was a long-limbed youngster of seventeen, as tall as I am now, and fair, so fair that I was still boyish-faced while most of my contemporaries and Philip (who favored his father) were at least smudgy with moustaches. With the head-master's valediction and the grave elder-brotherliness of old Henson, and the shrill cheers of a little crowd of juniors still echoing in my head, I very naturally came home in a mood of exalted gravity, and I can still remember pacing up and down the oblong lawn behind the rockery and the fig-tree wall with my father, talking of my outlook with all the tremendous *savoir faire* that was natural to my age, and noting with a secret gratification that our shoulders were now on a level. No doubt we were discussing Oxford and all that I was to do at Oxford; I don't remember a word of our speech though I recall the exact tint of its color and the distinctive feeling of our measured equal paces in the sunshine. . . .

I must have gone up to Burnmore House the following afternoon. I went up alone and I was sent out through the little door at the end of the big gallery into the garden. In those days Lady Ladislaw had made an Indian pavilion under the tall trees at the east end of the house, and here I found her with her cousin Helena Christian entertaining a mixture of people, a carriageful from Hampton End, the two elder Fawneys and a man in brown who had I think ridden over from Chestoxter Castle. Lady Ladislaw welcomed me with ample graciousness—as though I was a personage. "The children" she said were still at tennis, and as she spoke I saw Guy, grown nearly beyond recognition, and then a shining being in white, very straight and graceful, with a big soft hat and overshadowed eyes that smiled, come out from the hurried endearments of the sunflakes under the shadows of the great chestnuts, into the glow of summer light before the pavilion.

"Steve arrived!" she cried, and waved a welcoming racquet.

I do not remember what I said to her or what else she said or what anyone said. But I believe I could paint every detail of her effect. I know that when she came out of the brightness into the shadow of the pavilion it was like a regal condescension, and I know that she was wonderfully self-possessed and helpful with her mother's hospitalities, and that I marvelled I had never before perceived the subtler sweetness in the cadence of her voice. I seem also to remember a severe internal struggle for my self-possession, and that I had to recall my exalted position in the sixth form to save myself from becoming tongue-tied and abashed and awkward and utterly shamed.

You see she had her hair up and very prettily dressed, and those aggressive lean legs of hers had vanished, and she was sheathed in muslin that showed her the most delicately slender and beautiful of young women. And she seemed so radiantly sure of herself!

After our first greeting I do not think I spoke to her or looked at her again throughout the meal. I took things that she handed me with an appearance of supreme indifference, was politely attentive to the elder Miss Fawney, and engaged with Lady Ladislaw and the horsey little man in brown in a discussion of the possibility of mechanical vehicles upon the high road. That was in the early nineties. We were all of opinion that it was impossible to make a sufficiently light engine for the purpose. Afterwards Mary confessed to me how she had been looking forward to our meeting, and how snubbed I had made her feel. . . .

Then a little later than this meeting in the pavilion, though I am not clear now whether it was the same or some subsequent afternoon, we are walking in the sunken garden, and great clouds of purple clematis and some less lavish heliotrope-colored creeper, foam up against the ruddy stone balustrading. Just in front of us a fountain gushes out of a grotto of artificial stalagmite and bathes the pedestal of an absurd little statuette of the God of Love. We are talking almost easily. She looks sideways at my face, already with the quiet controlled watchfulness of a woman interested in a man, she smiles and she talks of flowers and sunshine, the Canadian winter—and with an abrupt transition, of old times we've had together in the shrubbery and the wilderness of bracken out beyond. She seems tremendously grown-up and womanly to me. I am talking my best, and glad, and in a manner scared at the thrill her newly discovered beauty gives me, and keeping up my dignity and coherence with an effort. My attention is constantly being distracted to note how prettily she moves, to wonder why it is I never noticed the sweet fall, the faint delightful whisper of a lisp in her voice before.

We agree about the flowers and the sunshine and the Canadian winter — about everything. "I think so often of those games we used to invent," she declares. "So do I," I say, "so do I." And then with a sudden boldness: "Once I broke a stick of yours, a rotten stick you thought a sound one. Do you remember?"

Then we laugh together and seem to approach across a painful, unnecessary distance that has separated us. It vanishes for ever. "I couldn't now," she says, "smack your face like that, Stephen."

That seems to me a brilliantly daring and delightful thing for her to say, and jolly of her to use my Christian name too! "I believe I scratched," she adds.

"You never scratched," I assert with warm conviction. "Never."

"I did," she insists and I deny. "You couldn't."

"We're growing up," she cries. "That's what has happened to us. We shall never fight again with our hands and feet, never—until death do us part."

"For better, or worse," I say, with a sense of wit and enterprise beyond all human precedent.

"For richer, or poorer," she cries, taking up my challenge with a lifting laugh in her voice.

And then to make it all nothing again, she exclaims at the white lilies that rise against masses of sweet bay along the further wall. . . .

How plainly I can recall it all! How plainly and how brightly! As we came up the broad steps at the further end towards the tennis lawn, she turned suddenly upon me and with a novel assurance of command told me to stand still. "*There*," she said with a hand out and seemed to survey me with her chin up and her white neck at the level of my eyes. "Yes. A whole step," she estimated, "and more, taller than I. You will look down on me, Stephen, now, for all the rest of our days."

"I shall always stand," I answered, "a step or so below you."

"No," she said, "come up to the level. A girl should be smaller than a man. You are a man, Stephen—almost. . . . You must be near six feet. . . . Here's Guy with the box of balls."

She flitted about the tennis court before me, playing with Philip against Guy and myself. She punished some opening condescensions with a wicked vigor—and presently Guy and I were straining every nerve to save the set. She had a low close serve I remember that seemed perfectly straightforward and simple, and was very difficult to return.

§ 6

All that golden summer on the threshold of my manhood was filled by Mary. I loved her with the love of a boy and a man. Either I was with Mary or I was hoping and planning to be with Mary or I was full of some vivid new impression of her or some enigmatical speech, some pregnant nothing, some glance or gesture engaged and perplexed my mind. In those days I slept the profound sweet sleep of youth, but whenever that deep flow broke towards the shallows, as I sank into it at night and came out of it at morning, I passed through dreams of Mary to and from a world of waking thought of her.

There must have been days of friendly intercourse when it seemed we talked nothings and wandered and meandered among subjects, but always we had our eyes on one another. And afterwards I would spend long hours in recalling and analyzing those nothings, questioning their nothingness, making out of things too submerged and impalpable for the rough drags of recollection, promises and indications. I would invent ingenious things to say, things pushing out suddenly from nothingness to extreme significance. I rehearsed a hundred declarations.

It was easy for us to be very much together. We were very free that summer and life was all leisure. Lady Ladislaw was busied with her own concerns; she sometimes went away for two or three days leaving no one but an attenuated governess with even the shadow of a claim to interfere with Mary. Moreover she was used to seeing me with her children at Burnmore; we were still in her eyes no more than children. . . . And also perhaps she did not greatly mind if indeed we did a little fall in love together. To her that may have seemed a very natural and slight and transitory possibility. . . .

One afternoon of warm shadows in the wood near the red-lacquered Chinese bridge, we two were alone together and we fell silent. I was trembling and full of a wild courage. I can feel now the exquisite surmise, the doubt of that moment. Our eyes met. She looked up at me with an unwonted touch of fear in her expression and I laid my hands on her. She did not recoil, she stood mute with her lips pressed together, looking at me steadfastly. I can feel that moment now as a tremendous hesitation, blank and yet full of light and life, like a clear sky in the moment before dawn. . . .

She made a little move towards me. Impulsively, with no word said, we kissed.

§ 7

I would like very much to give you a portrait of Mary as she was in those days. Every portrait I ever had of her I burnt in the sincerity of what was to have been our final separation, and now I have nothing of her in my possession. I suppose that in the files of old illustrated weeklies somewhere, a score of portraits must be findable. Yet photographs have a queer quality of falsehood. They have no movement and always there was a little movement about Mary just as there is always a little scent about flowers. She was slender and graceful, so that she seemed taller than she was, she had beautifully shaped arms and a brightness in her face; it seemed to me always that there was light in her face, more than the light that shone upon it. Her fair, very slightly reddish hair—it was warm like Australian gold—flowed with a sort of joyous bravery back from her low broad forehead; the color under her delicate skin was bright and quick, and her mouth always smiled faintly. There was a peculiar charm for me about her mouth, a whimsicality, a sort of humorous resolve in the way in which the upper lip fell upon the lower and in a faint obliquity that increased with her quickening smile. She spoke with a very clear delicate intonation that made one want to hear her speak again; she often said faintly daring things, and when she did, she had that little catch in the breath—of one who dares. She did not talk hastily; often before she spoke came a brief grave pause. Her eyes were brightly blue except when the spirit of mischief took her and then they became black, and there was something about the upper and lower lids that made them not only the prettiest but the sweetest and kindliest eyes in the world. And she moved with a quiet rapidity, without any needless movements, to do whatever she had a mind to do. . . .

But how impossible it is to convey the personal charm of a human being. I catalogue these things and it is as if she moved about silently behind my stumbling enumeration and smiled at me still, with her eyes a little darkened, mocking me. That phantom will never be gone from my mind. It was all of these things and none of these things that made me hers, as I have never been any other person's. . . .

We grew up together. The girl of nineteen mingles in my memory with the woman of twenty-five.

Always we were equals, or if anything she was the better of us two. I never made love to her in the commoner sense of the word, a sense in which the woman is conceived of as shy, unawakened, younger, more plastic, and the man as tempting, creating responses, persuading and compelling. We made love to each other as youth should, we were friends lit by a passion. . . . I think that is the best love. If I could wish your future I would have you love someone neither older and stronger nor younger and weaker than yourself. I would have you have neither a toy nor a devotion, for the one makes the woman contemptible and the other the man. There should be something almost sisterly between you. Love neither a goddess nor a captive woman. But I would wish you a better fate in your love than chanced to me.

Mary was not only naturally far more quick-minded, more swiftly understanding than I, but more widely educated. Mine was the stiff limited education of the English public school and university; I could not speak and read and think French and German as she could for all that I had a pedantic knowledge of the older forms of those tongues; and the classics and mathematics upon which I had spent the substance of my years were indeed of little use to me, have never been of any real use to me, they were ladders too clumsy to carry about and too short to reach anything. My general ideas came from the newspapers and the reviews. She on the other hand had read much, had heard no end of good conversation, the conversation of people who mattered, had thought for herself and had picked the brains of her brothers. Her mother had let her read whatever books she liked, partly because she believed that was the proper thing to do, and partly because it was so much less trouble to be liberal in such things.

We had the gravest conversations.

I do not remember that we talked much of love, though we were very much in love. We kissed; sometimes greatly daring we walked hand in hand; once I took her in my arms and carried her over a swampy place beyond the Killing Wood, and held her closely to me; that was a great event between us; but we were shy of one another, shy even of very intimate words; and a thousand daring and beautiful things I dreamt of saying to her went unsaid. I do not remember any endearing names from that time. But we jested and shared our humors, shaped our developing ideas in quaint forms to amuse one another and talked —as young men talk together.

We talked of religion; I think she was the first person to thaw the private silences that had kept me bound in these matters even from myself for years. I can still recall her face, a little flushed and coming nearer to mine after avowals and comparisons. "But Stephen," she says; "if none of these things are really true, why do they keep on telling them to us? What *is* true? What are we for? What is Everything for?"

I remember the awkwardness I felt at these indelicate thrusts into topics I had come to regard as forbidden.

"I suppose there's a sort of truth in them," I said, and then more Siddonsesquely: "endless people wiser than we are——"

"Yes," she said. "But that doesn't matter to us. Endless people wiser than we are have said one thing, and endless people wiser than we are have said exactly the opposite. It's *we* who have to understand—for ourselves. . . . We don't understand, Stephen."

I was forced to a choice between faith and denial. But I parried with questions. "Don't you," I asked, "feel there is a God?"

She hesitated. "There is something—something very beautiful," she said and stopped as if her breath had gone. "That is all I know, Stephen. . . ."

And I remember too that we talked endlessly about the things I was to do in the world. I do not remember that we talked about the things she was to do, by some sort of instinct and some sort of dexterity she evaded that, from the very first she had reserves from me, but my career and purpose became as it were the form in which we discussed all the purposes of life. I became Man in her imagination, the protagonist of the world. At first I displayed the modest worthy desire for respectable service that Harbury had taught me, but her clear, sceptical little voice pierced and tore all those pretences to shreds. "Do some decent public work," I said, or some such phrase.

"But is that All you want?" I hear her asking. "Is that All you want?"

I lay prone upon the turf and dug up a root of grass with my penknife. "Before I met you it was," I said.

"And now?"

"I want you."

"I'm nothing to want. I want you to want all the world. . . . *Why shouldn't you?*"

I think I must have talked of the greatness of serving the empire. "Yes, but splendidly," she insisted. "Not doing little things for other people—who aren't doing anything at all. I want you to conquer people and lead people. . . . When I see you, Stephen, sometimes—I almost wish I were a man. In order to be able to do all the things that you are going to do."

"For you," I said, "for you."

I stretched out my hand for hers, and my gesture went disregarded.

She sat rather crouched together with her eyes gazing far away across the great spaces of the park.

"That is what women are for," she said. "To make

men see how splendid life can be. To lift them up—out of a sort of timid grubbiness——" She turned upon me suddenly. "Stephen," she said, "promise me. Whatever you become, you promise and swear here and now never to be grey and grubby, never to be humpy and snuffy, never to be respectable and modest and dull and a little fat, like—like everybody. Ever."

"I swear," I said.

"By me."

"By you. No book to kiss! Please, give me your hand."

§ 8

All through that summer we saw much of each other. I was up at the House perhaps every other day; we young people were supposed to be all in a company together down by the tennis lawns, but indeed we dispersed and came and went by a kind of tacit understanding, Guy and Philip each with one of the Fawney girls and I with Mary. I put all sorts of constructions upon the freedom I was given with her, but I perceive now that we still seemed scarcely more than children to Lady Ladislaw, and that the idea of our marriage was as inconceivable to her as if we had been brother and sister. Matrimonially I was as impossible as one of the stable boys. All the money I could hope to earn for years to come would not have sufficed even to buy Mary clothes. But as yet we thought little of matters so remote, glad in our wonderful new discovery of love, and when at last I went off to Oxford, albeit the parting moved us to much tenderness and vows and embraces, I had no suspicion that never more in all our lives would Mary and I meet freely and gladly without restriction. Yet so it was. From that day came restraints and difficulties; the shadow of furtiveness fell between us; our correspondence had to be concealed.

I went to Oxford as one goes into exile; she to London. I would post to her so that the letters reached Landor House before lunch time when the sun of Lady Ladislaw came over the horizon, but indeed as yet no one was watching her letters. Afterwards as she moved about she gave me other instructions, and for the most part I wrote to her in envelopes addressed for her by one of the Fawney girls, who was under her spell and made no enquiry for what purpose these envelopes were needed.

To me of course Mary wrote without restraint. All her letters to me were destroyed after our crisis, but some of mine to her she kept for many years; at last they came back to me so that I have them now. And for all their occasional cheapness and crudity, I do not find anything in them to be ashamed of. They reflect, they are chiefly concerned with that search for a career of fine service which was then the chief preoccupation of my mind, the bias is all to a large imperialism, but it is manifest that already the first ripples of a rising tide of criticism against the imperialist movement had reached and were exercising me. In one letter I am explaining that imperialism is not a mere aggressiveness, but the establishment of peace and order throughout half the world. "We may never withdraw," I wrote with all the confidence of a Foreign Secretary, "from all these great territories of ours, but we shall stay only to raise their peoples ultimately to an equal citizenship with ourselves." And

5

then in the same letter: "and if I do not devote myself to the Empire what else is there that gives anything like the same opportunity of a purpose in life." I find myself in another tolerantly disposed to "accept socialism," but manifestly hostile to "the narrow mental habits of the socialists." The large note of youth! And in another I am clearly very proud and excited and a little mock-modest over the success of my first two speeches in the Union.

On the whole I like the rather boyish, tremendously serious young man of those letters. An egotist, of course, but what youth was ever anything else? I may write that much freely now, for by this time he is almost as much outside my personality as you or my father. He is the young Stratton, one of a line. I like his gravity; if youth is not grave with all the great spectacle of life opening at its feet, then surely no age need be grave. I love and envy his simplicity and honesty. His sham modesty and so forth are so translucent as scarcely to matter. It is clear I was opening my heart to myself as I opened it to Mary. I wasn't acting to her. I meant what I said. And as I remember her answers she took much the same high tone with me, though her style of writing was far lighter than mine, more easy and witty and less continuous. She flashed and flickered. As for confessed love-making there is very little,—I find at the end of one of my notes after the signature, "I love you, I love you." And she was even more restrained. Such little phrases as "Dear Stevenage"—that was one of her odd names for me— "I wish you were here," or "Dear, *dear* Stevenage," were epistolary events, and I would re-read the blessed wonderful outbreak a hundred times. . . .

INTENTIONS

Our separation lengthened. There was a queer detached unexpected meeting in London in December, for some afternoon gathering. I was shy and the more disconcerted because she was in winter town clothes that made her seem strange and changed. Then came the devastating intimation that all through the next summer the Ladislaws were to be in Scotland.

I did my boyish utmost to get to Scotland. They were at Lankart near Invermoriston, and the nearest thing I could contrive was to join a reading party in Skye, a reading party of older men who manifestly had no great desire for me. For more than a year we never met at all, and all sorts of new things happened to us both. I perceived they happened to me, but I did not think they happened to her. Of course we changed. Of course in a measure and relatively we forgot. Of course there were weeks when we never thought of each other at all. Then would come phases of hunger. I remember a little note of hers. "Oh Stevenage," it was scrawled, "perhaps next Easter!" Next Easter was an aching desolation. The blinds of Burnmore House remained drawn; the place was empty except for three old servants on board-wages. The Christians went instead to the Canary Isles, following some occult impulse of Lady Ladislaw's. Lord Ladislaw spent the winter in Italy.

What an empty useless beauty the great Park possessed during those seasons of intermission! There were a score of places in it we had made our own. . . .

Her letters to Oxford would cease for weeks, and suddenly revive and become frequent. Now and then would come a love-letter that seemed to shine like stars as I read it; for the most part they were low-pitched,

63

friendly or humorous letters in a roundish girlish writing that was maturing into a squarely characteristic hand. My letters to her too I suppose varied as greatly. We began to be used to living so apart. There were weeks of silence. . . .

Yet always when I thought of my life as a whole, Mary ruled it. With her alone I had talked of my possible work and purpose; to her alone had I confessed to ambitions beyond such modest worthiness as a public school drills us to affect. . . .

Then the whole sky of my life lit up again with a strange light of excitement and hope. I had a note, glad and serenely friendly, to say they were to spend all the summer at Burnmore.

I remember how I handled and scrutinized that letter, seeking for some intimation that our former intimacy was still alive. We were to meet. How should we meet? How would she look at me? What would she think of me?

§ 9

Of course it was all different. Our first encounter in this new phase had a quality of extreme disillusionment. The warm living creature, who would whisper, who would kiss with wonderful lips, who would say strange daring things, who had soft hair one might touch with a thrilling and worshipful hand, who changed one at a word or a look into a God of pride, became as if she had been no more than a dream. A self-possessed young aristocrat in white and brown glanced at me from amidst a group of brilliant people on the terrace, nodded as it seemed quite carelessly in acknowledgment of my salutation, and resumed her confident conversation with a tall stooping man, no less a person than Evesham, the Prime Minister. He was lunching at Burnmore on his way across country to the Rileys. I heard that dear laugh of hers, as ready and easy as when she laughed with me. I had not heard it for nearly three years—nor any sound that had its sweetness. "But Mr. Evesham," she was saying, "nowadays we don't believe that sort of thing——"

"There are a lot of things still for you to believe," says Mr. Evesham beaming. "A lot of things! One's capacity increases. It grows with exercise. Justin will bear me out."

Beyond her stood an undersized, brown-clad middle-aged man with a big head, a dark face and expressive brown eyes fixed now in unrestrained admiration on Mary's laughing face. This then was Justin, the incredibly rich and powerful, whose comprehensive operations could make and break a thousand fortunes in a day. He answered Evesham carelessly, with his gaze still on Mary, and in a voice too low for my straining ears. There was some woman in the group also, but she has left nothing upon my mind whatever except an effect of black and a very decorative green sunshade. She greeted Justin's remark, I remember, with the little yelp of laughter that characterized that set. I think too there was someone else in the group; but I cannot clearly recall who. . . .

Presently as I and Philip made unreal conversation together I saw Mary disengage herself and come towards us. It was as if a princess came towards a beggar. Absurd are the changes of phase between women and men. A year or so ago and all of us had been but "the children" together; now here were I and Philip mere youths still, nobodies, echoes and aspirations, crude promises at the best, and here was Mary in full flower, as glorious and central as the Hampton Court azaleas in spring.

"And this is Stephen," she said, aglow with happy confidence.

I made no memorable reply, and there was a little pause thick with mute questionings.

"After lunch," she said with her eye on mine, "I am going to measure against you on the steps. I'd hoped —when you weren't looking—I might creep up——"

"I've taken no advantage," I said.

"You've kept your lead."

Justin had followed her towards us, and now held out a hand to Philip. "Well, Philip my boy," he said, and defined our places. Philip made some introductory gesture with a word or so towards me. Justin glanced at me as one might glance at someone's new dog, gave an expressionless nod to my stiff movement of recognition, and addressed himself at once to Mary.

"Lady Mary," he said, "I've wanted to tell you——"

I caught her quick eye for a moment and knew she had more to say to me, but neither she nor I had the skill and alacrity to get that said.

"I wanted to tell you," said Justin, "I've found a little Japanese who's done exactly what you wanted with that group of dwarf maples."

She clearly didn't understand.

"But what did I want, Mr. Justin?" she asked.

"Don't say that you forget?" cried Justin. "Oh don't

tell me you forget! You wanted a little exact copy of a
Japanese house—— I've had it done. Beneath the
trees. . . ."

"And so you're back in Burnmore, Mr. Stratton," said
Lady Ladislaw intervening between me and their duo-
logue. And I never knew how pleased Mary was with
this faithful realization of her passing and forgotten fancy.
My hostess greeted me warmly and pressed my hand,
smiled mechanically and looked over my shoulder all the
while to Mr. Evesham and her company generally, and
then came the deep uproar of a gong from the house and
we were all moving in groups and couples luncheonward.

Justin walked with Lady Mary, and she was I saw
an inch taller than his squat solidity. A tall lady in
rose-pink had taken possession of Guy, Evesham and
Lady Ladislaw made the two centres of a straggling group
who were bandying recondite political allusions. Then
came one or two couples and trios with nothing very
much to say and active ears. Philip and I brought up
the rear silently and in all humility. Even young Guy
had gone over our heads. I was too full of a stupendous
realization for any words. Of course, during those years,
she had been doing—no end of things! And while I had
been just drudging with lectures and books and theorizing
about the Empire and what I could do with it, and taking
exercise, she had learnt, it seemed—the World.

§ 10

Lunch was in the great dining-room. There was a big
table and two smaller ones; we sat down anyhow, but
the first comers had grouped themselves about Lady

Ladislaw and Evesham and Justin and Mary in a central orb, and I had to drift perforce to one of the satellites. I secured a seat whence I could get a glimpse ever and again over Justin's assiduous shoulders of a delicate profile, and I found myself immediately engaged in answering the innumerable impossible questions of Lady Viping, the widow of terrible old Sir Joshua, that devastating divorce court judge who didn't believe in divorces. His domestic confidences had I think corrupted her mind altogether. She cared for nothing but evidence. She was a rustling, incessant, sandy, peering woman with a lorgnette and rapid, confidential lisping undertones, and she wanted to know who everybody was and how they were related. This kept us turning towards the other tables—and when my information failed she would call upon Sir Godfrey Klavier, who was explaining, rather testily on account of her interruptions, to Philip Christian and a little lady in black and the elder Fawney girl just why he didn't believe Lady Ladislaw's new golf course would succeed. There were two or three other casual people at our table; one of the Roden girls, a young guardsman and, I think, some other man whom I don't clearly remember.

"And so that's the great Mr. Justin," rustled Lady Viping and stared across me.

(I saw Evesham leaning rather over the table to point some remark at Mary, and noted her lips part to reply.)

"What *is* the word?" insisted Lady Viping like a fly in my ear.

I turned on her guiltily.

"Whether it's brachy," said Lady Viping, "or whether it's dolly—*I* can never remember?"

I guessed she was talking of Justin's head. "Oh!—brachycephalic," I said.

I had lost Mary's answer.

"They say he's a woman hater," said Lady Viping. "It hardly looks like it now, does it?"

"Who?" I asked. "What?—oh!—Justin."

"The great financial cannibal. Suppose she turned him into a philanthropist! Stranger things have happened. Look!—now. The man's face is positively tender."

I hated looking, and I could not help but look. It was as if this detestable old woman was dragging me down and down, down far below all dignity to her own level of a peeping observer. Justin was saying something to Mary in an undertone, something that made her glance up swiftly and at me before she answered, and there I was with my head side by side with those quivering dyed curls, that flighty black bonnet, that remorseless observant lorgnette. I could have sworn aloud at the hopeless indignity of my pose.

I saw Mary color quickly before I looked away.

"Charming, isn't she?" said Lady Viping, and I discovered those infernal glasses were for a moment honoring me. They shut with a click. "Ham," said Lady Viping. "I told him no ham—and now I remember—I like ham. Or rather I like spinach. I forgot the spinach. One has the ham for the spinach,—don't you think? Yes,—tell him. She's a perfect Dresden ornament, Mr. Stratton. She's adorable . . . (lorgnette and search for fresh topics). Who is the dark lady with the slight moustache—sitting there next to Guy? Sir Godfrey, who is the dark lady? No, I don't mean Mary

Fitton. Over there! Mrs. Roperstone. Ooh *The* Mrs. Roperstone. (Renewed lorgnette and click.) Yes—ham. With spinach. A lot of spinach. There's Mr. Evesham laughing again. He's greatly amused. Unusual for him to laugh twice. At least, aloud. (Rustle and adjustment of lorgnette.) Mr. Stratton, don't you think?—exactly like a little shepherdess. Only I can't say I think Mr. Justin is like a shepherd. On the whole, more like a large cloisonné jar. Now Guy would do. As a pair they're beautiful. Pity they're brother and sister. Curious how that boy manages to be big and yet delicate. H'm. Mixed mantel ornaments. Sir Godfrey, how old *is* Mrs. Roperstone? . . . You never know on principle. I think I shall make Mr. Stratton guess. What do you think, Mr. Stratton? . . . You never guess on principle! Well, we're all very high principled. (Fresh exploratory movements of the lorgnette.) Mr. Stratton, tell me; is that little peaked man near Lady Ladislaw Mr. Roperstone? I thought as much!''

All this chatter is mixed up in my mind with an unusual sense of hovering attentive menservants, who seemed all of them to my heated imagination to be watching me (and particularly one clean-shaven, reddish-haired, full-faced young man) lest I looked too much at the Lady Mary Christian. Of course they were merely watching our plates and glasses, but my nerves and temper were now in such a state that if my man went off to the buffet to get Sir Godfrey the pickled walnuts, I fancied he went to report the progress of my infatuation, and if a strange face appeared with the cider cup, that this was a new observer come to mark the revelation of my behavior. My food embarrassed me. I found hidden meanings in the talk of the Roden girl and her guardsman, and an ironical discovery in Sir Godfrey's eye. . . .

I felt indignant with Mary. I felt she disowned me and deserted me and repudiated me, that she ought in some manner to have recognized me. I gave her no credit for her speech to me before the lunch, or her promise to measure against me again. I blinded myself to all her frank friendliness. I felt she ought not to notice Justin, ought not to answer him. . . .

Clearly she liked those men to flatter her, she liked it. . . .

I remember too, so that I must have noted it and felt it then as a thing perceived for the first time, the large dignity of the room, the tall windows and splendid rich curtains, the darkened Hoppners upon the walls. I noted too the quality and abundance of the table things, and there were grapes and peaches, strawberries, cherries and green almonds, piled lavishly above the waiting dessert plates with the golden knives and forks, upon a table in the sunshine of the great bay. The very sunshine filtered through the tall narrow panes from the great chestnut trees without, seemed of a different quality from the common light of day. . . .

I felt like a poor relation. I sympathized with Anarchists. We had come out of the Park now finally, both Mary and I—into this. . . .

"Mr. Stratton I am sure agrees with me."

For a time I had been marooned conversationally, and Lady Viping had engaged Sir Godfrey. Evidently he was refractory and she was back at me.

"Look at it now in profile," she said, and directed me once more to that unendurable grouping. Justin again!

"It's a heavy face," I said.

"It's a powerful face. I wouldn't care anyhow to be up against it—as people say." And the lorgnette shut with a click. "What is this? Peaches!—Yes, and give me some cream." . . .

I hovered long for that measuring I had been promised on the steps, but either Mary had forgotten or she deemed it wiser to forget.

§ 11

I took my leave of Lady Ladislaw when the departure of Evesham broke the party into dispersing fragments. I started down the drive towards the rectory and then vaulted the railings by the paddock and struck across beyond the mere. I could not go home with the immense burthen of thought and new ideas and emotions that had come upon me. I felt confused and shattered to incoherence by the new quality of Mary's atmosphere. I turned my steps towards the wilder, lonelier part of the park beyond the Killing Wood, and lay down in a wide space of grass between two divergent thickets of bracken, and remained there for a very long time.

There it was in the park that for the first time I pitted myself against life upon a definite issue, and prepared my first experience of defeat. "I *will* have her," I said, hammering at the turf with my fist. "I will. I do not care if I give all my life . . ."

Then I lay still and bit the sweetness out of joints of grass, and presently thought and planned.

CHAPTER THE FOURTH

THE MARRIAGE OF THE LADY MARY CHRISTIAN

§ 1

FOR three or four days I could get no word with Mary. I could not now come and go as I had been able to do in the days when we were still "the children." I could not work, I could not rest, I prowled as near as I could to Burnmore House hoping for some glimpse of her, waiting for the moment when I could decently present myself again at the house.

When at last I called, Justin had gone and things had some flavor of the ancient time. Lady Ladislaw received me with an airy intimacy, all the careful responsibility of her luncheon party manner thrown aside. "And how goes Cambridge?" she sang, sailing through the great saloon towards me, and I thought that for the occasion Cambridge instead of Oxford would serve sufficiently well. "You'll find them all at tennis," said Lady Ladislaw, and waved me on to the gardens. There I found all four of them and had to wait until their set was finished.

"Mary," I said at the first chance, "are we never to talk again?"

"It's all different," she said.

73

"I am dying to talk to you—as we used to talk."

"And I—Stevenage. But—— You see?"

"Next time I come," I said, "I shall bring you a letter. There is so much——"

"No," she said. "Can't you get up in the morning? Very early—five or six. No one is up until ever so late."

"I'd stay up all night."

"Serve!" said Maxton, who was playing the two of us and had stopped I think to tighten a shoe.

Things conspired against any more intimacy for a time. But we got our moment on the way to tea. She glanced back at Philip, who was loosening the net, and then forward to estimate the distance of Maxton and Guy. "They're all three going," she said, "after Tuesday. Then—before six."

"Wednesday?"

"Yes."

"Suppose after all," she threw out, "I can't come."

"Fortunes of war."

"If I can't come one morning I may come another," she spoke hastily, and I perceived that Guy and Maxton had turned and were waiting for us.

"You know the old Ice House?"

"Towards the gardens?"

"Yes. On the further side. Don't come by the road, come across by the end of the mere. Lie in the bracken until you see me coming. . . . I've not played tennis a dozen times this year. Not half a dozen."

This last was for the boys.

"You've played twenty times at least since you've been here," said Guy, with the simple bluntness of a brother. "I'm certain."

74

§ 2

To this day a dewy morning in late August brings back the thought of Mary and those stolen meetings. I have the minutest recollection of the misty bloom upon the turf, and the ragged, filmy carpet of gossamer on either hand, of the warm wetness of every little blade and blossom and of the little scraps and seeds of grass upon my soaking and discolored boots. Our footsteps were dark green upon the dew-grey grass. And I feel the same hungry freshness again at the thought of those stolen meetings. Presently came the sunrise, blinding, warming, dew-dispelling arrows of gold smiting through the tree stems, a flood of light foaming over the bracken and gilding the under sides of the branches. Everything is different and distinctive in those opening hours; everything has a different value from what it has by day. All the little things upon the ground, fallen branches, tussocks, wood-piles, have a peculiar intensity and importance, seem magnified, because of the length of their shadows in the slanting rays, and all the great trees seem lifted above the light and merged with the sky. And at last, a cool grey outline against the blaze and with a glancing iridescent halo about her, comes Mary, flitting, adventurous, friendly, wonderful.

"Oh Stevenage!" she cries, "to see you again!"

We each hold out both our hands and clasp and hesitate and rather shyly kiss.

"Come!" she says, "we can talk for an hour. It's still not six. And there is a fallen branch where we can

75

sit and put our feet out of the wet. Oh! it's so good to be out of things again—clean out of things—with you. Look! there is a stag watching us."

"You're glad to be with me?" I ask, jealous of the very sunrise.

"I am always glad," she says, "to be with you. Why don't we always get up at dawn, Stevenage, every day of our lives?"

We go rustling through the grass to the prostrate timber she has chosen. (I can remember even the thin bracelet on the wrist of the hand that lifted her skirt.) I help her to clamber into a comfortable fork from which her feet can swing. . . .

Such fragments as this are as bright, as undimmed, as if we had met this morning. But then comes our conversation, and that I find vague and irregularly obliterated. But I think I must have urged her to say she loved me, and beat about the bush of that declaration, too fearful to put my heart's wish to the issue, that she would promise to wait three years for me—until I could prove it was not madness for her to marry me. "I have been thinking of it all night and every night since I have been here," I said. "Somehow I will do something. In some way—I will get hold of things. Believe me!— with all my strength."

I was standing between the forking boughs, and she was looking down upon me.

"Stephen dear," she said, "dear, dear Boy; I have never wanted to kiss you so much in all my life. Dear, come close to me."

She bent her fresh young face down to mine, her fingers were in my hair.

"My Knight," she whispered close to me. "My beautiful young Knight."

I whispered back and touched her dew fresh lips. . . .

"And tell me what you would do to conquer the world for me?" she asked.

I cannot remember now a word of all the vague threatenings against the sundering universe with which I replied. Her hand was on my shoulder as she listened. . . .

But I do know that even on this first morning she left me with a sense of beautiful unreality, of having dipped for some precious moments into heroic gossamer. All my world subjugation seemed already as evanescent as the morning haze and the vanishing dews as I stood, a little hidden in the shadows of the Killing Wood and ready to plunge back at the first hint of an observer, and watched her slender whiteness flit circumspectly towards the house.

§ 3

Our next three or four meetings are not so clearly defined. We did not meet every morning for fear that her early rising should seem too punctual to be no more than a chance impulse, nor did we go to the same place. But there stands out very clearly a conversation in a different mood. We had met at the sham ruins at the far end of the great shrubbery, a huge shattered Corinthian portico of rather damaged stucco giving wide views of the hills towards Alfridsham between its three erect pillars, and affording a dry seat upon its fallen ones. It was an overcast morning, I remember probably the hour was earlier; a kind of twilight clearness made the world seem strange and the bushes and trees between us and the house very heavy and still and dark. And we were at cross purpose, for now it was becoming clear to me that Mary did not mean to marry me, that she dreaded making any promise to me for the future, that all the heroic common cause I wanted with her, was quite alien to her dreams.

"But Mary," I said looking at her colorless delicate face, "don't you love me? Don't you want me?"

"You know I love you, Stevenage," she said. "You know."

"But if two people love one another, they want to be always together, they want to belong to each other."

She looked at me with her face very intent upon her meaning. "Stevenage," she said after one of those steadfast pauses of hers, "I want to belong to myself."

"Naturally," I said with an air of disposing of an argument, and then paused.

"Why should one have to tie oneself always to one other human being?" she asked. "Why must it be like that?"   .

I do not remember how I tried to meet this extraordinary idea. "One loves," I may have said. The subtle scepticisms of her mind went altogether beyond my habits of thinking; it had never occurred to me that there was any other way of living except in these voluntary and involuntary mutual servitudes in which men and women live and die. "If you love me," I urged, "if you love me—— I want nothing better in all my life but to love and serve and keep you and make you happy."

She surveyed me and weighed my words against her own.

"I love meeting you," she said. "I love your going

because it means that afterwards you will come again. I love this—this slipping out to you. But up there, there is a room in the house that is *my* place—me—my own. Nobody follows me there. I want to go on living, Stevenage, just as I am living now. I don't want to become someone's certain possession, to be just usual and familiar to anyone. No, not even to you."

"But if you love," I cried.

"To you least of all. Don't you see?—I want to be wonderful to you, Stevenage, more than to anyone. I want—I want always to make your heart beat faster. I want always to be coming to you with my own heart beating faster. Always and always I want it to be like that. Just as it has been on these mornings. It has been beautiful—altogether beautiful."

"Yes," I said, rather helplessly, and struggled with great issues I had never faced before.

"It isn't," I said, "how people live."

"It is how I want to live," said Mary.

"It isn't the way life goes."

"I want it to be. Why shouldn't it be? Why at any rate shouldn't it be for me?"

§ 4

I made some desperate schemes to grow suddenly rich and powerful, and I learnt for the first time my true economic value. Already my father and I had been discussing my prospects in life and he had been finding me vague and difficult. I was full of large political intentions, but so far I had made no definite plans for a living that would render my political ambitions possible. It was becoming apparent to me that for a poor man in England, the only possible route to political distinction is the bar, and I was doing my best to reconcile myself to the years of waiting and practice that would have to precede my political début.

My father disliked the law. And I do not think it reconciled him to the idea of my being a barrister that afterwards I hoped to become a politician. "It isn't in our temperament, Stephen," he said. "It's a pushing, bullying, cramming, base life. I don't see you succeeding there, and I don't see myself rejoicing even if you do succeed. You have to shout, and Strattons don't shout; you have to be smart and tricky and there's never been a smart and tricky Stratton yet; you have to snatch opportunities and get the better of the people and misrepresent the realities of every case you touch. You're a paid misrepresenter. They say you'll get a fellowship, Stephen. Why not stay up, and do some thinking for a year or so. There'll be enough to keep you. Write a little."

"The bar," I said, "is only a means to an end."

"If you succeed."

"If I succeed. One has to take the chances of life everywhere."

"And what is the end?"

"Constructive statesmanship."

"Not in that way," said my father, pouring himself a second glass of port, and turned over my high-sounding phrase with a faint hint of distaste; "Constructive Statesmanship. No. Once a barrister always a barrister. You'll only be a party politician. . . . Vulgar men. . . . Vulgar. . . . If you succeed that is. . . ."

He criticized me but he did not oppose me, and already in the beginning of the summer we had settled that I should be called to the bar.

Now suddenly I wanted to go back upon all these determinations. I began to demand in the intellectual slang of the time "more actuality," and to amaze my father with talk about empire makers and the greatness of Lord Strathcona and Cecil Rhodes. Why, I asked, shouldn't I travel for a year in search of opportunity? At Oxford I had made acquaintance with a son of Pramley's, the big Mexican and Borneo man, and to him I wrote, apropos of a half-forgotten midnight talk in the rooms of some common friend. He wrote back with the suggestion that I should go and talk to his father, and I tore myself away from Mary and went up to see that great exploiter of undeveloped possibilities and have one of the most illuminating and humiliating conversations in the world. He was, I remember, a little pale-complexioned, slow-speaking man with a humorous blue eye, a faint, just perceptible northern accent and a trick of keeping silent for a moment after you had finished speaking, and he talked to me as one might talk to a child of eight who wanted to know how one could become a commander-in-chief. His son had evidently emphasized my Union reputation, and he would have been quite willing, I perceived, to give me employment if I had displayed the slightest intelligence or ability in any utilizable direction. But quite dreadfully he sounded my equipment with me and showed me the emptiness of my stores.

"You want some way that gives you a chance of growing rich rapidly," he said. "Aye. It's not a bad idea.

But there's others, you know, have tried that game before ye.

"You don't want riches just for riches but for an end. Aye! Aye! It's the spending attracts ye. You'd not have me think you'd the sin of avarice. I'm clear on that about ye.

"Well," he explained, "it's all one of three things we do, you know—prospecting and forestalling and—just stealing, and the only respectable way is prospecting. You'd prefer the respectable way, I suppose? . . . I knew ye would. Well, let's see what chances ye have."

And he began to probe my practical knowledge. It was like an unfit man stripping for a medical inspection. Did I know anything of oil, of rubber, of sugar, of substances generally, had I studied mineralogy or geology, had I any ideas of industrial processes, of technical chemistry, of rare minerals, of labor problems and the handling of alien labor, of the economics of railway management or of camping out in dry, thinly populated countries, or again could I maybe speak Spanish or Italian or Russian? The little dons who career about Oxford afoot and awheel, wearing old gowns and mortarboards, giggling over Spooner's latest, and being tremendous "characters" in the intervals of concocting the ruling-class mind, had turned my mind away from such matters altogether. I had left that sort of thing to Germans and east-end Jews and young men from the upper-grade board schools of Sheffield and Birmingham. I was made to realize appalling wildernesses of ignorance. . . .

"You see," said old Pramley, "you don't seem to know anything whatever. It's a deeficulty. It 'll stand in your way a little now, though no doubt you'd be quick at the uptake—after all the education they've given ye. . . . But it stands in your way, if ye think of setting out to do something large and effective, just immediately. . . ."

Moreover it came out, I forget now how, that I hadn't clearly grasped the difference between cumulative and non-cumulative preference shares. . . .

I remember too how I dined alone that evening in a mood between frantic exasperation and utter abasement in the window of the Mediated Universities Club, of which I was a junior member under the undergraduate rule. And I lay awake all night in one of the austere club bedrooms, saying to old Pramley a number of extremely able and penetrating things that had unhappily not occurred to me during the progress of our interview. I didn't go back to Burnmore for several days. I had set my heart on achieving something, on returning with some earnest of the great attack I was to make upon the separating great world between myself and Mary. I am far enough off now from that angry and passionate youngster to smile at the thought that my subjugation of things in general and high finance in particular took at last the form of proposing to go into the office of Bean, Medhurst, Stockton, and Schnadhorst upon half commission terms. I was awaiting my father's reply to this startling new suggestion when I got a telegram from Mary. "We are going to Scotland unexpectedly. Come down and see me." I went home instantly, and told my father I had come to talk things over with him. A note from Mary lay upon the hall-table as I came in and encountered my father. "I thought it better to come down to you," I said with my glance roving to find that, and then I met his eye. It wasn't altogether an unkindly eye, but I winced dishonestly.

"Talking is better for all sorts of things," said my father, and wanted to know if the weather had been as hot in London as it had been in Burnmore.

Mary's note was in pencil, scribbled hastily. I was to wait after eleven that night near the great rose bushes behind the pavilion. Long before eleven I was there, on a seat in a thick shadow looking across great lakes of moonlight towards the phantom statuary of the Italianate garden and the dark laurels that partly masked the house. I waited nearly an hour, an hour of stillness and small creepings and cheepings and goings to and fro among the branches.

In the bushes near by me a little green glow-worm shared my vigil.

And then, wrapped about in a dark velvet cloak, still in her white dinner dress, with shining, gleaming, glancing stones about her dear throat, warm and wonderful and glowing and daring, Mary came flitting out of the shadows to me.

"My dear," she whispered, panting and withdrawing a little from our first passionate embrace, "Oh my dear! . . . How did I come? Twice before, when I was a girl, I got out this way. By the corner of the conservatory and down the laundry wall. You can't see from here, but it's easy—easy. There's a tree that helps. And now I have come that way to you. *You!* . . .

"Oh! love me, my Stephen, love me, dear. Love me as if we were never to love again. Am I beautiful, my dear? Am I beautiful in the moonlight? Tell me! . . .

"Perhaps this is the night of our lives, dear! Perhaps never again will you and I be happy! . . .

"But the wonder, dear, the beauty! Isn't it still? It's as if nothing really stood solid and dry. As if everything floated. . . .

"Everyone in all the world has gone to sleep to-night and left the world to us. Come! Come this way and peep at the house, there. Stoop—under the branches. See, not a light is left! And all its blinds are drawn and its eyes shut. One window is open, *my* little window, Stephen! but that is in the shadow where that creeper makes everything black.

"Along here a little further is night-stock. Now —Now! Sniff, Stephen! Sniff! The scent of it! It lies—like a bank of scented air. . . . And Stephen, there! Look! . . . A star—a star without a sound, falling out of the blue! It's gone!"

There was her dear face close to mine, soft under the soft moonlight, and the breath of her sweet speech mingled with the scent of the night-stock. . . .

That was indeed the most beautiful night of my life, a night of moonlight and cool fragrance and adventurous excitement. We were transported out of this old world of dusty limitations; it was as if for those hours the curse of man was lifted from our lives. No one discovered us, no evil thing came near us. For a long time we lay close in one another's arms upon a bank of thyme. Our heads were close together; her eyelashes swept my cheek, we spoke rarely and in soft whispers, and our hearts were beating, beating. We were as solemn as great mountains and as innocent as sleeping children. Our kisses were kisses of moonlight. And it seemed to me that nothing that had ever happened or could happen afterwards, mattered against that happiness. . . .

It was nearly three when at last I came back into my father's garden. No one had missed me from my room and the house was all asleep, but I could not get in because I had closed a latch behind me, and so I stayed in the little arbor until day, watching the day break upon long beaches of pale cloud over the hills towards Alfridsham. I slept at last with my head upon my arms upon the stone table, until the noise of shooting bolts and doors being unlocked roused me to watch my chance and slip back again into the house, and up the shuttered darkened staircase to my tranquil, undisturbed bedroom.

§ 5

It was in the vein of something evasive in Mary's character that she let me hear first of her engagement to Justin through the *Times*. Away there in Scotland she got I suppose new perspectives, new ideas; the glow of our immediate passion faded. The thing must have been drawing in upon her for some time. Perhaps she had meant to tell me of it all that night when she had summoned me to Burnmore. Looking back now I am the more persuaded that she did. But the thing came to me in London with the effect of an immense treachery. Within a day or so of the newspaper's announcement she had written me a long letter answering some argument of mine, and saying nothing whatever of the people about her. Even then Justin must have been asking her to marry him. Her mind must have been full of that question. Then came a storm of disappointment, humiliation and anger with this realization. I can still feel myself writing and destroying letters to her, letters of satire, of protest. Oddly enough I cannot recall the letter that at last I sent her, but it is eloquent of the weak boyishness of my position that I sent it in our usual furtive manner, accepted every precaution that confessed the impossibility of our relationship. "No," she scribbled back, "you do not understand. I cannot write. I must talk to you."

We had a secret meeting.

With Beatrice Normandy's connivance she managed to get away for the better part of the day, and we spent a long morning in argument in the Botanical Gardens— that obvious solitude—and afterwards we lunched upon ham and ginger beer at a little open-air restaurant near the Broad Walk and talked on until nearly four. We were so young that I think we both felt, beneath our very real and vivid emotions, a gratifying sense of romantic resourcefulness in this prolonged discussion. There is something ridiculously petty and imitative about youth, something too, naïvely noble and adventurous. I can never determine if older people are less generous and imaginative or merely less absurd. I still recall the autumnal melancholy of that queer, neglected-looking place, in which I had never been before, and which I have never revisited—a memory of walking along narrow garden paths beside queer leaf-choked artificial channels of water under yellow-tinted trees, of rustic bridges going nowhere in particular, and of a kind of brickwork ruined castle, greatly decayed and ivy-grown, in which we sat for a long time looking out upon a lawn and a wide gravel path leading to a colossal frontage of conservatory.

I must have been resentful and bitter in the beginning of that talk. I do not remember that I had any command of the situation or did anything but protest throughout that day. I was too full of the egotism of the young lover to mark Mary's moods and feelings. It was only afterwards that I came to understand that she was not wilfully and deliberately following the course that was to separate us, that she was taking it with hesitations and regrets. Yet she spoke plainly enough, she spoke with a manifest sincerity of feeling. And while I had neither the grasp nor the subtlety to get behind her mind I perceive now as I think things out that Lady Ladislaw had both watched and acted, had determined her daughter's ideas, sown her mind with suggestions, imposed upon her a conception of her situation that now dominated all her thoughts.

"Dear Stephen," reiterated Mary, "I love you. I do, clearly, definitely, deliberately love you. Haven't I told you that? Haven't I made that plain to you?"

"But you are going to marry Justin!"

"Stephen dear, can I possibly marry you? Can I?"

"Why not? Why not make the adventure of life with me? Dare!"

She looked down on me. She was sitting upon a parapet of the brickwork and I was below her. She seemed to be weighing possibilities.

"Why not?" I cried. "Even now. Why not run away with me, throw our two lives together? Do as lovers have dared to do since the beginning of things! Let us go somewhere together——"

"But Stephen," she asked softly, "*where?*"

"Anywhere!"

She spoke as an elder might do to a child. "No! tell me where—exactly. Where would it be? Where should we go? How should we live? Tell me. Make me see it, Stephen."

"You are too cruel to me, Mary," I said. "How can I—on the spur of the moment—arrange——?"

"But dear, suppose it was somewhere very grimy and narrow! Something—like some of those back streets I came through to get here. Suppose it was some dreadful place. And you had no money. And we were both worried and miserable. One gets ill in such places. If I loved you, Stephen—I mean if you and I—if you and I were to be together, I should want it to be in sunshine, I should want it to be among beautiful forests and mountains. Somewhere very beautiful. . . ."

"Why not?"

"Because—to-day I know. There are no such places in the world for us. Stephen, they are dreams."

"For three years now," I said, "I have dreamed such dreams.

"Oh!" I cried out, stung by my own words, "but this is cowardice! Why should we submit to this old world! Why should we give up—things you have dreamed as well as I! You said once—to hear my voice—calling in the morning. . . . Let us take each other, Mary, now. *Now!* Let us take each other, and"—I still remember my impotent phrase—"afterwards count the cost!"

"If I were a queen," said Mary. "But you see I am not a queen." . . .

So we talked in fragments and snatches of argument,

and all she said made me see more clearly the large hopelessness of my desire. "At least," I urged, "do not marry Justin now. Give me a chance. Give me three years, Mary, three short years, to work, to do something!"

She knew so clearly now the quality of her own intentions.

"Dear Stephen," she explained, "if I were to come away with you and marry you, in just a little time I should cease to be your lover, I should be your squaw. I should have to share your worries and make your coffee—and disappoint you, disappoint you and fail you in a hundred ways. Think! Should I be any good as a squaw? How can one love when one knows the coffee isn't what it should be, and one is giving one's lover indigestion? And I don't *want* to be your squaw. I don't want that at all. It isn't how I feel for you. I don't *want* to be your servant and your possession."

"But you will be Justin's—squaw, you are going to marry him!"

"That is all different, Stevenage. Between him and me there will be space, air, dignity, endless servants——"

"But," I choked. "You! He! He will make love to you, Mary."

"You don't understand, Stephen."

"He will make love to you, Mary. Mary! don't you understand? These things—— We've never talked of them. . . . You will bear him children!"

"No," she said.

"But——"

"No. He promises. Stephen,—I am to own myself."

"But— He marries you!"

"Yes. Because he—he admires me. He cannot live without me. He loves my company. He loves to be seen with me. He wants me with him to enjoy all the things he has. Can't you understand, Stephen?"

"But do you mean——?"

Our eyes met.

"Stephen," she said, "I swear."

"But—— He hopes."

"I don't care. He has promised. I have his promise. I shall be free. Oh! I shall be free—free! He is a different man from you, Stephen. He isn't so fierce; he isn't so greedy."

"But it parts us!"

"Only from impossible things."

"It parts us."

"It does not even part us, Stevenage. We shall see one another! we shall talk to one another."

"I shall lose you."

"I shall keep you."

"But I—do you expect me to be content with *this?*"

"I will make you content. Oh! Stephen dear, can't there be love—love without this clutching, this gripping, this carrying off?"

"You will be carried altogether out of my world."

"If I thought that, Stephen, indeed I would not marry him."

But I insisted we should be parted, and parted in the end for ever, and there I was the wiser of the two. I knew the insatiable urgency within myself. I knew that if I continued to meet Mary I should continue to desire her until I possessed her altogether.

§ 6

I cannot reproduce with any greater exactness than this the quality and gist of our day-long conversation. Between us was a deep affection, and instinctive attraction, and our mental temperaments and our fundamental ideas were profoundly incompatible. We were both still very young in quality, we had scarcely begun to think ourselves out, we were greatly swayed by the suggestion of our circumstances, complex, incoherent and formless emotions confused our minds. But I see now that in us there struggled vast creative forces, forces that through a long future, in forms as yet undreamt of, must needs mould the destiny of our race. Far more than Mary I was accepting the conventions of our time. It seemed to me not merely reasonable but necessary that because she loved me she should place her life in my youthful and inexpert keeping, share my struggles and the real hardships they would have meant for her, devote herself to my happiness, bear me children, be my inspiration in imaginative moments, my squaw, helper and possession through the whole twenty-four hours of every day, and incidentally somehow rear whatever family we happened to produce, and I was still amazed in the depths of my being that she did not reciprocate this simple and comprehensive intention. I was ready enough I thought for equivalent sacrifices. I was prepared to give my whole life, subordinate all my ambitions, to the effort to maintain our home. If only I could have her, have her for my own, I was ready to pledge every hour I had still to live to that service. It seemed mere perversity to me then that she should turn even such vows as that against me.

"But I don't want it, Stevenage," she said. "I don't want it. I want you to go on to the service of the empire, I want to see you do great things, do all the things we've talked about and written about. Don't you see how much better that is for you and for me—and for the world and our lives? I don't want you to become a horrible little specialist in feeding and keeping me."

"Then—then *wait* for me!" I cried.

"But—I want to live myself! I don't want to wait. I want a great house, I want a great position, I want space and freedom. I want to have clothes—and be as splendid as your career is going to be. I want to be a great and shining lady in your life. I can't always live as I do now, dependent on my mother, whirled about by her movements, living in her light. Why should I be just a hard-up Vestal Virgin, Stephen, in your honor? You will not be able to marry me for years and years and years—unless you neglect your work, unless you throw away everything that is worth having between us in order just to get me."

"But I want *you*, Mary," I cried, drumming at the little green table with my fist. "I want you. I want nothing else in all the world unless it has to do with you."

"You've got me—as much as anyone will ever have me. You'll always have me. Always I will write to you, talk to you, watch you. Why are you so greedy, Stephen? Why are you so ignoble? If I were to come now and marry you, it wouldn't help you. It would turn you into—a wife-keeper, into the sort of uninteresting pre-

7   93

occupied man one sees running after and gloating over the woman he's bought—at the price of his money and his dignity—and everything. . . . It's not proper for a man to live so for a woman and her children. It's dwarfish. It's enslaving. It's—it's indecent. Stephen! I'd hate you so." . . .

§ 7

We parted at last at a cab-rank near a bridge over the Canal at the western end of Park Village. I remember that I made a last appeal to her as we walked towards it, and that we loitered on the bridge, careless of who might see us there, in a final conflict of our wills. "Before it is too late, Mary, dear," I said.

She shook her head, her white lips pressed together.

"But after the things that have happened. That night —the moonlight!"

"It's not fair," she said, "for you to talk of that. It isn't fair."

"But Mary. This is parting. This indeed is parting."

She answered never a word.

"Then at least talk to me again for one time more."

"Afterwards," she said. "Afterwards I will talk to you. Don't make things too hard for me, Stephen."

"If I could I would make this impossible. It's—it's hateful."

She turned to the kerb, and for a second or so we stood there without speaking. Then I beckoned to a hansom.

She told me Beatrice Normandy's address.

I helped her into the cab. "Good-bye," I said with a

weak affectation of an everyday separation, and I turned to the cabman with her instructions.

Then again we looked at one another. The cabman waited. "All right, sir?" he asked.

"Go ahead!" I said, and lifted my hat to the little white face within.

I watched the cab until it vanished round the curve of the road. Then I turned about to a world that had become very large and empty and meaningless.

§ 8

I struggled feebly to arrest the course of events. I wrote Mary some violent and bitter letters. I treated her as though she alone were responsible for my life and hers; I said she had diverted my energies, betrayed me, ruined my life. I hinted she was cold-blooded, mercenary, shameless. Someday you, with that quick temper of yours and your power of expression, will understand that impulse to write, to pour out a passionately unjust interpretation of some nearly intolerable situation, and it is not the least of all the things I owe to Mary that she understood my passion and forgave those letters and forgot them. I tried twice to go and see her. But I do not think I need tell you, little son, of these self-inflicted humiliations and degradations. An angry man is none the less a pitiful man because he is injurious. The hope that had held together all the project of my life was gone, and all my thoughts and emotions lay scattered in confusion. . . .

You see, my little son, there are two sorts of love;

95

we use one name for very different things. The love that a father bears his children, that a mother feels, that comes sometimes, a strange brightness and tenderness that is half pain, at the revelation of some touching aspect of one long known to one, at the sight of a wife bent with fatigue and unsuspicious of one's presence, at the wretchedness and perplexity of some wrong-doing brother, or at an old servant's unanticipated tears, that is love—like the love God must bear us. That is the love we must spread from those of our marrow until it reaches out to all mankind, that will some day reach out to all mankind. But the love of a young man for a woman takes this quality only in rare moments of illumination and complete assurance. My love for Mary was a demand, it was a wanton claim I scored the more deeply against her for every moment of happiness she gave me. I see now that as I emerged from the first abjection of my admiration and began to feel assured of her affection, I meant nothing by her but to possess her, I did not want her to be happy as I want you to be happy even at the price of my life; I wanted her. I wanted her as barbarians want a hunted enemy, alive or dead. It was a flaming jealousy to have her mine. That granted, then I was prepared for all devotions. . . .

This is how men love women. Almost as exclusively and fiercely I think do women love men. And the deepest question before humanity is just how far this jealous greed may be subdued to a more generous passion. The fierce jealousy of men for women and women for men is the very heart of all our social jealousies, the underlying tension of this crowded modern life that has grown out of the ampler, simpler, ancient life of men. That is why we compete against one another so bitterly, refuse association and generous co-operations, keep the struggle for existence hard and bitter, hamper and subordinate the women as they in their turn would if they could hamper and subordinate the men—because each must thoroughly have his own.

And I knew my own heart too well to have any faith in Justin and his word. He was taking what he could, and his mind would never rest until some day he had all. I had seen him only once, but the heavy and resolute profile above his bent back and slender shoulders stuck in my memory.

If he was cruel to Mary, I told her, or broke his least promise to her, I should kill him.

§ 9

My distress grew rather than diminished in the days immediately before her marriage, and that day itself stands out by itself in my memory, a day of wandering and passionate unrest. My imagination tormented me with thoughts of Justin as a perpetual privileged wooer.

Well, well,—I will not tell you, I will not write the ugly mockeries my imagination conjured up. I was constantly on the verge of talking and cursing aloud to myself, or striking aimlessly at nothing with clenched fists. I was too stupid to leave London, too disturbed for work or any distraction of my mind. I wandered about the streets of London all day. In the morning I came near going to the church and making some preposterous interruptions.

97

And I remember discovering three or four carriages adorned with white favors and a little waiting crowd outside that extinguisher-spired place at the top of Regent Street, and wondering for a moment or so at their common preoccupation, and then understanding. Of course, another marriage! Of all devilish institutions!

What was I to do with my life now? What was to become of my life? I can still recall the sense of blank unanswerableness with which these questions dominated my mind, and associated with it is an effect of myself as a small human being, singular and apart, wandering through a number of London landscapes. At one time I was in a great grey smoke-rimmed autumnal space of park, much cut up by railings and worn by cricket pitches, far away from any idea of the Thames, and in the distance over the tops of trees I discovered perplexingly the clustering masts and spars of ships. I have never seen that place since. Then the Angel at Islington is absurdly mixed up with the distresses of this day. I attempted some great detour thence, and found myself with a dumb irritation returning to the place from another direction. I remember too a wide street over which passes a thundering railway bridge borne upon colossal rounded pillars of iron, and carrying in white and blue some big advertisement, I think of the *Daily Telegraph*. Near there I thought a crowd was gathered about the victim of some accident, and thrusting myself among the people with a vague idea of help, discovered a man selling a remedy for corns. And somewhere about this north region I discovered I was faint with hunger, and got some bread and cheese and beer in a gaudily decorated saloon bar with a sanded floor. I resisted a monstrous impulse to stay in that place and drink myself into inactivity and stupefaction with beer.

Then for a long time I sat upon an iron seat near some flower beds in a kind of garden that had the headstones of graves arranged in a row against a yellow brick wall. The place was flooded with the amber sunshine of a September afternoon. I shared the seat with a nursemaid in charge of a perambulator and several scuffling uneasy children, and I kept repeating to myself: "By now it is all over. The thing is done."

My sense of the enormity of London increased with the twilight, and began to prevail a little against my intense personal wretchedness. I remember wastes of building enterprise, interminable vistas of wide dark streets, with passing trams, and here and there at strategic corners coruscating groups of shops. And somewhere I came along a narrow street suddenly upon the distant prospect of a great monstrous absurd place on a steep hill against the last brightness of the evening sky, a burlesque block of building with huge truncated pyramids at either corner, that I have since learnt was the Alexandra Palace. It was so queer and bulky that it arrested and held my attention, struck on my memory with an almost dreamlike quality, so that years afterwards I went to Muswell Hill to see if indeed there really was such a place on earth, or whether I had had a waking nightmare during my wanderings. . . .

I wandered far that night, very far. Some girl accosted me, a thin-faced ruined child younger by a year or so than myself. I remembered how I talked to her, foolish rambling talk. "If you loved a man, and he was poor, you'd wait," I said, "you'd stick to him. You'd not leave him just to get married to a richer man."

We prowled talking for a time, and sat upon a seat somewhere near the Regent's Park canal. I rather think I planned to rescue her from a fallen 'life, but somehow we dropped that topic. I know she kissed me. I have a queer impression that it came into my head to marry her. I put all my loose money in her hands at last and went away extraordinarily comforted by her, I know not how, leaving her no doubt wondering greatly.

I did not go to bed that night at all, nor to the office next morning. I never showed myself in the office again. Instead I went straight down to my father, and told him I wanted to go to the war forthwith. I had an indistinct memory of a promise I had made Mary to stay in England, but I felt it was altogether unendurable that I should ever meet her again. My father sat at table over the remains of his lunch, and regarded me with astonishment, with the beginnings of protest.

"I want to get away," I said, and to my own amazement and shame I burst into tears.

"My boy!" he gasped, astonished and terrified. "You've—you've not done—some foolish thing?"

"No," I said, already wiping the tears from my face, "nothing. . . . But I want to go away."

"You shall do as you please," he said, and sat for a moment regarding his only son with unfathomable eyes.

Then he got up with a manner altogether matter-of-fact, came half-way round the table and mixed me a whisky and soda. "It won't be much of a war, I'm told," he said with the syphon in his hands, breaking a silence. "I sometimes wish—I had seen a bit of soldiering. And this seems to be an almost unavoidable war. Now, at any rate, it's unavoidable. . . . Drink this and have a biscuit."

He turned to the mantelshelf, and filled his pipe with his broad back to me. "Yes," he said, "you—— You'll be interested in the war. I hope—— I hope you'll have a good time there. . . ."

CHAPTER THE FIFTH

THE WAR IN SOUTH AFRICA

§ 1

MARY and I did not meet again for five years, and for nearly all that time I remained in South Africa. I went from England a boy; I came back seasoned into manhood. They had been years of crowded experience, rapid yet complicated growth, disillusionment and thought. Responsibility had come to me. I had seen death, I had seen suffering, and held the lives of men in my hands.

Of course one does not become a soldier on active service at once for the wishing, and there was not at first that ready disposition on the part of the home military authorities which arose later, to send out young enthusiasts. I could ride and shoot fairly well, and accordingly I decided to go on my own account to Durban —for it was manifest that things would begin in Natal— and there attach myself to some of the local volunteer corps that would certainly be raised. This took me out of England at once, a thing that fell in very well with my mood. I would, I was resolved, begin life afresh. I would force myself to think of nothing but the war. I would never if I could help it think of Mary again.

The war had already begun when I reached Durban. The town was seething with the news of a great British victory at Dundee. We came into the port through rain and rough weather and passed a big white liner loaded up feverishly from steam tenders with wealthy refugees going England-ward. From two troopships against the wharves there was a great business of landing horses—the horses of the dragoons and hussars from India. I spent the best part of my first night in South Africa in the streets looking in vain for a bedroom, and was helped at last by a kindly rickshaw Zulu to a shanty where I slept upon three chairs. I remember I felt singularly unwanted.

The next day I set about my volunteering. By midday I had opened communications with that extremely untried and problematical body, the Imperial Light Horse, and in three days more I was in the company of a mixed batch of men, mostly Australian volunteers, on my way to a place I had never heard of before called Ladysmith, through a country of increasing picturesqueness and along a curious curving little line whose down traffic seemed always waiting in sidings, and consisted of crowded little trains full of pitiful fugitives, white, brown, and black, stifled and starving. They were all clamoring to buy food and drink—and none seemed forthcoming. We shunted once to allow a southbound train to pass, a peculiar train that sent everyone on to the line to see—prisoners of war! There they were, real live enemies, rather glum, looking out at us with faces very like our own—but rather more unshaven. They had come from the battle of Elandslaagte. . . .

I had never been out of England before except for a little mountaineering in the French Alps and one walking excursion in the Black Forest, and the scenery of lower Natal amazed me. I had expected nothing nearly so tropical, so rich and vivid. There were little Mozambique monkeys chattering in the thick-set trees beside the line and a quantity of unfamiliar birds and gaudy flowers amidst the abundant deep greenery. There were aloe and cactus hedges, patches of unfamiliar cultivation upon the hills; bunchy, frondy growths that I learnt were bananas and plantains, and there were barbaric insanitary-looking Kaffir kraals which I supposed had vanished before our civilization. There seemed an enormous quantity of Kaffirs all along the line—and all of them, men, women, and children, were staring at the train. The scenery grew finer and bolder, and more bare and mountainous, until at last we came out into the great basin in which lay this Ladysmith. It seemed a poor unimportant, dusty little street of huts as we approached it, but the great crests beyond struck me as very beautiful in the morning light. . . .

I forgot the beauty of those hills as we drew into the station. It was the morning after the surrender of Nicholson's Nek. I had come to join an army already tremendously astonished and shattered. The sunny prospect of a triumphal procession to Pretoria which had been still in men's minds at Durban had vanished altogether. In rather less than a fortnight of stubborn fighting we had displayed a strategy that was flighty rather than brilliant, and lost a whole battery of guns and nearly twelve hundred prisoners. We had had compensations, our common soldiers were good stuff at any rate, but the fact was clear that we were fighting an army not only very much bigger than ours but better equipped, with bigger guns, better information, and it seemed superior strategy. We were being shoved back into this Ladysmith and encircled. This confused, disconcerted, and thoroughly bad-tempered army, whose mules and bullocks cumbered the central street of the place, was all that was left of the British Empire in Natal. Behind it was an unprotected country and the line to Pietermaritzburg, Durban, and the sea.

You cannot imagine how amazed I felt at it. I had been prepared for a sort of Kentucky quality in the enemy, illiteracy, pluck, guile and good shooting, but to find them with more modern arms than our own, more modern methods! Weren't we there, after all, to teach *them!* Weren't we the Twentieth and they the Eighteenth Century? The town had been shelled the day before from those very hills I had admired; at any time it might be shelled again. The nose of a big gun was pointed out to me by a blasphemous little private in the Devons. It was a tremendous, a profoundly impressive, black snout. His opinions of the directing wisdom at home were unquotable. The platform was a wild confusion of women and children and colored people,— there was even an invalid lady on a stretcher. Every non-combatant who could be got out of Ladysmith was being hustled out that day. Everyone was smarting with the sense of defeat in progress, everyone was disappointed and worried; one got short answers to one's questions. For a time I couldn't even find out where I had to go. . . .

§ 2

I fired my first shot at a fellow-creature within four days of my arrival. We rode out down the road to the south to search some hills, and found the Boers in fair strength away to the east of us. We were dismounted and pushed up on foot through a wood to a grassy crest. There for the first time I saw the enemy, little respectable-looking unsoldierlike figures, mostly in black, dodging about upon a ridge perhaps a mile away. I took a shot at one of these figures just before it vanished into a gully. One or two bullets came overhead, and I tried to remember what I had picked up about cover. They made a sound, *whiff-er-whiff*, a kind of tearing whistle, and there was nothing but a distant crackling to give one a hint of their direction until they took effect. I remember the peculiar smell of the grass amidst which I crouched, my sudden disgust to realize I was lying, and had to lie now for an indefinite time, in the open sunlight and far from any shade, and how I wondered whether after all I had wanted to come to this war.

We lay shooting intermittently until the afternoon, I couldn't understand why; we went forward a little, and at last retired upon Ladysmith. On the way down to the horses, I came upon my first dead man. He was lying in a crumpled heap not fifty yards from where I had been shooting. There he lay, the shattered mirror of a world. One side of his skull over the ear had been knocked away by a nearly spent bullet, and he was crumpled up and face upward as though he had struggled to his feet and fallen back. He looked rather horrible, with blue eyes wide open and glassily amazed, and the black flies clustering upon his clotted wound and round his open mouth. . . .

I halted for a moment at the sight, and found the keen scrutiny of a fellow trooper upon me. "No good waiting for him," I said with an affectation of indifference. But all through the night I saw him again, and marvelled at the stupendous absurdity of such a death. I was a little feverish, I remember, and engaged in an interminable theological argument with myself, why when a man is dead he should leave so queer and irrelevant a thing as a body to decay. . . .

I was already very far away from London and Burnmore Park. I doubt if I thought of Mary at all for many days.

§ 3

It isn't my business to write here any consecutive story of my war experiences. Luck and some latent quality in my composition made me a fairly successful soldier. Among other things I have an exceptionally good sense of direction, and that was very useful to me, and in Burnmore Park I suppose I had picked up many of the qualities of a scout. I did some fair outpost work during the Ladysmith siege, I could report as well as crawl and watch, and I was already a sergeant when we made a night attack and captured and blew up Long Tom. There, after the fight, while we were covering the engineers, I got a queer steel ball about the size of a pea in my arm, a bicycle bearings ball it was, and had my first experience of an army surgeon's knife next day. It was much less painful than I had expected. I was also hit during the big assault on the sixth of January in the left shoulder, but so very slightly that I wasn't technically disabled. They were the only wounds I got in the war, but I went under with dysentery before the relief; and though I was by no means a bad case I was a very yellow-faced, broken-looking convalescent when at last the Boer hosts rolled northward again and Buller's men came riding across the flats. . . .

I had seen some stimulating things during those four months of actual warfare, a hundred intense impressions of death, wounds, anger, patience, brutality, courage, generosity and wasteful destruction—above all, wasteful destruction—to correct the easy optimistic patriotism of my university days.   There is a depression in the opening stages of fever and a feebleness in a convalescence on a starvation diet that leads men to broad and sober views. (Heavens! how I hated the horse extract—'chevril' we called it—that served us for beef tea.)   When I came down from Ladysmith to the sea to pick up my strength I had not an illusion left about the serene, divinely appointed empire of the English.   But if I had less national conceit, I had certainly more patriotic determination. That grew with every day of returning health.   The reality of this war had got hold of my imagination, as indeed for a time it got hold of the English imagination altogether, and I was now almost fiercely keen to learn and do.   At the first chance I returned to active service, and now I was no longer a disconsolate lover taking war for a cure, but an earnest, and I think reasonably able, young officer, very alert for chances.

I got those chances soon enough.   I rejoined our men beyond Kimberley, on the way to Mafeking,—we were the extreme British left in the advance upon Pretoria—and I rode with Mahon and was ambushed with him in a little affair beyond Koodoosrand.   It was a sudden brisk encounter.   We got fired into at close quarters, but we knew our work by that time, and charged home and brought in a handful of prisoners to make up for the men we had lost. A few days later we came into the flattened ruins of the quaintest siege in history. . . .

Three days after we relieved Mafeking I had the luck to catch one of Snyman's retreating guns rather easily, the only big gun that was taken at Mafeking. I came upon it unexpectedly with about twenty men, spotted a clump of brush four hundred yards ahead, galloped into it before the Boers realized the boldness of our game, shot all the draught oxen while they hesitated, and held them up until Chambers arrived on the scene. The incident got perhaps a disproportionate share of attention in the papers at home, because of the way in which Mafeking had been kept in focus. I was mentioned twice again in despatches before we rode across to join Roberts in Pretoria and see what we believed to be the end of the war. We were too late to go on up to Komatipoort, and had some rather blank and troublesome work on the north side of the town. That was indeed the end of the great war; the rest was a struggle with guerillas.

Everyone thought things were altogether over. I wrote to my father discussing the probable date of my return. But there were great chances still to come for an active young officer; the guerilla war was to prolong the struggle yet for a whole laborious, eventful year, and I was to make the most of those later opportunities. . . .

Those years in South Africa are stuck into my mind like—like those pink colored pages about something else one finds at times in a railway *Indicateur*. Chance had put this work in my way, and started me upon it with a reputation that wasn't altogether deserved, and I found I could only live up to it and get things done well by a fixed and extreme concentration of my attention. But the whole business was so interesting that I found it possible to make that concentration. Essentially warfare is a game of elaborate but witty problems in precaution and anticipation, with amazing scope for invention. You so saturate your mind with the facts and possibilities of the situation that intuitions emerge. It did not do to think of anything beyond those facts and possibilities and dodges and counterdodges, for to do so was to let in irrelevant and distracting lights. During all that concluding year of service I was not so much myself as a forced and artificial thing I made out of myself to meet the special needs of the time. I became a Boer-outwitting animal. When I was tired of this specialized thinking, then the best relief, I found, was some quite trivial occupation—playing poker, yelling in the chorus of some interminable song one of the men would sing, or coining South African Limericks or playing burlesque *bouts-rimés* with Fred Maxim, who was then my second in command. . . .

Yet occasionally thought overtook me. I remember lying one night out upon a huge dark hillside, in a melancholy wilderness of rock-ribbed hills, waiting for one of the flying commandoes that were breaking northward from Cape Colony towards the Orange River in front of Colonel Eustace. We had been riding all day, I was taking risks in what I was doing, and there is something very cheerless in a fireless bivouac. My mind became uncontrollably active.

It was a clear, still night. The young moon set early in a glow of white that threw the jagged contours of a hill to the south-east into strange, weird prominence. The patches of moonshine evaporated from the summits of the nearer hills, and left them hard and dark. Then there was nothing but a great soft black darkness below that jagged edge and above it the stars very large and bright. Somewhere under that enormous serenity to the south of us the hunted Boers must be halting to snatch an hour or so of rest, and beyond them again extended the long thin net of the pursuing British. It all seemed infinitely small and remote, there was no sound of it, no hint of it, no searchlight at work, no faintest streamer of smoke nor the reflection of a solitary fire in the sky. . . .

All this business that had held my mind so long was reduced to insignificance between the blackness of the hills and the greatness of the sky; a little trouble, it seemed of no importance under the Southern Cross. And I fell wondering, as I had not wondered for long, at the forces that had brought me to this occupation and the strangeness of this game of war which had filled the minds and tempered the spirit of a quarter of a million of men for two hard-living years.

I fell thinking of the dead.

No soldier in a proper state of mind ever thinks of the dead. At times of course one suspects, one catches a man glancing at the pair of boots sticking out stiffly from under a blanket, but at once he speaks of other things. Nevertheless some suppressed part of my being had been stirring up ugly and monstrous memories, of distortion, disfigurement, torment and decay, of dead men in stained and ragged clothes, with their sole-worn boots drawn up under them, of the blood trail of a dying man who had crawled up to a dead comrade rather than die alone, of Kaffirs heaping limp, pitiful bodies together for burial, of the voices of inaccessible wounded in the rain on Waggon Hill crying in the night, of a heap of men we found in a donga three days dead, of the dumb agony of shell-torn horses, and the vast distressful litter and heavy brooding stench, the cans and cartridge-cases and filth and bloody rags of a shelled and captured laager. I will confess I have never lost my horror of dead bodies; they are dreadful to me—dreadful. I dread their stiff attitudes, their terrible intent inattention. To this day such memories haunt me. That night they nearly overwhelmed me. . . . I thought of the grim silence of the surgeon's tent, the miseries and disordered ravings of the fever hospital, of the midnight burial of a journalist at Ladysmith with the distant searchlight on Bulwana flicking suddenly upon our faces and making the coffin shine silver white. What a vast trail of destruction South Africa had become! I thought of the black scorched stones of burnt and abandoned farms, of wretched natives we had found shot like dogs and flung aside, rottenly amazed, decaying in infinite indignity; of stories of treachery and fierce revenges sweeping along in the trail of the greater fighting. I knew too well of certain atrocities,—one had to believe them incredibly stupid to escape the conviction that they were incredibly evil.

For a time my mind could make no headway against its monstrous assemblage of horror. There was something in that jagged black hill against the moonshine and the gigantic basin of darkness out of which it rose that seemed to gather all these gaunt and grisly effects into one appalling heap of agonizing futility. That rock rose up and crouched like something that broods and watches.

WAR

I remember I sat up in the darkness staring at it.

I found myself murmuring: "Get the proportions of things, get the proportions of things!" I had an absurd impression of a duel between myself and the cavernous antagonism of the huge black spaces below me. I argued that all this pain and waste was no more than the selvedge of a proportionately limitless fabric of sane, interested, impassioned and joyous living. These stiff still memories seemed to refute me. But why us? they seemed to insist. In some way it's essential,—this margin. I stopped at that.

"If all this pain, waste, violence, anguish is essential to life, why does my spirit rise against it? What is wrong with me?" I got from that into a corner of self-examination. Did I respond overmuch to these painful aspects in life? When I was a boy I had never had the spirit even to kill rats. Siddons came into the meditation, Siddons, the essential Englishman, a little scornful, throwing out contemptuous phrases. Soft! Was I a soft? What was a soft? Something not rough, not hearty and bloody! I felt I had to own to the word—after years of resistance. A dreadful thing it is when a great empire has to rely upon soft soldiers.

Was civilization breeding a type of human being too tender to go on living? I stuck for a time as one does on these nocturnal occasions at the word "hypersensitive," going round it and about it. . . .

I do not know now how it was that I passed from a mood so darkened and sunless to one of exceptional exaltation, but I recall very clearly that I did. I believe that I made a crowning effort against this despair and horror that had found me out in the darkness and overcome. I cried in my heart for help, as a lost child cries, to God. I seem to remember a rush of impassioned prayer, not only for myself, not chiefly for myself, but for all those smashed and soiled and spoilt and battered residues of men whose memories tormented me. I prayed to God that they had not lived in vain, that particularly those poor Kaffir scouts might not have lived in vain. "They are like children," I said. "It was a murder of children. . . . *By children!*"

My horror passed insensibly. I have to feel the dreadfulness of these things, I told myself, because it is good for such a creature as I to feel them dreadful, but if one understood it would all be simple. Not dreadful at all. I clung to that and repeated it,—"it would all be perfectly simple." It would come out no more horrible than the things that used to frighten me as a child,—the shadow on the stairs, the white moonrise reflected on a barked and withered tree, a peculiar dream of moving geometrical forms, an ugly illustration in the "Arabian Nights." . . .

I do not know how long I wrestled with God and prayed that night, but abruptly the shadows broke; and very suddenly and swiftly my spirit seemed to flame up into space like some white beacon that is set alight. Everything became light and clear and confident. I was assured that all was well with us, with us who lived and fought and with the dead who rotted now in fifty thousand hasty graves. . . .

For a long time it seemed I was repeating again and again with soundless lips and finding the deepest comfort in my words:—"And out of our agonies comes victory, out of our agonies comes victory! Have pity on us, God our Father!"

WAR

I think that mood passed quite insensibly from waking to a kind of clear dreaming. I have an impression that I fell asleep and was aroused by a gun. Yet I was certainly still sitting up when I heard that gun.

I was astonished to find things darkly visible about me. I had not noted that the stars were growing pale until the sound of this gun very far away called my mind back to the grooves in which it was now accustomed to move. I started into absolute wakefulness. A gun? . . .

I found myself trying to see my watch.

I heard a slipping and clatter of pebbles near me, and discovered Fred Maxim at my side. "Look!" he said, hoarse with excitement. "Already!" He pointed to a string of dim little figures galloping helter-skelter over the neck and down the gap in the hills towards us.

They came up against the pale western sky, little nodding swaying black dots, and flashed over and were lost in the misty purple groove towards us. They must have been riding through the night—the British following. To them we were invisible. Behind us was the shining east, we were in a shadow still too dark to betray us.

In a moment I was afoot and called out to the men, my philosophy, my deep questionings, all torn out of my mind like a page of scribbled poetry plucked out of a business note-book. Khaki figures were up all about me passing the word and hurrying to their places. All the dispositions I had made overnight came back clear and sharp into my mind. We hadn't long for preparations. . . .

It seems now there were only a few busy moments before the fighting began. It must have been much longer in reality. By that time we had seen their gun come over and a train of carts. They were blundering right into us. Every moment it was getting lighter, and the moment of contact nearer. Then "Crack!" from down below among the rocks, and there was a sudden stoppage of the trail of dark shapes upon the hillside. "Crack!" came a shot from our extreme left. I damned the impatient men who had shot away the secret of our presence. But we had to keep them at a shooting distance. Would the Boers have the wit to charge through us before the daylight came, or should we hold them? I had a swift, disturbing idea. Would they try a bolt across our front to the left? Had we extended far enough across the deep valley to our left? But they'd hesitate on account of their gun. The gun couldn't go that way because of the gullies and thickets. . . . But suppose they tried it! I hung between momentous decisions. . . .

Then all up the dim hillside I could make out the Boers halting and riding back. One rifle across there flashed.

We held them! . . .

We had begun the fight of Pieters Nek, which ended before midday with the surrender of Simon Botha and over seven hundred men. It was the crown of all my soldiering.

§ 4

I came back to England at last when I was twenty-six. After the peace of Vereeniging I worked under the Repatriation Commission which controlled the distribution of returning prisoners and concentrated population to their homes; for the most part I was distributing stock and grain, and presently manœuvring a sort of ploughing flying column that the dearth of horses and oxen made necessary, work that was certainly as hard as if far less exciting than war. That particular work of replanting the desolated country with human beings took hold of my imagination, and for a time at least seemed quite straightforward and understandable. The comfort of ceasing to destroy!

No one has written anything that really conveys the quality of that repatriation process; the queer business of bringing these suspicious, illiterate, despondent people back to their desolated homes, reuniting swarthy fathers and stockish mothers, witnessing their touchingly inexpressive encounters, doing what one could to put heart into their resumption. Memories come back to me of great littered heaps of luggage, bundles, blankets, rough boxes, piled newly purchased stores, ready-made doors, window sashes heaped ready for the waggons, slow-moving, apathetic figures sitting and eating, an infernal squawking of parrots, sometimes a wailing of babies. Repatriation went on to a parrot obligato, and I never hear a parrot squawk without a flash of South Africa across my mind. All the prisoners, I believe, brought back parrots—some two or three. I had to spread these people out, over a country still grassless, with teams of war-worn oxen, mules and horses that died by the dozen on my hands. The end of each individual instance was a handshake, and one went lumbering on, leaving the children one had deposited behind one already playing with old ration-tins or hunting about for cartridge-cases, while adults stared at the work they had to do.

There was something elementary in all that redistribution. I felt at times like a child playing in a nursery and putting out its bricks and soldiers on the floor. There was a kind of greatness too about the process, a quality of atonement. And the people I was taking back, the men anyhow, were for the most part charming and wonderful people, very simple and emotional, so that once a big bearded man, when I wanted him in the face of an overflowing waggon to abandon about half-a-dozen great angular colored West Indian shells he had lugged with him from Bermuda, burst into tears of disappointment. I let him take them, and at the end I saw them placed with joy and reverence in a little parlor, to become the war heirlooms no doubt of a long and bearded family. As we shook hands after our parting coffee he glanced at them with something between gratitude and triumph in his eyes.

Yes, that was a great work, more especially for a ripening youngster such as I was at that time. The memory of long rides and tramps over that limitless veld returns to me, lonely in spite of the creaking, lumbering waggons and transport riders and Kaffirs that followed behind. South Africa is a country not only of immense spaces but of an immense spaciousness. Everything is far apart; even the grass blades are far apart. Sometimes one crossed wide stony wastes, sometimes came great stretches of tall, yellow-green grass, wheel-high, sometimes a little green patch of returning cultivation drew nearer for an hour or so, sometimes the blundering, toilsome passage of a torrent interrupted our slow onward march. And constantly one saw long lines of torn and twisted barbed wire stretching away and away, and here and there one found archipelagoes as it were in this dry ocean of the skeletons of cattle, and there were places where troops had halted and their scattered ration-tins shone like diamonds in the sunshine. Occasionally I struck talk, some returning prisoner, some group of discharged British soldiers become carpenters or bricklayers again and making their pound a day by the work of rebuilding; always everyone was ready to expatiate upon the situation. Usually, however, I was alone, thinking over this immense now vanished tornado of a war and this equally astonishing work of healing that was following it.

I became keenly interested in all this great business, and thought at first of remaining indefinitely in Africa. Repatriation was presently done and finished. I had won Milner's good opinion, and he was anxious for me to go on working in relation to the labor difficulty that rose now more and more into prominence behind the agricultural re-settlement. But when I faced that I found myself in the middle of a tangle infinitely less simple than putting back an agricultural population upon its land.

§ 5

For the first time in my life I was really looking at the social fundamental of Labor.

There is something astonishingly naïve in the unconsciousness with which people of our class float over the great economic realities. All my life I had been hearing of the Working Classes, of Industrialism, of Labor Problems and the Organization of Labor; but it was only now in South Africa, in this chaotic, crude illuminating period of putting a smashed and desolated social order together again, that I perceived these familiar phrases represented something—something stupendously real. There were, I began to recognize, two sides to civilization; one traditional, immemorial, universal, the side of the homestead, the side I had been seeing and restoring; and there was another, ancient, too, but never universal, as old at least as the mines of Syracuse and the building of the pyramids, the side that came into view when I emerged from the dusty station and sighted the squat shanties and slender chimneys of Johannesburg, that uprooted side of social life, that accumulation of toilers divorced from the soil, which is Industrialism and Labor and which carries such people as ourselves, and whatever significance and possibilities we have, as an elephant carries its rider.

Now all Johannesburg and Pretoria were discussing Labor and nothing but Labor. Bloemfontein was in conference thereon. Our work of repatriation which had loomed so large on the southernward veld became here a business at once incidental and remote. One felt that a little sooner or a little later all that would resume and go on, as the rains would, and the veld-grass. But this was something less kindred to the succession of the seasons and the soil. This was a hitch in the upper fabric. Here in the great ugly mine-scarred basin of the Rand, with its bare hillsides, half the stamps were standing idle, machinery was eating its head off, time and water were running to waste amidst an immense exasperated disputation. Something had given way. The war had spoilt the Kaffir "boy," he was demanding enormous wages, he was away from Johannesburg, and above all, he would no longer "go underground."

Implicit in all the argument and suggestion about me was this profoundly suggestive fact that some people, quite a lot of people, scores of thousands, had to "go underground." Implicit too always in the discourse was the assumption that the talker or writer in question wasn't for a moment to be expected to go there. Those others, whoever they were, had to do that for us. Before the war it had been the artless Portuguese Kaffir, but he alas! was being diverted to open-air employment at Delagoa Bay. Should we raise wages and go on with the fatal process of "spoiling the workers," should we by imposing a tremendous hut-tax *drive* the Kaffir into our toils, should we carry the labor hunt across the Zambesi into Central Africa, should we follow the lead of Lord Kitchener and Mr. Creswell and employ the rather dangerous unskilled white labor (with "ideas" about strikes and socialism) that had drifted into Johannesburg, should we do tremendous things with labor-saving machinery, or were we indeed (desperate yet tempting resort!) to bring in the cheap Indian or Chinese coolie?

Steadily things were drifting towards that last tremendous experiment. There was a vigorous opposition in South Africa and in England (growing there to an outcry), but behind that proposal was the one vitalizing conviction in modern initiative: — indisputably it would pay, *it would pay!* . . .

The human mind has a much more complex and fluctuating process than most of those explanatory people who write about psychology would have us believe. Instead of that simple, direct movement, like the movement of a point, forward and from here to there, one's thoughts advance like an army, sometimes extended over an enormous front, sometimes in échelon, sometimes bunched in a column throwing out skirmishing clouds of emotion, some flying and soaring, some crawling, some stopping and dying. . . . In this matter of Labor, for example, I have thought so much, thought over the ground again and again, come into it from this way and from that way, that for the life of me I find it impossible to state at all clearly how much I made of these questions during that Johannesburg time. I cannot get back into those ancient ignorances, revive my old astonishments and discoveries. Certainly I envisaged the whole process much less clearly than I do now, ignored difficulties that have since entangled me, regarded with a tremendous perplexity aspects that have now become lucidly plain. I came back to England confused, and doing what confused people are apt to do, clinging to an inadequate phrase that seemed at any rate to define a course of action. The word "efficiency" had got hold of me. All our troubles came, one assumed, from being "inefficient." One turned towards politics with a bustling air, and was all for fault-finding and renovation.

I sit here at my desk, pen in hand, and trace figures on the blotting-paper, and wonder how much I understood at that time. I came back to England to work on the side of "efficiency," that is quite certain. A little later I was writing articles and letters about it, so that much is documented. But I think I must have apprehended too by that time some vague outline at least of those wider issues in the sæcular conflict between the new forms of human association and the old, to which contemporary politics and our national fate are no more than transitory eddies and rufflings of the surface waters. It was all so nakedly plain there. On the one hand was the primordial, on the other the rankly new. The farm on the veld stood on the veld, a thing of the veld, a thing rooted and established there and nowhere else. The dusty, crude, brick-field desolation of the Rand on the other hand did not really belong with any particularity to South Africa at all. It was one with our camps and armies. It was part of something else, something still bigger: a monstrous shadowy arm had thrust out from Europe and torn open this country, erected these chimneys, piled these heaps—and sent the ration-tins and cartridge-cases to follow them. It was gigantic kindred with that ancient predecessor which had built the walls of Zimbabwe. And this hungry, impatient demand for myriads of toilers, this threatening inundation of black or brown or yellow bond-serfs was just the natural voice of this colossal system to which I belonged, which had brought me hither, and which I now perceived I did not even begin to understand. . . .

One day when asking my way to some forgotten destination, I had pointed out to me the Grey and Roberts Deep Mine. Some familiarity in the name set me thinking until I recalled that this was the mine in which I had once heard Lady Ladislaw confess large holdings, this mine in which gangs of indentured Chinamen would presently be sweating to pay the wages of the game-keepers and roadmenders in Burnmore Park. . . .

Yes, this was what I was taking in at that time, but it found me—inexpressive; what I was saying on my return to England gave me no intimation of the broad conceptions growing in my mind. I came back to be one of the many scores of energetic and ambitious young men who were parroting "Efficiency," stirring up people and more particularly stirring up themselves with the utmost vigor,—and all the time within their secret hearts more than a little at a loss. . . .

§ 6

While I had been in South Africa circumstances had conspired to alter my prospects in life very greatly. Unanticipated freedoms and opportunities had come to me, and it was no longer out of the question for me to think of a parliamentary career. Our fortunes had altered. My father had ceased to be rector of Burnmore, and had become a comparatively wealthy man.

My second cousin, Reginald Stratton, had been drowned in Finland, and his father had only survived the shock of his death a fortnight; his sister, Arthur Mason's first wife, had died in giving birth to a stillborn child the year before, and my father found himself suddenly the owner of all that large stretch of developing downland and building land which old Reginald had bought between Shaddock and Golding on the south and West Esher station on the north, and in addition of considerable investments in northern industrials. It was an odd collusion of mortality; we had had only the coldest relations with our cousins, and now abruptly through their commercial and speculative activities, which we had always affected to despise and ignore, I was in a position to attempt the realization of my old political ambitions.

My cousins' house had not been to my father's taste. He had let it, and I came to a new home in a pleasant, plain red-brick house, a hundred and fifty years old perhaps, on an open and sunny hillside, sheltered by trees eastward and northward, a few miles to the south-west of Guilford. It had all the gracious proportions, the dignified simplicity, the roomy comfort of the good building of that time. It looked sunward; we breakfasted in sunshine in the library, and outside was an old wall with peach trees and a row of pillar roses heavily in flower. I had a little feared this place; Burnmore Rectory had been so absolutely home to me with its quiet serenities, its ample familiar garden, its greenhouses and intimately known corners, but I perceived I might have trusted my father's character to preserve his essential atmosphere. He was so much himself as I remembered him that I did not even observe for a day or so that he had not only aged considerably but discarded the last vestiges of clerical costume in his attire. He met me in front of the house and led me into a wide panelled hall and wrung my hand again and again, deeply moved and very inexpressive. "Did you have a good journey?" he asked again and again, with tears in his eyes. "Did you have a comfortable journey?"

"I've not seen the house," said I. "It looks fine."

"You're a man," he said, and patted my shoulder. "Of course! It was at Burnmore."

"*You're* not changed," I said. "You're not an atom changed."

"How could I?" he replied. "Come—come and have something to eat. You ought to have something to eat."

We talked of the house and what a good house it was, and he took me out into the garden to see the peaches and grape vine and then brought me back without showing them to me in order to greet my cousin. "It's very like Burnmore," he said with his eyes devouring me, "very

like. A little more space and—no services. No services
at all. That makes a gap of course. There's a little
chap about here, you'll find—his name is Wednesday—
who sorts my papers and calls himself my secretary. . . .
Not necessary perhaps but—*I missed the curate.*"

He said he was reading more than he used to do now
that the parish was off his hands, and he was preparing
material for a book. It was, he explained later, to take
the form of a huge essay ostensibly on Secular Canons,
but its purport was to be no less than the complete
secularization of the Church of England. At first he
wanted merely to throw open the cathedral chapters to
distinguished laymen, irrespective of their theological
opinions, and to make each English cathedral a centre of
intellectual activity, a college as it were of philosophers
and writers. But afterwards his suggestions grew bolder,
the Articles of Religion were to be set aside, the creeds
made optional even for the clergy. His dream became
more and more richly picturesque until at last he saw
Canterbury a realized Thelema, and St. Paul's a new
Academic Grove. He was to work at that remarkable
proposal intermittently for many years, and to leave
it at last no more than a shapeless mass of memoranda,
fragmentary essays, and selected passages for quotation.
Yet mere patchwork and scrapbook as it would be, I
still have some thought of publishing it. There is a
large human charity about it, a sun too broad and warm, a
reasonableness too wide and free perhaps for the timid
convulsive quality of our time, yet all good as good wine
for the wise. Is it incredible that a day should come when
our great grey monuments to the Norman spirit should
cease to be occupied by narrow-witted parsons and be-

sieged by narrow-souled dissenters, the soul of our race in exile from the home and place our fathers built for it? . . .

If he was not perceptibly changed, I thought my cousin Jane had become more than a little sharper and stiffer. She did not like my uncle's own personal secularization, and still less the glimpses she got of the ampler intentions of his book. She missed the proximity to the church and her parochial authority. But she was always a silent woman, and made her comments with her profile and not with her tongue. . . .

"I'm glad you've come back, Stephen," said my father as we sat together after dinner and her departure, with port and tall silver candlesticks and shining mahogany between us. "I've missed you. I've done my best to follow things out there. I've got, I suppose, every press mention there's been of you during the war and since. I've subscribed to two press-cutting agencies, so that if one missed you the other fellow got you. Perhaps you'll like to read them over one of these days. . . . You see, there's not been a soldier in the family since the Peninsular War, and so I've been particularly interested. . . . You must tell me all the things you're thinking of, and what you mean to do. This last stuff—this Chinese business— it puzzles me. I want to know what you think of it—and everything."

I did my best to give him my ideas such as they were. And as they were still very vague ideas I have no doubt he found me rhetorical. I can imagine myself talking of the White Man's Burthen, and how in Africa it had seemed at first to sit rather staggeringly upon our under-trained shoulders. I spoke of slackness and planless-ness.

"I've come back in search of efficiency." I have no doubt I said that at any rate.

"We're trying to run this big empire," I may have explained, "with under-trained, under-educated, poor-spirited stuff, and we shall come a cropper unless we raise our quality. I'm still Imperialist, more than ever I was. But I'm an Imperialist on a different footing. I've no great illusions left about the Superiority of the Anglo-Saxons. All that has gone. But I do think it will be a monstrous waste, a disaster to human possibilities if this great liberal-spirited empire sprawls itself asunder for the want of a little gravity and purpose. And it's here the work has to be done, the work of training and bracing up and stimulating the public imagination. . . ."

Yes, that would be the sort of thing I should have said in those days. There's an old *National Review* on my desk as I write, containing an article by me with some of those very phrases in it. I have been looking at it in order to remind myself of my own forgotten eloquence.

"Yes," I remember my father saying. "Yes." And then after reflection, "But those coolies, those Chinese coolies. You can't build up an imperial population by importing coolies."

"I don't like that side of the business myself," I said. "It's detail."

"Perhaps. But the Liberals will turn you out on it next year. And then start badgering public houses and looting the church. . . . And then this Tariff talk! Everybody on our side seems to be mixing up the unity of the empire with tariffs. It's a pity. Salisbury wouldn't have stood it. Unity! Unity depends on a common literature and a common language and common ideas and sympathies. It doesn't unite people for them to be forced to trade with each other. Trading isn't friendship. I don't trade with my friends and I don't make friends with my tradesmen. Natural enemies—polite of course but antagonists. Are you keen over this Tariff stuff, Steve?"

"Not a bit," I said. "That too seems a detail."

"It doesn't seem to be keeping its place as a detail," said my father. "Very few men can touch tariffs and not get a little soiled. I hate all this international sharping, all these attempts to get artificial advantages, all this making poor people buy inferior goods dear, in the name of the flag. If it comes to that, damn the flag! Custom-houses are ugly things, Stephen; the dirty side of nationality. Dirty things, ignoble, cross, cunning things. . . . They wake you up in the small hours and rout over your bags. . . . An imperial people ought to be an urbane people, a civilizing people—above such petty irritating things. I'd as soon put barbed wire along the footpath across that field where the village children go to school. Or claim that our mushrooms are cultivated. Or prosecute a Sunday-Society Cockney for picking my primroses. Custom-houses indeed! It's Chinese. There are things a Great Country mustn't do, Stephen. A country like ours ought to get along without the manners of a hard-breathing competitive cad. . . . If it can't I'd rather it didn't get along. . . . What's the good of a huckster country?—it's like having a wife on the streets. It's no excuse that she brings you money. But since the peace, and that man Chamberlain's visit to Africa, you Imperialists seem to have got this nasty spirit all over you. . . . The Germans do it, you say!"

My father shut one eye and regarded the color of his port against the waning light. "Let '*em*," he said. . . . "Fancy!—quoting the *Germans!* When I was a boy, there weren't any Germans. They came up after '70. Statecraft from Germany! And statesmen from Birmingham! German silver and Eloctroplated Empires. . . . No."

"It's just a part of our narrow outlook," I answered from the hearthrug, after a pause. "It's because we're so—limited that everyone is translating the greatness of empire into preferential trading and jealousy of Germany. It's for something bigger than that that I've returned."

"Those big things come slowly," said my father. And then with a sigh: "Age after age. They seem at times— to be standing still. Good things go with the bad; bad things come with the good. . . ."

I remember him saying that as though I could still hear him.

It must have been after dinner, for he was sitting, duskily indistinct, against the light, with a voice coming out to him. The candles had not been brought in, and the view one saw through the big plate glass window behind him was very clear and splendid. Those little Wealden hills in Surrey and Sussex assume at times, for all that by Swiss standards they are the merest ridges of earth, the dignity and mystery of great mountains. Now, the crests of Hindhead and Blackdown, purple black against the level gold of the evening sky, might have been some high-flung boundary chain. Nearer there gathered banks and pools of luminous lavender-tinted mist out of which hills of pinewood rose like islands out of

the sea.   The intervening spaces were magnified to continental dimensions.   And the closer lowlier things over
which we looked, the cottages below us, were grey and
black and dim, pierced by a few luminous orange windows
and with a solitary street lamp shining like a star; the
village might have been nestling a mountain's height
below instead of a couple of hundred feet.

I left my hearthrug, and walked to the window to
survey this.

"Who's got all that land stretching away there; that
little blunted sierra of pines and escarpments I mean?"

My father halted for an instant in his answer, and
glanced over his shoulder.

"Wardingham and Baxter share all those coppices,"
he remarked.   "They come up to my corner on each
side."

"But the dark heather and pine land beyond.   With
just the gables of a house among the trees."

"Oh? *that*," he said with a careful note of indifference.
"That's—Justin.   You know Justin.   He used to come
to Burnmore Park."

CHAPTER THE SIXTH

LADY MARY JUSTIN

§ 1

I DID not see Lady Mary Justin for nearly seven months after my return to England. Of course I had known that a meeting was inevitable, and I had taken that very carefully into consideration before I decided to leave South Africa. But many things had happened to me during those crowded years, so that it seemed possible that that former magic would no longer sway and distress me. Not only had new imaginative interests taken hold of me but—I had parted from adolescence. I was a man. I had been through a great war, seen death abundantly, seen hardship and passion, and known hunger and shame and desire. A hundred disillusioning revelations of the quality of life had come to me; once for example when we were taking some people to the concentration camps it had been necessary to assist at the premature birth of a child by the wayside, a startlingly gory and agonizing business for a young man to deal with. Heavens! how it shocked me! I could give a score of such grim pictures—and queer pictures. . . .

And it wasn't only the earthlier aspects of the life about me but also of the life within me that I had been

132

discovering. The first wonder and innocence, the worshipping, dawn-clear passion of youth, had gone out of me for ever. . . .

§ 2

We met at a dinner. It was at a house the Tarvrilles had taken for the season in Mayfair. The drawing-room was a big white square apartment with several big pictures and a pane of plate glass above the fireplace in the position in which one usually finds a mirror; this showed another room beyond, containing an exceptionally large, gloriously colored portrait in pastel—larger than I had ever thought pastels could be. Except for the pictures both rooms were almost colorless. It was a brilliant dinner, with a predominating note of ruby; three of the women wore ruby velvet; and Ellersley was present just back from Arabia, and Ethel Manton, Lady Hendon and the Duchess of Clynes. I was greeted by Lady Tarvrille, spoke to Ellersley and Lady Hendon, and then discovered a lady in a dress of blue and pearls standing quite still under a picture in the opposite corner of the room and regarding me attentively. It was Mary. Some man was beside her, a tall grey man with a broad crimson ribbon, and I think he must have spoken of me to her. It was as if she had just turned to look at me.

Constantly during those intervening months I had been thinking of meeting her. None the less there was a shock, not so much of surprise as of deferred anticipation. There she stood like something amazingly forgotten that was now amazingly recalled. She struck me in that brief crowded instant of recognition as being exactly

133

the person she had been when we had made love in Burnmore Park; there were her eyes, at once frank and sidelong, the old familiar sweep of her hair, the old familiar tilt of the chin, the faint humor of her lip, and at the same time she seemed to be something altogether different from the memories I had cherished, she was something graver, something inherently more splendid than they had recorded. Her face lit now with recognition.

I went across to her at once, with some dull obviousness upon my lips.

"And so you are back from Africa at last," she said, still unsmiling. "I saw about you in the papers. . . . You had a good time."

"I had great good luck," I replied.

"I never dreamt when we were boy and girl together that you would make a soldier."

I think I said that luck made soldiers.

Then I think we found a difficulty in going on with our talk, and began a dull little argument that would have been stupidly egotistical on my part if it hadn't been so obviously merely clumsy, about luck making soldiers or only finding them out. I saw that she had not intended to convey any doubt of my military capacity but only of that natural insensitiveness which is supposed to be needed in a soldier. But our minds were remote from the words upon our lips. We were like aphasiacs who say one thing while they intend something altogether different. The impulse that had brought me across to her had brought me up to a wall of impossible utterances. It was with a real quality of rescue that our hostess came between us to tell us our partners at the dinner-table, and to introduce me to mine. "You shall have him again on your other side," she said to Lady Mary with a charming smile for me, treating me as if I was a lion in request instead of the mere outsider I was.

We talked very little at dinner. Both of us I think were quite unequal to the occasion. Whatever meetings we had imagined, certainly neither of us had thought of this very possible encounter, a long disconcerting hour side by side. I began to remember old happenings with an astonishing vividness; there within six inches of me was the hand I had kissed; her voice was the same to its lightest shade, her hair flowed off her forehead with the same amazingly familiar wave. Was she too remembering? But I perhaps had changed altogether. . . .

"Why did you go away as you did?" she asked abruptly, when for a moment we were isolated conversationally. "Why did you never write?"

She had still that phantom lisp.

"What else could I do?"

She turned away from me and answered the man on her left, who had just addressed her. . . .

When the mid-dinner change came we talked a little about indifferent things, making a stiff conversation like a bridge over a torrent of unspoken intimacies. We discussed something; I think Lady Tarvrille's flowers and the Cape Flora and gardens. She told me she had a Japanese garden with three Japanese gardeners. They were wonderful little men to watch. "Humming-bird gardeners," she called them. "They wear their native costume."

"We are your neighbors in Surrey," she said, going off abruptly from that. "We are quite near to your father."

She paused with that characteristic effect of deliberation in her closed lips. Then she added: "I can see the trees behind your father's house from the window of my room."

"Yes," I said. ' You take all our southward skyline."

She turned her face to me with the manner of a great lady adding a new acquaintance to her collection. But her eyes met mine very steadily and intimately. "Mr. Stratton," she said—it was the first time in her life she had called me that—"when we come back to Surrey I want you to come and see me and tell me of all the things you are going to do. Will you?"

§ 3

That meeting, that revival, must have been late in November or early in December. Already by that time I had met your mother. I write to you, little son, not to you as you are now, but to the man you are someday to be. I write to understand myself, and, so far as I can understand, to make you understand. So that I want you to go back with me for a time into the days before your birth, to think not of that dear spirit of love who broods over you three children, that wise, sure mother who rules your life, but of a young and slender girl, Rachel More, younger then than you will be when at last this story comes into your hands. For unless you think of her as being a girl, if you let your present knowledge of her fill out this part in our story, you will fail to understand the proportions of these two in my life. So I shall write of her here as Rachel More, as if she were someone as completely dissociated from yourself as Lady Mary; as if she were someone in the story of my life who had as little to do with yours.

I had met her in September. The house my father lived in is about twelve miles away from your mother's home at Ridinghanger, and I was taken over by Percy Restall in his motor-car. Restall had just become a convert to this new mode of locomotion, and he was very active with a huge, malignant-looking French car that opened behind, and had a kind of poke bonnet and all sorts of features that have since disappeared from the automobile world. He took everyone that he could lay hands upon for rides,—he called it extending their range, and he called upon everyone else to show off the car; he was responsible for more introduction and social admixture in that part of Surrey than had occurred during the previous century. We punctured in the Ridinghanger drive, Restall did his own repairs, and so it was we stayed for nearly four hours and instead of a mere caller I became a familiar friend of the family.

Your mother then was still not eighteen, a soft white slip of being, tall, slender, brown-haired and silent, with very still deep dark eyes. She and your three aunts formed a very gracious group of young women indeed; Alice then as now the most assertive, with a gay initiative and a fluent tongue; Molly already a sun-brown gipsy, and Norah still a pig-tailed thing of lank legs and wild embraces and the pinkest of swift pink blushes; your uncle Sidney, with his shy lank moodiness, acted the brotherly part of a foil. There were several stray visitors, young men and maidens, there were always stray visitors in those days at Ridinghanger, and your grandmother, rosy and bright-eyed, maintained a gentle flow of creature comforts and kindly but humorous observations. I do not remember your grandfather on this occasion; probably he wasn't there.

There was tea, and we played tennis and walked about and occasionally visited Restall, who was getting dirtier and dirtier, and crosser and crosser at his repairs, and spreading a continually more remarkable assemblage of parts and instruments over the grass about him. He looked at last more like a pitch in the Caledonian market than a decent country gentleman paying an afternoon call. And then back to more tennis and more talk. We fell into a discussion of Tariff Reform as we sat taking tea. Two of the visitor youths were strongly infected by the new teachings which were overshadowing the outlook of British Imperialism. Some mean phrase about not conquering Africa for the German bagman, some ugly turn of thought that at a touch brought down Empire to the level of a tradesman's advantage, fell from one of them, and stirred me to sudden indignation. I began to talk of things that had been gathering in my mind for some time.

I do not know what I said. It was in the vein of my father's talk no doubt. But I think that for once I may have been eloquent. And in the midst of my demand for ideals in politics that were wider and deeper than artful buying and selling, that looked beyond a vulgar aggression and a churl's dread and hatred of foreign things, while I struggled to say how great and noble a thing empire might be, I saw Rachel's face. This, it was manifest, was a new kind of talk to her. Her dark eyes were alight with a beautiful enthusiasm for what I was trying to say, and for what in the light of that glowing reception I seemed to be.

I felt that queer shame one feels when one is taken suddenly at the full value of one's utmost expressions. I felt as though I had cheated her, was passing myself off for something as great and splendid as the Empire of my dreams. It is hard to dissociate oneself from the fine things to which one aspires. I stopped almost abruptly. Dumbly her eyes bade me go on, but when I spoke again it was at a lower level. . . .

That look in Rachel's eyes remained with me. My mind had flashed very rapidly from the realization of its significance to the thought that if one could be sure of that, then indeed one could pitch oneself high. Rachel, I felt, had something for me that I needed profoundly, without ever having known before that I needed it. She had the supreme gifts of belief and devotion; in that instant's gleam it seemed she held them out to me.

Never before in my life had it seemed credible to me that anyone could give me that, or that I could hope for such a gift of support and sacrifice. Love as I had known it had been a community and an alliance, a frank abundant meeting; but this was another kind of love that shone for an instant and promised, and vanished shyly out of sight as I and Rachel looked at one another.

Some interruption occurred. Restall came, I think, blackened by progress, to drink a cup of tea and negotiate the loan of a kitchen skewer. A kitchen skewer it appeared was all that was needed to complete his reconstruction in the avenue. Norah darted off for a kitchen skewer, while Restall drank. And then there was a drift to tennis, and Rachel and I were partners. All this time I was in a state of startled attention towards her, full of this astounding impression that something wonderful and unprecedented had flowed out from her towards my life, full too of doubts now whether that shining response had ever occurred, whether some trick of light and my brain had not deceived me. I wanted tremendously to talk to her, and did not know how to begin in any serious fashion. Beyond everything I wanted to see again that deep onset of belief. . . .

"Come again," said your grandmother to me, "come again!" after she had tried in vain to make Restall stay for an informal supper. I was all for staying, but Restall said darkly, "There are the Lamps."

"But they will be all right," said Mrs. More.

"I can't trust 'em," said Restall, with a deepening gloom. "Not after *that*." The motor-car looked self-conscious and uncomfortable, but said nothing by way of excuse, and Restall took me off in it like one whose sun has set for ever. "I wouldn't be surprised," said Restall as we went down the drive, "if the damned thing turned a somersault. It might do—anything." Those were the brighter days of motoring.

The next time I went over released from Restall's limitations, and stayed to a jolly family supper. I found remarkably few obstacles in my way to a better acquaintance with Rachel. You see I was an entirely eligible and desirable young man in Mrs. More's eyes. . . .

§ 4

When I recall these long past emotions again, I am struck by the profound essential difference between my feelings for your mother and for Mary. They were so different that it seems scarcely rational to me that they should be called by the same name. Yet each was love, profoundly deep and sincere. The contrast lies, I think, in our relative ages, and our relative maturity; that altered the quality of all our emotions. The one was the love of a man of six-and-twenty, exceptionally seasoned and experienced and responsible for his years, for a girl still at school, a girl attractively beautiful, mysterious and unknown to him; the other was the love of coevals, who had been playmates and intimate companions, and of whom the woman was certainly as capable and wilful as the man.

Now it is exceptional for men to love women of their own age, it is the commoner thing that they should love maidens younger and often much younger than themselves. This is true more particularly of our own class; the masculine thirties and forties marry the feminine twenties, all the prevailing sentiment and usage between the sexes rises naturally out of that. We treat this seniority as though it were a virile characteristic; we treat the man as though he were a natural senior, we expect a weakness, a timid deference, in the girl. I and Mary had loved one another as two rivers run together on the way to the sea, we had grown up side by side to the moment when we kissed; but I sought your mother, I watched her and desired her and chose her, very tenderly and worshipfully indeed, to be mine. I do not remember that there was any corresponding intention in my mind to be hers. I do not think that that idea came in at all. She was something to be won, something playing an inferior and retreating part. And I was artificial in all my attitudes to her, I thought of what would interest her, what would please her, I knew from the outset that what she saw in me to rouse that deep, shy glow of exaltation in her face was illusion, illusion it was my business to sustain. And so I won her, and long years had to pass, years of secret loneliness and hidden feelings, of preposterous pretences and covert perplexities, before we escaped from that crippling tradition of inequality and looked into one another's eyes with understanding and forgiveness, a woman and a man.

I made no great secret of the interest and attraction I found in Rachel, and the Mores made none of their entire approval of me. I walked over on the second occasion, and Ridinghanger opened out, a great flower of genial appreciation that I came alone, hiding nothing of its dawning perception that it was Rachel in particular I came to see.

Your grandmother's match-making was as honest as the day. There was the same salad of family and visitors as on the former afternoon, and this time I met Freshman, who was destined to marry Alice; there was tea, tennis, and, by your grandmother's suggestion, a walk to see the sunset from the crest of the hill. Rachel and I walked across the breezy moorland together, while I talked and tempted her to talk.

What, I wonder, did we talk about? English scenery, I think, and African scenery and the Weald about us, and the long history of the Weald and its present and future, and at last even a little of politics. I had never explored the mind of a girl of seventeen before; there was a surprise in all she knew and a delight in all she didn't know, and about herself a candor, a fresh simplicity of outlook that was sweeter than the clear air about us, sweeter than sunshine or the rising song of a lark. She believed so gallantly and beautifully, she was so perfectly, unaffectedly and certainly prepared to be a brave and noble person—if only life would let her. And she hadn't as yet any suspicion that life might make that difficult. . . .

I went to Ridinghanger a number of times in the spring and early summer. I talked a great deal with Rachel, and still I did not make love to her. It was always in my mind that I would make love to her, the heavens and earth and all her family were propitious, glowing golden with consent and approval, I thought she was the most wonderful and beautiful thing in life, and her eyes, the intonation of her voice, her hurrying color and a hundred little involuntary signs told me how she quickened at my coming. But there was a shyness. I loved her as one loves and admires a white flower or a beautiful child—some stranger's child. I felt that I might make her afraid of me. I had never before thought that to make love is a coarse thing. But still at high summer when I met Mary again no definite thing had been said between myself and Rachel. But we knew, each of us knew, that somewhere in a world less palpable, in fairyland, in dreamland, we had met and made our vows.

§ 5

You see how far my imagination had gone towards readjustment when Mary returned into my life. You see how strange and distant it was to meet her again, changed completely into the great lady she had intended to be, speaking to me with the restrained and practised charm of a woman who is young and beautiful and prominent and powerful and secure. There was no immediate sense of shock in that resumption of our broken intercourse, it seemed to me that night simply that something odd and curious had occurred. I do not remember how we parted that evening or whether we even saw each other after dinner was over, but from that hour forth Mary by insensible degrees resumed her old predominance in my mind. I woke up in the night and thought about her, and next day I found myself thinking of her, remembering things out of the past and recalling and examining every detail of the overnight encounter. How cold and ineffective we had been, both of us! We had been like people resuming a disused and partially forgotten language. Had she changed towards me? Did she indeed want to see me again or was that invitation a mere demonstration of how entirely unimportant seeing me or not seeing me had become?

Then I would find myself thinking with the utmost particularity of her face. Had it changed at all? Was it altogether changed? I seemed to have forgotten everything and remembered everything; that peculiar slight thickness of her eyelids that gave her eyes their tenderness, that light firmness of her lips. Of course she would want to talk to me, as now I perceived I wanted to talk to her

Was I in love with her still? It seemed to me then that I was not. It had not been that hesitating fierceness, that pride and demand and doubt, which is passionate love, that had made all my sensations strange to me as I sat beside her. It had been something larger and finer,

something great and embracing, a return to fellowship.
Here beside me, veiled from me only by our transient embarrassment and the tarnish of separation and silences, was
the one person who had ever broken down the crust of
shy insincerity which is so incurably my characteristic
and talked intimately of the inmost things of life to me.
I discovered now for the first time how intense had been
my loneliness for the past five years. I discovered now
that through all those years I had been hungry for such
talk as Mary alone could give me. My mind was filled
with talk, filled with things I desired to say to her; that
chaos began to take on a multitudinous expression at the
touch of her spirit. I began to imagine conversations
with her, to prepare reports for her of those new worlds of
sensation and activity I had discovered since that boyish
parting.

But when at last that talk came it was altogether
different from any of those I had invented.

She wrote to me when she came down into Surrey
and I walked over to Martens the next afternoon. I
found her in her own sitting-room, a beautiful characteristic apartment with tall French windows hung with
blue curtains, a large writing-desk and a great litter of
books. The room gave upon a broad sunlit terrace
with a balustrading of yellowish stone, on which there
stood great oleanders. Beyond was a flower garden and
then the dark shadows of cypresses. She was standing
as I came in to her, as though she had seen me coming
across the lawns and had been awaiting my entrance.
"I thought you might come to-day," she said, and told
the manservant to deny her to other callers. Again she
produced that queer effect of being at once altogether the

same and altogether different from the Mary I had known. "Justin," she said, "is in Paris. He comes back on Friday." I saw then that the change lay in her bearing, that for the easy confidence of the girl she had now the deliberate dignity and control of a married woman—a very splendidly and spaciously married woman. Her manner had been purged of impulse. Since we had met she had stood, the mistress of great houses, and had dealt with thousands of people.

"You walked over to me?"

"I walked," I said. "It is nearly a straight path. You know it?"

"You came over the heather beyond our pine wood," she confirmed. And then I think we talked some polite unrealities about Surrey scenery and the weather. It was so formal that by a common impulse we let the topic suddenly die. We stood through a pause, a hesitation. Were we indeed to go on at that altitude of cold civility? She turned to the window as if the view was to serve again.

"Sit down," she said and dropped into a chair against the light, looking away from me across the wide green space of afternoon sunshine. I sat down on a little sofa, at a loss also.

"And so," she said, turning her face to me suddenly, "you come back into my life." And I was amazed to see that the brightness of her eyes was tears. "We've lived—five years."

"You," I said clumsily, "have done all sorts of things. I hear of you—patronizing young artists—organizing experiments in village education."

"Yes," she said, "I've done all sorts of things. One

146

has to. Forced, unreal things for the most part. You I expect have done—all sorts of things also. . . . But yours have been real things. . . .''

"All things," I remarked sententiously, "are real. And all of them a little unreal. South Africa has been wonderful. And now it is all over one doubts if it really happened. Like that incredulous mood after a storm of passion."

"You've come back for good?"

"For good. I want to do things in England."

"Politics?"

"If I can get into that."

Again a pause. There came the characteristic moment of deliberation that I remembered so well.

"I never meant you," she said, "to go away. . . . You could have written. You never answered the notes I sent."

"I was frantic," I said, "with loss and jealousy. I wanted to forget."

"And you forgot?"

"I did my best."

"I did my best," said Mary. "And now—— Have you forgotten?"

"Nothing."

"Nor I. I thought I had. Until I saw you again. I've thought of you endlessly. I've wanted to talk to you. We had a way of talking together. But you went away. You turned your back as though all that was nothing—not worth having. You—you drove home my marriage, Stephen. You made me know what a thing of sex a woman is to a man—and how little else. . . ."

She paused.

"You see," I said slowly. "You had made me, as people say, in love with you. . . . I don't know—if you remember everything. . . ."

She looked me in the eyes for a moment.

"I hadn't been fair," she said with an abrupt abandonment of accusation. "But you know, Stephen, that night—— I meant to explain. And afterwards. . . . Things sometimes go as one hasn't expected them to go, even the things one has planned to say. I suppose—I treated you—disgustingly."

I protested.

"Yes," she said. "I treated you as I did—and I thought you would stand it. I *knew*, I knew then as well as you do now that male to my female you wouldn't stand it, but somehow—I thought there were other things. Things that could override that. . . ."

"Not," I said, "for a boy of one-and-twenty."

"But in a man of twenty-six?"

I weighed the question. "Things are different," I said, and then, "Yes. Anyhow now—if I may come back penitent,—to a friendship."

We looked at one another gravely. Faintly in our ears sounded the music of past and distant things. We pretended to hear nothing of that, tried honestly to hear nothing of it. I had not remembered how steadfast and quiet her face could be. "Yes," she said, "a friendship."

"I've always had you in my mind, Stephen," she said. "When I saw I couldn't marry you, it seemed to me I had better marry and be free of any further hope. I thought we could get over that. 'Let's get it over,' I thought. Now—at any rate—we have got over that." Her eyes verified her words a little doubtfully. "And we can talk

148

and you can tell me of your life, and the things you want to do that make life worth living. Oh! life has been *stupid* without you, Stephen, large and expensive and aimless. . . . Tell me of your politics. They say—Justin told me—you think of parliament?"

"I want to do that. I have been thinking—— In fact I am going to stand." I found myself hesitating on the verge of phrases in the quality of a review article. It was too unreal for her presence. And yet it was this she seemed to want from me. "This," I said, "is a phase of great opportunities. The war has stirred the Empire to a sense of itself, to a sense of what it might be. Of course this Tariff Reform row is a squalid nuisance; it may kill out all the fine spirit again before anything is done. Everything will become a haggle, a chaffering of figures. . . . All the more reason why we should try and save things from the commercial traveller. If the Empire is anything at all, it is something infinitely more than a combination in restraint of trade. . . ."

"Yes," she said. "And you want to take that line. The high line."

"If one does not take the high line," I said, "what does one go into politics for?"

"Stephen," she smiled, "you haven't lost a sort of simplicity—— People go into politics because it looks important, because other people go into politics, because they can get titles and a sense of influence and—other things. And then there are quarrels, old grudges to serve."

"These are roughnesses of the surface."

"Old Stephen!" she cried with the note of a mother. "They will worry you in politics."

I laughed. "Perhaps I'm not altogether so simple."

"Oh! you'll get through. You have a way of going on. But I shall have to watch over you. I see I shall have to watch over you. Tell me of the things you mean to do. Where are you standing?"

I began to tell her a little disjointedly of the probabilities of my Yorkshire constituency. . . .

§ 6

I have a vivid vignette in my memory of my return to my father's house, down through the pine woods and by the winding path across the deep valley that separated our two ridges. I was thinking of Mary and nothing but Mary in all the world and of the friendly sweetness of her eyes and the clean strong sharpness of her voice. That sweet white figure of Rachel that had been creeping to an ascendancy in my imagination was moonlight to her sunrise. I knew it was Mary I loved and had always loved. I wanted passionately to be as she desired, the friend she demanded, that intimate brother and confederate, but all my heart cried out for her, cried out for her altogether.

I would be her friend, I repeated to myself, I would be her friend. I would talk to her often, plan with her, work with her. I could put my meanings into her life and she should throw her beauty over mine. I began already to dream of the talk of to-morrow's meeting. . . .

§ 7

And now let me go on to tell at once the thing that changed life for both of us altogether, that turned us out of the courses that seemed set for us, our spacious, successful and divergent ways, she to the tragedy of her death and I from all the prospects of the public career that lay before me to the work that now, toilsomely, inadequately and blunderingly enough, I do. It was to pierce and slash away the appearances of life for me, it was to open my way to infinite disillusionment, and unsuspected truths. Within a few weeks of our second meeting Mary and I were passionately in love with one another; we had indeed become lovers. The arrested attractions of our former love released again, drew us inevitably to that. We tried to seem outwardly only friends, with this hot glow between us. Our tormented secret was half discovered and half betrayed itself. There followed a tragi-comedy of hesitations and dis-united struggle. Within four months the crisis of our two lives was past. . . .

It is not within my purpose to tell you, my son, of the particular events, the particular comings and goings, the chance words, the chance meetings, the fatal momentary misunderstandings that occurred between us. I want to tell of something more general than that. This misadventure is in our strain. It is our inheritance. It is a possibility in the inheritance of all honest and emotional men and women. There are no doubt people altogether cynical and adventurous to whom these passions and desires are at once controllable and permissible indulgences without any radiation of consequences, a secret and detachable part of life, and there may be people of convictions so strong and simple that these disturbances are eliminated, but we Strattons are of a quality neither so low nor so high, we stoop and rise, we are not convinced about our standards, and for many generations to come, with us and with such people as the Christians, and indeed with most of our sort of people, we shall be equally desirous of free and intimate friendship and prone to blaze into passion and disaster at that proximity.

This is one of the essential riddles in the adaptation of such human beings as ourselves to that greater civilized state of which I dream. It is the gist of my story. It is one of the two essential riddles that confront our kind. The servitude of sex and the servitude of labor are the twin conditions upon which human society rests to-day, the two limitations upon its progress towards a greater social order, to that greater community, those uplands of light and happy freedom, towards which that Being who was my father yesterday, who thinks in myself to-day, and who will be you to-morrow and your sons after you, by his very nature urges and must continue to urge the life of mankind. The story of myself and Mary is a mere incident in that gigantic, scarce conscious effort to get clear of toils and confusions and encumbrances, and have our way with life. We are like little figures, dots ascendant upon a vast hillside; I take up our intimacy for an instant and hold it under a lens for you. I become more than myself then, and Mary stands for innumerable women. It happened yesterday, and it is just a part of that same history that made Edmond Stratton of the Hays elope with Charlotte Anstruther and get himself run through the body at Haddington two hundred years ago, which drove the Laidlaw-Christians to Virginia in '45, gave Stratton Street to the moneylenders when George IV. was Regent, and broke the heart of Margaret Stratton in the days when Charles the First was king. With our individual variations and under changed conditions the old desires and impulses stirred us, the old antagonisms confronted us, the old difficulties and sloughs and impassable places baffled us. There are times when I think of my history among all those widespread repeated histories, until it seems to me that the human Lover is like a creature who struggles for ever through a thicket without an end. . . .

There are no universal laws of affection and desire, but it is manifestly true that for the most of us free talk, intimate association, and any real fellowship between men and women turns with an extreme readiness to love. And that being so it follows that under existing conditions the unrestricted meeting and companionship of men and women in society is a monstrous sham, a merely dangerous pretence of encounters. The safe reality beneath those liberal appearances is that a woman must be content with the easy friendship of other women and of one man only, letting a superficial friendship towards all other men veil impassable abysses of separation, and a man must in the same way have one sole woman intimate. To all other women he must be a little blind, a little deaf, politely inattentive. He must respect the transparent, intangible, tacit purdah about them, respect it but never allude to it. To me that is an intolerable state of affairs, but it is reality. If you live in the spirit of any other understanding you will court social disaster. I suppose it is a particularly intolerable state of affairs to us Strattons because it is in our nature to want things to seem what they are. That translucent yet impassible purdah outrages our veracity. And it is plain to me that our social order cannot stand and is not standing the tensions it creates.

The convention that passions and emotions are absent when they are palpably present broke down between Mary and myself, as it breaks down in a thousand other cases, as it breaks down everywhere. Our social life is honeycombed and rotten with secret hidden relationships. The rigid, the obtuse and the unscrupulously cunning escape; the honest passion sooner or later flares out and destroys. . . . Here is a difficulty that no bullying imposition of arbitrary rules on the one hand nor any reckless abandonment of law on the other, can solve. Humanity has yet to find its method in sexual things; it has to discover the use and the limitation of jealousy. And before it can even begin to attempt to find, it has to cease its present timid secret groping in shame and darkness and turn on the light of knowledge. None of us knows much and most of us do not even know what is known.

§ 8

The house is very quiet to-day. It is your mother's birthday, and you three children have gone with her and Mademoiselle Potin into the forest to celebrate the occasion. Presently I shall join you. The sunlit garden, with its tall dreaming lilies against the trellised vines upon the wall, the cedars and the grassy space about the sundial, have that distinguished stillness, that definite, palpable and almost outlined emptiness which is so to speak your negative presence. It is like a sheet of sunlit colored paper out of which your figures have been cut. There is a commotion of birds in the jasmine, and your Barker reclines with an infinite tranquillity, a masterless dog, upon the lawn. I take up this writing again after an interval of some weeks. I have been in Paris, attending the Sabotage Conference, and dealing with those intricate puzzles of justice and discipline and the secret sources of contentment that have to be solved if sabotage is ever to vanish from labor struggles again. I think a few points have been made clearer in that curious riddle of reconciliations. . . .

Now I resume this story. I turn over the sheets that were written and finished before my departure, and come to the notes for what is to follow.

Perhaps my days of work in Paris have carried my mind on beyond the point at which I left the narrative. I sit as it were among a pile of memories that are now all disordered and mixed up together, their proper sequences and connexions lost. I cannot trace the phases through which our mutual passion rode up through the restrained and dignified intentions of our friendship. But I know that presently we were in a white heat of desire. There must have been passages that I now altogether forget, moments of tense transition. I am more and more convinced that our swiftest, intensest, mental changes leave far less vivid memories than impressions one receives when one is comparatively passive. And of this phase in my life of which I am now telling I have clear memories of a time when we talked like brother and sister, or like angels if you will, and hard upon that came a time when we were planning in all our moments together how and when and where we might meet in secret and meet again.

Things drift with a phantom-like uncertainty into my mind and pass again; those fierce motives of our transition have lost now all stable form and feature, but I believe there was a curious tormenting urgency in our jealousy of those others, of Justin on my part and of Rachel on hers. At first we had talked quite freely about Rachel, had discussed my conceivable marriage with her. We had indeed a little forced that topic, as if to reassure ourselves of the honesty of our new footing. But the force that urged us nearer pervaded all our being. It was hard enough to be barred apart, to snatch back our hands from touching, to avoid each other's eyes, to hurry a little out of the dusk towards the lit house and its protecting servants, but the constant presence and suggestion of those others from whom there were no bars, or towards whom bars could be abolished at a look, at an impulse, exacerbated that hardship, roused a fierce insatiable spirit of revolt within us. At times we grew angry with each other's formalism, came near to quarrelling. . . .

I associate these moods with the golden stillnesses of a prolonged and sultry autumn, and with slowly falling leaves. . . .

I will not tell you how that step was taken, it matters very little to my story, nor will I tell which one of us it was first broke the barriers down.

§ 9

But I do want to tell you certain things. I want to tell you them because they are things that affect you closely. There was almost from the first a difference between Mary and myself in this, that I wanted to be public about our love, I wanted to be open and defiant, and she—hesitated. She wanted to be secret. She wanted to keep me; I sometimes think that she was moved to become my mistress because she wanted to keep me. But she also wanted to keep everything else in her life,—her position, her ample freedoms and wealth and dignity. Our love was to be a secret cavern, Endymion's cave. I was ready enough to do what I could to please her, and for a time I served that secrecy, lied, pretended, agreed to false addresses, assumed names, and tangled myself in a net-work of furtive proceedings. These are things that poison and consume honest love.

You will learn soon enough as you grow to be a man that beneath the respectable assumptions of our social life there is an endless intricate world of subterfuge and hidden and perverted passion,—for all passion that wears a mask is perversion—and that thousands of people of our sort are hiding and shamming about their desires, their gratifications, their true relationships. I do not mean the open offenders, for they are mostly honest and gallant people, but the men and women who sin in the shadows, the people who are not clean and scandalous, but immoral and respectable. This underworld is not for us. I wish that I who have looked into it could in some way inoculate you now against the repetition of my misadventure. We Strattons are daylight men, and if I work now for widened facilities of divorce, for an organized freedom and independence of women, and greater breadth of toleration, it is because I know in my own person the degradations, the falsity, the bitterness, that can lurk beneath the inflexible pretentions of the established code to-day.

And I want to tell you too of something altogether

unforeseen that happened to us, and that was this, that from the day that passion carried us and we became in the narrower sense of the word lovers, all the wider interests we had in common, our political intentions, our impersonal schemes, began to pass out of our intercourse. Our situation closed upon us like a trap and hid the sky. Something more intense had our attention by the feet, and we used our wings no more. I do not think that we even had the real happiness and beauty and delight of one another. Because, I tell you, there is no light upon kiss or embrace that is not done with pride. I do not know why it should be so, but people of our race and quality are a little ashamed of mere gratification in love. Always we seem in my memory to have been whispering with flushed cheeks, and discussing interminably—*situation*. Had something betrayed us, might something betray, was this or that sufficiently cunning? Had we perhaps left a footmark or failed to burn a note, was the second footman who was detailed as my valet even now pausing astonished in the brushing of my clothes with our crumpled secret in his hand? Between myself and the clear vision of this world about me this infernal net-work of precautions spread like a veil.

And it was not only a matter of concealments but of positive deceptions. The figure of Justin comes back to me. It is a curious thing that in spite of our bitter antagonism and the savage jealousy we were to feel for one another, there has always been, and there remains now in my thought of him, a certain liking, a regret at our opposition, a quality of friendliness. His broad face, which the common impression and the caricaturist make so powerful and eagle-like, is really not a brutal or heavy face at all. It is no doubt aquiline, after the fashion of an eagle-owl, the mouth and chin broad and the eyes very far apart, but there is a minute puckering of the brows which combines with that queer streak of brown discoloration that runs across his cheek and into the white of his eyes, to give something faintly plaintive and pitiful to his expression, an effect enhanced by the dark softness of his eyes. They are gentle eyes; it is absurd to suppose them the eyes of a violently forceful man. And indeed they do not belie Justin. It is not by vehemence or pressure that his wealth and power have been attained; it is by the sheer detailed abundance of his mind. In that queer big brain of his there is something of the calculating boy and not a little of the chess champion; he has a kind of financial gift, he must be rich, and grows richer. What else is there for him to do? How many times have I not tried to glance carelessly at his face and scrutinize that look in his eyes, and ask myself was that his usual look, or was it lit by an instinctive jealousy? Did he perhaps begin to suspect? I had become a persistent visitor in the house, he might well be jealous of such minor favors as she showed me, for with him she talked but little and shared no thoughts. His manner with her was tinctured by an habituated despair. They were extraordinarily polite and friendly with one another. . . .

I tried a hundred sophistications of my treachery to him. I assured myself that a modern woman is mistress and owner of herself; no chattel, and so forth. But he did not think so, and neither she nor I were behaving as though we thought so. In innumerable little things we were doing our best tacitly to reassure him. And so you see me shaking hands with this man, affecting an interest in his topics and affairs, staying in his house, eating his food and drinking his wine, that I might be the nearer to his wife. It is not the first time that has been done in the world, there are esoteric codes to justify all I did; I perceive there are types of men to whom such relationships are attractive by the very reason of their illicit excitement. But we Strattons are honest people, there is no secretive passion in our blood; this is no game for us; never you risk the playing of it, little son, big son as you will be when you read this story. Perhaps, but I hope indeed not, this may reach you too late to be a warning, come to you in mid-situation. Go through with it then, inheritor of mine, and keep as clean as you can, follow the warped honor that is still left to you—and if you can, come out of the tangle. . . .

It is not only Justin haunts the memories of that furtive time, but Rachel More. I see her still as she was then, a straight, white-dressed girl with big brown eyes that regarded me now with perplexity, now with a faint dismay. I still went over to see her, and my manner had changed. I had nothing to say to her now and everything to hide. Everything between us hung arrested, and nothing could occur to make an end.

I told Mary I must cease my visits to the Mores. I tried to make her feel my own sense of an accumulating cruelty to Rachel. "But it explains away so much," she said. "If you stop going there—everyone will talk. Everything will swing round—and point here."

"Rachel!" I protested.

"No," she said, overbearing me, "you must keep on going to Ridinghanger. You must. You must." . . .

For a long time I had said nothing to Mary of the burthen these pretences were to me; it had seemed a monstrous ingratitude to find the slightest flaw in the passionate love and intimacy she had given me. But at last the divergence of our purposes became manifest to us both. A time came when we perceived it clearly and discussed it openly. I have still a vivid recollection of a golden October day when we had met at the edge of the plantation that overlooks Bearshill. She had come through the gardens into the pine-wood, and I had jumped the rusty banked stream that runs down the Bearshill valley, and clambered the barbed wire fence. I came up the steep bank and through a fringe of furze to where she stood in the shade; I kissed her hand, and discovered mine had been torn open by one of the thorns of the wire and was dripping blood. "Mind my dress," she said, and we laughed as we kissed with my arm held aloof.

We sat down side by side upon the warm pine needles that carpeted the sand, and she made a mothering fuss about my petty wound, and bound it in my handkerchief. We looked together across the steep gorge at the blue ridge of trees beyond. "Anyone," she said, "might have seen us this minute."

"I never thought," I said, and moved a foot away from her.

"It's too late if they have," said she, pulling me back to her. "Over beyond there, that must be Hindhead. Someone with a telescope——!"

"That's less credible," I said. And it occurred to me that the grey stretch of downland beyond must be the ridge to the west of Ridinghanger.

"I wish," I said, "it didn't matter. I wish I could come and go and fear nobody—and spend long hours with you—oh! at our ease."

"Now," she said, "we spend short hours. I wonder if I would like—— It's no good, Stephen, letting ourselves think of things that can't be. Here we are. Kiss that hand, my lover, there, just between wrist and thumb —the little hollow. Yes, exactly there."

But thoughts had been set going in my mind. "Why," I said presently, "should you always speak of things that can't be? Why should we take all this as if it were all that there could be? I want long hours. I want you to shine all the day through on my life. Now, dear, it's as if the sun was shown ever and again, and then put back behind an eclipse. I come to you half-blinded, I go away unsatisfied. All the world is dark in between, and little phantom *yous* float over it."

She rested her cheek on her hand and looked at me gravely.

"You are hard to satisfy, brother heart," she said.

"I live in snatches of brightness and all the rest of life is waiting and thinking and waiting."

"What else is there? Haven't we the brightness?"

"I want you," I said. "I want *you* altogether."

"After so much?"

"I want the more. Mary, I want you to come away with me. No, listen! this life—don't think I'm not full of the beauty, the happiness, the wonder—— But it's a suspense. It doesn't go on. It's just a dawn, dear, a splendid dawn, a glory of color and brightness and freshness and hope, and—no sun rises. I want the day. Everything else has stopped with me and stopped with

you. I do nothing with my politics now,—I pretend.
I have no plans in life except plans for meeting you and
again meeting you. I want to go on, I want to go on with
you and take up work and the world again—you beside
me. I want you to come out of all this life—out of all
this immense wealthy emptiness of yours———"

"Stop," she said, "and listen to me, Stephen."

She paused with her lips pressed together, her brows a
little knit.

"I won't," she said slowly. "I am going on like this.
I and you are going to be lovers—just as we are lovers
now—secret lovers. And I am going to help you in all
your projects, hold your party together—for you will have
a party—my house shall be its centre———"

"But Justin———"

"He takes no interest in politics. He will do what
pleases me."

I took some time before I answered. "You don't
understand how men feel," I said.

She waited for what else I had to say. I lay prone, and
gathered together and shaped and reshaped a little heap
of pine needles. "You see—— I can't do it. I want
you."

She gripped a handful of my hair, and tugged hard
between each word. "Haven't you got me?" she asked
between her teeth. "What more *could* you have?"

"I want you openly."

She folded her arms beneath her. "*No*," she said.

For a little while neither of us spoke.

"It's the trouble of the deceit?" she asked.

"It's—the deceit."

"We can stop all that," she said.

I looked up at her face enquiringly.

"By having no more to hide," she said, with her eyes full of tears. "If it's nothing to you——"

"It's everything to me," I said. "It's overwhelming me. Oh Mary, heart of my life, my dear, come out of this! Come with me, come and be my wife, make a clean thing of it! Let me take you away, and then let me marry you. I know it's asking you—to come to a sort of poverty——"

But Mary's blue eyes were alight with anger. "Isn't it a clean thing *now*, Stephen?" she was crying. "Do you mean that you and I aren't clean now? Will you never understand?"

"Oh clean," I answered, "clean as Eve in the garden. But can we keep clean? Won't the shadow of our falsehoods darken at all? Come out of it while we are still clean. Come with me. Justin will divorce you. We can stay abroad and marry and come back."

Mary was kneeling up now with her hands upon her knees.

"Come back to what?" she cried. "Parliament?—after that? You *boy!* you sentimentalist! you—you duffer! Do you think I'd let you do it for your own sake even? Do you think I want you—spoilt? We should come back to mope outside of things, we should come back to fret our lives out. I won't do it, Stephen, I won't do it. End *this* if you like, break our hearts and throw them away and go on without them, but to turn all our lives into a scandal, to give ourselves over to the mean and the malicious, a prey to old women—and *you* damned out of everything! A man partly forgiven! A man who went wrong for a woman! *No!*"

She sprang lightly to her feet and stood over me as I knelt before her. "And I came here to be made love to, Stephen! I came here to be loved! And you talk that nonsense! You remind me of everything—wretched!"

She lifted up her hands and then struck down with them, a gesture of infinite impatience. Her face as she bent to me was alive with a friendly anger, her eyes suddenly dark. "You *duffer!*" she repeated. . . .

§ 10

Discovery followed hard upon that meeting. I had come over to Martens with some book as a pretext; the man had told me that Lady Mary awaited me in her blue parlor, and I went unannounced through the long gallery to find her. The door stood a little ajar, I opened it softly so that she did not hear me, and saw her seated at her writing-desk with her back to me, and her cheek and eyebrow just touched by the sunlight from the open terrace window. She was writing a note. I put my hand about her shoulder, and bent to kiss her as she turned. Then as she came round to me she started, was for a moment rigid, then thrust me from her and rose very slowly to her feet.

I turned to the window and became as rigid, facing Justin. He was standing on the terrace, staring at us, with a face that looked stupid and inexpressive and— very white. The sky behind him, appropriately enough, was full of the tattered inky onset of a thunderstorm. So we remained for a lengthy second perhaps, a trite *tableau vivant.* We two seemed to hang helplessly upon Justin, and he was the first of us to move.

He made a queer, incomplete gesture with one hand, as if he wanted to undo the top button of his waistcoat and then thought better of it. He came very slowly into the room. When he spoke his voice had neither rage nor denunciation in it. It was simply conversational. "I felt this was going on," he said. And then to his wife with the note of one who remarks dispassionately on a peculiar situation. "Yet somehow it seemed wrong and unnatural to think such a thing of you."

His face took on something of the vexed look of a child who struggles with a difficult task. "Do you mind," he said to me, "will you go?"

I took a moment for my reply. "No," I said. "Since you know at last—— There are things to be said."

"No," said Mary, suddenly. "Go! Let me talk to him."

"No," I said, "my place is here beside you."

He seemed not to hear me. His eyes were fixed on Mary. He seemed to think he had dismissed me, and that I was no longer there. His mind was not concerned about me, but about her. He spoke as though what he said had been in his mind, and no doubt it had been in his mind, for many days. "I didn't deserve this," he said to her. "I've tried to make your life as you wanted your life. It's astonishing to find—I haven't. You gave no sign. I suppose I ought to have felt all this happening, but it comes upon me surprisingly. I don't know what I'm to do." He became aware of me again. "And *you!*" he said. "What am I to do? To think that you —while I have been treating her like some sacred thing. . . ."

The color was creeping back into his face. Indignation had come into his voice, the first yellow lights of rising jealousy showed in his eyes.

"Stephen," I heard Mary say, "will you leave me to talk to my husband?"

"There is only one thing to do," I said. "What is the need of talking? We two are lovers, Justin." I spoke to both of them. "We two must go out into the world, go out now together. This marriage of yours—it's no marriage, no real marriage. . . ."

I think I said that. I seem to remember saying that; perhaps with other phrases that I have forgotten. But my memory of what we said and did, which is so photographically clear of these earlier passages that I believe I can answer for every gesture and nearly every word that I have set down, becomes suddenly turbid. The high tension of our first confrontation was giving place to a flood of emotional impulse. We all became eager to talk, to impose interpretations and justifications upon our situation. We all three became divided between our partial attention to one another and our urgent necessity to keep hold of our points of view. That I think is the common tragedy of almost all human conflicts, that rapid breakdown from the first cool apprehension of an issue to heat, confusion, and insistence. I do not know if indeed we raised our voices, but my memory has an effect of raised voices, and when at last I went out of the house it seemed to me that the men-servants in the hall were as hushed as beasts before a thunderstorm, and all of them quite fully aware of the tremendous catastrophe that had come to Martens. And moreover, as I recalled afterwards with astonishment, I went past them and out into the driving rain unprotected, and not one of them stirred a serviceable hand. . . .

What was it we said? I have a vivid sense of declaring not once only but several times that Mary and I were husband and wife "in the sight of God." I was full of the idea that now she must inevitably be mine. I must have spoken to Justin at times as if he had come merely to confirm my view of the long dispute there had been between us. For a while my mind resisted his extraordinary attitude that the matter lay between him and Mary, that I was in some way an interloper. It seemed to me there was nothing for it now but that Mary should stand by my side and face Justin with the world behind him. I remember my confused sense that presently she and I would have to go straight out of Martens. And she was wearing a tea-gown, easy and open, and the flimsiest of slippers. Any packing, any change of clothing, struck me as an incredible anti-climax. I had visions of our going forth, hand in hand. Outside was the soughing of a coming storm, a chill wind drove a tumult of leaves along the terrace, the door slammed and yawned open again, and then came the rain. Justin, I remember, still talking, closed the door. I tried to think how I could get to the station five miles away, and then what we could do in London. We should seem rather odd visitors to an hotel—without luggage. All this was behind my valiant demand that she should come with me, and come now.

And then my mind was lanced by the thin edge of realization that she did not intend to come now, and that Justin was resolved she should not do so. After the first shock of finding herself discovered she had stood pale but uncowed before her bureau, with her eyes

rather on him than on me. Her hands, I think, were
behind her upon the edge of the writing flap, and she was
a little leaning upon them. She had the watchful alert
expression of one who faces an unanticipated but by no
means overwhelming situation. She cast a remark to
me. "But I do not want to come with you," she said.
"I have told you I do not want to come with you." All
her mind seemed concentrated upon what she should do
with Justin. "You must send him away," he was saying.
"It's an abominable thing. It must stop. How can you
dream it should go on?"

"But you said when you married me I should be free,
I should own myself! You gave me this house——"

"What! To disgrace myself!"

I was moved to intervene.

"You must choose between us, Mary," I cried. "It
is impossible you should stay here! You cannot stay
here."

She turned upon me, a creature at bay. "Why
shouldn't I stay here? Why must I choose between
two men? I want neither of you. I want myself. I'm
not a thing. I'm a human being. I'm not your thing,
Justin—nor yours, Stephen. Yet you want to quarrel
over me—like two dogs over a bone. I am going to stay
here—in my house! It's my house. I made it. Every
room of it is full of me. Here I am!"

She stood there making this magnificently extravagant
claim; her eyes blazing blue, her hair a little dishevelled
with a strand across her cheek.

Both I and Justin spoke together, and then turned in
helpless anger upon one another. I remember that with
the clumsiest of weak gestures he bade me begone from

the house, and that I with a now rather deflated rhetoric answered I would go only with Mary at my side. And there she stood, less like a desperate rebel against the most fundamental social relations than an indignant princess, and demanded of us and high heaven, "Why should I be fought for? Why should I be fought for?"

And then abruptly she gathered her skirts in her hand and advanced. "Open that door, Stephen," she said, and was gone with a silken whirl and rustle from our presence.

We were left regarding one another with blank expressions.

Her departure had torn the substance out of our dispute. For the moment we found ourselves left with a new situation for which there is as yet no tradition of behavior. We had become actors in that new human comedy that is just beginning in the world, that comedy in which men still dispute the possession and the manner of the possession of woman according to the ancient rules, while they on their side are determining ever more definitely that they will not be possessed. . . .

We had little to say to one another,—mere echoes and endorsements of our recent declarations. "She must come to me," said I. And he, "I will save her from that at any cost."

That was the gist of our confrontation, and then I turned about and walked along the gallery towards the entrance, with Justin following me slowly. I was full of the wrath of baffled heroics; I turned towards him with something of a gesture. Down the perspective of the white and empty gallery he appeared small and perplexed. The panes of the tall French windows were slashed with rain. . . .

§ 11

I forget now absolutely what I may have expected to happen next. I cannot remember my return to my father's house that day. But I know that what did happen was the most unanticipated and incredible experience of my life. It was as if the whole world of mankind were suddenly to turn upside down and people go about calmly in positions of complete inversion. I had a note from Mary on the morning after this discovery that indeed dealt with that but was otherwise not very different from endless notes I had received before our crisis. It was destroyed, so that I do not know its exact text now, but it did not add anything material to the situation, or give me the faintest shadow to intimate what crept close upon us both. She repeated her strangely thwarting refusal to come away and live with me. She seemed indignant that we had been discovered—as though Justin had indulged in an excess of existence by discovering us. I completed and despatched to her a long letter I had already been writing overnight in which I made clear the hopeless impossibility of her attitude, vowed all my life and strength to her, tried to make some picture of the happiness that was possible for us together, sketched as definitely as I could when and where we might meet and whither we might go. It must have made an extraordinary jumble of protest, persuasion and practicality. It never reached her; it was intercepted by Justin.

I have gathered since that after I left Martens he sent telegrams to Guy and Philip and her cousin Lord Tarvrille. He was I think amazed beyond measure at this revelation of the possibilities of his cold and distant wife, with a vast passion of jealousy awaking in him, and absolutely incapable of forming any plan to meet the demands of his extraordinary situation. Guy and Philip got to him that night, Tarvrille came down next morning, and Martens became a debate. Justin did not so much express views and intentions as have them extracted from him; it was manifest he was prepared for the amplest forgiveness of his wife if only I could be obliterated from their world. Confronted with her brothers, the two men in the world who could be frankly brutal to her, Mary's dignity suffered; she persisted she meant to go on seeing me, but she was reduced to passionate tears.

Into some such state of affairs I came that morning on the heels of my letter, demanding Lady Mary of a scared evasive butler.

Maxton and Tarvrille appeared: "Hullo, Stratton!" said Tarvrille, with a fine flavor of an agreeable chance meeting. Philip had doubts about his greeting me, and then extended his reluctant hand with a nervous grin to excuse the delay.

"I want to see Lady Mary," said I, stiffly.

"She's not up yet," said Tarvrille, with a hand on my shoulder. "Come and have a talk in the garden."

We went out with Tarvrille expanding the topic of the seasons. "It's a damned good month, November, say what you like about it." Philip walked grimly silent on my other hand.

"And it's a damned awkward situation you've got us into, Stratton," said Tarvrille, "say what you like about it."

"It isn't as though old Justin was any sort of beast,"

he reflected, "or anything like that, you know. He's a most astonishing decent chap, clean as they make them."

"This isn't a beastly intrigue," I said.

"It never is," said Tarvrille genially.

"We've loved each other a long time. It's just flared out here."

"No doubt of that," said Tarvrille. "It's been like a beacon to all Surrey."

"It's one of those cases where things have to be re-adjusted. The best thing to do is for Mary and me to go abroad——"

"Yes, but does Mary think so?"

"Look here!" said Philip in a voice thick with rage. "I won't have Mary divorced. I won't. See? I won't."

"What the devil's it got to do with *you?*" I asked with an answering flash of fury.

Tarvrille's arm ran through mine. "Nobody's going to divorce Mary," he said reassuringly. "Not even Justin. He doesn't want to, and nobody else can, and there you are!"

"But we two——"

"You two have had a tremendously good time. You've got found out—and there you are!"

"This thing has got to stop absolutely *now,*" said Philip and echoed with a note of satisfaction in his own phrasing, "absolutely *now.*"

"You see, Stratton," said Tarvrille as if he were expanding Philip's assertion, "there's been too many divorces in society. It's demoralizing people. It's discrediting us. It's setting class against class. Everybody is saying why don't these big people either set about respecting the law or altering it. Common people are getting too infernally clear-headed. Hitherto it's mattered so little. . . . But we can't stand any more of it, Stratton, now. It's something more than a private issue; it's a question of public policy. We can't stand any more divorces."

He reflected. "We have to consider something more than our own personal inclinations. We've got no business to be here at all if we're not a responsible class. We owe something—to ourselves."

It was as if Tarvrille was as concerned as I was for this particular divorce, as if he struggled with a lively desire to see me and Mary happily married after the shortest possible interval. And indeed he manifestly wasn't unsympathetic; he had the strongest proclivity for the romantic and picturesque, and it was largely the romantic picturesqueness of renunciation that he urged upon me. Philip for the most part maintained a resentful silence; he was a clenched anger against me, against Mary, against the flaming possibilities that threatened the sister of Lord Maxton, that most promising and distinguished young man.

Of course their plans must have been definitely made before this talk, probably they had made them overnight, and probably it was Tarvrille had given them a practicable shape, but he threw over the whole of our talk so satisfying a suggestion of arrest and prolonged discussion that it never occurred to me that I should not be able to come again on the morrow and renew my demand to see Mary. Even when next day I turned my face to Martens and saw the flag had vanished from the flagstaff, it seemed merely a token of that household's perturbation. I thought the house looked oddly blank

and sleepy as I drew near, but I did not perceive that this
was because all the blinds were drawn. The door upon
the lawn was closed, and presently the butler came to
open it. He was in an old white jacket, and collarless.
"Lady Mary!" he said. "Lady Mary has gone, sir.
She and Mr. Justin went yesterday after you called."

"Gone!" said I. "But where?"

"I *think* abroad, sir."

"Abroad!"

"I *think* abroad."

"But—— They've left an address?"

"Only to Mr. Justin's office," said the man. "Any
letters will be forwarded from there."

I paused upon the step. He remained stiffly def-
erential, but with an air of having disposed of me. He
reproved me tacitly for forgetting that I ought to conceal
my astonishment at this disappearance. He was indeed
an admirable man-servant. "Thank you," said I, and
dropped away defeated from the door.

I went down the broad steps, walked out up the lawn,
and surveyed house and trees and garden and sky. To
the heights and the depths and the uttermost, I knew now
what it was to be amazed. . . .

§ 12

I had felt myself an actor in a drama, and now I had
very much the feeling an actor would have who answers
to a cue and finds himself in mid-stage with the scenery
and the rest of the cast suddenly vanished behind him.
By that mixture of force and persuasion which avails

175

itself of a woman's instinctive and cultivated dread of disputes and raised voices and the betrayal of contention to strangers, by the sheer tiring down of nerves and of sleepless body and by threats of an immediate divorce and a campaign of ruin against me, these three men had obliged Mary to leave Martens and go with them to Southampton, and thence they took her in Justin's yacht, the *Water-Witch*, to Waterford, and thence by train to a hired house, an adapted old castle at Mirk near Crogham in Mayo. There for all practical purposes she was a prisoner. They took away her purse, and she was four miles from a pillar-box and ten from a telegraph office. This house they had taken furnished without seeing it on the recommendation of a London agent, and in the name of Justin's solicitor. Thither presently went Lady Ladislaw, and an announcement appeared in the *Times* that Justin and Lady Mary had gone abroad for a time and that no letters would be forwarded.

I have never learnt the particulars of that abduction, but I imagine Mary astonished, her pride outraged, humiliated, helpless, perplexed and maintaining a certain outward dignity. Moreover, as I was presently to be told, she was ill. Guy and Philip were, I believe, the moving spirits in the affair; Tarvrille was their apologetic accomplice, Justin took the responsibility for what they did and bore the cost, he was bitterly ashamed to have these compulsions applied to his wife, but full now of a gusty fury against myself. He loved Mary still with a love that was shamed and torn and bleeding, but his ruling passion was that infinitely stronger passion than love in our poor human hearts, jealousy. He was prepared to fight for her now as men fight for a flag, tearing it to pieces in the struggle. He meant now to keep Mary. That settled, he was prepared to consider whether he still loved her or she him. . . .

Now here it may seem to you that we are on the very verge of romance. Here is a beautiful lady carried off and held prisoner in a wild old place, standing out half cut off from the mainland among the wintry breakers of the west coast of Ireland. Here is the lover, baffled but insistent. Here are the fierce brothers and the stern dragon husband, and you have but to make out that the marriage was compulsory, irregular and, on the ground of that irregularity, finally dissoluble, to furnish forth a theme for Marriott Watson in his most admirable and adventurous vein. You can imagine the happy chances that would have guided me to the hiding-place, the trusty friend who would have come with me and told the story, the grim siege of the place—all as it were *sotto voce* for fear of scandal—the fight with Guy in the little cave, my attempted assassination, the secret passage. Would to heaven life had those rich simplicities, and one could meet one's man at the end of a sword! My siege of Mirk makes a very different story from that.

In the first place I had no trusted friend of so extravagant a friendship as such aid would demand. I had no one whom it seemed permissible to tell of our relations. I was not one man against three or four men in a romantic struggle for a woman. I was one man against something infinitely greater than that, I was one man against nearly all men, one man against laws, traditions, instincts, institutions, social order. Whatever my position had been before, my continuing pursuit of Mary was open social rebellion. And I was in a state of extreme uncertainty how far Mary was a willing agent in this abrupt disappearance. I was disposed to think she had consented far more than she had done to this astonishing step. Carrying off an unwilling woman was outside my imaginative range. It was luminously clear in my mind that so far she had never countenanced the idea of flight with me, and until she did I was absolutely bound to silence about her. I felt that until I saw her face to face again, and was sure she wanted me to release her, that prohibition held. Yet how was I to get at her and hear what she had to say? Clearly it was possible that she was under restraint, but I did not know; I was not certain, I could not prove it. At Guildford station I gathered, after ignominious enquiries, that the Justins had booked to London. I had two days of nearly frantic inactivity at home, and then pretended business that took me to London, for fear that I should break out to my father. I came up revolving a dozen impossible projects of action in my mind. I had to get into touch with Mary, at that my mind hung and stopped. All through the twenty-four hours my nerves jumped at every knock upon my door; this might be the letter, this might be the telegram, this might be herself escaped and come to me. The days passed like days upon a painful sick-bed, grey or foggy London days of an appalling length and emptiness. If I sat at home my imagination tortured me; if I went out I wanted to be back and see if any communication had come. I tried repeatedly to see Tarvrille. I had an idea of obtaining a complete outfit for an elopement, but I was restrained by my entire ignorance of what a woman may need. I tried to equip myself for a sudden crisis by the completest preparation of every possible aspect. I did some absurd and ill-advised things. I astonished a respectable solicitor in a grimy little office behind a queer little court with trees near Cornhill, by asking him to give advice to an anonymous client and then putting my anonymous case before him. "Suppose," said I, "it was for the plot of a play." He nodded gravely.

My case as I stated it struck me as an unattractive one.

"Application for a Writ of Habeas Corpus," he considered with eyes that tried to remain severely impartial, "by a Wife's Lover, who wants to find out where she is. . . . It's unusual. You will be requiring the husband to produce her Corpus. . . . I don't think—speaking in the same general terms as those in which you put the circumstances, it would be likely to succeed. . . . No."

Then I overcame a profound repugnance and went to a firm of private detectives. It had occurred to me that if I could have Justin, Tarvrille, Guy or Philip traced I might get a clue to Mary's hiding-place. I remember a queer little office, a blusterous, frock-coated creature with a pock-marked face, iron-grey hair, an eyeglass and a strained tenor voice, who told me twice that he was a gentleman and several times that he would prefer not to do business than to do it in an ungentlemanly manner, and who was quite obviously ready and eager to blackmail either side in any scandal into which spite or weakness admitted his gesticulating fingers. He alluded vaguely to his staff, to his woman helpers, "some personally attached to me," to his remarkable underground knowledge of social life—"the illicit side." What could he do for me? There was nothing, I said, illicit about me. His interest waned a little. I told him that

I was interested in certain financial matters, no matter what they were, and that I wanted to have a report of the movements of Justin and his brothers-in-law for the past few weeks and for a little time to come. "You want them watched?" said my private enquiry agent, leaning over the desk towards me and betraying a slight squint. "Exactly," said I. "I want to know what sort of things they are looking at just at present."

"Have you any inkling——?"

"None."

"If our agents have to travel——"

I expressed a reasonable generosity in the matter of expenses, and left him at last with a vague discomfort in my mind. How far mightn't this undesirable unearth the whole business in the course of his investigations? And then what could he do? Suppose I went back forthwith and stopped his enquiries before they began! I had a disagreeable feeling of meanness that I couldn't shake off; I felt I was taking up a weapon that Justin didn't deserve. Yet I argued with myself that the abduction of Mary justified any such course.

As I was still debating this I saw Philip. He was perhaps twenty yards ahead of me, he was paying off a hansom which had just put him down outside Blake's. "Philip," I cried, following him up the steps and overtaking him and seizing his arm as the commissionaire opened the door for him. "Philip! What have you people done with Mary? Where is Mary?"

He turned a white face to me. "How dare you," he said with a catch of the breath, "mention my sister?"

I spoke in an undertone, and stepped a little between him and the man at the door in order that the latter might not hear what I said. "I want to see her," I expostulated. "I *must* see her. What you are doing is not playing the game. I've *got* to see her."

"Let go of my arm, sir!" cried he, and suddenly I felt a whirlwind of rage answering the rage in his eyes. The pent-up exasperation of three weeks rushed to its violent release. He struck me in the face with the hand that was gripped about his umbrella. He meant to strike me in the face and then escape into his club, but before he could get away from me after his blow I had flung out at him, and had hit him under the jawbone. My blow followed his before guard or counter was possible. I hit with all my being. It was an amazing flare up of animal passion; from the moment that I perceived he was striking at me to the moment when both of us came staggering across the door-mat into the dignified and spacious hall-way of Blake's, we were back at the ancestral ape, and we did exactly what the ancestral ape would have done. The arms of the commissionaire about my waist, the rush of the astonished porter from his little glass box, two incredibly startled and delighted pages, and an intervening member bawling out "Sir! Sir!" converged to remind us that we were a million years or so beyond those purely arboreal days. . . .

We seemed for a time to be confronted before an audience that hesitated to interfere. "How dare you name my sister to me?" he shouted at me, and brought to my mind the amazing folly of which he was capable. I perceived Mary's name flung to the four winds of heaven.

"You idiot, Philip!" I cried. "I don't *know* your sister. I've not seen her—scarcely seen her for years.

I ask you—I ask you for a match-box or something and you hit me."

"If you dare to speak to her——!"

"You fool!" I cried, going nearer to him and trying to make him understand. But he winced and recoiled defensively. "I'm sorry," I said to the commissionaire who was intervening. "Lord Maxton has made a mistake."

"Is he a member?" said someone in the background, and somebody else suggested calling a policeman. I perceived that only a prompt retreat would save the whole story of our quarrel from the newspapers. So far as I could see nobody knew me there except Philip. I had to take the risks of his behavior; manifestly I couldn't control it. I made no further attempt to explain anything to anybody. Everyone was a little too perplexed for prompt action, and so the advantage in that matter lay with me. I walked through the door, and with what I imagined to be an appearance of the utmost serenity down the steps. I noted an ascending member glance at me with an expression of exceptional interest, but it was only after I had traversed the length of Pall Mall that I realized that my lip and the corner of my nostril were both bleeding profusely. I called a cab when I discovered my handkerchief scarlet, and retreated to my flat and cold ablutions. Then I sat down to write a letter to Tarvrille, with a clamorous "Urgent, Please forward if away" above the address, and tell him at least to suppress Philip. But within the club that blockhead, thinking of nothing but the appearances of our fight and his own credit, was varying his assertion that he had thrashed me, with denunciations of me as a "blackguard," and giving half a dozen men a highly colored, improvised, and altogether improbable account of my relentless pursuit and persecution of Lady Mary Justin, and how she had left London to avoid me. They listened, no doubt, with extreme avidity. The matrimonial relations of the Justins had long been a matter for speculative minds.

And while Philip was doing this, Guy, away in Mayo still, was writing a tender, trusting, and all too explicit letter to a well-known and extremely impatient lady in London to account for his continued absence from her house. "So that is it!" said the lady, reading, and was at least in the enviable position of one who had confirmatory facts to impart. . . .

And so quite suddenly the masks were off our situation and we were open to an impertinent world. For some days I did not realize what had happened, and lived in hope that Philip had been willing and able to cover his lapse. I went about with my preoccupation still, as I imagined, concealed, and with an increasing number of typed letters from my private enquiry agent in my pocket containing inaccurate and worthless information about the movements of Justin, which appeared to have been culled for the most part from a communicative young policeman stationed at the corner nearest to the Justins' house, or expanded from *Who's Who* and other kindred works of reference. The second letter, I remember, gave some particulars about the financial position of the younger men, and added that Justin's credit with the west-end tradesmen was "limitless," points upon which I had no sort of curiosity whatever. . . .

I suppose a couple of hundred people in London knew before I did that Lady Mary Justin had been carried off to Ireland and practically imprisoned there by her husband because I was her lover. The thing reached me at last through little Fred Riddling, who came to my rooms in the morning while I was sitting over my breakfast. "Stratton!" said he, "what is all this story of your shaking Justin by the collar, and threatening to kill him if he didn't give up his wife to you? And why do you want to fight a duel with Maxton? What's it all about? Fire-eater you must be! I stood up for you as well as I could, but I heard you abused for a solid hour last night, and there was a chap there simply squirting out facts and dates and names. Got it all. . . . What have you been up to?"

He stood on my hearthrug with an air of having called for an explanation to which he was entitled, and he very nearly got one. But I just had some scraps of reserve left, and they saved me. "Tell me first," I said, delaying myself with the lighting of a cigarette, "the particulars . . . as you heard them."

Riddling embarked upon a descriptive sketch, and I got a minute or so to think.

"Go on," I said with a note of irony, when he paused. "Go on. Tell me some more. Where did you say they have taken her; let us have it right."

By the time his little store had run out I knew exactly what to do with him. "Riddling," said I, and stood up beside him suddenly and dropped my hand with a little added weight upon his shoulder, "Riddling, do you know the only right and proper thing to do when you hear scandal about a friend?"

"Come straight to him," said Riddling virtuously, "as I have done."

"No. Say you don't believe it. Ask the scandal-monger how he knows and insist on his telling you—insist. And if he won't—be very, very rude to him. Insist up to the quarrelling point. Now who were those people?"

"Well—that's a bit stiff. . . . One chap I didn't know at all."

"You should have pulled him up and insisted upon knowing who he was, and what right he had to lie about me. For it's lying, Riddling. Listen! It isn't true that I'm besieging Lady Mary Justin. So far from besieging her I didn't even know where she was until you told me. Justin is a neighbor of my father's and a friend of mine. I had tea with him and his wife not a month ago. I had tea with them together. I knew they were going away, but it was a matter of such slight importance to me, such slight importance"—I impressed this on his collarbone—"that I was left with the idea that they were going to the south of France. I believe they are in the south of France. And there you are. I'm sorry to spoil sport, but that's the bleak unromantic truth of the matter."

"You mean to say that there is nothing in it all?"

"Nothing."

He was atrociously disappointed. "But everybody," he said, "everybody has got something."

"Somebody will get a slander case if this goes on. I don't care what they've got."

"Good Lord!" he said, and stared at the rug. "You'll take your oath——" He glanced up and met my eye. "Oh, of course it's all right what you say." He was profoundly perplexed. He reflected. "But then, I say Stratton, why did you go for Maxton at Blake's? *That*

I had from an eye-witness. You can't deny a scrap like that—in broad daylight. Why did you do that?"

"Oh *that's* it," said I. "I begin to have glimmerings. There's a little matter between myself and Maxton. . . ." I found it a little difficult to improvise a plausible story.

"But he said it was his sister," persisted Riddlings. "He said so afterwards, in the club."

"Maxton," said I, losing my temper, "is a fool and a knave and a liar. His sister indeed! Lady Mary! If he can't leave his sister out of this business I'll break every bone of his body." . . . I perceived my temper was undoing me. I invented rapidly but thinly. "As a matter of fact, Riddling, it's quite another sort of lady has set us by the ears."

Riddling stuck his chin out, tucked in the corners of his mouth, made round eyes at the breakfast things and, hands in pockets, rocked from heels to toes and from toes to heels. "I see Stratton, yes, I see. Yes, all this makes it very plain, of course. Very plain. . . . Stupid thing, scandal is. . . . Thanks! no, I won't have a cigarette."

And he left me presently with an uncomfortable sense that he did see, and didn't for one moment intend to restrain his considerable histrionic skill in handing on his vision to others. For some moments I stood savoring this all too manifest possibility, and then my thoughts went swirling into another channel. At last the curtain was pierced. I was no longer helplessly in the dark. I got out my Bradshaw, and sat with the map spread out over the breakfast things studying the routes to Mayo. Then I rang for Williams, the man I shared with the two adjacent flat-holders, and told him to pack my kit-bag because I was suddenly called away.

§ 13

Many of the particulars of my journey to Ireland have faded out of my mind altogether. I remember most distinctly my mood of grim elation that at last I had to deal with accessible persons again. . . .

The weather was windy and violent, and I was sea-sick for most of the crossing, and very tired and exhausted when I landed. Williams had thought of my thick over-coat and loaded me with wraps and rugs, and I sat in the corner of a compartment in that state of mental and bodily fatigue that presses on the brows like a painless headache. I got to some little junction at last where I had to wait an hour for a branch-line train. I tasted all the bitterness of Irish hospitality, and such coffee as Ireland alone can produce. Then I went on to a station called Clumber or Clumboye, or some such name, and thence after some difficulty I got a car for my destination. It was a wretched car in which hens had been roosting, and it was drawn by a steaming horse that had sores under its mended harness.

An immense wet wind was blowing as we came over the big hill that lies to the south of Mirk. Everything was wet, the hillside above me was either intensely green sodden turf or great streaming slabs of limestone, seaward was a rocky headland, a ruin of a beehive shape, and beyond a vast waste of tumbling waters unlit by any sun. Not a tree broke that melancholy wilderness, nor any living thing but ourselves. The horse went stumblingly under the incessant stimulation of the driver's lash and tongue. . . .

"Yonder it is," said my man, pointing with his whip,

and I twisted round to see over his shoulder, not the Rhine-like castle I had expected, but a long low house of stone upon a headland, backed by a distant mountain that vanished in a wild driven storm of rain as I looked. But at the sight of Mirk my lassitude passed, my nerves tightened, and my will began to march again. Now, thought I, we bring things to an issue. Now we come to something personal and definite. The vagueness is at an end. I kept my eyes upon the place, and thought it more and more like a prison as we drew nearer. Perhaps from that window Mary was looking for me now. Had she wondered why I did not come to her before? Now at any rate I had found her. I sprang off the car, found a bell-handle, and set the house jangling.

The door opened, and a little old man appeared with his fingers thrust inside his collar as though he were struggling against strangulation. He regarded me for a second, and spoke before I could speak.

"What might you be wanting?" said he, as if he had an answer ready.

"I want to see Lady Mary Justin," I said.

"You can't," he said. "She's gone."

"Gone!"

"The day before yesterday she went to London. You'll have to be getting back there."

"She's gone to London."

"No less."

"Willingly?"

The little old man struggled with his collar. "Anyone would go willingly," he said, and seemed to await my further commands. He eyed me obliquely with a shadow of malice in his eyes.

It was then my heart failed, and I knew that we lovers were beaten. I turned from the door without another word to the janitor. "Back," said I to my driver, and got up behind him.

But it is one thing to decide to go back, and another to do it. At the little station I studied time-tables, and I could not get to England again without a delay of half a day. Somewhere I must wait. I did not want to wait where there was any concourse of people. I decided to stay in the inn by the station for the intervening six hours, and get some sleep before I started upon my return, but when I saw the bedroom I changed my plan and went down out of the village by a steep road towards the shore. I wandered down through the rain and spindrift to the very edge of the sea, and there found a corner among the rocks a little sheltered from the wind, and sat, inert and wretched; my lips salt, my hair stiff with salt, and my body wet and cold; a miserable defeated man. For I had now an irrational and entirely overwhelming conviction of defeat. I saw as if I ought always to have seen that I had been pursuing a phantom of hopeless happiness, that my dream of ever possessing Mary again was fantastic and foolish, and that I had expended all my strength in vain. Over me triumphed a law and tradition more towering than those cliffs and stronger than those waves. I was overwhelmed by a sense of human weakness, of the infinite feebleness of the individual man against wind and wave and the stress of tradition and the ancient usages of mankind. "We must submit," I whispered, crouching close, "we must submit." . . .

Far as the eye could reach the waves followed one another in long unhurrying lines, an inexhaustible succession, rolling, hissing, breaking, and tossing white manes of foam, to gather at last for a crowning effort and break thunderously, squirting foam two hundred feet up the streaming faces of the cliffs. The wind tore and tugged at me, and wind and water made together a clamor as though all the evil voices in the world, all the violent passions and all the hasty judgments were seeking a hearing above the more elemental uproar. . . .

§ 14

And while I was in this phase of fatigue and despair in Mayo, the scene was laid and all the other actors were waiting for the last act of my defeat in London. I came back to find two letters from Mary and a little accumulation of telegrams and notes, one written in my flat, from Tarvrille.

Mary's letters were neither of them very long, and full of a new-born despair. She had not realized how great were the forces against her and against us both. She let fall a phrase that suggested she was ill. She had given in, she said, to save herself and myself and others from the shame and ruin of a divorce, and I must give in too. We had to agree not to meet or communicate for three years, and I was to go out of England. She prayed me to accept this. She knew, she said, she seemed to desert me, but I did not know everything,—I did not know everything,—I must agree; she could not come with me; it was impossible. *Now* certainly it was impossible. She had been weak, but I did not know all. If I knew all I should be the readier to understand and forgive her, but it was part of the conditions that I could not know all. Justin had been generous, in his way. . . . Justin had everything in his hands, the whole world was behind him against us, and I must give in. Those letters had a quality I had never before met in her, they were broken-spirited. I could not understand them fully, and they left me perplexed, with a strong desire to see her, to question her, to learn more fully what this change in her might mean.

Tarvrille's notes recorded his repeated attempts to see me, I felt that he alone was capable of clearing up things for me, and I went out again at once and telegraphed to him for an appointment.

He wired to me from that same house in Mayfair in which I had first met Mary after my return. He asked me to come to him in the afternoon, and thither I went through a November fog, and found him in the drawing-room that had the plate glass above the fireplace. But now he was vacating the house, and everything was already covered up, the pictures and their frames were under holland, the fine furniture all in covers of faded stuff, the chandeliers and statues wrapped up, the carpets rolled out of the way. Even the window-curtains were tucked into wrappers, and the blinds, except one he had raised, drawn down. He greeted me and apologized for the cold inhospitality of the house. "It was convenient here," he said. "I came here to clear out my papers and boxes. And there's no chance of interruptions."

He went and stood before the empty fireplace, and plunged into the middle of the matter.

"You know, my dear Stratton, in this confounded business my heart's with you. It has been all along. If

I could have seen a clear chance before you—for you and Mary to get away—and make any kind of life of it—though she's my cousin—I'd have helped you. Indeed I would. But there's no sort of chance—not the ghost of a chance. . . ."

He began to explain very fully, quite incontrovertibly, that entire absence of any chance for Mary and myself together. He argued to the converted. "You know as well as I do what that romantic flight abroad, that Ouidaesque *casa* in some secluded valley, comes to in reality. All round Florence there's no end of such scandalous people, I've been among them, the nine circles of the repenting scandalous, all cutting one another."

"I agree," I said. "And yet——"

"What?"

"We could have come back."

Tarvrille paused, and then leant forward. "No."

"But people have done so. It would have been a clean sort of divorce."

"You don't understand Justin. Justin would ruin you. If you were to take Mary away. . . . He's a queer little man. Everything is in his hands. Everything always is in the husband's hands in these affairs. If he chooses. And keeps himself in the right. For an injured husband the law sanctifies revenge. . . .

"And you see, you've got to take Justin's terms. He's changed. He didn't at first fully realize. He feels —cheated. We've had to persuade him. There's a case for Justin, you know. He's had to stand—a lot. I don't wonder at his going stiff at last. No doubt it's hard for you to see that. But you have to see it. You've got to go away as he requires—three years out of England, you've got to promise not to correspond, not to meet afterwards——"

"It's so extravagant a separation."

"The alternative is—not for you to have Mary, but for you two to be flung into the ditch together—that's what it comes to, Stratton. Justin's got his case. He's set like—steel. You're up against the law, up against social tradition, up against money—any one of those a man may fight, but not all three. And she's ill, Stratton. You owe her consideration. You of all people. That's no got-up story; she's truly ill and broken. She can no longer fly with you and fight with you, travel in uncomfortable trains, stay in horrible little inns. You don't understand. The edge is off her pluck, Stratton."

"What do you mean?" I asked, and questioned his face.

"Just exactly what I say."

A gleam of understanding came to me. . . .

"Why can't I see her?" I broke in, with my voice full of misery and anger. "Why can't I see her? As if seeing her once more could matter so very greatly now!"

He appeared to weigh something in his mind. "You can't," he said.

"How do I know that she's not being told some story of my abandonment of her? How do I know she isn't being led to believe I no longer want her to come to me?"

"She isn't," said Tarvrille, still with that arrested judicial note in his voice. "You had her letters?" he said.

"Two."

"Yes. Didn't they speak?"

"I want to see her. Damn it, Tarvrille!" I cried with

sudden tears in my smarting eyes. "Let *her* send me away. This isn't—— Not treating us like human beings."

"Women," said Tarvrille and looked at his boot toes, "are different from men. You see, Stratton——"

He paused. "You always strike me, Stratton, as not realizing that women are weak things. We've got to take *care* of them. You don't seem to feel that as I do. Their moods—fluctuate—more than ours do. If you hold 'em to what they say in the same way you hold a man—it isn't fair. . . ."

He halted as though he awaited my assent to that proposition.

"If you were to meet Mary now, you see, and if you were to say to her, come—come and we'll jump down Etna together, and you said it in the proper voice and with the proper force, she'd do it, Stratton. You know that. Any man knows a thing like that. And she wouldn't *want* to do it. . . ."

"You mean that's why I can't see her."

"That's why you can't see her."

"Because we'd become—dramatic."

"Because you'd become—romantic and uncivilized."

"Well," I said sullenly, realizing the bargain we were making, "I won't."

"You won't make any appeal?"

"No."

He made no answer, and I looked up to discover him glancing over his shoulder through the great glass window into the other room. I stood up very quickly, and there in the further apartment were Guy and Mary, standing side by side. Our eyes met, and she came forward towards the window impulsively, and paused, with that unpitying pane between us. . . .

Then Guy was opening the door for her and she stood in the doorway. She was in dark furs wrapped about her, but in the instant I could see how ill she was and how broken. She came a step or so towards me and then stopped short, and so we stood, shyly and awkwardly under Guy and Tarvrille's eyes, two yards apart. "You see," she said, and stopped lamely.

"You and I," I said, "have to part, Mary. We—— We are beaten. Is that so?"

"Stephen, there is nothing for us to do. We've offended. We broke the rules. We have to pay."

"By parting?"

"What else is there to do?"

"No," I said. "There's nothing else." . . .

"I tried," she said, "that you shouldn't be sent from England."

"That's a detail," I answered.

"But your politics—your work?"

"That does not matter. The great thing is that you are ill and unhappy—that I can't help you. I can't do anything. . . . I'd go anywhere . . . to save you. . . . All I can do, I suppose, is to part like this and go."

"I shan't be—altogether unhappy. And I shall think of you——"

She paused, and we stood facing one another, tongue-tied. There was only one word more to say, and neither of us would say it for a moment.

"Good-bye," she whispered at last, and then, "Don't think I deserted you, Stephen my dear. Don't think ill of me. I couldn't come—I couldn't come to you," and suddenly her face changed slowly and she began to weep, my fearless playmate whom I had never seen weeping before; she began to weep as an unhappy child might weep.

"Oh my Mary!" I cried, weeping also, and held out my arms, and we clung together and kissed with tear-wet faces.

"No," cried Guy belatedly, "we promised Justin!"

But Tarvrille restrained his forbidding arm, and then after a second's interval put a hand on my shoulder. "Come," he said. . . .

And so it was Mary and I parted from one another.

CHAPTER THE SEVENTH
BEGINNING AGAIN

§ 1

IN operas and romances one goes from such a parting in a splendid dignity of gloom. But I am no hero, and I went down the big staircase of Tarville's house the empty shuck of an abandoned desire. I was acutely ashamed of my recent tears. In the centre of the hall was a marble figure swathed about with yellow muslin. "On account of the flies," I said, breaking our silence.

My words were far too unexpected for Tarville to understand. "The flies," I repeated with an air of explanation.

"You're sure she'll be all right?" I said abruptly.

"You've done the best thing you can for her."

"I suppose I have. I have to go." And then I saw ahead of me a world full of the tiresome need of decisions and arrangements and empty of all interest. "Where the *devil* am I to go, Tarville? I can't even get out of things altogether. . . ."

And then with a fresh realization of painful difficulties ahead: "I have to tell this to my father. I've got to explain—— And he thought—he expected——"

Tarville opened the half of the heavy front door

197

for me, hesitated, and came down the broad steps into the chilly grey street and a few yards along the pavement with me. He wanted to say something that he found difficult to say. When at last he did find words they were quite ridiculous in substance, and yet at the time I took them as gravely as he intended them. "It's no good quoting Marcus Aurelius," said Tarvrille, "to a chap with his finger in the crack of a door."

"I suppose it isn't," I said.

"One doesn't want to be a flatulent ass of course," said Tarvrille, "still——"

He resumed with an air of plunging. "It will sound just rot to you now, Stratton, but after all it comes to this. Behind us is a—situation—with half-a-dozen particular persons. Out here—I mean here round the world—before you've done with them—there's a thousand million people—men and women."

"Oh! what does that matter to me?" said I.

"Everything," said Tarvrille. "At least—it ought to."

He stopped and held out his hand. "Good-bye, Stratton—good luck to you! Good-bye."

"Yes," I said. "Good-bye."

I turned away from him. The image of Mary crying as a child cries suddenly blinded me and blotted out the world.

§ 2

I want to give you as clearly as I can some impression of the mental states that followed this passion and this collapse. It seems to me one of the most extraordinary aspects of all that literature of speculative attack which is called psychology, that there is no name and no description at all of most of the mental states that make up life. Psychology, like sociology, is still largely in the scholastic stage, it is ignorant and intellectual, a happy refuge for the lazy industry of pedants; instead of experience and accurate description and analysis it begins with the rash assumption of elements and starts out upon ridiculous syntheses. Who with a sick soul would dream of going to a psychologist? . . .

Now here was I with a mind sore and inflamed. I did not clearly understand what had happened to me. I had blundered, offended, entangled myself; and I had no more conception than a beast in a bog what it was had got me, or the method or even the need of escape. The desires and passionate excitements, the anger and stress and strain and suspicion of the last few months had worn deep grooves in my brain, channels without end or issue, out of which it seemed impossible to keep my thoughts. I had done dishonorable things, told lies, abused the confidence of a friend. I kept wrestling with these intolerable facts. If some momentary distraction released me for a time, back I would fall presently before I knew what was happening, and find myself scheming once more to reverse the accomplished, or eloquently restating things already intolerably overdiscussed in my mind, justifying the unjustifiable or avenging defeat. I would dream again and again of some tremendous appeal to Mary, some violent return and attack upon the situation. . . .

One very great factor in my mental and moral distress was the uncertain values of nearly every aspect of the case. There is an invincible sense of wild rightness about passionate love that no reasoning and no training will ever altogether repudiate; I had a persuasion that out of that I would presently extract a magic to excuse my deceits and treacheries and assuage my smarting shame. And round these deep central preoccupations were others of acute exasperation and hatred towards secondary people. There had been interventions, judgments upon insufficient evidence, comments, and often quite justifiable comments, that had filled me with an extraordinary savagery of resentment.

I had a persuasion, illogical but invincible, that I was still entitled to all the respect due to a man of unblemished honor. I clung fiercely to the idea that to do dishonorable things isn't necessarily to be dishonorable. . . . This state of mind I am describing is, I am convinced, the state of every man who has involved himself in any affair at once questionable and passionate. He seems free, but he is not free; he is the slave of the relentless paradox of his position.

And we were all of us more or less in deep grooves we had made for ourselves, Philip, Guy, Justin, the friends involved, and all in the measure of our grooves incapable of tolerance or sympathetic realization. Even when we slept, the clenched fist of the attitudes we had assumed gave a direction to our dreams.

You see the same string of events that had produced all this system of intense preoccupations had also severed me from the possible resumption of those wider interests out of which our intrigue had taken me. I had had to leave England and all the political beginnings I had been planning, and to return to those projects now, those now impossible projects, was to fall back promptly into hopeless exasperation. . . .

And then the longing, the longing that is like a physical pain, that hunger of the heart for some one intolerably dear! The desire for a voice! The arrested habit of phrasing one's thoughts for a hearer who will listen in peace no more! From that lonely distress even rage, even the concoction of insult and conflict, was a refuge. From that pitiless travail of emptiness I was ready to turn desperately to any offer of excitement and distraction.

From all those things I was to escape at last unhelped, but I want you to understand particularly these phases through which I passed; it falls to many and it may fall to you to pass through such a period of darkness and malign obsession. Make the groove only a little deeper, a little more unclimbable, make the temperament a little less sanguine, and suicide stares you in the face. And things worse than suicide, that suicide of self-respect which turns men to drugs and inflammatory vices and the utmost outrageous defiance of the dreaming noble self that has been so despitefully used. Into these same inky pools I have dipped my feet, where other men have drowned. I understand why they drown. And my taste of misdeed and resentment has given me just an inkling of what men must feel who go to prison. I know what it is to quarrel with a world.

§ 3

My first plan when I went abroad was to change my Harbury French, which was poor stuff and pedantic, into a more colloquial article, and then go into Germany to do the same thing with my German, and then perhaps to remain in Germany studying German social conditions—and the quality of the German army. It seemed to me that when the term of my exile was over I might return to England and re-enter the army. But all these were very anæmic plans conceived by a tired mind, and I set about carrying them out in a mood of slack lassitude. I got to Paris, and in Paris I threw them all overboard and went to Switzerland.

I remember very clearly how I reached Paris. I arrived about sunset—I suppose at St. Lazare or the Gare du Nord—sent my luggage to the little hotel in the Rue d'Antin where I had taken rooms, and dreading their loneliness decided to go direct to a restaurant and dine. I remember walking out into the streets just as shops and windows and street lamps were beginning to light up, and strolling circuitously through the clear bright stir of the Parisian streets to find a dinner at the Café de la Paix. Some day you will know that peculiar sharp definite excitement of Paris. All cities are exciting, and each I think in a different way. And as I walked down along some boulevard towards the centre of things I saw a woman coming along a side street towards me, a woman with something in her body and something in her carriage that reminded me acutely of Mary. Her face was downcast, and then as we converged she looked up at me, not with the meretricious smile of her class but with a steadfast, friendly look. Her face seemed to me sane and strong. I passed and hesitated. An extraordinary impulse took me. I turned back. I followed this woman across the road and a little way along the opposite pavement. I remember I did that, but I do not remember clearly what was

in my mind at the time; I think it was a vague rush towards the flash of companionship in her eyes. There I
had seemed to see the glimmer of a refuge from my
desolation. Then came amazement and reaction. I
turned about and went on my way, and saw her no more.

But afterwards, later, I went out into the streets of
Paris bent upon finding that woman. She had become
a hope, a desire.

I looked for her for what seemed a long time, half
an hour perhaps or two hours. I went along, peering
at the women's faces, through the blazing various lights,
the pools of shadowy darkness, the flickering reflections
and transient glitter, one of a vast stream of slow-moving
adventurous human beings. I crossed streams of traffic,
paused at luminous kiosks, became aware of dim rows of
faces looking down upon me from above the shining
enamel of the omnibuses. . . . My first intentness upon
one person, so that I disregarded any distracting intervention, gave place by insensible degrees to a more
general apprehension of the things about me. That
original woman became as it were diffused. I began to
look at the men and women sitting at the little tables
behind the panes of the cafés, and even on the terraces—
for the weather was still dry and open. I scrutinized the
faces I passed, faces for the most part animated by a sort
of shallow eagerness. Many were ugly, many vile with
an intense vulgarity, but some in that throng were pretty,
some almost gracious. There was something pathetic
and appealing for me in this great sweeping together of
people into a little light, into a weak community of desire
for joy and eventfulness. There came to me a sense of
tolerance, of fellowship, of participation. From an outer

darkness of unhappiness or at least of joylessness, they had all come hither—as I had come.

I was like a creature that slips back again towards some deep waters out of which long since it came, into the light and air. It was as if old forgotten things, pre-natal experiences, some magic of ancestral memories, urged me to mingle again with this unsatisfied passion for life about me. . . .

Then suddenly a wave of feeling between self-disgust and fear poured over me. This vortex was drawing me into deep and unknown things. . . . I hailed a passing *fiacre*, went straight to my little hotel, settled my account with the proprietor, and caught a night train for Switzerland.

All night long my head ached, and I lay awake swaying and jolting and listening to the rhythms of the wheels, Paris clean forgotten so soon as it was left, and my thoughts circling continually about Justin and Philip and Mary and the things I might have said and done.

§ 4

One day late in February I found myself in Vevey. I had come down with the break-up of the weather from Montana, where I had met some Oxford men I knew and had learned to ski. I had made a few of those vague acquaintances one makes in a winter-sport hotel, but now all these people were going back to England and I was thrown back upon myself once more. I was dull and angry and unhappy still, full of self-reproaches and dreary indignations, and then very much as the sky will sometimes break surprisingly through storm clouds there began in me a new series of moods. They came to me by surprise. One clear bright afternoon I sat upon the wall that runs along under the limes by the lake shore, envying all these people who were going back to England and work and usefulness. I thought of myself, of my career spoilt, my honor tarnished, my character tested and found wanting. So far as English politics went my prospects had closed for ever. Even after three years it was improbable that I should be considered by the party managers again. And besides, it seemed to me I was a man crippled. My other self, the mate and confirmation of my mind, had gone from me. I was no more than a mutilated man. My life was a thing condemned; I had joined the ranks of loafing, morally-limping, English exiles.

I looked up. The sun was setting, a warm glow fell upon the dissolving mountains of Savoy and upon the shining mirror of the lake. The luminous, tranquil breadth of it caught me and held me. "I am done for." The light upon the lake and upon the mountains, the downward swoop of a bird over the water and something in my heart, gave me the lie.

"What nonsense!" I said, and felt as if some dark cloud that had overshadowed me had been thrust back.

I stared across at Savoy as though that land had spoken. Why should I let all my life be ruled by the blunders and adventures of one short year of adventure? Why should I become the votary of a train of consequences? What had I been dreaming of all this time? Over there were gigantic uplands I had never seen and trodden; and beyond were great plains and cities, and

14   205

beyond that the sea, and so on, great spaces and multitudinous things all round about the world. What did the things I had done, the things I had failed to do, the hopes crushed out of me, the tears and the anger, matter to *that?* And in some amazing way this thought so took possession of me that the question seemed also to carry with it the still more startling collateral, what then did they matter to me? "Come out of yourself," said the mountains and all the beauty of the world. "Whatever you have done or suffered is nothing to the inexhaustible offer life makes you. We are you, just as much as the past is you."

It was as though I had forgotten and now remembered how infinitely multitudinous life can be. It was as if Tarvrille's neglected words to me had sprouted in the obscurity of my mind and borne fruit. . . .

I cannot explain how that mood came, I am doing my best to describe it, and it is not easy even to describe. And I fear that to you who will have had I hope no experience of such shadows as I had passed through, it is impossible to convey its immense elation. . . . I remember once I came in a boat out of the caves of Han after two hours in the darkness, and there was the common daylight that is nothing wonderful at all, and its brightness ahead there seemed like trumpets and cheering, like waving flags and like the sunrise. And so it was with this mood of my release.

There is a phrase of Peter E. Noyes', that queer echo of Emerson whom people are always rediscovering and forgetting again, a phrase that sticks in my mind,—"Every living soul is heir to an empire and has fallen into a pit." It's an image wonderfully apt to describe my change of mental attitude, and render the contrast between those intensely passionate personal entanglements that had held me tight and that wide estate of life that spreads about us all, open to all of us in just the measure that we can scramble out of our individual selves—to a more general self. I seemed to be hanging there at the brim of my stale and painful den, staring at the unthought-of greatness of the world, with an unhoped-for wind out of heaven blowing upon my face.

I suppose the intention of the phrase "finding salvation," as religious people use it, is very much this experience. If it is not the same thing it is something very closely akin. It is as if someone were scrambling out of a pit into a largeness—a largeness that is attainable by every man just in the measure that he realizes it is there.

I leave these fine discriminations to the theologian. I know that I went back to my hotel in Vevey with my mind healed, with my will restored to me, and my ideas running together into plans. And I know that I had come out that day a broken and apathetic man.

§ 5

The next day my mood declined again; it was as if that light, that sense of release that had shone so clear and strong in my mind, had escaped me. I sought earnestly to recover it. But I could not do so, and I found my old narrow preoccupations calling urgently to me again.

I thought that perhaps I might get back those intimations of outlook and relief if I clambered alone into some high solitude and thought. I had a crude attractive vision of myself far above the heat and noise, communing with the sky. It was the worst season for climbing, and on the spur of the moment I could do nothing but get up the Rochers de Naye on the wrong side, and try and find some eyrie that was neither slippery nor wet. I did not succeed. In one place I slipped down a wet bank for some yards and held at last by a root; if I had slipped much further I should not be writing here now; and I came back a very weary and bruised climber, without any meditation. . . .

Three nights after when I was in bed I became very lucidly awake—it must have been about two or three in the morning—and the vision of life returned to me, with that same effect of enlargement and illumination. It was as if the great stillness that is behind and above and around the world of sense did in some way communicate with me. It bade me rouse my spirit and go on with the thoughts and purposes that had been stirring and pro-liferating in my mind when I had returned to England from the Cape. "Dismiss your passion." But I urged that that I could not do; there was the thought of Mary sub-jugated and weeping, the smarting memory of injury and defeat, the stains of subterfuge and discovery, the aching separation. No matter, the stillness answered, in the end all that is just to temper you for your greater uses. . . . I cannot forget, I insisted. Do not forget, but for the present this leads you no whither; this chapter has ended; dismiss it and turn to those other things. You are not only Stephen Stratton who fell into adultery; in these silences he is a little thing and far away; here and with me you are Man—Everyman—in this round world in which your lot has fallen. But Mary, I urged, to forget Mary is a treason, an ingratitude, seeing that she loved me. But the stillness did not command me to forget her, but only to turn my face now to the great work that lies before mankind. And that work? That work, so far as your share goes, is first to understand, to solve, and then to achieve, to work out in the measure of yourself that torment of pity and that desire for order and justice which together saturate your soul. Go about the world, embrue yourself with life, make use of that confusedly striving brain that I have lifted so painfully out of the deadness of matter. . . .

"But who are you?" I cried out suddenly to the night. "Who are you?"

I sat up on the side of my bed. The dawn was just beginning to break up the featureless blackness of the small hours. "This is just some odd corner of my brain," I said. . . .

Yet—— How did I come to have this odd corner in my brain? What *is* this lucid stillness? . . .

§ 6

Let me tell you rather of my thoughts than of my moods, for there at least one comes to something with a form that may be drawn and a substance that is measurable; one ceases to struggle with things indefinable and the effort to convey by metaphors and imaginary voices things that are at once bodiless and soundless and lightless and yet infinitely close and real. And moreover with that mysterious and subtle change of heart in me there came also a change in the quality and range of my ideas. I seemed to rise out of a tangle of immediacies and misconceptions, to see more largely and more freely than I had ever done before.

I have told how in my muddled and wounded phase I had snatched at the dull project of improving my languages, and under the cloak of that spying a little upon German military arrangements. Now my mind set such petty romanticism on one side. It had recovered the strength to look on the whole of life and on my place in it. It could resume the ideas that our storm of passion had for a time thrust into the background of my thoughts. I took up again all those broad generalizations that had arisen out of my experiences in South Africa, and which I had been not so much fitting into as forcing into the formulæ of English politics; I recalled my disillusionment with British Imperialism, my vague but elaborating apprehension of a profound conflict between enterprise and labor, a profound conflict between the life of the farm and the life of trade and finance and wholesale production, as being something far truer to realities than any of the issues of party and patriotism upon which men were spending their lives. So far as this rivalry between England and Germany, which so obsessed the imagination of Europe, went, I found that any faith I may have had in its importance had simply fallen out of my mind. As a danger to civilization, as a conceivable source of destruction and delay, it was a monstrous business enough, but that in the long run it mattered how or when they fought and which won I did not believe. In the development of mankind the thing was of far less importance than the struggle for Flanders or the wars of France and

Burgundy. I was already coming to see Europe as no more than the dog's-eared corner of the page of history,—like most Europeans I had thought it the page—and my recovering mind was eager and open to see the world beyond and form some conception of the greater forces that lay outside our insularities. What is humanity as a whole doing? What is the nature of the world process of which I am a part? Why should I drift from cradle to grave wearing the blinkers of my time and nationality, a mere denizen of Christendom, accepting its beliefs, its stale antagonisms, its unreal purposes? That perhaps had been tolerable while I was still an accepted member of the little world into which my lot had fallen, but now that I was thrust out its absurdity glared. For me the alternative was to be a world-man or no man. I had seemed sinking towards the latter: now I faced about and began to make myself what I still seek to make myself to-day, a son of mankind, a conscious part of that web of effort and perplexity which wraps about our globe. . . .

All this I say came into my mind as if it were a part of that recovery of my mind from its first passionate abjection. And it seemed a simple and obvious part of the same conversion to realize that I was ignorant and narrow, and that, too, in a world which is suffering like a beast in a slime pit by reason of ignorance and narrowness of outlook, and that it was my manifest work and purpose to make myself less ignorant and to see and learn with all my being. It came to me as a clear duty that I I should get out of the land of hotels and leisure and go seeking the facts and clues to human inter-relationship nearer the earthy roots of things, and I turned my thoughts to India and China, those vast enigmas of human accumulation, in a spirit extraordinarily like that of some mystic who receives a call. I felt I must go to Asia and from Asia perhaps round the world. But it was the greatness of Asia commanded me. I wanted to see the East not as a spectacle but as the simmering vat in which the greater destiny of man brews and brews. . . .

§ 7

It was necessary to tell my father of my intentions. I made numerous beginnings. I tore up several letters and quarrelled bitterly with the hotel pens. At first I tried to describe the change that had happened to my mind, to give him some impression of the new light, the release that had come to me. But how difficult this present world is with its tainted and poisoned phrases and its tangled misunderstandings! Here was I writing for the first time in my life of something essentially religious and writing it to him whose profession was religion, and I could find no words to convey my meaning to him that did not seem to me fraught with the possibilities of misinterpretation. One evening I made a desperate resolve to let myself go, and scrawled my heart out to him as it seemed that night, a strange, long letter. It was one of the profoundest regrets that came to me when I saw him dead last winter that I did not risk his misunderstanding and post that letter. But when I re-read it in the next morning's daylight it seemed to me so rhetorical, so full of—what shall I call it?—spiritual bombast, it so caricatured and reflected upon the deep feelings sustaining me, that I could not post it for shamefacedness, and I tore it up into little pieces and sent instead the briefest of notes.

"I am doing no good here in Switzerland," I wrote. "Would you mind if I went east? I want to see something of the world outside Europe. I have a fancy I may find something to do beyond there. Of course, it will cost rather more than my present allowance. I will do my best to economize. Don't bother if it bothers you—I've been bother enough to you. . . ."

He replied still more compactly. "By all means. I will send you some circular notes, Poste Restante, Rome. That will be on your way. Good wishes to you, Stephen. I'm glad you want to go east instead of just staying in Switzerland."

I sit here now and wonder, little son, what he thought, what he supposed, what he understood.

I loved my father, and I began to perceive he loved me wonderfully. I can imagine no man I would have sooner had for a priest than him; all priestcraft lays hands if it can, and with an excellent wisdom, upon the titles and dignity of fatherhood; and yet here am I left to guessing—I do not know whether my father ever worshipped, whether he ever prayed with his heart bared to God. There are times when the inexpressiveness of life comes near to overwhelming me, when it seems to me we are all asleep or entranced, and but a little way above the still cows who stand munching slowly in a field. Why couldn't we and why didn't we talk together? . . . We fear bathos too much, are shyly decent to the pitch of mania. We have neither the courage of our bodies nor of our souls. . . .

I went almost immediately to Rome. I stayed in

Rome some days, getting together an outfit, and incidentally seeing that greater city of the dead in whose embrace the modern city lies. I was now becoming interested in things outside my grooves, though my grooves were still there, deep and receptive, and I went about the place at last almost eagerly, tracing the outlines of that great departed city on whose colossal bones the churches and palaces of the middle ages cluster like weeds in the spaces and ruins of a magnificent garden. I found myself one day in the Forum, thinking of that imperialism that had built the Basilica of Julius Cæsar, and comparing its cramped vestiges with that vaster second administrative effort which has left the world the monstrous arches of Constantine. I sat down over against these last among the ruins of the Vestals' House, and mused on that later reconstruction when the Empire, with its science aborted and its literature and philosophy shrivelled to nothing, its social fabric ruined by the extravagances of financial adventure and its honor and patriotism altogether dead, united itself, in a desperate effort to continue, with all that was most bickeringly intolerant and destructive in Christianity—only to achieve one common vast decay. All Europe to this day is little more than the sequel to that failure. It is the Roman Empire in disintegration. The very churches whose domes rise to the northward of the ancient remains are built of looted stones and look like parasitic and fungoid growths, and the tourists stream through those spaces day by day, stare at the marble fragments, the arches, the fallen carvings and rich capitals, with nothing greater in their minds and nothing clearer. . . .

I discovered I was putting all this into the form of a

letter to Mary. I was writing to her in my mind, as many people talk to themselves. And I remember that I wandered upon the Palatine Hill musing over the idea of writing a long letter to her, a long continuous letter to her, a sort of diary of impressions and ideas, that somewhen, years ahead, I might be able to put into her hands.

One does not carry out such an idea into reality; it is so much easier to leave the letter imagined and unwritten if there lives but little hope of its delivery; yet for many years I kept up an impalpable correspondence in my thoughts, a stream of expression to which no answer came —until at last the habits of public writing and the gathering interests of a new rôle in life diverted it to other ends.

§ 8

One morning on the way from Brindisi to Egypt I came up on deck at dawn because my mind was restless and I could not sleep. Another solitary passenger was already up, so intently watching a pink-lit rocky coast-line away to the north of us that for a time he did not observe me.

"That's Crete," he said, when at last he became aware of me close at hand.

"Crete!" said I.

"Yes," he said, "Crete."

He came nearer to me. "That, sir," he said with a challenging emphasis, "is the most wonderful island I've ever yet set eyes on,—quite the most wonderful."

"Five thousand years ago," he remarked after a pause that seemed to me to be calculated, "they were building palaces there, better than the best we can build to-day.

And things—like modern things. They had bathrooms there, beautifully fitted bathrooms—and admirable sanitation—admirable. Practically—American. They had better artists to serve them than your King Edward has, why! Minos would have laughed or screamed at all that Windsor furniture. And the things they made of gold, sir—you couldn't get them done anywhere to-day. Not for any money. There was a Go about them. . . . They had a kind of writing, too—before the Phœnicians. No man can read it now, and there it is. Fifty centuries ago it was; and to-day— They grow oranges and lemons. And they riot. . . . Everything else gone. . . . It's as if men struggled up to a certain pitch and then—grew tired. . . . All this Mediterranean; it's a tired sea. . . ."

That was the beginning of a curious conversation. He was an American, a year or so younger than myself, going, he said, "to look at Egypt."

"In our country," he explained, "we're apt to forget all these worked-out regions. Too apt. We don't get our perspectives. We think the whole blessed world is one everlasting boom. It hit me first down in Yucatan that that wasn't so. Why! the world's littered with the remains of booms and swaggering beginnings. Americanism!—there's always been Americanism. This Mediterranean is just a Museum of old Americas. I guess Tyre and Sidon thought they were licking creation all the time. It's set me thinking. What's *really* going on? Why—anywhere,—you're running about among ruins—anywhere. And ruins of something just as good as anything we're doing to-day. Better—in some ways. It takes the heart out of you. . . ."

It was Gidding, who is now my close friend and ally.

I remember very vividly the flavor of morning freshness as we watched Crete pass away northward and I listened to his talk.

"I was coming out of New York Harbor a month ago and looking back at the skyscrapers," he said, "and suddenly it hit me in the mind;—'That's just the next ruin,' I thought."

I remember that much of our first talk, but the rest of it now is indistinct.

We had however struck up an acquaintance, we were both alone, and until he left me on his way to Abydos we seem now to have been conversing all the time. And almost all the time we were discussing human destiny and the causes of effort and decay, and whether the last few ascendant centuries the world has seen have in them anything more persistent than the countless beginnings that have gone before.

"There's Science," said I a little doubtfully.

"At Cnossus there they had Dædalus, sir, fifty centuries ago. Dædalus! He was an F.R.S. all right. I haven't a doubt he flew. If they hadn't steel they had brass. We're too conceited about our little modern things."

§ 9

I found something very striking and dramatic in the passage from Europe to Asia. One steams slowly through a desert that comes up close to the ship; the sand stretches away, hillock and mound beyond hillock and mound; one sees camels in the offing stringing out to some ancient destination; one is manifestly passing across a barrier,—

the canal has changed nothing of that. Suez is a first dab of tumultuous Orientalism, noisy and vivid. And then, after that gleam of turmoil, one opens out into the lonely dark blue waters of the Red Sea. Right and left the shore is a bitter, sun-scorched desolation; eastward frowns a great rampart of lowering purple mountains towering up to Sinai. It is like no European landscape. The boat goes slowly as if uncharted dangers lurked ahead. It is a new world with a new atmosphere. Then comes wave upon wave of ever more sultry air, and the punkahs begin to swing and the white clothes appear. Everyone casts off Europe, assumes an Asiatic livery. The very sun, rushing up angrily and abruptly after a heated night, is unfamiliar, an Asiatic sun.

And so one goes down that reef-fringed waterway to Aden; it is studded with lonely-looking lighthouses that burn, it seems, untended, and sometimes in their melancholy isolation swing great rhythmic arms of light. And then, land and the last lateen sails of Aden vanishing together, one stands out into the hot thundery monotonies of the Indian Ocean; into imprisonment in a blue horizon across whose Titan ring the engines seem to throb in vain. How one paces the ship day by day, and eats and dozes and eats again, and gossips inanely and thanks Heaven even for a flight of flying fish or a trail of smoke from over the horizon to take one's mind a little out of one's oily quivering prison! . . . A hot portentous delay; a sinister significant pause; that is the voyage from Europe to India still.

I suppose by the time that you will go to India all this prelude will have vanished, you will rattle through in a train-de-luxe from Calais, by way of Baku or Constantinople; you will have none of this effect of a deliberate sullen approach across limitless miles of sea. But that is how I went to India. Everything seemed to expand; I was coming out of the frequent landfalls, the neighborly intimacies and neighborly conflicts of the Mediterranean into something remoter; into larger seas and greater lands, rarer communications and a vaster future. . . .

To go from Europe to Asia is like going from Norway to Russia, from something slight and "advanced" to something massive and portentous. I felt that nearly nine years ago; to-day all Asia seems moving forward to justify my feelings. . . .

And I remember too that as I went down the Red Sea and again in the Indian Ocean I had a nearly intolerable passion of loneliness. A wound may heal and still leave pain. I was coming out of Europe as one comes out of a familiar house into something larger and stranger, I seemed but a little speck of life, and behind me, far away and silent and receding, was the one other being to whom my thoughts were open. It seemed very cruel to me that I could not write to her.

Such moods were to come to me again and again, and particularly during the inactivities of voyages and in large empty spaces and at night when I was weary. At other times I could banish and overcome them by forcing myself to be busy and by going to see novel and moving things.

CHAPTER THE EIGHTH

THIS SWARMING BUSINESS OF MANKIND

§ 1

I DO not think I could now arrange into a consecutive history my travellings, my goings and returnings in my wandering effort to see and comprehend the world. And certainly even if I could arrange my facts I should still be at a loss to tell of the growth of ideas that is so much more important than any facts, to trace the increasing light to its innumerable sources, to a chink here, to a glowing reflection there, to a leap of burning light from some long inert darkness close at hand. But steadily the light grew, and this vast world of man, in which *our* world, little son, is the world of a limited class in a small island, began to take on definite forms, to betray broad universal movements; what seemed at first chaotic, a drift and tangle of passions, traditions, foolish ideas, blundering hostilities, careless tolerances, became confusedly systematic, showed something persistent and generalized at work among its multitudinous perplexity.

I wonder now if I can put before you very briefly the main generalizations that were growing up in my mind during my exile, the simplified picture into which I translated the billions of sights and sounds and—smells, for every part of the world has its distinctive olfactory palette as much as its palette of colors—that rained daily and nightly upon my mind.

Before my eyes again as I sit here in this quiet walled French garden, the great space before the Jumna Musjid at Delhi reappears, as I saw it in the evening stillness against a glowing sky of gold, and the memory of countless worshippers within, praying with a devotion no European displays. And then comes a memory of that long reef of staircases and temples and buildings, the ghats of Benares, in the blazing morning sun, swarming with a vast multitude of multicolored people and the water also swarming with brown bodies. It has the colors of a bed of extravagantly splendid flowers and the light that is Indian alone. Even as I sit here these places are alive with happening. It is just past midday here; at this moment the sun sinks in the skies of India, the Jumna Musjid flushes again with the glow of sunset, the smoke of evening fires streams heavenward against its subtle lines, and upon those steps at Benares that come down the hillside between the conquering mosque of Aurangzeb and the shining mirror of the Ganges a thousand silent seated figures fall into meditation. And other memories recur and struggle with one another; the crowded river-streets of Canton, the rafts and houseboats and junks innumerable, riding over inky water, begin now to twinkle with a thousand lights. They are ablaze in Osaka and Yokohama and Tokio, and the swarming staircase streets of Hong Kong glitter with a wicked activity now that night has come. I flash a glimpse of Burmese temples, of villages in Java, of the sombre purple masses of the walls of the Tartar city at Pekin with squat pagoda-guarded gates. How those great outlines lowered at me in the twilight, full of fresh memories and grim anticipations of baseness and violence and bloodshed! I sit here recalling it—feeling it all out beyond the trellised vine-clad wall that bounds my physical vision. . . . Vast crowded world that I have seen! going from point to point seeking for clues, for generalities, until at last it seems to me that there emerges—something understandable.

I think I have got something understandable out of it all.

What a fantastically courageous thing is this mind of ours! My thoughts seem to me at once presumptuous and inevitable. I do not know why it is that I should dare, that any of us should dream of this attempt to comprehend. But we who think are everyone impelled to this amazing effort to get it all together into some simple generality. It is not reason but a deep-seated instinct that draws our intelligence towards explanations, that sets us perpetually seeking laws, seeking statements that will fit into infinite, incessantly interweaving complexities, and be true of them all! There is I perceive a valiant and magnificent stupidity about the human mind, a disregard of disproportion and insufficiency—like the ferret which will turn from the leveret it has seized to attack even man if he should interfere. By these desperate feats of thinking it is that our species has achieved its victories. By them it survives. By them it must stand the test of ultimate survival. Some forgotten man in our ancestry—for every begetting man alive was in my individual ancestry and yours three thousand years ago—first dared to think of the world as round,—an astounding temerity. He rolled up the rivers and mountains, the forests and plains and broad horizons that stretched beyond his ken, that seemed to commonsense to go on certainly for ever, into a ball, into a little ball "like an orange." Magnificent feat of the imagination, outdoing Thor's deep draught of the sea! And once he had done it, all do it and no one falters at the deed. You are not yet seven as I write and already you are serenely aware that you live upon a sphere. And in much the same manner it is that we, who are sociologists and economists, publicists and philosophers and what not, are attempting now to roll up the vast world of facts which concern human intercourse, the whole indeed of history and archæology, into some similar imaginable and manageable shape, that presently everyone will be able to grasp.

I suppose there was a time when nobody bothered at all about the shape of the earth, when nobody had even had the idea that the earth could be conceived as having a shape, and similarly it is true that it is only in recent centuries that people have been able to suppose that there was a shape to human history. It is indeed not much more than a century since there was any real emergence from theological assumptions and pure romanticism and accidentalism in these matters. Old Adam Smith it was, probing away at the roots of economics, who set going the construction of ampler propositions. From him spring all those new interpretations which have changed the writing of history from a record of dramatic reigns and wars and crises to an analysis of economic forces. How impossible it would be for anyone now to write that great chapter of Gibbon's in which he sweeps together into one contempt the history of sixty Emperors and six hundred years of time. His note of weariness and futility vanishes directly one's vision penetrates the immediate surface. Those Heraclians and Isaurians and Comneni were not history, a schoolboy nowadays knows that their record is not history, knows them for the mere scum upon the stream.

And still to-day we have our great interpretations to make. Ours is a time of guesses, theories and provisional generalizations. Our phase corresponds to the cosmography that was still a little divided between discs and domes and spheres and cosmic eggs; that was still a thousand years from measuring and weighing a planet. For a long time my mind hovered about the stimulating theories of Socialism and particularly about those more systematic forms of Socialist teaching that centre about Karl Marx. He rose quite naturally out of those early economists who saw all the world in terms of production and saving. He was a necessary step for me at least, on the way to understanding. For a time I did so shape the world in my mind that it seemed to me no more than a vast enterprise for the organization and exploitation of labor. For a time I thought human life was essentially a labor problem, that working and controlling work and lending and selling and "speculating" made the essential substance of human life, over which the forms of politics ran as the stripes of a tiger's skin run and bend over its living muscles. I followed my period in thinking that. You will find in Ferrero's "Roman Decline," which was published early in this century, and which waits for you in the library, almost exactly the method of interpretation that was recommending itself to me in 1904 and 1905.

Well, the labor problem concerns a great—*substantial,* shall I say?—in human society. It is only I think the basis and matter of society, not its shape and life and reality, but it had to be apprehended before I could get on to more actual things. Insensibly the idea that contemporary political forms mattered very fundamentally to men, was fading out of my mind. The British Empire and the German Empire, the Unity of Italy, and Anglo-Saxon ascendency, the Yellow Peril and all the other vast phantoms of the World-politician's mythology were fading out of my mind in those years, as the Olympic cosmogony must have faded from the mind of some inquiring Greek philosopher in the days of Heraclitus. And I revised my history altogether in the new light. The world had ceased to be chaotic in my mind; it had become a vast if as yet a quite inconclusive drama between employer and employed.

It makes a wonderful history, this history of mankind as a history of Labor, as a history of the perpetual attempts of an intelligent minority to get things done by other people. It does not explain how that aggression of the minority arose nor does it give any conception of a primordial society which corresponds with our knowledge of the realities of primitive communities. One begins rather in the air with a human society that sells and barters and sustains contracts and permits land to be privately owned, and having as hastily as possible got away from that difficulty of beginnings, having ignored the large areas of the world which remain under a pacific and unprogressive agriculture to this day, the rest of the story becomes extremely convincing and illuminating. It does indeed give a sustaining explanation to a large part of recorded history, this generalization about the proclivity of able and energetic people to make other people do things. One ignores what is being done as if that mattered nothing, and concentrates upon the use and enslavement of men.

One sees that enslavement to labor progressing from crude directness to the most subtly indirect methods. The first expedient of enterprise was the sword and then the whip, and still there are remote and ugly corners of the world, in the Mexican Valle Nazionale or in Portuguese South Africa, where the whip whistles still and the threat of great suffering and death follows hard upon the reluctant toiler. But the larger part of our modern slavery is past the stage of brand and whip. We have fallen into methods at once more subtle and more effective. We stand benevolently in front of our fellow man, offering, almost as if it were food and drink and shelter and love, the work we want him to do; and behind him, we are acutely aware, is necessity, sometimes quite of our making, as when we drive him to work by a hut-tax or a poll tax or a rent, that obliges him to earn money, and sometimes not so obviously of our making, sometimes so little of our making that it is easy to believe we have no power to remove it. Instead of flicking the whip, we groan at last with Harriet Martineau at the inexorable laws of political economy that condemn us to comfort and direction, and those others to toil and hardship and indignity. . . .

And through the consideration of these latter later aspects it was that I came at last to those subtler problems of tacit self-deception, of imperfect and unwilling apprehension, of innocently assumed advantages, of wilfully disregarded unfairness; and also to all those other problems of motive, those forgotten questions of why we make others work for us long after our personal needs are satisfied, why men aggrandize and undertake, which gradually have become in my mind the essential problems of human relationship, replacing the crude problems of labor altogether in that position, making *them* at last only questions of contrivance and management on the way to greater ends.

I have come to believe now that labor problems are problems merely by the way. They have played their part in a greater scheme. This phase of expropriation and enslavement, this half designed and half unconscious driving of the duller by the clever, of the pacific by the bolder, of those with weak appetites and imaginations by those with stronger appetites and imaginations, has been a necessary phase in human development. With my innate passionate desire to find the whole world purposeful, I cannot but believe that. But however necessary it has been, it is necessary no longer. Strangest of saviors, there rises over the conflicts of mankind the glittering angular promise of the machine. There is no longer any need for slavery, open or disguised. We do not need slaves nor toilers nor mere laborers any more; they are no longer essential to a civilization. Man has ridden on his brother man out of the need of servitude. He struggles through to a new phase, a phase of release, a phase when leisure and an unexampled freedom is possible to every human being. Is possible. And it is there one halts seeing that splendid possibility of aspiration and creation before mankind—and seeing mankind for the most part still downcast, quite unaware or incredulous, following the old rounds, the grooves of ancient and superseded assumptions and subjections. . . .

But here I will not trace in any detail the growth of my conviction that the ancient and heavy obligation to work hard and continually throughout life has already slipped from man's shoulders. Suffice it that now I conceive of the task before mankind as a task essentially of rearrangement, as a problem in relationships, extremely complex and difficult indeed, but credibly solvable. During my Indian and Chinese journey I was still at the Marxist stage. I went about the east looking at labor, watching its organization and direction, seeing great interests and enterprises replace the diffused life of an earlier phase; the disputes and discussions in the Transvaal which had first opened my mind to these questions came back to me, and steadily I lost my interest in those mere political and national issues with their paraphernalia of kings and flags and governments and parties that had hitherto blinded me to these more fundamental interactions.

§ 2

It happened that in Bombay circumstances conspired to bring the crude facts of labor enslavement vividly before me. I found a vigorous agitation raging in the English press against the horrible sweating that was going on in the cotton mills, I met the journalist most intimately concerned in the business on my second day in India, and before a week was out I was hard at work getting up the question and preparing a memorandum with him on the possibility of immediate legislative intervention. The very name of Bombay, which for most people recalls a spacious and dignified landfall, lateen sails, green islands and jutting precipices, a long city of trees and buildings like a bright and various breakwater between the great harbor and the sea, and then exquisite little temples, painted bullock carriages, Towers of Silence, Parsis, and an amazingly kaleidoscopic population,—is for me a reminder of narrow, fœtid, plague-stricken streets and tall insanitary tenement-houses packed and dripping with humanity, and of terrible throbbing factories working far into the night, blazing with electric light against the velvet-black night-sky of India, damp with the steam-clouds that are maintained to moisten the thread, and swarming with emaciated overworked brown children—for even the adults, spare and small, in those mills seem children to a western eye.

I plunged into this heated dreadful business with a passionate interest and went back to the Yacht Club only when the craving for air and a good bath and clean clothes and space and respect became unendurable. I waded deep in labor, in this process of consuming humanity for gain, chasing my facts through throbbing quivering sheds reeking of sweat and excrement under the tall black-smoking chimneys,—chasing them in very truth, because when we came prying into the mills after the hour when child-labor should cease, there would be a shrill whistle, a patter of feet and a cuffing and hiding of the naked little creatures we were trying to rescue. They would be hidden under rugs, in boxes, in the most impossible places, and we dragged them out scared and lying. Many of them were perhaps seven years old at most; and the adults—men and women of fourteen that is to say—we could not touch at all, and they worked in that Indian heat, in a noisome air drenched with steam for fourteen and fifteen hours a day. And essential to that general impression is a memory of a slim Parsi mill-manager luminously explaining the inherited passion for toil in the Indian weaver, and a certain bulky Hindu with a lemon-yellow turban and a strip of plump brown stomach showing between his clothes, who was doing very well, he said, with two wives and five children in the mills.

That is my Bombay, that and the columns of crossed circles marking plague cases upon the corners of houses and a peculiar acrid smell, and the polychromatic stir of crowded narrow streets between cliffs of architecture with carved timbers and heavy ornamentations, into which the sun strikes obliquely and lights a thousand vivid hues. . . .

Bombay, the gateway of what silly people were still calling in those days "the immemorial East," Bombay, which is newer than Boston or New York, Bombay which has grown beneath the Englishman's shadow out of a Portuguese fort in the last two hundred years. . . .

§ 3

I came out of these dark corners presently into the sunblaze of India. I was now intensely interested in the whole question of employment and engaged in preparing matter for my first book, "Enterprise and India," and therein you may read how I went first to Assam and then down to Ceylon following up this perplexing and complicated business of human enslavement to toil, exercised by this great spectacle of human labor, and at once attracted by and stimulated by and dissatisfied with those socialist generalizations that would make all this vast harsh spectacle of productive enterprise a kind of wickedness and outrage upon humanity. And behind and about the things I was looking for were other things for which I was not looking, that slowly came into and qualified the problem. It dawned upon me by degrees that India is not so much one country as a vast spectacle of human development at every stage, in infinite variety. One ranges between naked savages and the most sophisticated of human beings. I pursued my enquiries about great modern enterprises, about railway labor, canal labor, tea-planting, across vast stretches of country where men still lived, illiterate, agricultural, unprogressive and simple, as men lived before the first stirrings of recorded history. One sees by the tanks of those mud-built villages groups of women with brass vessels who are identical in pose and figure and quality with the women modelled in Tanagra figures, and the droning wall-wheel is the same that irrigated the fields of ancient Greece, and the crops and beasts and all the life is as it was in Greece and Italy, Phœnicia and Judea before the very dawn of history.

By imperceptible degrees I came to realize that this matter of expropriation and enslavement and control, which bulks so vastly upon the modern consciousness, which the Socialists treat as though it was the comprehensive present process of mankind, is no more than one aspect of an overlife that struggles out of a massive ancient and traditional common way of living, struggles out again and again—blindly and always so far with a disorderly insuccess. . . .

I began to see in their proper proportion the vast enduring normal human existence, the peasant's agricultural life, unlettered, laborious and essentially unchanging on the one hand, and on the other those excrescences of multitudinous city aggregation, those stormy excesses of productive energy that flare up out of that life, establish for a time great unstable strangenesses of human living, palaces, cities, roads, empires, literatures, and then totter and fall back again into ruin. In India even more than about the Mediterranean all this is spectacular. There the peasant goes about his work according to the usage of fifty thousand years. He has a primitive version of religion, a moral tradition, a social usage, closely adapted by countless years of trial and survival to his needs, and the whole land is littered with the vestiges and abandoned material of those newer, bolder, more experimental beginnings, beginnings that merely began.

It was when I was going through the panther-haunted palaces of Akbar at Fatehpur Sikri that I first felt how tremendously the ruins of the past may face towards the future; the thing there is like a frozen wave that rose and never broke; and once I had caught that light upon things, I found the same quality in all the ruins I saw, in Amber and Vijayanagar and Chitor, and in all that I have seen or heard of, in ancient Rome and ancient Verona, in Pæstum and Cnossus and ancient Athens. None of these places was ever really finished and done with; the Basilicas of Cæsar and Constantine just as much as the baths and galleries and halls of audience at Fatehpur Sikri express not ends achieved but thwarted intentions of permanence. They embody repulse and rejection. They are trials, abandoned trials, towards ends vaguely apprehended, ends felt rather than known. Even so was I moved by the Bruges-like emptinesses of Pekin, in the vast pretensions of its Forbidden City, which are like a cry, long sustained, that at last dies away in a wail. I saw the place in 1905 in that slack interval after the European looting and before the great awakening that followed the Russo-Japanese war. Pekin in a century or so may be added in its turn to the list of abandoned endeavors. Insensibly the sceptre passes. . . . Nearer home than any of these places have I imagined the same thing; in Paris it seemed to me I felt the first chill shadow of that same arrest, that impalpable ebb and cessation at the very crest of things, that voice which opposes to all the hasty ambitions and gathering eagerness of men: "It is not here, it is not yet."

Only the other day as I came back from Paris to this quiet place and walked across the fields from the railway station to this house, I saw an old woman, a grandmother, a bent old crone with two children playing about her as she cut grass by the wayside, and she cut it, except that her sickle was steel, exactly as old women were cutting grass before there was writing, before the dawn of history, before men laid the first stones one upon the other of the first city that ever became a ruin. . . .

You see Civilization has never yet existed, it has only continually and obstinately attempted to be. Our Civilization is but the indistinct twilight before the dawn. It is still only a confused attempt, a flourish out of barbarism, and the normal life of men, the toiling earthy life of the field and the byre, goes on still like a stream that at once supports and carries to destruction the experimental ships of some still imperfect inventor. India gives it all from first to last, and now the modern movement, the latest half-conscious struggle of the New Thing in mankind, throws up Bombay and Calcutta, vast feverish pustules upon the face of the peninsula, bridges the sacred rivers with hideous iron lattice-work and smears the sky of the dusty ruin-girdled city of Delhi,—each ruin is the vestige of an empire,—with the black smoke of factory chimneys.

Altogether scattered over that sun-burnt plain there are the remains of five or six extinguished Delhis, that played their dramas of frustration before the Delhi of the Great Mogul. This present phase of human living —its symbol at Delhi is now, I suppose, a scaffold-bristling pile of neo-Georgian building—is the latest of the constructive synthetic efforts to make a newer and fuller life for mankind. Who dares call it the last? I question myself constantly whether this life we live to-day, whether that too, is more than a trial of these blind constructive forces, more universal perhaps, more powerful perhaps than any predecessor but still a trial, to litter the world with rusting material when the phase of recession recurs.

But yet I can never quite think that is so. This time, surely, it is different. This time may indeed be the beginning of a permanent change; this time there are new elements, new methods and a new spirit at work upon construction that the world has never known before. Mankind may be now in the dawn of a fresh phase of living altogether. It is possible. The forces of construction are proportionally gigantic. There was never so much clear and critical thought in the world as there is now, never so large a body of generally accessible knowledge and suggestion, never anything like the same breadth of outlook, the same universality of imaginative freedom. That is so in spite of infinite turmoil and confusion. Moreover the effort now is less concentrated, less dramatic. There is no one vital center to the modern movement which disaster can strike or decay undermine. If Paris or New York slacken and grow dull and materialist, if Berlin and London conspire for a mutual destruction, Tokio or Baku or Valparaiso or Christiania or Smyrna or Delhi will shelter and continue the onward impetus.

And this time too it is not any one person, any one dynasty, any one cult or race which carries our destiny. Human thought has begun to free itself from individual entanglements and dramatic necessities and accidental standards. It becomes a collective mind, a collective will towards achievement, greater than individuals or cities or kingdoms or peoples, a mind and will to which we all contribute and which none of us may command nor compromise by our private errors. It ceases to be aristocratic; it detaches itself from persons and takes possession of us all. We are involved as it grows free and dominant, we find ourselves, in spite of ourselves, in spite of quarrels and jealousies and conflicts, helping and serving in the making of a new world-city, a new greater State above our legal States, in which all human life becomes a splendid enterprise, free and beautiful, whose aptest symbol in all our world is a huge Gothic Cathedral lit to flame by the sun, whose scheme is the towering conquest of the universe, whose every little detail is the wrought-out effort of a human soul. . . .

Such were the ideas that grew together in my mind as I went about India and the East, across those vast sunlit plains, where men and women still toil in their dusty fields for a harsh living and live in doorless hovels on floors of trampled cow-dung, persecuted by a hundred hostile beasts and parasites, caught and eaten by tigers and panthers as cats eat mice, and grievously afflicted by periodic famine and pestilence, even as men and women lived before the dawn of history, for untold centuries, for hundreds of thousands of years.

§ 4

How strange we English seem in India, a little scattered garrison. Are we anything more than accidental, anything more than the messenger-boy who has brought the impetus of the new effort towards civilization through the gates of the East? Are we makers or just a means, casually taken up and used by the great forces of God?

I do not know, I have never been able to tell. I have never been able to decide whether we are the greatest or the dullest of peoples.

I think we are an imaginative people with an imagination at once gigantic, heroic and shy, and also we are a strangely restrained and disciplined people who are yet neither subdued nor subordinated. . . . These are flat contradictions to state, and yet how else can one render the paradox of the English character and this spectacle of a handful of mute, snobbish, not obviously clever and quite obviously ill-educated men, holding together kingdoms, tongues and races, three hundred millions of them, in a restless fermenting peace? Again and again in India I would find myself in little circles of the official English,— supercilious, pretentious, conventional, carefully "turned out" people, living gawkily, thinking gawkily, talking nothing but sport and gossip, relaxing at rare intervals into sentimentality and levity as mean as a banjo tune, and a kind of despairful disgust would engulf me. And then in some man's work, in some huge irrigation scheme, some feat of strategic foresight, some simple, penetrating realization of deep-lying things, I would find an effect, as if out of a thickly rusted sheath one had pulled a sword and found it—flame. . . .

I recall one evening I spent at a little station in Bengal, between Lucknow and Delhi, an evening given over to private theatricals. The theatre was a huge tent, and the little roughly improvised stage was lit by a row of oil footlights and so small as barely to give a foothold for the actors and actresses in the more crowded scenes. About me were the great people, the colonel's wife, a touring young man of family, officers and the wife of the manager of the big sugar refinery close at hand. Behind were English of a more dubious social position, also connected with the sugar refinery, a Eurasian family or so, very dressy and aggressive and terribly snubbed, and then I think various Portuguese and other nondescripts and groups of non-commissioned officers and men, some with their wives. The play, admirably chosen, was that crystallization of liberal Victorian snobbery, *Caste*, and I remember there was a sub-current of amusement because the young officer who played—what *is* the name of the hero's friend? I forget — had in the haste of his superficiality adopted a moustache that would not keep on and an eyeglass that would not keep in.

Everybody was acting very badly, nobody was word-perfect and a rasping prompter would not keep ahead as he ought to have done; the scenery and the make-ups were daubs, and I was filled with amazement that having quite wantonly undertaken to do this thing these people could then do it so slackly. Then a certain sudden warmth in the applause about me quickened my attention, and I realized the satirical purport of drunken old father Eccles, and the moral intention of his son-in-law, the plumber. Between them they expressed the whole duty of the workingman as the prosperous Victorians conceived it. He was to work hard always at any job he could find for any wages he could get, and if he didn't he was a "drunken shirker" and the dupe of "paid agitators." A comforting but misleading doctrine. And here were these people a decade on in the twentieth century, with Time, Death, and Judgment close upon them, still eagerly applauding, eager to excuse their minds with this one-sided, ungracious, old-fashioned nonsense, that has done so much to intensify the deepening class antagonisms that strain us now at home almost to the breaking point!

How amazingly, it seemed, those people didn't understand and wouldn't understand any class but their own, any race but their own, any usage other than their use! Covertly I surveyed the colonel's profile. It expressed nothing but entire satisfaction with these disastrous interpretations. What a weather-worn thought-free face that grizzled veteran showed the world!

I was seized with a sudden curiosity to see how the private soldiers behind me were taking old Eccles. I turned round to discover cropped heads and faces as expressionless as masks, and behind them dusky faces watching very alertly, and then other dusky faces, Eurasians, inferiors, servants, natives.

Then at a sharp edge the glare of our lighting ceased and the canvas walls of our narrow world of illusion opened into a vast blue twilight. At the opening stood two white-clad Sikhs, very, very still and attentive, watching the performance, and beyond them was a great space of sky over a dim profile of trees and roofs and a minaret, a sky darkling down to the flushed red memory—such a short memory it is in India—of a day that had gone for ever.

I remained staring at that for some time.

"Isn't old Eccles *good?*" whispered the colonel's wife beside me, and recalled me to the play. . . .

Somehow that picture of a narrow canvas tent in the midst of immensities has become my symbol for the whole life of the governing English, the English of India and Switzerland and the Riviera and the West End and the public services. . . .

But they are not England, they are not the English reality, which is a thing at once bright and illuminating and fitful, a thing humorous and wise and adventurous —Shakespeare, Dickens, Newton, Darwin, Nelson, Bacon, Shelley—English names every one—like the piercing light of lanterns swinging and swaying among the branches of dark trees at night.

§ 5

I went again to Ceylon to look into the conditions of Coolie importation, and then I was going back into Assam once more, still in the wake of indentured labor, when I chanced upon a misadventure. I had my first and only experience of big game shooting in the Garo Hills, I was clawed out of a tree by a wounded panther, he missed his hold and I got back to my branch, but my shoulder was put out, my thigh was badly torn, and my

239

blood was poisoned by the wound. I had an evil uncomfortable time. My injury hampered me greatly, and for a while it seemed likely I should be permanently lamed. I had to keep to vehicles and reasonably good roads. I wound up my convalescence with a voyage to Singapore, and from thence I went on rather disconnectedly to a number of exploratory journeys—excursions rather than journeys—into China. I got to Pekin and then suddenly faced back to Europe, returning overland through Russia.

I wanted now to study the conditions of modern industrialism at its sources, and my disablement did but a little accelerate a return already decided upon. I had got my conception of the East as a whole and of the shape of the historical process. I no longer felt adrift in a formless chaos of forces. I preceived now very clearly that human life is essentially a creative struggle out of the usage of immemorial years, that the synthesis of our contemporary civilization is this creative impulse rising again in its latest and greatest effort, the creative impulse rising again, as a wave rises from the trough of its predecessors, out of the ruins of our parent system, imperial Rome. But this time, and for the first time, the effort is world-wide, and China and Iceland, Patagonia and Central Africa all swing together with us to make—or into another catastrophic failure to make—the Great State of mankind. All this I had now distinctly in my mind. The new process I perceive had gone further in the west; was most developed in the west. The lighter end lifts first. So back I came away from the great body of mankind, which is Asia, to its head. And since I was still held by my promise from returning to England I betook myself first to the Pas de Calais and then to Belgium and thence into industrial Germany, to study the socialistic movement at its sources.

And I was beginning to see too very clearly by the time of my return that what is confusedly called the labor problem is really not one problem at all, but two. There is the old problem, the problem as old as Zimbabwe and the pyramids, the declining problem, the problem of organizing masses of unskilled labor to the constructive ends of a Great State, and there is the new modification due to machinery, which has rendered unskilled labor and labor of a low grade of skill almost unnecessary to mankind, added coal, oil, wind and water, the elementary school and the printing-press to our sources of power, and superseded the ancient shepherding and driving of men by the possibility of their intelligent and willing co-operation. The two are still mixed in every discussion, even as they are mixed in the practice of life, but inevitably they will be disentangled. We break free from slavery, open or disguised, just as we illuminate and develop this disentanglement. . . .

I have long since ceased to trouble about the economics of human society. Ours are not economic but psychological difficulties. There is enough for everyone, and only a fool can be found to deny it. But our methods of getting and making are still ruled by legal and social traditions from the time before we had tapped these new sources of power, before there was more than enough for everyone, and when a bare supply was only secured by jealous possession and unremitting toil. We have no longer to secure enough by a stern insistence. We have come to a plenty. The problem now is to make that plenty go round, and *keep it enough* while we do.

Our real perplexities are altogether psychological. There are no valid arguments against a great-spirited Socialism but this, that people will not. Indolence, greed, meanness of spirit, the aggressiveness of authority, and above all jealousy, jealousy for our pride and vanity, jealousy for what we esteem our possessions, jealousy for those upon whom we have set the heavy fetters of our love, a jealousy of criticism and association, these are the real obstacles to those brave large reconstructions, those profitable abnegations and brotherly feats of generosity that will yet turn human life—of which our individual lives are but the momentary parts—into a glad, beautiful and triumphant co-operation all round this sunlit world.

If but humanity could have its imagination touched——

I was already beginning to see the great problem of mankind as indeed nothing other than a magnification of the little problem of myself, as a problem in escape from grooves, from preoccupations and suspicions, precautions and ancient angers, a problem of escape from these spiritual beasts that prowl and claw, to a new generosity and a new breadth of view.

For all of us, little son, as for each of us, salvation is that. We have to get away from ourselves to a greater thing, to a giant's desire and an unending life, ours and yet not our own.

§ 6

It is a queer experience to be even for a moment in the grip of a great beast. I had been put into the fork of a tree, so that I could shoot with the big stem behind my back. The fork wasn't, I suppose, more than a score of feet from the ground. It was a safe enough place from a tiger, and that is what we expected. We had been misled by our tracker, who had mistaken the pugs of a big leopard for a tiger's,—they were over rocky ground for the most part and he had only the spoor of a chance patch of half-dried mud to go upon. The beast had killed a goat and was beaten out of a thicket near by me in which he had been lying up. The probability had seemed that he would go away along a tempting ravine to where Captain Crosby, who was my host, awaited him; I, as the amateur, was intended to be little more than a spectator. But he broke back towards the wing of the line of beaters and came across the sunlit rocks within thirty yards of my post.

Seen going along in that way, flattened almost to the ground, he wasn't a particularly impressive beast, and I shot at his shoulder as one might blaze away at a rabbit,—perhaps just a little more carefully, feeling as a Lord of Creation should who dispenses a merited death. I expected him either to roll over or bolt.

Then instantly he was coming in huge bounds towards me. . . .

He came so rapidly that he was covered by the big limb of the tree on which I was standing until he was quite beneath me, and my second shot, which I thought in the instant must have missed him, was taken rapidly as he crouched to spring up the trunk.

Then you know came a sort of astonishment, and I think,—because afterwards Crosby picked up a dropped cartridge at the foot of the tree—that I tried to reload. I believe I was completely incredulous that the beast was going to have me until he actually got me. The thing was too completely out of my imaginative picture. I don't believe I thought at all while he was coming up the tree. I merely noted how astonishingly he resembled an angry cat. Then he'd got my leg, he was hanging on to it first by two claws and then by one claw, and the whole weight of him was pulling me down. It didn't seem to be my leg. I wasn't frightened, I felt absolutely nothing, I was amazed. I slipped, tried to get a hold on the tree trunk, felt myself being hauled down, and then got my arm about the branch. I still clung to my unloaded gun as an impoverished aristocrat might cling to his patent of nobility. That was, I felt, my answer for him yet.

I suppose the situation lasted a fraction of a second, though it seemed to me to last an interminable time. Then I could feel my leggings rip and his claw go scoring deeply down my calf. That hurt in a kind of painless, impersonal interesting way. Was my leg coming off? Boot? The weight had gone, that enormous weight!

He'd missed his hold altogether! I heard his claws tear down the bark of the tree and then his heavy, soft fall upon the ground.

I achieved a cat-like celerity. In another second I was back in my fork reloading, my legs tucked up as tightly as possible.

I peered down through the branches ready for him. He wasn't there. Not up the tree again? . . . Then I saw him making off, with a halting gait, across the scorching rocks some thirty yards away, but I could not get my gun into a comfortable position before he was out of sight behind a ridge. . . . I wondered why the sunlight seemed to be flickering like an electric light that fails, was somehow aware of blood streaming from my leg down the tree-stem; it seemed a torrent of blood, and there was a long, loose ribbon of flesh very sickening to see; and then I fainted and fell out of the tree, bruising my arm and cheek badly and dislocating my shoulder in the fall. . . . Some of the beaters saw me fall, and brought Crosby in sufficient time to improvise a *torniquet* and save my life.

CHAPTER THE NINTH

THE SPIRIT OF THE NEW WORLD

§ 1

I MET Rachel again in Germany through the devices of my cousin the Fürstin Letzlingen. I had finished seeing what I wanted to see in Westphalia and I was preparing to go to the United States. There I thought I should be able to complete and round off that large view of the human process I had been developing in my mind. But my departure was delayed by an attack of influenza that I picked up at a Socialist Congress in Munich, and the dear Durchlaucht, hearing of this and having her own views of my destiny, descended upon me while I was still in bed there, made me get up and carried me off in her car, to take care of me herself at her villa at Boppard, telling me nothing of any fellow-guests I might encounter.

She had a villa upon the Rhine under a hill of vineyards, where she devoted herself—she was a widow—to matchmaking and belated regrets for the childlessness that necessitated a perpetual borrowing of material for her pursuit. She had a motor-car, a steam-launch, several rowing boats and canoes, a tennis-lawn, a rambling garden, a devious house and a rapid mind, and in fact

246

everything that was necessary for throwing young people together. She made her surprise seem easy and natural, and with returning health I found myself already back upon my old footing of friendly intimacy with Rachel.

I found her a new and yet a familiar Rachel. She had grown up, she was no longer a schoolgirl, crystalline clear with gleams of emotion and understanding, and what she had lost in transparency she had gained in depth. And she had become well-informed, she had been reading very widely and well, I could see, and not simply reading but talking and listening and thinking. She showed a vivid interest in the current of home politics,—at that time the last government of Mr. Balfour was ebbing to its end and my old Transvaal friends, the Chinese coolies, were to avenge themselves on their importers. The Tariff Reformers my father detested were still struggling to unseat the Premier from his leadership of Conservatism. . . .

It was queer to hear once more, after my Asiatic wanderings and dreamings, those West-End dinner-table politics, those speculations about "Winston's" future and the possibility of Lloyd George or Ramsay Macdonald or Macnamara taking office with the Liberals and whether there might not ultimately be a middle party in which Haldane and Balfour, Grey and the Cecils could meet upon common ground. It seemed now not only very small but very far off. She told me too of the huge popularity of King Edward. He had proved to be interested, curious, understanding and clever, an unexpectedly successful King. She described how he was breaking out of the narrow official limits that had kept his mother in a kind of social bandbox, extending his solvent informality of friendliness to all sorts of men. He had won the heart of Will Crooks, the labor member for Poplar, for example, made John Burns a social success and warmed all France for England.

I surveyed this novel picture of the English throne diffusing amiability.

"I suppose it's what the throne ought to do," said Rachel. "If it can't be inspiration, at any rate it can tolerate and reconcile and take the ill-bred bitterness out of politics."

"My father might have said that."

"I got that from your father," she said; and added after a momentary pause, "I go over and talk to him."

"You talk to my father!"

"I like to. Or rather I listen and take it in. I go over in the afternoon. I go sometimes twice or three times a week."

"That's kind of you."

"Not at all. You see—— It sounds impudent, I know, for a girl to say so, but we've so many interests in common."

§ 2

I was more and more interested by Rachel as the days went on. A man must be stupid who does not know that a woman is happy in his presence, and for two years now and more I had met no one with a very strong personal feeling for me. And quite apart from that, her mind was extraordinarily interesting to me because it was at once so active and so clear and so limited by her entirely English circumstances. She had the prosperous

English outlook. She didn't so much see the wide world as get glimpses of it through the tangle of Westminster and of West End and week-end limitations. She wasn't even aware of that greater unprosperous England, already sulking and darkling outside her political world, that greater England which was presently to make its first audible intimations of discontent in that remarkable anticlimax to King George's Coronation, the Railway Strike. India for her was the land of people's cousins, Germany and the German Dreadnoughts bulked far larger, and all the tremendous gathering forces of the East were beyond the range of her imagination. I set myself to widen her horizons.

I told her something of the intention and range of my travels, and something of the views that were growing out of their experiences.

I have a clear little picture in my mind of an excursion we made to that huge national Denkmal which rears its head out of the amiable vineyards of Assmannshausen and Rudesheim over against Bingen. We landed at the former place, went up its little funicular to eat our lunch and drink its red wine at the pleasant inn above, and then strolled along through the woods to the monument.

The Fürstin fell behind with her unwilling escort, a newly arrived medical student from England, a very pleasant youngster named Berwick, who was all too obviously anxious to change places with me. She devised delays, and meanwhile I, as yet unaware of the state of affairs, went on with Rachel to that towering florid monument with its vast gesticulating Germania, which triumphs over the conquered provinces.

We fell talking of war and the passions and delusions

that lead to war. Rachel's thoughts were strongly colored by those ideas of a natural rivalry between Germany and England and of a necessary revenge for France which have for nearly forty years diverted the bulk of European thought and energy to the mere waste of military preparations. I jarred with an edifice of preconceptions when I scoffed and scolded at these assumptions.

"Our two great peoples are disputing for the leadership of the world," I said, "and meanwhile the whole world sweeps past us. We're drifting into a quarrelsome backwater."

I began to tell of the fermentation and new beginnings that were everywhere perceptible throughout the East, of the vast masses of human ability and energy that were coming into action in China and India, of the unlimited future of both North and South America, of the mere accidentalness of the European advantage. "History," I said, "is already shifting the significance out of Western Europe altogether, and we English cannot see it; we can see no further than Berlin, and these Germans can think of nothing better than to taunt the French with such tawdry effigies as *this!* Europe goes on to-day as India went on in the eighteenth century, making aimless history. And the sands of opportunity run and run. . . ."

I shrugged my shoulders and we stood for a little while looking down on the shining crescent of the Rhine.

"Suppose," said Rachel, "that someone were to say that—in the House."

"The House," I said, "doesn't hear things at my pitch. Bat outcries. Too shrill altogether."

"It might. If *you*——"

She halted, hesitated for a moment on the question and asked abruptly:

"When are you coming back to England, Mr. Stratton?"

"Certainly not for six months," I said.

A movement of her eyes made me aware of the Fürstin and Berwick emerging from the trees. "And then?" asked Rachel.

I didn't want to answer that question, in which the personal note sounded so clearly. "I am going to America to see America," I said, "and America may be rather a big thing to see."

"You must see it?"

"I want to be sure of it—as something comprehensive. I want to get a general effect of it. . . ."

Rachel hesitated, looked back to measure the distance of the Fürstin and her companion and put her question again, but this time with a significance that did not seem even to want to hide itself. "*Then* will you come back?" she said.

Her face flamed scarlet, but her eyes met mine boldly. Between us there was a flash of complete understanding.

My answer, if it was lame and ungallant to such a challenge, was at least perfectly honest. "I can't make up my mind," I said. "I've been near making plans—taking steps. . . . Something holds me back. . . ."

I had no time for an explanation.

"I can't make up my mind," I repeated.

She stood for a moment rather stiffly, staring away towards the blue hills of Alsace.

Then she turned with a smiling and undisturbed countenance to the Fürstin. Her crimson had given place to white. "The triumph of it," she said with a slight gesture to the flamboyant Teutonism that towered over us, and boldly repeating words I had used scarcely five minutes before, "makes me angry. They conquered—ungraciously. . . ."

She had overlooked something in her effort to seem entirely self-possessed. She collapsed. "My dear!" she cried,—"I forgot!"

"Oh! I'm only a German by marriage!" cried the Fürstin. "And I can assure you I quite understand—about the triumph of it. . . ." She surveyed the achievement of her countrymen. "It is—ungracious. But indeed it's only a sort of artlessness if you see the thing properly. . . . It's not vulgarity—it's childishness. . . . They've hardly got over it yet—their intense astonishment at being any good at war. . . . That large throaty Victory! She's not so militant as she seems. She's too plump. . . . Of course what a German really appreciates is nutrition. But I quite agree with you both. . . . I'm beginning to want my tea, Mr. Stratton. . . . Rachel!"

Her eyes had been on Rachel as she chattered. The girl had turned to the distant hills again, and had forgotten even to pretend to listen to the answer she had evoked. Now she came back sharply to the sound of her name.

"Tea?" said the Fürstin.

"Oh!" cried Rachel. "Yes. Yes, certainly. Rather. Tea."

§ 3

It was clear to me that after that I must as people say "have things out" with Rachel. But before I could do anything of the sort the Fürstin pounced upon me. She made me sit up that night after her other guests had gone to their rooms, in the cosy little turret apartment she called her study and devoted to the reading of whatever was most notorious in contemporary British fiction. "Sit down," said she, "by the fire in that chair there and tell me all about it. It's no good your pretending you don't know what I mean. What are you up to with her, and why don't you go straight to your manifest destiny as a decent man should?"

"Because manifestly it isn't my destiny," I said.

"Stuff," said the Fürstin.

"You know perfectly well why I am out of England."

"Everybody knows—except of course quite young persons who are being carefully brought up."

"Does *she* know?"

"She doesn't seem to."

"Well, that's what I want to know."

"Need she know?"

"Well, it does seem rather essential——"

"I suppose if you think so——"

"Will you tell her?"

"Tell her yourself, if she must be told. Down there in Surrey, she *must* have seen things and heard things. But I don't see that she wants a lot of ancient history."

"If it is ancient history!"

"Oh! two years and a half,—it's an Era."

I made no answer to that, but sat staring into the fire while my cousin watched my face. At length I made my confession. "I don't think it is ancient history at all," I said. "I think if I met Mary again now——"

"You mean Lady Mary Justin?"

17   253

"Of course."

"It would be good for your mind if you remembered to call her by her proper name. . . . You think if you met her again you two would begin to carry on. But you see, —you aren't going to meet her. Everybody will see that doesn't happen."

"I mean that I—— Well——"

"You'd better not say it. Besides, it's nonsense. I doubt if you've given her a thought for weeks and weeks."

"Until I came here perhaps that was almost nearly true. But you've stirred me up, sweet cousin, and old things, old memories and habits have come to the surface again. Mary wrote herself over my life—in all sorts of places. . . . I can't tell you. I've never talked of her to anyone. I'm not able, very well, to talk about my feelings. . . . Perhaps a man of my sort—doesn't love twice over."

I disregarded a note of dissent from my cousin. "That was all so magic, all my youth, all my hope, all the splendid adventure of it. Why should one pretend? . . . I'm giving none of that to Rachel. It isn't there any more to give. . . ."

"One would think," remarked the Fürstin, "there was no gift of healing."

She waited for me to speak, and then irritated by my silence struck at me sharply with that wicked little tongue of hers.

"Do you think that Lady Mary Justin thinks of you—as you think of her? Do you think she hasn't settled down?"

I looked up at her quickly.

"She's just going to have a second child," the Fürstin flung out.

Yes, that did astonish me. I suppose my face showed it.

"That girl," said the Fürstin, "that clean girl would have sooner died—ten thousand deaths. . . . And she's never—never been anything to you."

I think that for an instant she had been frightened at her own words. She was now quite angry and short of breath. She had contrived a rapid indignation against Mary and myself.

"I didn't know Mary had had any child at all," I said.

"This makes two," said the Fürstin, and held up a brace of fingers, "with scarcely a year and a half between them. Not much more anyhow. . . . It was natural, I suppose. A natural female indecency. I don't blame her. When a woman gives in she ought to do it thoroughly. But I don't see that it leaves *you* much scope for philandering, Stephen, does it? . . . And there you are, and here is Rachel. And why don't you make a clean job of your life? . . ."

"I didn't understand."

"I wonder what you imagined."

I reflected. "I wonder what I did. I suppose I thought of Mary—just as I had left her—always."

I remained with my mind filled with confused images of Mary, memories, astonishment. . . .

I perceived the Fürstin was talking.

"Maundering about," she was saying, "like a huntsman without a horse. . . . You've got work to do—blood in your veins. I'm not one of your ignorant women, Stephen. You ought to have a wife. . . ."

"Rachel's too good," I said, at the end of a pause and

perceiving I had to say something, "to be that sort of wife."

"No woman's too good for a man," said the Fürstin von Letzlingen with conviction. "It's what God made her for."

§ 4

My visit to Boppard was drawing to an end before I had a clear opportunity to have things out with Rachel. It was in a little garden, under the very shadow of that gracious cathedral at Worms, the sort of little garden to which one is admitted by ringing a bell and tipping a custodian. I think Worms is in many respects one of the most beautiful cathedrals I have ever seen, so perfectly proportioned, so delicately faded, so aloof, so free from pride or presumption, and it rises over this green and flowery peace, a towering, lithe, light brown, sunlit, easy thing, as unconsciously and irrelevantly splendid as a tall ship in the evening glow under a press of canvas. We looked up at it for a time and then went on with the talk to which we had been coming slowly since the Fürstin had packed us off for it, while she went into the town with Berwick to buy toys for her gatekeeper's children. I had talked about myself, and the gradual replacement of my ambition to play a part in imperial politics by wider intentions. "You know," I asked abruptly, "why I left England?"

She thought through the briefest of pauses. "No," she decided at last.

"I made love," I said, "to Lady Mary Justin, and we were found out. We couldn't go away together——"

"Why not?" she interjected.

"It was impossible."

For some moments neither of us spoke. "Something," she said, and then, "Some vague report," and left these fragments to be her reply.

"We were old playmates; we were children together. We have—something—that draws us to each other. She—she made a mistake in marrying. We were both very young and the situation was difficult. And then afterwards we were thrown together. . . . But you see that has made a great difference to my life; it's turned me off the rails on which men of my sort usually run. I've had to look to these other things. . . . They've become more to me than to most people if only because of that. . . ."

"You mean these ideas of yours—learning as much as you can about the world, and then doing what you can to help other people to a better understanding."

"Yes," I said.

"And that—will fill your life."

"It ought to."

"I suppose it ought. I suppose—you find—it does."

"Don't you think it ought to fill my life?"

"I wondered if it did."

"But why shouldn't it?"

"It's so—so cold."

My questioning silence made her attempt to explain.

"One wants life more beautiful than that," she said. "One wants—— There are things one needs, things nearer one."

We became aware of a jangling at the janitor's bell. Our opportunity for talk was slipping away. And we were both still undecided, both blunderingly nervous and insecure. We were hurried into clumsy phrases that afterwards we would have given much to recall.

"But how could life be more beautiful," I said, "than when it serves big human ends?"

Her brows were knit. She seemed to be listening for the sound of the unlocking gate.

"But," she said, and plunged, "one wants to be loved. Surely one needs that."

"You see, for me—that's gone."

"Why should it be gone?"

"It is. One doesn't begin again. I mean — myself. *You*—can. You've never begun. Not when you've loved —loved really." I forced that on her. I over empha- sized. "It was real love, you know; the real thing. . . . I don't mean the mere imaginative love, blindfold love, but love that sees. . . . I want you to understand that. I loved—altogether. . . ."

Across the lawn under its trim flowering-trees appeared Berwick loaded with little parcels, and manifestly eager to separate us, and the Fürstin as manifestly putting on the drag.

"There's a sort of love," I hurried, "that doesn't renew itself ever. Don't let yourself believe it does. Some- thing else may come in its place, but that is different. It's youth,—a wonderful newness. . . . Look at that youngster. *He* can love you like that. I've watched him. He does. You know he does. . . ."

"Yes," she said, as hurriedly; "but then, you see, I don't love him."

"You don't?"

"I can't."

"But he's such a fresh clean human being——"

"That's not all," said Rachel. "That's not all. . . . You don't understand."

The two drew near. "It is so hard to explain," she said. "Things that one hardly sees for oneself. Sometimes it seems one cannot help oneself. You can't choose. You are taken. . . ." She seemed about to say something more, and stopped and bit her lip.

In another moment I was standing up, and the Fürstin was calling to us across ten feet of space. "Such amoosin' little toyshops. We've got a heap of things. Just look at him!"

He smiled over his load with anxious eyes upon our faces.

"Ten separate parcels," he said, appealing for Rachel's sympathy. "I'm doing my best not to complain."

And rather adroitly he contrived to let two of them slip, and captured Rachel to assist him.

He didn't relinquish her again.

§ 5

The Fürstin and I followed them along the broad, pleasant, tree-lined street towards the railway station.

"A boy of that age ought not to marry a girl of that age," said the Fürstin, breaking a silence.

I didn't answer.

"Well?" she said, domineering.

"My dear cousin," I said, "I know all that you have in your mind. I admit—I covet her. You can't make me more jealous than I am. She's clean and sweet— it is marvellous how the God of the rest of the world can

259

have made a thing so brave and honest and wonderful. She's better than flowers. But I think I'm going away to-night, nevertheless."

"You don't mean you're going to carry chivalry to the point of giving that boy a chance—for he hasn't one while you're about."

"No. You see—I want to give Rachel a chance. You know as well as I do—the things in my mind."

"That you've got to forget."

"That I don't forget."

"That you're bound in honor to forget. And who could help you better?"

"I'm going," I said and then, wrathfully, "If you think I want to use Rachel as a sort of dressing—for my old sores——"

I left the sentence unfinished.

"Oh *nonsense!*" cried the Fürstin, and wouldn't speak to me again until we got to that entirely Teutonic "art" station that is not the least among the sights of Worms.

"Sores, indeed!" said the Fürstin presently, as we walked up the end of the platform.

"There's nothing," said the Fürstin, with an unusual note of petulance, "she'd like better."

"I can't think what men are coming to," she went on. "You're in love with her, or you wouldn't be so generous. And she's head over heels with you. And here you are! I'll give you one more chance——"

"I won't take it," I interrupted. "It isn't fair. I tell you I won't take it. I'll go two days earlier to prevent you. Unless you promise me—— Of course I see how things are with her. She's not a sphinx. But it isn't fair. It isn't. Not to her, or to him—or myself. *He's* got some claims. He's got more right to her than I. . . ."

"A boy like that! No man has any rights about women —until he's thirty. And as for me and all the pains *I've* taken—— Oh! I *hate* Worms. Dust and ashes! Well here thank heaven! comes the train. If nothing else could stir you, Stephen, at least I could have imagined some decent impulse of gratitude to me. Stephen, you're disgusting. You've absolutely spoilt this trip for me— absolutely. When only a little reasonableness on *your* part—— Oh!"

She left her sentence unfinished.

Berwick and I had to make any conversation that was needed on the way back to Boppard. Rachel did not talk and the Fürstin did not want to.

§ 6

Directly I had parted from Rachel's questioning eyes I wanted to go back to them. It seems to me now that all the way across to America, in that magnificent German liner I joined at Hamburg, I was thinking in confused alternations of her and of Mary. There are turns of thought that still bring back inseparably with them the faint echo of the airs of the excellent but industrious band that glorified our crossing.

I had been extraordinarily shocked and concerned at the thought of Mary bearing children. It is a grotesque thing to confess but I had never let myself imagine the possibility of such a thing for her who had been so immensely mine. . . .

We are the oddest creatures, little son, beasts and barbarians and brains, neither one nor the other but all confusedly, and here was I who had given up Mary and resigned her and freed myself from her as I thought altogether, cast back again into my old pit by the most obvious and necessary consequence of her surrender and mine.   And it's just there and in that relation that we men and women are so elaborately insecure.   We try to love as equals and behave as equals and concede a level freedom, and then comes a crisis,—our laboriously contrived edifice of liberty collapses and we perceive that so far as sex goes the woman remains to the man no more than a possession—capable of loyalty or treachery.

There, still at that barbaric stage, the situation stands. You see I had always wanted to own Mary, and always she had disputed that.   That is our whole story, the story of an instinctive subjugation struggling against a passionate desire for fellowship.   She had denied herself to me, taken herself away; that much I could endure; but now came this blazing fact that showed her as it seemed in the most material and conclusive way—overcome.   I had storms of retrospective passion at the thoroughness of her surrender. . . . Yes, and that's in everyone of us,— in everyone.   I wonder if in all decent law-abiding London there lives a single healthy adult man who has not at times longed to trample and kill. . . .

For once I think the Fürstin miscalculated consequences. I think I should have engaged myself to Rachel before I went to America if it had not been for the Fürstin's revelation, but this so tore me that I could no longer go on falling in love again, naturally and sweetly.   No man falls in love if he has just been flayed. . . . I could no longer think of Rachel except as a foil to Mary. I was moved to marry her by a new set of motives; to fling her so to speak in Mary's face, and from the fierce vulgarity of that at least I recoiled—and let her go as I have told you.

§ 7

I had thought all that was over.

I remember my struggles to recover my peace.

I remember how very late one night I went up to the promenade deck to smoke a cigar before turning in. It was a warm moonlight night. The broad low waves of ebony water that went seething past below, foamed luminous and were streaked and starred with phosphorescence. The recumbent moon, past its full and sinking westward, seemed bigger than I had ever seen it before, and the roundness of the watery globe was manifest about the edge of the sky. One had that sense so rare on land, so common in the night at sea, of the world as a conceivable sphere, and of interstellar space as of something clear and close at hand.

There came back to me again that feeling I had lost for a time in Germany of being not myself but Man consciously on his little planet communing with God.

But my spirit was saying all the time, "I am still in my pit, in my pit. After all I am still in my pit."

And then there broke the answer on my mind, that all our lives we must struggle out of our pits, that to struggle out of our pit is this life, there is no individual life but that, and that there comes no escape here, no end to that effort, until the release of death. Continually or frequently we may taste salvation, but never may we achieve it while we are things of substance. Each moment in our lives we come to the test and are lost again or saved again. To be assured of one's security is to forget and fall away.

And standing at the rail with these thoughts in my mind, suddenly I prayed. . . .

I remember how the engine-throbs beat through me like the beating of a heart, and that far below, among the dim lights that came up from the emigrants in the steerage, there was a tinkling music as I prayed and a man's voice singing a plaintive air in some strange Slavonic tongue.

That voice of the invisible singer and the spirit of the unknown song-maker and the serenity of the sky, they were all, I perceived, no more and no less than things in myself that I did not understand. They were out beyond the range of understanding. And yet they fell into the completest harmony that night with all that I seemed to understand. . . .

§ 8

The onset of New York was extraordinarily stimulating to me. I write onset. It is indeed that. New York rides up out of the waters, a cliff of man's making; its great buildings at a distance seem like long Chinese banners held up against the sky. From Sandy Hook to the great landing stages and the swirling hooting traffic of the Hudson River there fails nothing in that magnificent crescendo of approach.

And New York keeps the promise of its first appearance. There is no such fulness of life elsewhere in all the world. The common man in the streets is a bigger common man than any Old World city can show, physically bigger; there is hope in his eyes and a braced defiance. New York may be harsh and blusterous and violent, but there is a breeze from the sea and a breeze of fraternity in the streets, and the Americans of all peoples in the world are a nation of still unbroken men.

I went to America curious, balancing between hope and scepticism. The European world is full of the criticism of America, and for the matter of that America too is full of it; hostility and depreciation prevail,—overmuch, for in spite of rawness and vehemence and a scum of blatant, oh! quite asinine folly, the United States of America remains the greatest country in the world and the living hope of mankind. It is the supreme break with the old tradition; it is the freshest and most valiant beginning that has ever been made in human life.

Here was the antithesis of India; here were no peasants whatever, no traditional culture, no castes, no established differences (except for the one schism of color); this amazing place had never had a famine, never a plague; here were no temples and no priesthoods dominating the lives of the people,—old Trinity church embedded amidst towering sky-scrapers was a symbol for as much as they had of all that; and here too there was no crown, no affectations of an ancient loyalty, no visible army, no traditions of hostility, for the old defiance of Britain is a thing now ridiculous and dead; and everyone I met had an air as if he knew that to-morrow must be different from to-day and different and novel and remarkable by virtue of himself and such as himself.

I went about New York, with the incredulous satisfaction of a man who has long doubted, to find that after all America was coming true. The very clatter pleased me, the crowds, the camp-like slovenliness, a disorder so entirely different from the established and accepted untidiness of China or India. Here was something the old world had never shown me, a new enterprise, a fresh vigor. In the old world there is Change, a mighty wave now of Change, but it drives men before it as if it were a power outside them and not in them; they do not know, they do not believe; but here the change is in the very blood and spirit of mankind. They breathe it in even before the launch has brought their feet to Ellis Island soil. In six months they are Americanized. Does it matter that a thing so gigantic should be a little coarse and blundering in detail, if this stumbling giant of the new time breaks a gracious relic or so in his eager clutch and treads a little on the flowers?

§ 9

And in this setting of energy and activity, towering city life and bracing sea breezes, I met Gidding again, whom I had last seen departing into Egypt to look more particularly at the prehistoric remains and the temples of the first and second dynasty at Abydos. It was at a dinner-party, one of those large gatherings that welcome interesting visitors. It wasn't, of course, I who was the centre of interest, but a distinguished French portrait painter; I was there as just any guest. I hadn't even perceived Gidding until he came round to me in that precious gap of masculine intercourse that ensues upon the departure of the ladies. That gap is one of the rare opportunities for conversation men get in America.

"I don't know whether you will remember me," he said, "but perhaps you remember Crete—in the sunrise."

"And no end of talk afterwards," I said, grasping his hand, "no end—for we didn't half finish. Did you have a good time in Egypt?"

"I'm not going to talk to you about Egypt," said Gidding. "I'm through with ruins. I'm going to ask you—you know what I'm going to ask you."

"What I think of America. It's the same inevitable question. I think everything of it. It's the stepping-off place. I've come here at last, because it matters most."

"That's what we all want to believe," said Gidding. "That's what we want you to tell us."

He reflected. "It's immense, isn't it, perfectly immense? But—— I am afraid at times we're too disposed to forget just what it's all about. We've got to be reminded. That, you know, is why we keep on asking."

He went on to question me where I had been, what I had done, what I made of things. He'd never, he said, forgotten our two days' gossip in the Levant, and all the wide questions about the world and ourselves that we had broached then and left so open. I soon found myself talking very freely to him. I am not a ready or abundant talker, but Gidding has the knack of precipitating my ideas. He is America to my Europe, and at his touch all that has been hanging in concentrated solution in my mind comes crystallizing out. He has to a peculiar degree that directness and simplicity which is the distinctive American quality. I tried to explain to his solemnly nodding head and entirely intelligent eyes just exactly what I was making of things, of the world, of humanity, of myself. . . .

It was an odd theme for two men to attempt after dinner, servants hovering about them, their two faces a little flushed by wine and good eating, their keen interest masked from the others around them by a gossiping affectation, their hands going out as they talked for matches or cigarette, and before we had gone further than to fling out a few intimations to each other our colloquy was interrupted by our host standing up and by the general stir that preluded our return to feminine society. "We've got more to say than this," said Gidding. "We've got to *talk*." He brought out a little engagement book that at once drew out mine in response. And a couple of days after, we spent a morning and afternoon together and got down to some very intimate conversation. We motored out to lunch at a place called Nyack, above the Palisades, we crossed on a ferry to reach it, and we visited the house of Washington Irving near Yonkers on our way.

I've still a vivid picture in my mind of the little lawn at Irvington that looks out upon the rushing steel of Hudson River, where Gidding opened his heart to me. I can see him now as he leant a little forward over the table, with his wrists resting upon it, his long clean-shaven face very solemn and earnest and grey against the hard American sunlight in the greenery about us, while he told me in that deliberate American voice of his and with the deliberate American solemnity, of his desire to "do some decent thing with life."

He was very anxious to set himself completely before me, I remember, on that occasion. There was a peculiar mental kinship between us that even the profound differences of our English and American trainings could not mask. And now he told me almost everything material about his life. For the first time I learnt how enormously rich he was, not only by reason of his father's acquisitions, but also because of his own almost instinctive aptitude for business. "I've got," he said, "to begin with, what almost all men spend their whole lives in trying to get. And it amounts to nothing. It leaves me with life like a blank sheet of paper, and nothing in particular to write on it."

"You know," he said, "it's—exasperating. I'm already half-way to three-score and ten, and I'm still wandering about wondering what to do with this piece of life God has given me. . . ."

He had "lived" as people say, he had been in scrapes and scandals, tasted to the full the bitter intensities of the personal life; he had come by a different route to the same conclusions as myself, was as anxious as I to escape from memories and associations and feuds and that excessive vividness of individual feeling which blinds us to the common humanity, the common interest, the gentler, larger reality, which lies behind each tawdrily emphatic self. . . .

"It's a sort of inverted homœopathy I want," he said. "The big thing to cure the little thing. . . ."

But I will say no more of that side of our friendship, because the ideas of it are spread all through this book from the first page to the last. . . . What concerns me now is not our sympathy and agreement, but that other aspect of our relations in which Gidding becomes impulse and urgency. "Seeing we have these ideas," said he,—"and mind you there must be others who have them or are getting to them, for nobody thinks all alone in this world, —seeing we have these ideas what are we going to *do?*"

§ 10

That meeting was followed by another before I left New York, and presently Gidding joined me at Denver, where I was trying to measure the true significance of a labor paper called *The Appeal to Reason* that, in spite of a rigid boycott by the ordinary agencies for news distribution went out in the middle west to nearly half a million subscribers, and was filled with such a fierceness of insurrection against labor conditions, such a hatred, blind and impassioned, as I had never known before. Gidding remained with me there and came back with me to Chicago, where I wanted to see something of the Americanization of the immigrant, and my survey of America, the social and economic problem of America, resolved itself more and more into a conference with him.

There is no more fruitless thing in the world than to speculate how life would have gone if this thing or that had not happened. Yet I cannot help but wonder how far I might have travelled along the lines of my present work if I had gone to America and not met Gidding, or if I had met him without visiting America. The man and his country are inextricably interwoven in my mind. Yet I do think that his simplicity and directness, his force of initiative that turned me from a mere enquirer into an active writer and organizer, are qualities less his in particular than America's in general. There is in America a splendid crudity, a directness that cleared my spirit as a bracing wind will sweep the clouds from mountain scenery. Compared with our older continents America is mankind stripped for achievement. So many things are not there at all, need not be considered; no institutional aristocracy, no Kaisers, Czars, nor King-Emperors to maintain a litigious sequel to the Empire of Rome; it has no uneducated immovable peasantry rooted to the soil, indeed it has no rooting to the soil at all; it is, from the Forty-ninth Parallel to the tip of Cape Horn, one triumphant embodiment of freedom and deliberate agreement. For I mean all America, Spanish-speaking as well as English-speaking; they have this detachment from tradition in common. See how the United States, for example, stands flatly on that bare piece of eighteenth-century intellectualism the Constitution, and is by virtue of that a structure either wilful and intellectual or absurd. That sense of incurable servitude to fate and past traditions, that encumbrance with ruins, pledges, laws and ancient institutions, that perpetual complication of considerations and those haunting memories of preceding human failures which dwarf the courage of destiny in Europe and Asia, vanish from the mind within a week of one's arrival in the New World. Naturally one begins to do things. One is inspired to do things. One feels that one has escaped, one feels that the time is *now*. All America, North and South alike, is one tremendous escape from ancient obsessions into activity and making.

And by the time I had reached America I had already come to see that just as the issues of party politics at home and international politics abroad are mere superficialities above the greater struggle of an energetic minority to organize and exploit the labor of the masses of mankind, so that struggle also is only a huge incident in the still more than half unconscious impulse to replace the ancient way of human living by a more highly organized world-wide social order, by a world civilization embodying itself in a World State. And I saw now how that impulse could neither cease nor could it on the other hand realize itself until it became conscious and deliberate and merciful, free from haste and tyranny, persuasive and sustained by a nearly universal sympathy and understanding. For until that arrives the creative forces must inevitably spend themselves very largely in blind alleys, futile rushes and destructive conflicts. Upon that our two minds were agreed.

"We have," said Gidding, "to understand and make understanding. That is the real work for us to do, Stratton, that is our job. The world, as you say, has been floundering about, half making civilization and never achieving it. Now *we*, I don't mean just you and me, Stratton, particularly, but every intelligent man among us, have got to set to and make it thorough. There is no other sane policy for a man outside his private passions but that. So let's get at it——"

I find it now impossible to trace the phases by which I reached these broad ideas upon which I rest all my work, but certainly they were present very early in my discussions with Gidding. We two men had been thinking independently but very similarly, and it is hard to say just what completing touches either of us gave to the other's propositions. We found ourselves rather than arrived at the conception of ourselves as the citizens neither of the United States nor of England but of a state that had still to come into being, a World State, a great unity behind and embracing the ostensible political fabrics of to-day—a unity to be reached by weakening antagonisms, by developing understandings and toleration, by fostering the sense of brotherhood across the ancient bounds.

We believed and we believe that such a creative conception of a human commonweal can be fostered in exactly the same way that the idea of German unity was fostered behind the dukedoms, the free cities and kingdoms of Germany, a conception so creative that it can dissolve traditional hatreds, incorporate narrower loyalties and replace a thousand suspicions and hostilities by a common passion for collective achievement, so creative that at last the national boundaries of to-day may become obstacles as trivial to the amplifying good-will of men as the imaginary line that severs Normandy from Brittany, or Berwick from Northumberland.

And it is not only a great peace about the earth that this idea of a World State means for us, but social justice also. We are both convinced altogether that there survives no reason for lives of toil, for hardship, poverty, famine, infectious disease, for the continuing cruelties of wild beasts and the greater multitude of crimes, but mismanagement and waste, and that mismanagement and waste spring from no other source than ignorance and from stupid divisions and jealousies, base patriotisms, fanaticisms, prejudices and suspicions that are all no more than ignorance a little mingled with viciousness. We have looked closely into this servitude of modern labor, we

have seen its injustice fester towards syndicalism and
revolutionary socialism, and we know these things for the
mere aimless, ignorant resentments they are; punishments,
not remedies. We have looked into the portentous
threat of modern war, and it is ignorant vanity and
ignorant suspicion, the bargaining aggression of the
British prosperous and the swaggering vulgarity of the
German junker that make and sustain that monstrous
European devotion to arms. And we are convinced
there is nothing in these evils and conflicts that light may
not dispel. We believe that these things can be dispelled,
that the great universals, Science which has limitations
neither of race nor class, Art which speaks to its own in
every rank and nation, Philosophy and Literature which
broaden sympathy and banish prejudice, can flood and
submerge and will yet flow over and submerge every one
of these separations between man and man.

I will not say that this Great State, this World Re-
public of civilized men, is our dream, because it is not a
dream, it is a manifestly reasonable possibility. It is our
intention. It is what we are deliberately making and what
in a little while very many men and women will be making.
We are secessionists from all contemporary nationalities
and loyalties. We have set ourselves with all the capacity
and energy at our disposal to create a world-wide common
fund of ideas and knowledge, and to evoke a world-wide
sense of human solidarity in which the existing limitations
of political structure must inevitably melt away.

It was Gidding and his Americanism, his inborn pre-
disposition to innovation and the large freedom of his
wealth that turned these ideas into immediate concrete
undertakings. I see more and more that it is here that

we of the old European stocks, who still grow upon the old wood, differ most from those vigorous grafts of our race in America and Africa and Australia on the one hand and from the renascent peoples of the East on the other: that we have lost the courage of youth and have not yet gained the courage of desperate humiliations, in taking hold of things. To Gidding it was neither preposterous nor insufferably magnificent that we should set about a propaganda of all science, all knowledge, all philosophical and political ideas, round about the habitable globe. His mind began producing concrete projects as a fire-work being lit produces sparks, and soon he was "figuring out" the most colossal of printing and publishing projects, as a man might work out the particulars for an alteration to his bathroom. It was so entirely natural to him, it was so entirely novel to me, to go on from the proposition that understanding was the primary need of humanity to the systematic organization of free publishing, exhaustive discussion, intellectual stimulation. He set about it as a company of pharmacists might organize the distribution of some beneficial cure.

"Say, Stratton," he said, after a conversation that had seemed to me half fantasy; "Let's *do* it."

There are moments still when it seems to me that this life of mine has become the most preposterous of adventures. We two absurd human beings are spending our days and nights in a sustained and growing attempt to do what? To destroy certain obsessions and to give the universal human mind a form and a desire for expression. We have put into the shape of one comprehensive project that force of released wealth that has already dotted America with universities, libraries, institutions for research and enquiry. Already there are others at work with us, and presently there will be a great number. We have started an avalanche above the old politics and it gathers mass and pace. . . .

And there never was an impulse towards endeavor in a human heart that wasn't preposterous. Man is a preposterous animal. Thereby he ceases to be a creature and becomes a creator, he turns upon the powers that made him and subdues them to his service; by his sheer impudence he establishes his claim to possess a soul. . . .

But I need not write at all fully of my work here. This book is not about that but about my coming to that. Long before this manuscript reaches your hands—if ultimately I decide that it shall reach your hands—you will be taking your share, I hope, in this open conspiracy against potentates and prejudices and all the separating powers of darkness.

§ 11

I would if I could omit one thing that I must tell you here, because it goes so close to the very core of all this book has to convey. I wish I could leave it out altogether. I wish I could simplify my story by smoothing out this wrinkle at least and obliterating a thing that was at once very real and very ugly. You see I had at last struggled up to a sustaining idea, to a conception of work and duty to which I could surely give my life. I had escaped from my pit so far. And it was natural that now with something to give I should turn not merely for consolation and service but for help and fellowship to that dear human being across the seas who had offered them to me so straightly and sweetly. All that is brave and good and as you would have me, is it not? Only, dear son, that is not all the truth.

There was still in my mind, for long it remained in my mind, a bitterness against Mary. I had left her, I had lost her, we had parted; but from Germany to America and all through America and home again to my marriage and with me after my marriage, it rankled that she could still go on living a life independent of mine. I had not yet lost my desire to possess her, to pervade and dominate her existence; my resentment that though she loved me she had first not married me and afterwards not consented to come away with me was smouldering under the closed hatches of my mind. And so while the better part of me was laying hold of this work because it gave me the hope of a complete distraction and escape from my narrow and jealous self, that lower being of the pit was also rejoicing in the great enterprises before me and in the marriage upon which I had now determined, because it was a last trampling upon my devotion to Mary, because it defied and denied some lurking claims to empire I could suspect in her. I want to tell you that particularly because so I am made, so you are made, so most of us are made. There is scarcely a high purpose in all the world that has no dwarfish footman at its stirrup, no base intention over which there does not ride at least the phantom of an angel.

Constantly in those days, it seems to me now, I was haunted by my own imagination of Mary amiably reconciled to Justin, bearing him children, forgetful of or repudiating all the sweetness, all the wonder and beauty we had shared. . . . It was an unjust and ungenerous con-

277

ception, I knew it for a caricature even as I entertained it, and yet it tormented me. It stung me like a spur. It kept me at work, and if I strayed into indolence brought me back to work with a mind galled and bleeding. . . .

§ 12

And I suppose it is mixed up with all this that I could not make love easily and naturally to Rachel. I could not write love-letters to her. There is a burlesque quality in these scruples, I know, seeing that I was now resolved to marry her, but that is the quality, that is the mixed texture of life. We overcome the greater things and are conscience-stricken by the details.

I wouldn't, even at the price of losing her—and I was now passionately anxious not to lose her—use a single phrase of endearment that did not come out of me almost in spite of myself. At any rate I would not cheat her. And my offer of marriage when at last I sent it to her from Chicago was, as I remember it, almost business-like. I atoned soon enough for that arid letter in ten thousand sweet words that came of themselves to my lips. And she paid me at any rate in my own coin when she sent me her answer by cable, the one word "Yes."

And indeed I was already in love with her long before I wrote. It was only a dread of giving her a single undeserved cheapness that had held me back so long. It was that and the perplexity that Mary still gripped my feelings; my old love for her was there in my heart in spite of my new passion for Rachel, it was blackened perhaps and ruined and changed but it was there. It was as if a new crater burnt now in the ampler circumference of an old volcano, which showed all the more desolate and sorrowful and obsolete for the warm light of the new flames. . . .

How impatiently I came home! Thoughts of England I had not dared to think for three long years might now do what they would in me. I dreamt of the Surrey Hills and the great woods of Burnmore Park, of the changing skies and stirring soft winds of our grey green Motherland. There was fog in the Irish Sea, and we lost the better part of a day hooting our way towards Liverpool while I fretted about the ship with all my luggage packed, staring at the grey waters that weltered under the mist. It was the longest day in my life. My heart was full of desire, my eyes ached for the little fields and golden October skies of England, England that was waiting to welcome me back from my exile with such open arms. I was coming home,—home.

I hurried through London into Surrey and in my father's study, warned by a telegram, I found a bright-eyed, resolute young woman awaiting me, with the quality about her of one who embarks upon a long premeditated adventure. And I found too a family her sisters and her brother all gladly ready for me, my father too was a happy man, and on the eighth of November in 1906 Rachel and I were married in the little church at Shere. We stayed for a week or so in Hampshire near Ringwood, the season was late that year and the trees still very beautiful; and then we went to Portofino on the Ligurian coast.

There presently Gidding joined us and we began to work out the schemes we had made in America, the schemes that now fill my life.

CHAPTER THE TENTH

MARY WRITES

§ 1

IT was in the early spring of 1909 that I had a letter from Mary.

By that time my life was set fully upon its present courses, Gidding and I had passed from the stage of talking and scheming to definite undertakings. Indeed by 1909 things were already organized upon their present lines. We had developed a huge publishing establishment with one big printing plant in Barcelona and another in Manchester, and we were studying the peculiar difficulties that might attend the establishment of a third plant in America. Our company was an English company under the name of Alphabet and Mollentrave, and we were rapidly making it the broadest and steadiest flow of publication the world had ever seen. Its streams already reached further and carried more than any single firm had ever managed to do before. We were reprinting, in as carefully edited and revised editions as we could, the whole of the English, Spanish and French literature, and we were only waiting for the release of machinery to attack German, Russian and Italian, and were giving each language not only its own but a very complete series of good translations of the classical writers in every other tongue. We had a little band of editors and translators permanently in our service at each important literary centre. We had, for example, more than a score of men at work translating Bengali fiction and verse into English, —a lot of that new literature is wonderfully illuminating to an intelligent Englishman—and we had a couple of men hunting about for new work in Arabic. We meant to give so good and cheap a book, and to be so comprehensive in our choice of books, excluding nothing if only it was real and living, on account of any inferiority of quality, obscurity of subject or narrowness of demand, that in the long run anybody, anywhere, desiring to read anything would turn naturally and inevitably to our lists.

Ours was to be in the first place a world literature. Then afterwards upon its broad currents of distribution and in the same forms we meant to publish new work and new thought. We were also planning an encyclopædia. Behind our enterprise of translations and reprints we were getting together and putting out a series of guide-books, gazetteers, dictionaries, text-books and books of reference, and we were organizing a revising staff for these, a staff that should be constantly keeping them up to date. It was our intention to make every copy we printed bear the date of its last revision in a conspicuous place, and we hoped to get the whole line of these books ultimately upon an annual basis, and to sell them upon repurchasing terms that would enable us to issue a new copy and take back and send the old one to the pulping mill at a narrow margin of profit. Then we meant to spread our arms wider, and consolidate and offer our whole line of text-books, guide-books and gazet-

teers, bibliographies, atlases, dictionaries and directories
as a new World Encyclopædia, that should also annually
or at longest biennially renew its youth.

So far we had gone in the creation of a huge international organ of information, and of a kind of gigantic
modern Bible of world literature, and in the process of
its distribution we were rapidly acquiring an immense
detailed knowledge of the book and publishing trade,
finding congestions here, neglected opportunities there,
and devising and drawing up a hundred schemes for
relief, assistance, amalgamation and rearrangement. We
had branches in China, Japan, Peru, Iceland and a thousand remote places that would have sounded as far off
as the moon to an English or American bookseller in the
seventies. China in particular was a growing market.
We had a subsidiary company running a flourishing line
of book shops in the east-end of London, and others in
New Jersey, Chicago, Buenos Ayres, the South of France,
and Ireland. Incidentally we had bought up some
thousands of miles of Labrador forest to ensure our paper
supply, and we could believe that before we died there
would not be a corner of the world in which any book of
interest or value whatever would not be easily attainable
by any intelligent person who wanted to read it. And
already we were taking up the more difficult and ambitious phase of our self-appointed task, and considering
the problem of using these channels we were mastering
and deepening and supplementing for the stimulation
and wide diffusion of contemporary thought.

· There we went outside the province of Alphabet and
Mollentrave and into an infinitely subtler system of
interests. We wanted to give sincere and clear-thinking

writers encouragement and opportunity, to improve the critical tribunal and make it independent of advertising interests, so that there would be a readier welcome for luminous thinking and writing and a quicker explosion of intellectual imposture. We sought to provide guides and intelligencers to contemporary thought. We had already set up or subsidized or otherwise aided a certain number of magazines and periodicals that seemed to us independent-spirited, out-spoken and well handled, but we had still to devise our present scheme of financing groups of men to create magazines and newspapers, which became their own separate but inalienable property after so many years of success.

But all this I hope you will already have become more or less familiar with when this story reaches your hands, and I hope by the time it does so we shall be far beyond our present stage of experiment and that you will have come naturally to play your part in this most fascinating business of maintaining an onward intellectual movement in the world, a movement not simply independent of but often running counter to all sorts of political and financial interests. I tell you this much here for you to understand that already in 1909 and considering the business side of my activities alone, I was a hard worker and very strenuously employed. And in addition to all this huge network of enterprises I had developed with Gidding, I was still pretty actively a student. I wasn't—I never shall be—absolutely satisfied with my general ideas. I was enquiring keenly and closely into those problems of group and crowd psychology from which all this big publishing work has arisen, and giving particular attention to the war-panics and outbreaks of international hostility that were then passing in deepening waves across Europe. I had already accumulated a mass of notes for the book upon "Group Jealousy in Religious Persecution, Racial Conflicts and War" which I hope to publish the year after next, and which therefore I hope you will have read long before this present book can possibly come to you. And moreover Rachel and I had established our home in London—in the house we now occupy during the winter and spring—and both you and your little sister had begun your careers as inhabitants of this earth. Your little sister had indeed but just begun.

And then one morning at the breakfast-table I picked a square envelope out of a heap of letters, and saw the half-forgotten and infinitely familiar handwriting of Lady Mary Justin. . . . The sight of it gave me an odd mixture of sensations. I was startled, I was disturbed, I was a little afraid. I hadn't forgiven her yet; it needed but this touch to tell me how little I had forgotten. . . .

§ 2

I sat with it in my hand for a moment or so before I opened it, hesitating as one hesitates before a door that may reveal a dramatic situation. Then I pushed my chair a little back from the table and ripped the envelope.

It was a far longer letter than Mary had ever written me in the old days, and in a handwriting as fine as ever but now rather smaller. I have it still, and here I open its worn folds and, except for a few trifling omissions, copy it out for you. . . . A few trifling omissions, I say,—

just one there is that is not trifling, but that I must needs make. . . .

You will never see any of these letters because I shall destroy them so soon as this copy is made. It has been difficult—or I should have destroyed them before. But some things can be too hard for us. . . .

This first letter is on the Martens note-paper; its very heading was familiar to me. The handwriting of the earlier sentences is a little stiff and disjointed, and there are one or two scribbled obliterations; it is like someone embarrassed in speaking; and then it passes into her usual and characteristic ease. . . .

And as I read, slowly my long-cherished anger evaporated, and the real Mary, outspoken and simple, whom I had obscured by a cloud of fancied infidelities, returned to me. . . .

"My dear Stephen," she begins, "About six weeks ago I saw in the *Times* that you have a little daughter. It set me thinking, picturing you with a mite of a baby in your arms—what *little* things they are, Stephen!— and your old face bent over it, so that presently I went to my room and cried. It set me thinking about you so that I have at last written you this letter. . . . I love to think of you with wife and children about you Stephen,— I heard of your son for the first time about a year ago, but—don't mistake me,—something wrings me too. . . .

"Well, I too have children. Have you ever thought of me as a mother? I am. I wonder how much you know about me now. I have two children and the youngest is just two years old. And somehow it seems to me that now that you and I have both given such earnests of our good behavior, such evidence that *that* side of life anyhow is effectually settled for us, there is no reason remaining why we shouldn't correspond. You are my brother, Stephen, and my friend and my twin and the core of my imagination, fifty babies cannot alter that, we can live but once and then die, and, promise or no promise, I will not be dead any longer in your world when I'm not dead, nor will I have you, if I can help it, a cold unanswering corpse in mine. . . .

"Too much of my life and being, Stephen, has been buried, and I am in rebellion. This is a breach of the tomb if you like, an irregular private premature resurrection from an interment in error. Out of my alleged grave I poke my head and say Hello! to you. Stephen, old friend! dear friend! how are you getting on? What is it like to you? How do you feel? I want to know about you. . . . I'm not doing this at all furtively, and you can write back to me, Stephen, as openly as your heart desires. I have told Justin I should do this. I rise, you see, blowing my own Trump. Let the other graves do as they please. . . .

"Your letters will be respected, Stephen. . . . If you choose to rise also and write me a letter.

"Stephen, I've been wanting to do this for—for all the time. If there was thought-reading you would have had a thousand letters. But formerly I was content to submit, and latterly I've chafed more. I think that as what they call passion has faded, the immense friendliness has become more evident, and made the bar less and less justifiable. You and I have had so much between us beyond what somebody the other day—it was in a report in the *Times*, I think—was calling *Materia Matrimoniala*. And of course I hear about you from all sorts of people, and in all sorts of ways—whatever you have done about me I've had a woman's sense of honor about you and I've managed to learn a great deal without asking forbidden questions. I've pricked up my ears at the faintest echo of your name.

"They say you have become a publisher with an American partner, a sort of Harmsworth and Nelson and Times Book Club and Hooper and Jackson all rolled into one. That seems so extraordinary to me that for that alone I should have had to write to you. I want to know the truth of that. I never see any advertisement of Stratton & Co. or get any inkling of what it is you publish. Are you the power behind the respectable Murgatroyd and the honest Milvain? I know them both and neither has the slightest appearance of being animated by you. And equally perplexing is your being mixed up with an American like that man Gidding in Peace Conferences and Social Reform Congresses and so forth. It's so— Carnegieish. There I'm surer because I've seen your name in reports of meetings and I've read your last two papers in the *Fortnightly*. I can't imagine you of all people, with your touch of reserve, launching into movements and rubbing shoulders with faddists. What does it mean, Stephen? I had expected to find you coming back into English politics—speaking and writing on the lines of your old beginning, taking up that work you dropped—it's six years now ago. I've been accumulating disappointment for two years. Mr. Arthur, you see, on our side,"—this you will remember was in 1909—"still steers our devious party courses, and the Tariff Reformers have still to capture us. Weston Massinghay was comparing them the other night, at a dinner at the Clynes',

287

to a crowded piratical galley trying to get alongside a good seaman in rough weather. He was very funny about Leo Maxse in the poop, white and shrieking with passion and the motion, and all the capitalists armed to the teeth and hiding snug in the hold until the grappling-irons were fixed. . . . Why haven't you come into the game? I'd hoped it if only for the sake of meeting you again. What are you doing out beyond there?

"We are in it so far as I can contrive. But I contrive very little. We are pillars of the Conservative party—on that Justin's mind is firmly settled—and every now and then I clamor urgently that we must do more for it. But Justin's ideas go no further than writing cheques—doing more for the party means writing a bigger cheque—and there are moments when I feel we shall simply bring down a peerage upon our heads and bury my ancient courtesy title under the ignominy of a new creation. He would certainly accept it. He writes his cheque and turns back at the earliest opportunity to his miniature gardens and the odd little freaks of collecting that attract him. Have you ever heard of chintz oil jars? 'No,' you will say. Nor has anyone else yet except our immediate circle of friends and a few dealers who are no doubt industriously increasing the present scanty supply. We possess three. They are matronly shaped jars about two feet or a yard high, of a kind of terra-cotta with wooden tops surmounted by gilt acorns, and they have been covered with white paint and on this flowers and birds and figures from some very rich old chintz have been stuck very cunningly, and then everything has been varnished—and there you are. Our first and best was bought for seven-and-sixpence, brought home in the car, put upon a console table on the second landing and worshipped. It's really a very pleasant mellow thing to see. Nobody had ever seen the like. Guests, sycophantic people of all sorts were taken to consider it. It was looked at with heads at every angle, one man even kept his head erect and one went a little upstairs and looked at it under his arm. Also the most powerful lenses have been used for a minute examination, and one expert licked the varnish and looked extremely thoughtful and wise at me as he turned the booty over his gifted tongue. And now, God being with us, we mean to possess every specimen in existence—before the Americans get hold of the idea. Yesterday Justin got up and motored sixty miles to look at an alleged fourth. . . .

"Oh my dear! I am writing chatter. You perceive I've reached the chattering stage. It is the fated end of the clever woman in a good social position nowadays, her mind beats against her conditions for the last time and breaks up into this carping talk, this spume of observation and comment, this anecdotal natural history of the restraining husband, as waves burst out their hearts in a foam upon a reef. But it isn't chatter I want to write to you.

"Stephen, I'm intolerably wretched. No creature has ever been gladder to have been born than I was for the first five and twenty years of my life. I was full of hope and I was full, I suppose, of vanity and rash confidence. I thought I was walking on solid earth with my head reaching up to the clouds, and that sea and sky and all mankind were mine for the smiling. And I am nothing and worse than nothing, I am the ineffectual

mother of two children, a daughter whom I adore—but
of her I may not tell you—and a son,—a son who is too
like his father for any fury of worship, a stolid little creature. . . . That is all I have done in the world, a mere
blink of maternity, and my blue Persian who is scarcely
two years old, has already had nine kittens. My husband
and I have never forgiven each other the indefinable
wrong of not pleasing each other; that embitters more
and more; to take it out of each other is our rôle; I have
done my duty to the great new line of Justin by giving
it the heir it needed, and now a polite and silent separation has fallen between us. We hardly speak except in
company. I have not been so much married, Stephen,
I find, as collected, and since our tragic misadventure—
but there were beautiful moments, Stephen, unforgettable glimpses of beauty in that — thank God, I say
impenitently for that—the door of the expensively splendid cabinet that contains me, when it is not locked, is
very discreetly—watched. I have no men friends, no
social force, no freedom to take my line. My husband is
my official obstacle. We barb the limitations of life for
one another. A little while ago he sought to chasten me—
to rouse me rather—through jealousy, and made me aware
indirectly but a little defiantly of a young person of ar-
tistic gifts in whose dramatic career he was pretending
a conspicuous interest. I was jealous and roused, but
scarcely in the way he desired. 'This,' I said quite
cheerfully, 'means freedom for *me*, Justin,' — and the
young woman vanished from the visible universe with
an incredible celerity. I hope she was properly paid off
and not simply made away with by a minion, but I become more and more aware of my ignorance of a great

financier's methods as I become more and more aware of them. . . .

"Stephen, my dear, my brother, I am intolerably unhappy. I do not know what to do with myself, or what there is to hope for in life. I am like a prisoner in a magic cage and I do not know the word that will release me. How is it with you? Are you unhappy beyond measure or are you not; and if you are not, what are you doing with life? Have you found any secret that makes living tolerable and understandable? Write to me, write to me at least and tell me that. . . . Please write to me.

"Do you remember how long ago you and I sat in the old Park at Burnmore, and how I kept pestering you and asking you what is all this *for?* And you looked at the question as an obstinate mule looks at a narrow bridge he could cross but doesn't want to. Well, Stephen, you've had nearly—how many years is it now?—to get an answer ready. What *is* it all for? What do you make of it? Never mind my particular case, or the case of Women with a capital *W*, tell me *your* solution. You are active, you keep doing things, you find life worth living. Is publishing a way of peace for the heart? I am prepared to believe even that. But justify yourself. Tell me what you have got there to keep your soul alive."

§ 3

I read this letter to the end and looked up, and there was my home about me, a room ruddy-brown and familiar, with the row of old pewter things upon the dresser, the steel engravings of former Strattons that came to me from my father, a convex mirror exaggerating my upturned face. And Rachel just risen again sat at the other end of the table, a young mother, fragile and tender-eyed. The clash of these two systems of reality was amazing. It was as though I had not been parted from Mary for a day, as though all that separation and all that cloud of bitter jealousy had been a mere silence between two people in the same room. Indeed it was extraordinarily like that, as if I had been sitting at a desk, imagining myself alone, reading my present life as one reads in a book at a shaded lamp, and then suddenly that silent other had spoken.

And then I looked at the page of my life before me and became again a character in the story.

I met the enquiry in Rachel's eyes. "It's a letter from Mary Justin," I said.

She did not answer for a few moments. She became interested in the flame of the little spirit lamp that kept her coffee hot. She finished what she had to do with that and then remarked, "I thought you two were not to correspond."

"Yes," I said, putting the letter down; "that was the understanding."

There was a little interval of silence, and then I got up and went to the fireplace where the bacon and sausages stood upon a trivet.

"I suppose," said Rachel, "she wants to hear from you again."

"She thinks that now we have children, and that she has two, we can consider what was past, past and closed and done with, and she wants to hear—about me. . . . Apart from everything else—we were very great friends."

"Of course," said Rachel with lips a little awry, "of course. You must have been great friends. And it's natural for her to write."

"I suppose," she added, "her husband knows."

"She's told him, she says. . . ."

Her eye fell on the letter in my hand for the smallest fraction of a second, and it was as if hastily she snatched away a thought from my observation. I had a moment of illuminating embarrassment. So far we had contrived to do as most young people do when they marry, we had sought to make our lives unreservedly open to one another, we had affected an entire absence of concealments about our movements, our thoughts. If perhaps I had been largely silent to her about Mary it was not so much that I sought to hide things from her as that I myself sought to forget. It is one of the things that we learn too late, the impossibility of any such rapid and wilful coalescences of souls. But we had maintained a convention of infinite communism since our marriage; we had shown each other our letters as a matter of course, shared the secrets of our friends, gone everywhere together as far as we possibly could.

I wanted now to give her the letter in my hand to read —and to do so was manifestly impossible. Something had arisen between us that made out of our unity two abruptly separated figures masked and veiled. Here were things I knew and understood completely and that I could not even describe to Rachel. What would she make of Mary's "Write to me. Write to me"? A mere wish to resume. . . . I would not risk the exposure of Mary's mind and heart and unhappiness, to her possible misinterpretation. . . .

That letter fell indeed like a pitiless searchlight into all that region of differences ignored, over which we had built the vaulted convention of our complete mutual understanding. In my memory it seems to me now as though we hung silent for quite a long time over the evasions that were there so abruptly revealed.

Then I put the letter into my pocket with a clumsy assumption of carelessness, and knelt down to the fender and sausages.

"It will be curious," I said, "to write to her again. . . . To tell her about things. . . ."

And then with immense interest, "Are these Chichester sausages you've got here, Rachel, or some new kind?"

Rachel roused herself to respond with an equal affectation, and we made an eager conversation about bacon and sausages—for after that startling gleam of divergence we were both anxious to get back to the superficialities of life again.

§ 4

I did not answer Mary's letter for seven or eight days.

During that period my mind was full of her to the exclusion of every other interest. I re-read all that she had to say many times, and with each reading the effect of her personality deepened. It was all so intensely familiar, the flashes of insight, the blazing frankness, the quick turns of thought, and her absurd confidence in a sort of sane stupidity that she had always insisted upon my possessing. And her unembarrassed affectionateness. Her quick irregular writing seemed to bring back with it the changing light in her eyes, the intonations of her voice, something of her gesture. . . .

I didn't go on discussing with myself whether we two ought to correspond; that problem disappeared from my thoughts. Her challenge to me to justify myself took possession of my mind. That thrust towards self-examination was the very essence of her ancient influence. How did I justify myself? I was under a peculiar compulsion to answer that to her satisfaction. She had picked me up out of my work and accumulating routines with that demand, made me look at myself and my world again as a whole. . . . I had a case. I have a case. It is a case of passionate faith triumphing over every doubt and impossibility, a case real enough to understand for those who understand, but very difficult to state. I tried to convey it to her.

I do not remember at all clearly what I wrote to her. It has disappeared from existence. But it was certainly a long letter. Throughout this book I have been trying to tell you the growth of my views of life and its purpose, from my childish dreams and Harbury attitudes to those ideas of human development that have made me under-take the work I do. It is not glorious work I know, as the work of great artists and poets and leaders is glorious, but it is what I find best suits my gifts and my want of gifts. Greater men will come at last to build within my scaffoldings. In some summary phrasing I must have set out the gist of this. I must have explained my sense of the supreme importance of mental clarification in human life. All this is manifest in her reply. And I think too I did my best to tell her plainly the faith that was in me, and why life seemed worth while to me. . . .

Her second letter came after an interval of only a few days from the despatch of mine. She began abruptly.

"I won't praise your letter or your beliefs. They are fine and large—and generous—like you. Just a little artificial (but you will admit that), as though you had felt them *give* here and there and had made up your mind they shouldn't. At times it's oddly like looking at the Alps, the real Alps, and finding that every now and then the mountains have been eked out with a plank and canvas Earl's Court background. . . . Yes, I like what you say about Faith. I believe you are right. I wish I could—perhaps some day I shall—light up and *feel* you are right. But—but—— That large, *respectable* project, the increase of wisdom and freedom and self-knowledge in the world, the calming of wars, the ending of economic injustice and so on and so on——

"When I read it first it was like looking at a man in profile and finding him solid and satisfactory, and then afterwards when I thought it all over and looked for the particular things that really matter to me and tried to translate it into myself—nothing is of the slightest importance in the world that one cannot translate into oneself—then I began to realize just how amazingly deficient you are. It was like walking round that person in profile and finding his left side wasn't there—with everything perfect on the right, down to the buttons. A kind of intellectual Lorelei—sideways. You've planned out your understandings and tolerances and enquiries and clearings-up as if the world were all just men—or citizens—and nothing doing but racial and national and class prejudices and the exacting and shirking of labor, and you seem to ignore altogether that man is a sexual

296

animal first—first, Stephen, first—that he has that in common with all the animals, that it made him indeed because he has it more than they have—and after that, a long way after that, he is the labor-economizing, war- and feud-making creature you make him out to be. A long way after that. . . .

"Man is the most sexual of all the beasts, Stephen. Half of him, womankind, rather more than half, isn't simply human at all, it's specialized, specialized for the young, not only naturally and physically as animals are, but mentally and artificially. Womankind isn't human, it's reduced human. It's 'the sex' as the Victorians used to say, and from the point of view of the Lex Julia and the point of view of Mr. Malthus, and the point of view of biologists and saints and artists and everyone who deals in feeling and emotion—and from the point of view of all us poor specialists, smothered up in our clothes and restrictions—the future of the sex is the centre of the whole problem of the human future, about which you are concerned. All this great world-state of your man's imagination is going to be wrecked by us if you ignore us, we women are going to be the Goths and Huns of another Decline and Fall. We are going to sit in the conspicuous places of the world and *loot* all your patient accumulations. We are going to abolish your offspring and turn the princes among you into undignified slaves. Because, you see, specialized as we are, we are not quite specialized, we are specialized under duress, and at the first glimpse of a chance we abandon our cradles and drop our pots and pans and go for the vast and elegant side possibilities— of our specialization. Out we come, looking for the fun the men are having. Dress us, feed us, play with us!

We'll pay you in excitement,—tremendous excitement. The State indeed! All your little triumphs of science and economy, all your little accumulations of wealth that you think will presently make the struggle for life an old story and the millennium possible—*we spend*. And all your dreams of brotherhood!—we will set you by the ears. We hold ourselves up as my little Christian nephews—Philip's boys—do some coveted object, and say *Quis?* and the whole brotherhood shouts '*Ego!*' to the challenge. . . . Back you go into Individualism at the word and all your Brotherhood crumbles to dust again.

"How are you going to remedy it, how are you going to protect that Great State of your dreams from this anti-citizenship of sex? You give no hint.

"You are planning nothing, Stephen, nothing to meet this. You are fighting with an army all looting and undisciplined, frantic with the private jealousies that centre about *us*, feuds, cuts, expulsions, revenges, and you are giving out orders for an army of saints. You treat us as a negligible quantity, and we are about as negligible as a fire in the woodwork of a house that is being built. . . .

"I read what I have written, Stephen, and I perceive I have the makings of a fine scold in me. Perhaps under happier conditions—— . . . I should certainly have scolded you, constantly, continually. . . . Never did a man so need scolding. . . . And like any self-respecting woman I see that I use half my words in the wrong meanings in order to emphasize my point. Of course when I write woman in all that has gone before I don't mean woman. It is a woman's privilege to talk or write

298

incomprehensibly and insist upon being understood. So
that I expect you already to understand that what I mean
isn't that men are creative and unselfish and brotherly and
so forth and that women are spoiling and going to spoil
the game—although and notwithstanding that is exactly
what I have written—but that humans are creative and
unselfish et cetera and so forth, and that it is their sexual,
egotistical, passionate side (which is ever so much bigger
relatively in a woman than in a man, and that is why I
wrote as I did) which is going to upset your noble and
beautiful apple-cart. But it is not only that by nature we
are more largely and gravely and importantly sexual than
men but that men have shifted the responsibility for attraction and passion upon us and made us pay in servitude
and restriction and blame for the common defect of the
species. So that you see really I was right all along in
writing of this as though it was women when it wasn't,
and I hope now it is unnecessary for me to make my
meaning clearer than it is now and always has been in this
matter. And so, resuming our discourse, Stephen, which
only my sense of your invincible literalness would ever have
interrupted, what are you going to do with us?

"I gather from a hint rather than accept as a statement
that you propose to give us votes.

"Stephen!—do you really think that we are going to
bring anything to bear upon public affairs worth having?
I know something of the contemporary feminine intelligence. Justin makes no serious objection to a large and
various circle of women friends, and over my little sitting-
room fire in the winter and in my corners of our various
gardens in the summer and in walks over the heather at
Martens and in Scotland there are great talks and confes-

sions of love, of mental freedom, of ambitions, and belief and unbelief—more particularly of unbelief. I have sometimes thought of compiling a dictionary of unbelief, a great list of the things that a number of sweet, submissive, value-above-rubies wives have told me they did not believe in. It would amaze their husbands beyond measure. The state of mind of women about these things, Stephen, is dreadful—I mean about all these questions— you know what I mean. The bold striving spirits do air their views a little, and always in a way that makes one realize how badly they need airing—but most of the nicer women are very chary of talk, they have to be drawn out, a hint of opposition makes them start back or prevaricate, and I see them afterwards with their husbands, pretty silken furry feathery jewelled *silences*. All their suppression doesn't keep them orthodox, it only makes them furtive and crumpled and creased in their minds— in just the way that things get crumpled and creased if they are always being shoved back into a drawer. You have only to rout about in their minds for a bit. They pretend at first to be quite correct, and then out comes the nasty little courage of the darkness. Sometimes there is even an apologetic titter. They are quite emancipated, they say; I have misunderstood them. Their emancipation is like those horrid white lizards that grow in the Kentucky caves out of the sunlight. They tell you they don't see why they shouldn't do this or that—mean things, underhand things, cheap, vicious, sensual things. . . . Are there, I wonder, the same dreadful little caverns in men? I doubt it. And then comes a situation that really tries their quality. . . . Think of the quandary I got into with you, Stephen. And for my sex I'm rather a daring person. The way in which I went so far—and then ran away. I had a kind of excuse—in my illness. That illness! Such a queer untimely feminine illness. . . .

"We're all to pieces, Stephen. That's what brought down Rome. The women went to pieces then, and the women are going to pieces to-day. What's the good of having your legions in the Grampians and marching up to Philae, while the wives are talking treason in your houses? It's no good telling us to go back to the Ancient Virtues. The Ancient Virtues haven't *kept*. The Ancient Virtues in an advanced state of decay is what was the matter with Rome and what is the matter with us. You can't tell a woman to go back to the spinning-wheel and the kitchen and the cradle, when you have power-looms, French cooks, hotels, restaurants and modern nurseries. We've overflowed. We've got to go on to a lot of New Virtues. And in all the prospect before me—I can't descry one clear simple thing to do. . . .

"But I'm running on. I want to know, Stephen, why you've got nothing to say about all this. It must have been staring you in the face ever since I spent my very considerable superfluous energies in wrecking your career. Because you know I wrecked it, Stephen. I *knew* I was wrecking it and I wrecked it. I knew exactly what I was doing all the time. I had meant to be so fine a thing for you, a mothering friend, to have that dear consecutive kindly mind of yours steadying mine, to have seen you grow to power over men, me helping, me admiring. It was to have been so fine. So fine! Didn't I urge you to marry Rachel, make you talk of her. Don't you remember that? And one day when I saw you thinking of Rachel, saw a kind of pride in your eyes!—suddenly I

20   301

couldn't stand it. I went to my room after you had gone and thought of you and her until I wanted to scream. I couldn't bear it. It was intolerable. I was violent to my toilet things. I broke a hand-glass. Your dignified, selfish, self-controlled Mary *smashed* a silver hand-mirror. I never told you that. You know what followed. I pounced on you and took you. Wasn't I—a soft and scented hawk? Was either of us better than some creature of instinct that does what it does because it must? It was like a gust of madness—and I cared, I found, no more for your career than I cared for any other little thing, for honor, for Rachel, for Justin, that stood between us. . . .

"My dear, wasn't all that time, all that heat and hunger of desire, all that secret futility of passion, the very essence of the situation between men and women now? We are all trying most desperately to be human beings, to walk erect, to work together—what was your phrase?—'in a multitudinous unity,' to share what you call a common collective thought that shall rule mankind, and this tremendous force which seizes us and says to us: 'Make that other being yours, bodily yours, mentally yours, wholly yours—at any price, no matter the price,' bars all our unifications. It splits the whole world into couples watching each other. Until all our laws, all our customs seem the servants of that. It is the passion of the body swamping the brain; it's an ape that has seized a gun, a beautiful modern gun. Here am I, Justin's captive, and he mine, he mine because at the first escapade of his I get my liberty. Here are we two, I and you, barred for ever from the sight of one another, and I and you writing—I at any rate—in spite of the ill-concealed resentment of my partner. We're just two, peeping through our bars, of a universal multitude. Everywhere this prison of sex. Have you ever thought just all that it means when every woman in the world goes dressed in a costume to indicate her sex, her cardinal fact, so that she dare not even mount a bicycle in knicker-bockers, she has her hair grown long to its longest because yours is short, and everything conceivable is done to emphasize and remind us (and you) of the fundamental trouble between us? As if there was need of reminding! Stephen, is there no way out of this? Is there no way at all? Because if there is not, then I had rather go back to the hareem than live as I do now imprisoned in glass— with all of life in sight of me and none in reach. I had rather Justin beat me into submission and mental tran-quillity and that I bore him an annual—probably deciduous—child. I can understand so well now that feminine attitude that implies, 'Well, if I must have a master, then the more master the better.' Perhaps that is the way; that Nature will not let us poor humans get away from sex, and I am merely—what is it?—an abnormality— with whiskers of enquiry sprouting from my mind. Yet I don't feel like that. . . .

"I'm pouring into these letters, Stephen, the concen-trated venom of years of brooding. My heart is black with rebellion against my lot and against the lot of woman. I have been given life and a fine position in the world, I made one fatal blunder in marrying to make these things secure, and now I can do nothing with it all and I have nothing to do with it. It astounds me to think of the size of our establishments, Stephen, of the extravagant way in which whole counties and great countries pay tribute to pile up the gigantic heap of wealth upon which we two lead our lives of futile entanglement. In this place alone there are fourteen gardeners and garden helps, and this is not one of our garden places. Three weeks ago I spent a thousand pounds on clothes in one great week of shopping, and our yearly expenditure upon personal effect, upon our magnificence and our margins cannot be greatly less than forty-five thousand pounds. I walk about our house and gardens, I take one of the carriages or one of the automobiles and go to some large pointless gathering of hundreds and thousands and thousands of pounds, and we walk about and say empty little things, and the servants don't laugh at us, the butlers don't laugh at us, the people in the street tolerate us. . . . It has an effect of collective insanity. . . . You know the story of one of those dear Barons of the Cinque Ports—a decent plumber-body from Rye or Winchelsea—one of the six—or eight—who claimed the privilege of carrying the canopy over the King"—she is speaking of King Edward's coronation of course—"how that he was discovered suddenly to be speaking quite audibly to the sacred presence so near to him: 'It is very remarkable—we should be here, your majesty—very remarkable.' And then he subsided—happily unheard—into hopeless embarrassment. That is exactly how I feel, Stephen. I feel I can't stand it much longer, that presently I shall splutter and spoil the procession. . . .

"Perhaps I don't properly estimate our position in the fabric, but I can't get away from the feeling that everything in social life leads up to this—to us,—the ridiculous canopy. If so, then the universe means—*nothing*; it's blowing great forms and shapes as a swamp blows bubbles; a little while ago it was megatheriums and plesiosauriums—if that's the name for them—and now it is country-houses and motor-cars and coronation festivals. And in the end—it is all nonsense, Stephen. It is utter nonsense.

"If it isn't nonsense, tell me what it is. For me at any rate it's nonsense, and for every intelligent woman about me—for I talk to some of them, we indulge in seditious whisperings and wit—and there isn't one who seems to have been able to get to anything solider than I have done. Each of us has had her little fling at maternity—about as much as a washerwoman does in her odd time every two or three years—and that is our uttermost reality. All the rest,—trimmings! We go about the world, Stephen, dressing and meeting each other with immense ceremony, we have our seasonal movements in relation to the ritual of politics and sport, we travel south for the Budget and north for the grouse, we play games to amuse the men who keep us—not a woman would play a game for its own sake—we dabble with social reform and politics, for which few of us care a rap except as an occupation, we 'discover' artists or musicians or lecturers (as though we cared), we try to believe in lovers or, still harder, try to believe in old or new religions, and most of us—I don't—do our best to give the gratifications and exercise the fascinations that are expected of us. . . .

"Something has to be done for women, Stephen. We are the heart of life, birth and begetting, the home where the future grows, and your schemes ignore us and slide about over the superficialities of things. We are spoiling the whole process of progress, we are turning all the achievements of mankind to nothingness. Men invent, create, do miracles with the world, and we translate it all into shopping, into a glitter of dresses and households, into an immense parade of pride and excitement. We excite men, we stir them to get us and keep us. Men turn from their ideas of brotherhood to elaborate our separate cages. . . .

"I am Justin's wife; not a thing in my heavens or my earth that is not subordinated to that.

"Something has to be done for women, Stephen, something—urgently—and nothing is done until that is done, some release from their intolerable subjection to sex, so that for us everything else in life, respect, freedom, social standing, is entirely secondary to that. But what has to be done? We women do not know. Our efforts to know are among the most desolating of spectacles. I read the papers of those suffrage women; the effect is more like agitated geese upon a common than anything human has a right to be. . . . That's why I turn to you. Years ago I felt, and now I know, there is about you a simplicity of mind, a foolishness of faith, that is stronger and greater than the cleverness of any woman alive. You are one of those strange men who take high and sweeping views—as larks soar. It isn't that you yourself are high and sweeping. . . . No, but still I turn to you. In the old days I used to turn to you and shake your mind and make you think about things you seemed too sluggish to think about without my clamor. Once do you remember at Martens I shook you by the ears. . . . And when I made you think, you thought, as I could never do. Think now—about women.

"Stephen, there are moments when it seems to me that

this futility of women, this futility of men's effort *through* women, is a fated futility in the very nature of things. We may be saddled with it as we are with all the animal infirmities we have, with appendixes and suchlike things inside of us, and the passions and rages of apes and a tail —I believe we have a tail curled away somewhere, haven't we? Perhaps mankind is so constituted that badly as they get along now they couldn't get along at all if they let women go free and have their own way with life. Perhaps you can't have *two* sexes loose together. You must shut up one. I've a horrible suspicion that all these anti-suffrage men like Lord Cromer and Sir Ray Lankester must know a lot about life that I do not know. And that other man Sir Something-or-other Wright, who said plainly that men cannot work side by side with women because they get excited. . . . And yet, you know, women have had glimpses of a freedom that was not mischievous. I could have been happy as a Lady Abbess—I must have space and dignity, Stephen—and those women had things in their hands as no women have things in their hands to-day. They came to the House of Lords. But they lost all that. Was there some sort of natural selection? . . .

"Stephen, you were made to answer my mind, and if you cannot do it nobody can. What is your outlook for women? Are we to go back to seclusion or will it be possible to minimize sex? If you are going to minimize sex how are you going to do it? Suppression? There is plenty of suppression now. Increase or diminish the pains and penalties? My nephew, Philip's boy, Philip Christian, was explaining to me the other day that if you boil water in an open bowl it just boils away, and that if you boil it in a corked bottle it bangs everything to pieces, and you have, he says, 'to look out.' But I feel that's a bad image. Boiling-water isn't frantically jealous, and men and women are. But still suppose, suppose you trained people not to make such an awful fuss about things. *Now* you train them to make as much fuss as possible. . . .

"Oh bother it all, Stephen! Where's your mind in these matters? Why haven't you tackled these things? Why do you leave it to *me* to dig these questions into you—like opening a reluctant oyster? Aren't they patent? You up and answer them, Stephen—or this correspondence will become abusive. . . ."

§ 5

It was true that I did ignore or minimize sexual questions as much as I could. I was forced now to think why I did this. That carried me back to those old days of passion, memories I had never stirred for many years. And I wrote to Mary that there was indeed no reason but a reasonable fear, that in fact I had dismissed them because they had been beyond my patience and self-control, because I could not think very much about them without an egotistical reversion to the bitterness of my own case. And in avoiding them I was only doing what the great bulk of men in business and men in affairs find themselves obliged to do. They train themselves not to think of the rights and wrongs of sexual life, not to tolerate liberties even in their private imaginations. They know it is like carrying a torch into a powder magazine. They feel they cannot trust their own minds beyond the experience, tested usages, and conventions of the ages, because they know how many of those who have ventured further have been blinded by mists and clouds of rhetoric, lost in inexplicable puzzles and wrecked disastrously. There in those half explored and altogether unsettled hinterlands, lurk desires that sting like adders and hatreds cruel as hell. . . .

And then I went on—I do not clearly remember now the exact line of argument I adopted—to urge upon her that our insoluble puzzles were not necessarily insoluble puzzles for the world at large, that no one soldier fights anything but a partial battle, and that it wasn't an absolute condemnation of me to declare that I went on living and working for social construction with the cardinal riddles of social order, so far as they affected her, unsolved. Wasn't I at any rate preparing apparatus for that huge effort at solution that mankind must ultimately make? Wasn't this dredging out and deepening of the channels of thought about the best that we could hope to do at the present time, seeing that to launch a keel of speculation prematurely was only to strand oneself among hopeless reefs and confusions? Better prepare for a voyage to-morrow than sail to destruction to-day.

Whatever I put in that forgotten part of my letter was put less strikingly than my first admissions, and anyhow it was upon these that Mary pounced to the disregard of any other point. "There you are," she wrote, with something like elation, "there is a tiger in the garden and you won't talk or think about it for fear of growing excited. That is my grievance against so much historical and political and social discussion; its hopeless futility because of its hopeless omissions. You plan the world's future, taking the women and children for granted, with Egotistical Sex, as you call it, a prowling monster upsetting everything you do. . . ."

But I will not give you that particular letter in its order, nor its successors. Altogether she wrote me twenty-two letters, and I one or two more than that number to her, and—a thing almost inevitable in a discussion by correspondence—there is a lot of overlapping and recapitulation. Those letters spread over a space of nearly two and a half years. Again and again she insists upon the monstrous exaggeration of the importance of sex in human life and of the need of some reduction of its importance, and she makes the boldest experimental suggestions for the achievement of that end. But she comes slowly to recognize that there is a justification for an indirect attack, that sex and the position of women do not constitute the primary problem in that bristling system of riddles that lies like a hostile army across the path of mankind. And she realized too that through art, through science and literature and the whole enquiring and creative side of man's nature, lies the path by which those positions are to be outflanked, and those eternal-looking impossibles and inconceivables overcome. Here is a fragment—saturated with the essence of her thought. Three-quarters of her earlier letters are variations on this theme. . . .

"What you call 'social order,' Stephen, all the arrangements seem to me to be *built* on subjection to sex even more than they are built (as you say) on labor subjection. And this is an age of release, you say it is an age of release for the workers and they know it. And so do the women. Just as much. 'Wild hopes' indeed! The workers' hopes are nothing to the women's! It is not only the workers who are saying let us go free, manage things differently so that we may have our lives relieved from this intolerable burthen of constant toil, but the women also are saying let us go free. They are demanding release just as much from their intolerable endless specialization as females. The tramp on the roads who won't work, the swindler and the exploiter who contrive not to work, the strikers who throw down their tools, no longer for twopences and sixpences as you say but because their way of living is no longer tolerable to them, and we women, who don't bear children or work or help; we are all in one movement together. We are part of the General Strike. I have been a striker all my life. We are doing nothing—by the hundred thousand. Your old social machine is working without us and in spite of us, it carries us along with it and we are sand in the bearings. I'm not a wheel, Stephen, I'm grit. What you say about the reactionaries and suppressionists who would stifle the complaints of labor and crush out its struggles to be free, is exactly true about the reactionaries and suppressionists who would stifle the discussion of the woman's position and crush out her hopes of emancipation. . . ."

And here is a page of the peculiar doubt that was as characteristic of her as the quick changes of her eyes. It gives just that pessimistic touch that tempered her valiant adventurousness, that gave a color at last to the tragedy of her death. . . .

"Have you ever thought, Stephen, that perhaps these (repressionist) people are righter than you are—that if the worker gets free he *won't* work and that if the woman gets free she won't furl her sex and stop disturbing things? Suppose she *is* wicked as a sex, suppose she *will* trade on her power of exciting imaginative men. A lot of these new women run with the hare and hunt with the hounds, beguile some poor innocent of a man to ruin them and then call in fathers, brother, husbands, friends, chivalry, all the rest of it, and make the best of both sides of a sex. Suppose we go on behaving like that. After we've got all our emancipations. Suppose that the liberation of common people simply means loafing, no discipline, nothing being done, an end to labor and the beginning of nothing to replace it, and that the liberation of women simply means the elaboration of mischief. Suppose that it is so. Suppose you are just tumbling the contents of the grate into the middle of the room. Then all this emancipation *is* a decay, even as conservative-minded people say,—it's none the less a decay because we want it, —and the only thing to stop it is to stop it, and to have more discipline and more suppression and say to women and the common people: 'Back to the Sterner Virtues; Back to Servitude!' I wish I hadn't these reactionary streaks in my thoughts, but I have and there you are. . . ."

And then towards the second year her letters began to break away from her preoccupation with her position as a woman and to take up new aspects of life, more general aspects of life altogether. It had an effect not of her having exhausted the subject but as if, despairing of a direct solution, she turned deliberately to the relief of other considerations. She ceased to question her own life, and taking that for granted, wrote more largely of less tangible things. She remembered that she had said that life, if it was no more than its present appearances, was "utter nonsense." She went back to that. "One says things like that," she wrote "and not for a moment does one believe it. I grumble at my life, I seem to be always weakly and fruitlessly fighting my life, and I love it. I would not be willingly dead—for anything. I'd rather be an old match-woman selling matches on a freezing night in the streets than be dead. Nothing nonsensical ever held me so tightly or kept me so interested. I suppose really I am full of that very same formless faith on which you rely. But with me it's not only shapeless but intangible. . . . I nibble at religion. I am immensely attracted. I stand in the doorway. Only when they come out to persuade me to come in I am like a shy child and I go away. The temples beguile me and the music, but not the men. I feel I want to join *it* and they say 'join *us*.' They are—like vergers. Such small things! Such dreadful little *arguing* men! They don't let you come in, they want you to say they are right. All the really religious people seem to be outside nowadays and all the pretending, cheating, atheistical, vain and limited people within. . . .

"But the beautiful things religion gives! The beauty! Do you know Saint Paul's, Stephen? Latterly I have been there time after time. It is the most beautiful interior in all the world, so great, so sombrely dignified, so perfectly balanced—and filled with such wonderful music, brimming with music just as crystal water brims in a bowl of crystal. The other day I went there, up into a little gallery high up under the dome, to hear Bach's Passion Music, the St. Matthew Passion. One hangs high and far above the little multitudes below, the white-robed singers, the white-robed musicians, ranks and ranks, the great organ, the rows and rows and rows of congregation, receding this way, that way, into the haze of the aisle and the transepts, and out of it all streams the sound and the singing, it pours up past you like a river, a river that rushes upward to some great sea, some unknown sea. The whole place is music and singing. . . . I hang on to the railings, Stephen, and weep—I have to weep—and I wonder and wonder. . . .

"One prays then as naturally as one drinks when one is thirsty and cold water comes to hand. I don't know whom I pray to, but I pray;—of course I pray. Latterly, Stephen, I have been reading devotional works and trying to catch that music again. I never do—definitely. Never. But at times I put down the book and it seems to me that surely a moment ago I heard it, that if I sit very still in a moment I shall hear it again. And I can feel it is there, I know it is there, like a bat's cry, pitched too high for my ears. I know it is there, just as I should still know there was poetry somewhere if some poor toothless idiot with no roof to his mouth and no knowledge of any but the commonest words tried to read Shelley to me. . . .

"I wish I could pray with you, Stephen; I wish I could kneel down somewhere with you of all people and pray."

§ 6

Presently our correspondence fell away. The gaps between our letters lengthened out. We never wrote regularly because for that there must be a free exchange upon daily happenings, and neither of us cared to dwell too closely on our immediate lives. We had a regard for one another that left our backgrounds vague and shadowy.

She had made her appeal across the sundering silences to me and I had answered, and we had poured out certain things from our minds. We could not go on discussing. I was a very busy man now, and she did not write except on my replies.

For a gap of nearly four months neither of us had anything to say in a letter at all. I think that in time our correspondence might have altogether died away. Then she wrote again in a more familiar strain to tell me of certain definite changes of relationship and outlook. She said that the estrangement between herself and Justin had increased during the past year; that they were going to live practically apart; she for the most part in the Surrey house where her two children lived with their governesses and maids. But also she meant to snatch weeks and seasons for travel. Upon that they had been disputing for some time. "I know it is well with the children," she wrote; "why should I be in perpetual attendance? I do nothing for them except an occasional kiss, or half-an-hour's romping. Why should one pretend? Justin and I have wrangled over this question of going away, for weeks, but at last feminine persistence has won. I am going to travel in my own fashion and see the world. With periodic appearances at his side in London and Scotland. We have agreed at least on one thing, and that is upon a companion; she is to be my secretary in title, my moral guarantor in fact, and her name which is her crowning glory is Stella Summersley Satchel. She is blonde, erect, huffy-mannered and thoroughly up to both sides of her work. I partly envy her independence and rectitude—partly only. It's odd and quite inconsistent of me that I don't envy her altogether. In theory I insist that a woman should not have charm,—it is our undoing. But when I meet one without it——!

"I shall also trail a maid, but I guess that young woman will learn what it is to be left behind in half the cities of Europe before I have done with her. I always lose my maids. They are so much more passive and forgettable than luggage—abroad that is. And Justin usually in the old days used to remember about them. And his valet used to see after them,—a most attentive man. Justin cannot, he says, have his wife abroad with merely a companion; people would talk; maid it must be as well. And so in a week or less I shall start, unusually tailormade, for South Germany and all that jolly country, companioned and maided. I shall tramp—on the feet God has given me—in stout boots. Miss Summersley Satchel marches, I understand, like the British infantry but on a vegetarian 'basis,'—fancy calling your nourishment a 'basis'!—the maid and so forth by *Eilgut*. . . ."

§ 7

After the letter containing that announcement she wrote to me twice again, once from Oban and then after a long interval from Siena. The former was a scornfully minute description of the English at their holidays and how the conversation went among the women after dinner. "They are like a row of Japanese lanterns, all blown out long ago and swinging about in a wind," she wrote—an extravagant image that yet conveys something of the large, empty, unilluminating effect of a sort of social intercourse very vividly. In the second letter she was concerned chiefly with the natural beauty of Italy and how latterly she had thrice wept at beautiful things, and what this mystery of beauty could be that had such power over her emotions.

"All up the hillside before the window as I write the herbage is thick with anemones. They aren't scattered evenly and anyhow amongst the other things but in little clusters and groups that die away and begin again, like the repetitions of an air in some musical composition. I have been sitting and looking at them for the better part of an hour, loving them more and then more, and the sweet sunlight that is on them and in among them. . . . How marvellous are these things, Stephen! All these little exquisite things that are so abundant in the world, the gleaming lights and blossoms, the drifting scents! At times these things bring me to weeping. . . . I can't help it. It is as if God who is so stern and high, so terrible to all our appeals, took pity for a moment and saw fit to speak very softly and tenderly. . . ."

That was the last letter I was ever to have from her.

21

CHAPTER THE ELEVENTH

The Last Meeting

§ 1

IN the summer of 1911 immediately after the coronation of King George there came one of those storms of international suspicion that ever and again threaten Europe with war. It seems to have been brewed by some German adepts at Welt-Politik, those privileged makers of giant bombs who sit at the ears of foreign ministers suggesting idiotic wickedness, and it was brewed with a sublime ignorance of nearly every reality in the case. A German warship without a word of notice seized Agadir on the Atlantic coast of Morocco, within the regions reserved to French influence; an English demand for explanations was uncivilly disregarded and England and France and presently Germany began vigorous preparations for war. All over the world it was supposed that Germany had at last flung down the gauntlet. In England the war party was only too eager to grasp what it considered to be a magnificent opportunity. Heaven knows what the Germans had hoped or intended by their remarkable coup; the amazing thing to note is that they were not prepared to fight, they had not even the necessary money ready and they could not get it; they had perhaps never intended to fight, and the autumn saw the danger disperse again into diplomatic bickerings and insincerely pacific professions. But in the high summer the danger had not dispersed, and in common with every reasonable man I found myself under the shadow of an impending catastrophe that would have been none the less gigantic and tragic because it was an imbecility. It was an occasion when everyone needs must act, however trivially disproportionate his action may be to the danger. I cabled Gidding who was in America to get together whatever influences were available there upon the side of pacific intervention, and I set such British organs as I could control or approach in the same direction. It seemed probable that Italy would be drawn into any conflict that might ensue; it happened that there was to be a Conference of Peace Societies in Milan early in September, and thither I decided to go in the not very certain hope that out of that assemblage some form of European protest might be evolved.

That August I was very much run down. I had been staying in London through almost intolerably hot weather to attend a Races Congress that had greatly disappointed me. I don't know particularly now why I had been disappointed nor how far the feeling was due to my being generally run down by the pressure of detailed work and the stress of thinking about large subjects in little scraps of time. But I know that a kind of despair came over me as I sat and looked at that multicolored assembly and heard in succession the heavy platitudes of white men, the slick, thin cleverness of Hindoos, the rich-toned florid rhetoric of negroes. I lost sight of any germ of splendid possibility in all those people, and saw all too plainly the vanity, the jealousy, the self-interests that show up so harshly against the professions of every altruistic movement. It seemed all such a windy business against the firm prejudices, the vast accumulated interests that grind race against race. We had no common purpose at all at that conference, no proposal to hold us together. So much of it was like bleating on a hillside. . . .

I wanted a holiday badly, and then came this war crisis and I felt unable to go away for any length of time. Even bleating it seemed to me was better than acquiescence in a crime against humanity. So to get heart to bleat at Milan I snatched at ten days in the Swiss mountains en route. A tour with some taciturn guide involving a few middling climbs and glacier excursions seemed the best way of recuperating. I had never had any time for Switzerland since my first exile there years ago. I took the advice of a man in the club whose name I now forget —if ever I knew it, a dark man with a scar—and went up to the Schwarzegg Hut above Grindelwald, and over the Strahlegg to the Grimsel. I had never been up into the central mass of the Bernese Oberland before, and I was amazed and extraordinarily delighted by the vast lonely beauty of those interminable uplands of ice. I wished I could have lingered up there. But that is the tragedy of those sunlit desolations; one may not stay; one sees and exclaims and then looks at a watch. I wonder no one has ever taken an arctic equipment up into that wilderness, and had a good healing spell of lonely exaltation. I found the descent from the Strahlegg as much of a climb as I was disposed to undertake; for an hour we were coming down frozen snow that wasn't so much a slope as a slightly inclined precipice. . . .

THE LAST MEETING

From the Grimsel I went over the Rhone glacier to the inn on the Furka Pass, and then, paying off my guide and becoming frankly a pedestrian, I made my way round by the Schöllenen gorge to Goeschenen, and over the Susten Joch to the Susten Pass and Stein, meaning to descend to Meiringen.

But I still had four days before I went on to Italy, and so I decided to take one more mountain. I slept at the Stein inn, and started in the morning to do that agreeable first mountain of all, the Titlis, whose shining genial head attracted me. I did not think a guide necessary, but a boy took me up by a track near Gadmen, and left me to my Siegfried map some way up the great ridge of rocks that overlooks the Engstlen Alp. I a little overestimated my mountaineering, and it came about that I was benighted while I was still high above the Joch Pass on my descent. Some of this was steep and needed caution. I had to come down slowly with my folding lantern, in which a reluctant candle went out at regular intervals, and I did not reach the little inn at Engstlen Alp until long after eleven at night. By that time I was very tired and hungry.

They told me I was lucky to get a room, only one stood vacant; I should certainly not have enjoyed sleeping on a billiard table after my day's work, and I ate a hearty supper, smoked for a time, meditated emptily, and went wearily to bed.

But I could not sleep. Usually, I am a good sleeper, but ever and again when I have been working too closely or over-exerting myself I have spells of wakefulness, and that night after perhaps an hour's heavy slumber I became thinly alert and very weary in body and spirit, and

I do not think I slept again. The pain in my leg that the panther had torn had been revived by the day's exertion. For the greater part of my life insomnia has not been disagreeable to me. In the night, in the stillness, one has a kind of detachment from reality, one floats there without light, without weight, feeling very little of one's body. One has a certain disembodiment and one can achieve a magnanimity of thought, forgiveness and self-forgetfulness that are impossible while the body clamors upon one's senses. But that night, because, I suppose, I was so profoundly fatigued, I was melancholy and despondent. I could feel again the weight of the great beast upon me as he clawed me down and I clung—desperately, in that interminable instant before he lost his hold. . . .

Yes, I was extraordinarily wretched that night. I was filled with self-contempt and self-disgust. I felt that I was utterly weak and vain, and all the pretensions and effort of my life mere florid, fruitless pretensions and nothing more. I had lost all control over my mind. Things that had seemed secondary before became primary, difficult things became impossible things. I had been greatly impeded and irritated in London by the manœuvres of a number of people who were anxious to make capital out of the crisis, self-advertising people who wanted at any cost to be lifted into a position of unique protest. . . . You see, that unfortunate Nobel prize has turned the advocacy of peace into a highly speculative profession; the qualification for the winner is so vaguely defined that a vast multitude of voluntary idealists has been created and a still greater number diverted from the unendowed pursuit of human welfare in other directions. Such a man as myself who is known to command a considerable publicity is necessarily a prey to those moral *entrepreneurs*. All sorts of ridiculous and petty incidents had forced this side of public effort upon me, but hitherto I had been able to say, with a laugh or sigh as the case warranted, "So much is dear old humanity and all of us"; and to remember the great residuum of nobility that remained. Now that last saving consideration refused to be credible. I lay with my body and my mind in pain thinking these people over, thinking myself over too with the rest of my associates, thinking drearily and weakly, recalling spites, dishonesties and vanities, feuds and absurdities, until I was near persuaded that all my dreams of wider human understandings, of great ends beyond the immediate aims and passions of common everyday lives, could be at best no more than the refuge of shy and weak and ineffective people from the failure of their personal lives. . . .

We idealists are not jolly people, not honest simple people; the strain tells upon us; even to ourselves we are unappetizing. Aren't the burly, bellowing fellows after all righter, with their simple natural hostility to everything foreign, their valiant hatred of everything unlike themselves, their contempt for aspiring weakness, their beer and lush sentiment, their here-to-day-and-gone-to-morrow conviviality and fellowship? Good fellows! While we others, lost in filmy speculations, in moon-and-star snaring and the chase of dreams, stumble where even they walk upright. . . .

You know I have never quite believed in myself, never quite believed in my work or my religion. So it has always been with me and always, I suppose, will be. I know I am purblind, I know I do not see my way clearly nor very far; I have to do with things imperfectly apprehended. I cannot cheat my mind away from these convictions. I have a sort of hesitation of the soul as other men have a limp in their gait. God, I suppose, has a need for lame men. God, I suppose, has a need for blind men and fearful and doubting men, and does not intend life to be altogether swallowed up in staring sight. Some things are to be reached best by a hearing that is not distracted by any clearer senses. But so it is with me, and this is the innermost secret I have to tell you.

I go valiantly for the most part I know, but despair ' is always near to me. In the common hours of my life it is as near as a shark may be near a sleeper in a ship; the thin effectual plank of my deliberate faith keeps me secure, but in these rare distresses of the darkness the plank seems to become transparent, to be on the verge of dissolution, a sense of life as of an abysmal flood, full of cruelty, densely futile, blackly aimless, penetrates my defences. . . .

I don't think I can call these stumblings from conviction unbelief; the limping man walks for all his limping, and I go on in spite of my falls. "Though he slay me yet will I trust in him. . . ."

I fell into an inconsecutive review of my life under this light that touched every endeavor with the pale tints of failure. And as that flow of melancholy reflection went on, it was shot more and more frequently with thoughts of Mary. It was not a discursive thinking about Mary but a definite fixed direction of thought towards her. I had not so thought of her for many years. I wanted her, I felt, to come to me and help me out of this distressful pit into which my spirit had fallen. I believed she could. I perceived our separation as an irreparable loss. She had a harder, clearer quality than I, a more assured courage, a readier, surer movement of the mind. Always she had "lift" for me. And then I had a curious impression that I had heard her voice calling my name, as one might call out in one's sleep. I dismissed it as an illusion, and then I heard it again. So clearly that I sat up and listened—breathless. . . .

Mixed up with all this was the intolerable uproar and talking of a little cascade not fifty yards from the hotel. It is curious how distressing that clamor of running water, which is so characteristic of the Alpine night, can become. At last those sounds can take the likeness of any voice whatever. The water, I decided, had called to me, and now it mocked and laughed at me. . . .

The next morning I descended at some late hour by Swiss reckoning, and discovered two ladies in the morning sunlight awaiting breakfast at a little green table. One rose slowly at the sight of me, and stood and surveyed me with a glad amazement.

§ 2

There she stood real and solid, a little unfamiliar in her tweeds and with her shining eyes intimate and unforgettable, as though I had never ceased to see them for all those intervening years. And bracing us both and holding back our emotion was, quite unmistakably, Miss Summersley Satchel, a blonde business-like young woman with a stumpy nose very cruelly corrugated and inflamed by a pince-nez that savagely did much more than its duty by its name. She remained seated, tilting her chair a little, pushing herself back from the table and regarding me—intelligently.

It was one of those moments in life when one is taken unawares. I think our common realization of the need of masking the reality of our encounter, the hasty search in our minds for some plausible face upon this meeting, must have been very obvious to the lady who observed us. Mary's first thought was for a pseudonym. Mine was to make it plain we met by accident.

"It's Mr.—Stephen!" said Mary.

"It's you!"

"Dropped out of the sky!"

"From over there. I was benighted and go there late."

"Very late?"

"One gleam of light—and a yawning waiter. Or I should have had to break windows. . . . And then I meet you!"

Then for a moment or so we were silent, with our sense of the immense gravity of this position growing upon us. A little tow-headed waiter-boy appeared with their coffee and rolls on a tray poised high on his hand.

"You'll have your coffee out here with us?" said Mary.

"Where else?" said I, as though there was no conceivable alternative, and told the tow-headed waiter.

Belatedly Mary turned to introduce me to her secretary: "My friend Miss Summersley Satchel. Mr.—Stephen." Miss Satchel and I bowed to each other and agreed that the lake was very beautiful in the morning light. "Mr. Stephen," said Mary, in entirely unnecessary explanation, "is an old friend of my mother's. And I haven't seen him for years. How is Mrs. Stephen—and the children?"

I answered briefly and began to tell of my climb down the Titlis. I addressed myself with unnecessary explicitness to Miss Satchel. I did perhaps over-accentuate the extreme fortuitousness of my appearance. . . . From where I stood, the whole course of the previous day after I had come over the shoulder was visible. It seemed a soft little shining pathway to the top, but the dangers of the descent had a romantic intensification in the morning light. "The rule of the game," said I, "is that one stops and waits for daylight. I wonder if anyone keeps that rule."

We talked for a time of mountains, I still standing a little aloof until my coffee came. Miss Summersley Satchel produced that frequent and most unpleasant byeproduct of a British education, an intelligent interest in etymology. "I wonder," she said, with a brow of ruffled omniscience and eyeing me rather severely with a magnified eye, "why it is *called* Titlis. There must be *some* reason. . . ."

Presently Miss Satchel was dismissed indoors on a transparent excuse and Mary and I were alone together. We eyed one another gravely. Perhaps all the more gravely because of the wild excitement that was quickening our pulse and breathing, and thrilling through our nerves. She pushed back the plate before her and put her dear elbows on the table and dropped her chin between her hands in an attitude that seemed all made of little memories.

"I suppose," she said, "something of this kind was bound to happen."

She turned her eyes to the mountains shining in the morning light. "I'm glad it has happened in a beautiful place. It might have been—anywhere."

"Last night," I said, "I was thinking of you and wanting to hear your voice again. I thought I did."

"I too. I wonder—if we had some dim perception. . . ."

She scanned my face. "Stephen, you're not much changed. You're looking well. . . . But your eyes,—they're dog-tired eyes. Have you been working too hard?"

"A conference—what did you call them once?—a Carnegieish conference in London. Hot weather and fussing work and endless hours of weak grey dusty speeches, and perhaps that clamber over there yesterday was too much. It *was* too much. In India I damaged a leg. . . . I had meant to rest here for a day."

"Well,—rest here."

"With you!"

"Why not? Now you are here."

"But—— After all, we've promised."

"It's none of our planning, Stephen."

"It seems to me I ought to go right on—so soon as breakfast is over."

She weighed that with just the same still pause, the same quiet moment of lips and eyes that I recalled so well. It was as things had always been between us that she should make her decision first and bring me to it.

"It isn't natural," she decided, "with the sun rising and the day still freshly beginning that you should go or that I should go. I've wanted to meet you like this and talk about things,—ten thousand times. And as for

me Stephen I *won't* go. And I won't let you go if I can
help it. Not this morning, anyhow. No. Go later in the
day if you will, and let us two take this one talk that
God Himself has given us. We've not planned it. It's
His doing, not ours."

I sat, yielding. "I am not so sure of God's participation," I said. "But I know I am very tired, and glad to
be with you. I can't tell you how glad. So glad—— I
think I should weep if I tried to say it. . . ."

"Three, four, five hours perhaps—even if people know.
Is it so much worse than thirty minutes? We've broken
the rules already; we've been flung together; it's not our
doing, Stephen. A little while longer—adds so little to
the offence and means to us——"

"Yes," I said, "but—if Justin knows?"

"He won't."

"Your companion?"

There was the briefest moment of reflection. "She's
discretion itself," she said.

"Still——"

"If he's going to know the harm is done. We may
as well be hung for a sheep as a lamb. And he won't
know. No one will know."

"The people here."

"Nobody's here. Not a soul who matters. I doubt
if they know my name. . . . No one ever talks to
me."

I sat in the bright sunshine, profoundly enervated and
quite convinced, but still maintaining out of mere indolence a show of hesitation. . . .

"You take the good things God sends you, Stephen—
as I do. You stay and talk with me now, before the cur-

tain falls again. We've tired of letters. You stay and talk to me.

"Here we are, Stephen, and it's the one chance that is ever likely to come to us in all our lives. We'll keep the point of honor; and you shall go to-day. But don't let's drive the point of honor into the quick. Go easy Stephen, old friend. . . . My dear, my dear! What has happened to you? Have you forgotten? Of course! Is it possible for you to go, mute, with so much that we can say. . . . And these mountains and this sunlight! . . ."

I looked up to see her with her elbows on the table and her hands clasped under her chin; that face close to mine, her dear blue eyes watching me and her lips a little apart.

No other human being has ever had that effect upon me, so that I seem to feel the life and stir in that other body more than I feel my own.

§ 3

From the moment when I confessed my decision to stay we gave no further thought to the rightfulness or wisdom of spending the next few hours together. We thought only of those hours. Things lent themselves to us. We stood up and walked out in front of the hotel and there moored to a stake at the edge of the water was a little leaky punt, the one vessel on the Engstlen See. We would take food with us as we decided and row out there to where the vast cliffs came sheer from the water, out of earshot or interference and talk for all the time we had. And I remember now how Mary stood and called to Miss Satchel's window to tell her of this intention, and how I discovered again that exquisite slender grace I knew so well.

You know the very rowing out from the shore had in it something sweet and incredible. It was as if we were but dreaming together and might at any moment awaken again, countless miles and a thousand things apart. I rowed slowly with those clumsy Swiss oars that one must thrust forward, breaking the smooth crystal of the lake, and she sat sideways looking forward, saying very little and with much the same sense I think of enchantment and unreality. And I saw now for the first time as I watched her over my oars that her face was changed; she was graver and, I thought, stronger than the Mary I had known.

Even now I can still doubt if that boat and lake were real. And yet I remember even minute and irrelevant details of the day's impressions with an extraordinary and exquisite vividness. Perhaps it is that very luminous distinctness which distinguishes these events from the common experiences of life and puts them so above the quality of things that are ordinarily real.

We rowed slowly past a great headland and into the bay at the upper end of the water. We had not realized at first that we could row beyond the range of the hotel windows. The rock that comes out of the lake is a clear dead white when it is dry, and very faintly tinted, but when it is wetted it lights warmly with flashes and blotches of color, and is seen to be full of the most exquisite and delicate veins. It splinters vertically and goes up in cliffs, very high and sculptured, with a quality almost of porcelain, that at a certain level suddenly become more rude and massive and begin to overhang. Under the cliffs the water is very deep and blue-green, and runs here and there into narrow clefts. This place where we landed was a kind of beach left by the recession of the ice, all the rocks immediately about us were ice-worn, and the place was paved with ice-worn boulders. Two huge bluffs put their foreheads together above us and hid the glacier from us, but one could feel the near presence of ice in the air. Out between them boiled a little torrent, and spread into a hundred intercommunicating channels amidst the great pebbles. And those pebbles were covered by a network of marvellously gnarled and twisted stems bearing little leaves and blossoms, a network at once very ancient and very fresh, giving a peculiar gentleness and richness to the Alpine severity that had dwarfed and tangled them. It was astounding that any plant could find nourishment among those stones. The great headland, with patches of yellowish old snow still lingering here and there upon its upper masses, had crept insensibly between us and the remote hotel and now hid it altogether. There was nothing to remind us of the world that had separated us, except that old and leaky boat we had drawn up upon the stones at the limpid water's edge.

"It is as if we had come out of life together," she whispered, giving a voice to my thought.

She sat down upon a boulder and I sat on a lower slab a yard or so away, and we looked at one another. "It's still unreal," she said.

I felt awkward and at a loss as I sat there before her, as a man unused to drawing-rooms might feel in the presence of a strange hostess.

"You are so *you*," I said; "so altogether my nearest thing—and so strange too, so far off, that I feel—shy. . . .

"I'm shy," I repeated. "I feel that if I speak loudly all this will vanish. . . ."

I looked about me. "But surely this is the most beautiful place in the whole world! Is it indeed in the world?"

"Stephen, my dear," she began presently, "what a strange thing life is! Strange! The disproportions! The things that will not fit together. The little things that eat us up, and the beautiful things that might save us and don't save us, don't seem indeed to have any meaning in regard to ordinary sensible affairs. . . . This *beauty*. . . .

"Do you remember, Stephen, how long ago in the old park you and I talked about immortality and you said then you did not want to know anything of what comes after life. Even now do you want to know? You are too busy and I am not busy enough. I want to be sure, not only to know, but to know that it is so, that this life—no, not *this* life, but that life, is only the bleak twilight of the morning. I think death—just dead death—after the life I have had is the most impossible of ends. . . . You don't want—particularly? I want to passionately. I *want* to live again—out of this body, Stephen, and all that it carries with it, to be free—as beautiful things are free. To be free as this is free—an exquisite clean freedom. . . .

"I can't believe that the life of this earth is all that there is for us—or why should we ever think it strange? Why should we still find the ordinary matter-of-fact things of everyday strange? We do—because they aren't

—*us*. . . . Eating. Stuffing into ourselves thin slices of what were queer little hot and eager beasts. . . . The perpetual need to do such things. And all the mad fury of sex, Stephen! . . . We don't live, we suffocate in our living bodies. They storm and rage and snatch; it isn't *us*, Stephen, really. It can't be us. It's all so excessive —if it is anything more than the first furious rush into existence of beings that will go on—go on at last to quite beautiful real things. Like this perhaps. To-day the world is beautiful indeed with the sun shining and love shining and you, my dear, so near to me. . . . It's so incredible that you and I must part to-day. It's as if— someone told me the sun was a little mad. It's so per- fectly natural to be with you again. . . ."

Her voice sank. She leant a little forward towards me. "Stephen, suppose that you and I were dead to-day. Suppose that when you imagined you were climbing yester- day, you died. Suppose that yesterday you died and that you just thought you were still climbing as you made your way to me. Perhaps you are dead up there on the moun- tain and I am lying dead in my room in this hotel, and this is the Great Beginning. . . .

"Stephen, I am talking nonsense because I am so happy to be with you here. . . ."

§ 4

For a time we said very little. Then irregularly, disconnectedly, we began to tell each other things about ourselves.

The substance of our lives seemed strangely objective

that day; we had as it were come to one another clean out of our common conditions. She told me of her troubles and her secret weaknesses; we bared our spirits and confessed. Both of us had the same tale of mean and angry and hasty impulses, both of us could find kindred inconsistencies, both had an exalted assurance that the other would understand completely and forgive and love. She talked for the most part, she talked much more than I, with a sort of wonder at the things that had happened to her, and for long spaces we did not talk at all nor feel the need of talking, and what seems very strange to me now, seeing that we had been impassioned lovers, we never kissed; we never kissed at all; I do not even remember that I thought of kissing her. We had a shyness between us that kept us a little apart, and I cannot remember that we ever touched one another except that for a time she took me and led me by the hand towards a little place of starry flowers that had drawn her eyes and which she wished me to see. Already for us two our bodies were dead and gone. We were shy, shy of any contact, we were a little afraid of one another, there was a kind of awe between us that we had met again.

And in that strange and beautiful place her fancy that we were dead together had a fitness that I cannot possibly convey to you. I cannot give you by any writing the light and the sweet freshness of that high desolation. You would need to go there. What was lovely in our talk, being said in that setting, would seem but a rambling discourse were I to write it down,—as I believe that even now I could write it down—word for word almost, every thought of it, so fresh does it remain with me. . . .

My dear, some moments are eternal. It seems to me

that as I write to tell you of this I am telling you not of something that happened two years ago but of a thing immortal. It is as if I and Mary were together there holding the realities of our lives before us as though they were little sorry tales written in books upon our knees. . . .

§ 5

It was still in the early afternoon that we came down again across the meandering ice-water streams to our old boat, and pushed off and rowed slowly out of that magic corner back to every-day again. . . .

Little we knew to what it was we rowed.

As we glided across the water and rounded the head-land and came slowly into view of the hotel again, Mary was reminded of our parting and for a little while she was disposed to make me remain. "If you could stay a little longer," she said,—"Another day? If any harm is done, it's done."

"It has been beautiful," I said, "this meeting. It's just as if—when I was so jaded and discouraged that I could have put my work aside and despaired altogether,—some power had said, 'Have you forgotten the friendship I gave you?' . . . But we shall have had our time. We've met,—we've seen one another, we've heard one another. We've hurt no one. . . ."

"You will go?"

"To-day. Before sunset. Isn't it right that I should go?"

"Stay," she whispered, with a light in her eyes.

"No. I dare not."

She did not speak for a long time.

"Of course," she said at last, "you're right. You only said—I would have said it for you if you had not. You're so right, Stephen. . . . I suppose, poor silly little things, that if you stayed we should certainly begin making love to each other. It would be—necessary. We should fence about a little and then there it would be. No barrier—to stop us. And neither of us wants it to happen. It isn't what we want. You would become urgent, I suppose, and I should be—coquettish. In spite of ourselves that power would make us puppets. As if already we hadn't made love. . . . I could find it in my heart now. . . . Stephen I could *make* you stay. . . .

"Oh! Why are we so tormented, Stephen? In the next world we shall meet, and this will trouble us no longer. The love will be there—oh, the love will be there, like something that has at last got itself fully born, got itself free from some queer clinging seed-case. . . .

"We shall be rid of jealousy, Stephen, that inflammation of the mind, that bitterness, that pitiless sore, so that I shan't be tormented by the thought of Rachel and she will be able to tolerate me. She was so sweet and wonderful a girl—with those dark eyes. And I've never done her justice—never. Nor she me. I snatched you from her. I snatched you. . . .

"Someday we shall be different. . . . All this putting oneself round another person like a fence, against everyone else, almost against everything else; it's so wicked, so fierce.

"It's so possible to be different. Sometimes now, sometimes for long parts of a day I have no base passions at all —even in this life. To be like that always! But I can't see clearly how these things can be; one dreams of them in a kind of luminous mist, and if one looks directly at them, they vanish again. . . ."

§ 6

And at last we came to the landing, and moored the little boat and walked up the winding path to the hotel. The dull pain of separation was already upon us.

I think we had forgotten Miss Summersley Satchel altogether. But she appeared as we sat down to tea at that same table at which we had breakfasted, and joined us as a matter of course. Conceivably she found the two animated friends of the morning had become rather taciturn. Indeed there came a lapse of silence so portentous that I roused myself to effort and told her, all over again, as I realized afterwards, the difficulties that had benighted me upon Titlis. Then Miss Satchel regaled Mary with some particulars of the various comings and goings of the hotel. I became anxious to end this tension and went into the inn to pay my bill and get my knapsack. When I came out Mary stood up.

"I'll come just a little way with you, Stephen," she said, and I could have fancied the glasses of the companion flashed to hear the surname of the morning reappear a Christian name in the afternoon. . . .

"Is that woman behind us safe?" I asked, breaking the silence as we went up the mountain-side.

Mary looked over her shoulder for a contemplative second.

"She's always been—discretion itself."

We thought no more of Miss Satchel.

THE LAST MEETING

"This parting," said Mary, "is the worst of the price we have to pay. . . . Now it comes to the end there seem a thousand things one hasn't said. . . ."

And presently she came back to that. "We shan't remember this so much perhaps. It was there we met, over there in the sunlight—among those rocks. I suppose —perhaps—we managed to say something. . . ."

As the ascent grew steeper it became clear that if I was to reach the Melch See Inn by nightfall, our moment for parting had come. And with a "Well," and a white-lipped smile and a glance at the Argus-eyed hotel, she held out her hand to me. "I shall live on this, brother Stephen," she said, "for years."

"I too," I answered. . . .

It was wonderful to stand and face her there, and see her real and living with the warm sunlight on her, and her face one glowing tenderness. We clasped hands; all the warm life of our hands met and clung and parted.

I went on alone up the winding path,—it zigzags up the mountain-side in full sight of the hotel for the better part of an hour—climbing steadily higher and looking back and looking back until she was just a little strip of white—that halted and seemed to wave to me. I waved back and found myself weeping. "You fool!" I said to myself, "Go on"; and it was by an effort that I kept on my way instead of running back to her again. Presently the curvature of the slope came up between us and hid her altogether, hid the hotel, hid the lakes and the cliffs. . . .

It seemed to me that I could not possibly see her any more. It was as if I knew that sun had set for ever.

§ 7

I lay at the Melch See Inn that night, and rose betimes and started down that wild grey gorge in the early morning light. I walked to Sachseln, caught an early train to Lucerne and went on in the afternoon to Como. And there I stayed in the sunshine taking a boat and rowing alone far up the lake and lying in it, thinking of love and friendship and the accidents and significance of my life, and for the most part not thinking at all but feeling, feeling the glow of our meeting and the finality of our separation, as one feels the clear glow of a sunset when the wind rises and the cold night draws near. Everything was pervaded by the sense of her. Just over those mountains, I thought, is Mary. I was alone in my boat, but her presence filled the sky. It seemed to me that at any moment I could go to her. And the last vestige of any cloud between us for anything we had done or failed to do in these crises of distress and separation, had vanished and gone altogether.

In the afternoon I wrote to Rachel. I had not written to her for three days, and even now I told her nothing of my meeting with Mary. I had not written partly because I could not decide whether I should tell her of that or not; in the end I tried to hide it from her. It seemed a little thing in regard to her, a thing that could not hurt her, a thing as detached from her life and as inconsecutive as a dream in my head.

Three days later I reached Milan, a day before the formal opening of the Peace Congress. But I found a telegram had come that morning to the Poste Restante to banish all thought of my pacific mission from my mind. It came from Paris and its blue ribbon of text ran:

"Come back at once to London. Justin has been told of our meeting and is resolved upon divorce. Will do all in my power to explain and avert but feel you should know at once."

There are some things so monstrously destructive to all we hold dear that for a time it is impossible to believe them. I remember now that as I read that amazing communication through—at the first reading it was a little difficult to understand because the Italian operator had guessed at one or two of the words, no real sense of its meaning came to me. That followed sluggishly. I felt as one might feel when one opens some offensive anonymous letter or hears some preposterous threat.

"What *nonsense!*" I said, faint-heartedly. I stood for a time at my bedroom window trying to shake this fact altogether off my mind. But it stayed, and became more and more real. Suddenly with a start I perceived it was real. I had to do things forthwith.

I rang the bell and asked for an *Orario*. "I shan't want these rooms. I have to go back to England," I said. "Yes,—I have had bad news." . . .

§ 8

"We've only got to explain," I told myself a hundred times during that long sleepless journey. The thundering wheels so close beneath my head echoed: "Explain. Oh yes! Explain! Explain! Explain!"

And something, a voice to which I would not listen, urged: "Suppose they do not choose to believe what you explain."

When I sat face to face with Maxwell Hartington, my solicitor, in his ink-splashed, dirty, yellow-grained room with its rows of black tin boxes, I could no longer ignore that possibility. Maxwell Hartington sat back in his chair after his fashion, listening to my story, breathing noisily through his open mouth, perspiring little beads and looking more out of condition than ever. I never knew a man so wine-sodden and so sharp-witted.

"That's all very well, Stratton," he said, "between ourselves. Very unfortunate and all that sort of thing. But it doesn't satisfy Justin evidently; and we've got to put a different look on it if we can, before we go before a jury. You see——" He seemed to be considering and rejecting unpalatable phrases. "They won't understand."

"But," I said, "after all—a mere chance of the same hotel. There must be more evidence than that."

"You spent the night in adjacent rooms," he said dryly.

"Adjacent rooms!" I cried.

He regarded me for a moment with something bordering on admiration. "Didn't you know?" he said.

"No."

"They've routed that out. You were sleeping with your two heads within a yard of one another anyhow. Thirty-six you had, and she had thirty-seven."

"But," I said and stopped.

Maxwell Hartington's admiration gave place I think to a slight resentment at my sustained innocence. "And Lady Mary changed rooms with her secretary two nights before—to be near the vacant room. The secretary went into number 12 on the floor below,—a larger room, at thirteen francs a day, and one not exposed to the early daylight. . . ."

He turned over a paper on his desk. "You didn't know, of course," he said. "But what I want to have" —and his voice grew wrathful—" is sure evidence that you didn't know. No jury on earth is going to believe you didn't know. No jury!—— Why,"—his mask dropped—"no man on earth is going to believe a yarn like that! If that's all you have, Stratton——"

§ 9

Our London house was not shut up—two servants were there on board-wages against the possibility of such a temporary return as I was now making—Rachel was away with you three children at Cromingham. I had not told her I was returning to London, and I had put up at one of my clubs. Until I had had a second interview with Maxwell Hartington I still would not let myself think that it was possible that Mary and I would fail with our explanations. We had the common confidence of habitually unchallenged people that our word would be accepted. I had hoped indeed to get the whole affair settled and abolished without anything of it coming to Rachel's ears. Then at my leisure I should be able to tell her exactly how things had come about. But each day made it clearer that things were not going to be settled, that the monstrous and the incredible was going to happen and that Justin had set

343

his mind implacably upon a divorce. My sense of complete innocence had already been shaken by Maxwell Hartington; I had come to perceive that we had been amazingly indiscreet, I was beginning to think we had been criminally indiscreet.

I saw Maxwell Hartington for a second time, and it became clear to me I must abandon any hope of keeping things further from Rachel. I took my luggage round to my house, to the great astonishment of the two servants, —they had supposed of course that I was in Italy—and then went down on the heels of a telegram to Rachel. I forget the wording of that telegram, but it was as little alarming as possible; I think I said something about "back in London for documents; shall try to get down to you." I did not specify any particular train or indeed state definitely that I was coming that day.

I had never been to Cromingham before. I went to the house you occupied on the Esplanade and learnt that you were all upon the beach. I walked along the sea-wall scrutinizing the various bright groups of children and nursemaids and holiday people that were scattered over the sands. It was a day of blazing sunshine, and between the bright sky and the silver drabs of the sand stretched the low levels of a sea that had its customary green-grey touched for once with something of the sapphire glow of the Mediterranean. Here and there were gay little umbrella tents or canvas shelters, and a bather or so and pink and white wading children broke the dazzling edge of foam. And I sought you with a kind of reluctance as though finding you would bring nearer the black irrational disaster that hung over us all.

And when I found you at last you were all radiantly

happy and healthy, the prettiest of families, and only your mother was touched with any gravity deeper than the joy of sunshine and sea. You and Mademoiselle Potin—in those days her ministrations were just beginning—were busy constructing a great sea-wall that should really and truly stop the advancing tide. Rachel Two was a little apart, making with infinite contentment an endless multitude of conical sand pies with her little tin pail. Margaret, a pink inarticulate lump, scrabbled in the warm sand under Jessica's care. Your mother sat and watched you—thoughtfully. And before any of you knew that I was there my shadow fell across you all.

You accepted my appearance when I ought to have been in Italy with the unquestioning confidence with which you still take all my comings and goings. For you, Italy, America, any place is just round the corner. I was kissed with affection but haste, and you got back to your sand-works as speedily as possible. I inspected Rachel Two's mounds,—she was giving them the names of her various aunts and uncles—and patted the crowing Margaret, who ignored me. Rachel had sprung to her feet and kissed me and now hovered radiant over me as I caressed you youngsters. It was all so warm, so real, that for an instant the dark threat that hung over us all vanished from my skies, to return with the force of a blow.

"And what has brought you back?" said Rachel. "I had expected a month of widowhood. What can have brought you back?"

The dancing gladness in her eyes vanished swiftly as she waited for an answer to her question. She caught the note of tragedy from my face. "Why have you come back from Italy?" she asked in an altered voice.

"Rachel," I said taking her arm, with a desolating sense of the futility in my gesture of protection; "let us walk along the beach. I want to tell you something——Something rather complicated."

"Is there going to be war, Stephen?" she asked abruptly.

It seemed then that this question which merely concerned the welfare of a hundred million people or so and pain, destruction and disaster beyond measure, was the most trivial of digressions.

"No," I said. "I haven't thought about the war."

"But I thought—you were thinking of nothing else."

"This has put it out of my head. It's something——Something disastrous to us."

"Something has happened to our money?"

"I wish that was all."

"Then what is it?" Her mind flashed out. "It has something to do with Mary Justin."

"How did you know that?"

"I guessed."

"Well. It is. You see—in Switzerland we met."

"You *met!*"

"By accident. She had been staying at the hotel on Engstlen Alp."

"You slept there!" cried Rachel.

"I didn't know she was in the hotel until the next day."

"And then you came away!"

"That day."

"But you talked together?"

"Yes."

"And for some reason—— You never told me, Stephen! You never told me. And you met. But—— Why is this, disaster?"

"Because Justin knows and he means to divorce her— and it may be he will succeed. . . ."

Rachel's face had become white, for some time she said nothing. Then slowly, "And if he had not known and done that—I should never have known."

I had no answer to make to that. It was true. Rachel's face was very still, and her eyes stared at the situation laid bare to her.

"When you began," she choked presently, "when she wrote—I knew—I felt——"

She ceased for fear she might weep, and for a time we walked in silence.

"I suppose," she said desperately at last, "he will get his divorce."

"I am afraid he will."

"There's no evidence—you didn't. . . ."

"No."

"And I never dreamt——!"

Then her passion tore at her. "Stephen my dear," she wept, "you didn't? you didn't? Stephen, indeed you didn't, did you? You kept faith with me as a husband should. It was an accident—a real accident—and there was no planning for you to meet together. It was as you say? I've never doubted your word ever—I've never doubted you."

Well, at any rate I could answer that plainly, and I did.

"And you know, Stephen," she said, "I believe you. And I *can't* believe you. My heart is tormented. Why did you write to her? Why did you two write and go on writing? And why did you tell me nothing of that meeting? I believe you because I can't do anything but believe you. It would kill me not to believe you in a thing that came so near to us. And yet, there it is, like a knife being twisted in my heart—that you met. Should I have known of your meeting, Stephen—ever? I know I'm talking badly for you. . . . But this thing strikes me suddenly. Out of this clear beautiful sky! And the children there—so happy in the sunshine! I was so happy. So happy. With you coming. . . . It will mean shames and law-courts and newspapers, losses of friends, losses of money and freedom. . . . My mother and my people! . . . And you and all the work you do! . . . People will never forget it, never forgive it. They will say you promised. . . . If she had never written, if she had kept to her bargain——"

"We should still have met."

"Stephen! . . . Stephen, you must bear with me. . . ."

"This is a thing," I said, "that falls as you say out of the sky. It seemed so natural—for her to write. . . . And the meeting . . . it is like some tremendous disaster of nature. I do not feel I have deserved it. It is—irrational. But there it is, little Rachel of my heart, and we have to face it. Whatever happens we have to go on. It doesn't alter the work we have to do. If it clips our wings—we have to hop along with clipped wings. . . . For you—I wish it could spare you. And she—she too is a victim, Rachel."

"She need not have written," said Rachel. "She need not have written. And then if you had met——"

She could not go on with that.

"It is so hard," I said, "to ask you to be just to her—and me. I wish I could have come to you and married you—without all that legacy—of things remembered.

. . . I was what I was. . . . One can't shake off a thing in one's blood. And besides—besides——"

I stopped helplessly.

§ 10

And then Mary came herself to tell me there would be no divorce.

She came to me unexpectedly. I had returned to town that evening, and next morning as I was sitting down in my study to answer some unimportant questions Maxwell Hartington had sent me, my parlormaid appeared. "Can you speak," she asked, "to Lady Mary Justin?"

I stood up to receive my visitor.

She came in, a tall dark figure, and stood facing me in silence until the door had closed behind her. Her face was white and drawn and very grave. She stooped a little, I could see she had had no sleep, never before had I seen her face marked by pain. And she hesitated. . . . "My dear!" I said; "why have you come to me?"

I put a chair for her and she sat down.

For a moment she controlled herself with difficulty. She put her hand over her eyes, she seemed on the verge of bitter weeping. . . .

"I came," she said at last. . . . "I came. I had to come . . . to see you."

I sat down in a chair beside her.

"It wasn't wise," I said. "But—never mind. You look so tired, my dear!"

She sat quite still for a little while.

Then she moved her arm as though she felt for me

blindly, and I put my arms about her and drew her head to my shoulder and she wept. . . .

"I knew," she sobbed, "if I came to you. . . ."

Presently her weeping was over.

"Get me a little cold water, Stephen," she said. "Let me have a little cold water on my face. I've got my courage now again. Just then,—I was down too low. Yes—cold water. Because I want to tell you—things you will be glad to hear." . . .

"You see, Stephen," she said—and now all her self-possession had returned; "there mustn't be a divorce. I've thought it all out. And there needn't be a divorce."

"Needn't be?"

"No."

"What do you mean?"

"I can stop it."

"But how?"

"I can stop it. I can manage—— I can make a bargain. . . . It's very sweet, dear Stephen, to be here talking to you again."

She stood up.

"Sit at your desk, my dear," she said. "I'm all right now. That water was good. How good cold things can be! Sit down at your desk and let me sit here. And then I will talk to you. I've had such a time, my dear. Ah!"

She paused and stuck her elbows on the desk and looked me in the eyes. And suddenly that sweet, frank smile of hers swept like sunshine across the wintry desolation of her face. "We've both been having a time," she said. "This odd little world,—it's battered us with its fists. For such a little. And we were both so ridiculously

350

happy. Do you remember it, the rocks and the sunshine and all those twisted and tangled little plants? And how the boat leaked and you baled it out! And the parting, and how you trudged up that winding path away from me! A grey figure that stopped and waved—a little figure—such a virtuous figure! And then, this storm! this *awful* hullabaloo! Lawyers, curses, threats——. And Stella Summersley Satchel like a Fury of denunciation. What hatred that woman has hidden from me! It must have accumulated. . . . It's terrible to think, Stephen, how much I must have tried her. . . . Oh! how far away those Alps are now, Stephen! Like something in another life. . . . And here we are!—among the consequences."

"But,—you were saying we could stop the divorce."

"Yes. We can. I can. But I wanted to see you, —before I did. Somehow I don't feel lonely with you. I had to see you. . . . It's good to see you."

She looked me in the face. Her tired eyes lit with a gleam of her former humor.

"Have you thought," she asked, "of all that will happen if there is a divorce?"

"I mean to fight every bit of it."

"They'll beat you."

"We'll see that."

"But they will. And then?"

"Why should one meet disaster half way?"

"Stephen!" she said; "what will happen to you when I am not here to make you look at things? Because I shan't be here. Not within reach of you. . . . There are times when I feel like a mother to you. Never more than now. . . ."

And then with rapid touches she began to picture

351

the disaster before me. She pictured the Court and our ineffectual denials, she made me realize the storm of hostility that was bound to burst over us. "And think of me," she said. "Stripped I shall be and outcast."

"Not while I live!"

"But what can you do for me? You will have Rachel. How can you stand by me? You can't be cruel to Rachel. You know you can't be cruel to Rachel. Look me in the face, Stephen; tell me. Yes. . . . Then how can you stand by me?"

"Somehow!" I cried foolishly and stopped.

"They'll use me to break your back with costs and damages. There'll be those children of yours to think of. . . ."

"My God!" I cried aloud. "Why do you torment me? Haven't I thought enough of those things? . . . Haven't I seen the ruin and the shame, the hopeless trap, men's trust in me gone, my work scattered and ended again, my children growing up to hear this and that exaggeration of our story. And you——. All the bravery of your life scattered and wasted. The thing will pursue us all, cling to us. It will be all the rest of our lives for us. . . ."

I covered my face with my hands.

When I looked up, her face was white and still, and full of a strange tenderness. "I wouldn't have you, Stephen —I wouldn't have you be cruel to Rachel. . . . I just wanted to know—something. . . . But we're wandering. We're talking nonsense. Because as I said, there need be no divorce. There will be no divorce at all. That's what I came to tell you. I shall have to pay—in a way, Stephen. . . . Not impossibly. Don't think it is anything impossible. . . ."

Then she bit her lips and sat still. . . .

"My dear," I whispered, "if we had taken one another at the beginning. . . ."

But she went on with her own thoughts.

"You love those little children of yours," she said. "And that trusting girl-wife. . . .Of course you love them. They're yours. Oh! they're so deeply — yours. . . . Yours. . . ."

"Oh my dear! don't torture me! I do love them. But I love you too."

"No," she said, "not as you do them."

I made a movement of protest.

"No," she said, whitely radiant with a serenity I had never seen before in her face. "You love me with your brain. With your soul if you like. I *know*, my poor bleeding Stephen!—Aren't those tears there? Don't mind my seeing them, Stephen. . . . Poor dear! Poor dear! . . . You love *them* with your inmost heart. Why should you mind that I see you do? . . . All my life I've been wrong, Stephen, and now I know too late. It's the things we own we love, the things we buy with our lives. . . . Always I have been hard, I've been a little hard. . . . Stephen, my dear, I loved you, always I have loved you, and always I have tried to keep myself. . . . It's too late. . . . I don't know why I am talking like this. . . . But you see I can make a bargain now—it's not an impossible bargain—and save you and save your wife and save your children——"

"But how?" I said, still doubting.

"Never mind how, Stephen. Don't ask me how now. Nothing very difficult. Easy. But I shall write you no more letters—see you—no more. Never. And that's why I had to come, you see, why I was able to come to you, just to see you and say good-bye to you, and take leave of you, dear Love that I threw away and loved too late. . . ."

She bit her lip and faced me there, a sweet flushed living thing, with a tear coursing down her cheek, and her mouth now firm and steady.

"You can stop this divorce?" I said, "But how, Mary?"

"No, don't ask me how. At a price. It's a bargain. No, no! Don't think that,—a bargain with Justin, but not degrading. Don't, my dear, let the thought of it distress you. I have to give earnests. . . . Never, dear, never through all the dusty rest of life again will you and I speak together. Never! Even if we come face to face once more—no word. . . ."

"Mary," I said, "what is it you have to do? You speak as if—— What is it Justin demands?"

"No! do not ask me that. . . . Tell me—you see we've so much to talk about, Stephen—tell me of all you are going to do. Everything. Because I've got to make a great vow of renunciation—of you. Not to think again—not even to think of you again. . . . No, no. I'm not even to look for you in the papers any more. There's to be no tricks this time. And so you see I want to fill up my mind with you. To store myself with you. Tell me your work is worth it—that it's not like the work of everyone. Tell me, Stephen—*that*. I want to believe that—tremendously. Don't be modest now. That will be cruel. I want to believe that I am at last to do something that is worth doing, something not fruitless. . . ."

"Are you to go into seclusion," I asked suddenly, "to be a nun——?"

"It is something like that," she said; "very like that. But I have promised—practically—not to tell you that. Tell me your soul, Stephen, now. Give me something I may keep in my mind through — through all those years of waiting. . . ."

"But where?" I cried. "What years of waiting?"

"In a lonely place, my dear—among mountains. High and away. Very beautiful, but lonely. A lake. Great rocks. . . . Yes,—like that place. So odd. . . . I shall have so much time to think, and I shall have no papers—no news. I mustn't talk to you of that. Don't let me talk to you of that. I want to hear about this world, this world I am going to leave, and how you think you are going on fighting in the hot and dusty struggle—to make the world cool and kind and reasonable, to train minds better, to broaden ideas . . . all those things you believe in. All those things you believe in and stick to—even when they are dull. Now I am leaving it, I begin to see how fine it is —to fight as you want to fight. A tiresome inglorious lifelong fight. . . . You really believe, Stephen?"

§ 11

And then suddenly I read her purpose.

"Mary," I cried, and stood up and laid my hand upon her arm, "Tell me what is it you mean to do. What do you mean to do?"

She looked up at me defensively and for a moment neither of us spoke.

"Mary," I said, and could not say what was in my thoughts.

"You are wrong," she lied at last. . . .

She stood up too and faced me. I held her shoulder and looked into her eyes.

The gong of my little clock broke the silence.

"I must go, Stephen," she said. "I did not see how the time was slipping by."

I began to entreat her and she to deny. "You don't understand," she said, "you don't understand. Stephen! —I had hoped you would understand. You see life,— not as I see it. I wanted—all sorts of splendid things and you—begin to argue. You are shocked, you refuse to understand. . . . No. No. Take your hands off me, Stephen dear, and let me go. Let me go!"

"But," I said, stupid and persistent, "what are you going to do?"

"I've told you, Stephen, I've told you. As much as I can tell you. And you think—this foolish thing. As though I could do that! Stephen, if I promise, will you let me go? . . ."

§ 12

My mind leaps from that to the moment in the afternoon, when torn by intolerable distresses and anxiety I knocked and rang, and again knocked at the door of the house she occupied in South Street, with the intention of making one last appeal to her to live—if, indeed, it was death she had in mind. I had let her go from me and instantly a hundred neglected things had come into my head. I could go away with her, I could threaten to die with her; it seemed to me that nothing in all the world mattered if only I could thrust back the dark hand of death to which

356

she had so manifestly turned. I knew, I knew all along that her extorted promise would not bind her. I knew and I let the faintest shadow of uncertainty weaken and restrain me. And I went to her too late. I saw instantly that I was too late when the door opened and showed me the scared face of a young footman whose eyes were red with tears.

"Are you Doctor —— ?" he asked of my silence.

"I want——" I said. "I must speak to Lady Mary."

He was wordless for a moment. "She—she died, sir," he said. "She's died suddenly." His face quivered, he was blubbering. He couldn't say anything more; he stood snivelling in the doorway.

For some moments I remained confronting him as if I would dispute his words. Some things the mind contests in the face of invincible conviction. One wants to thrust back time. . . .

CHAPTER THE TWELFTH

The Arraignment of Jealousy

§ 1

I SIT here in this graciously proportioned little room which I shall leave for ever next week, for already your mother begins to pack for England again. I look out upon the neat French garden that I have watched the summer round, and before me is the pile of manuscript that has grown here, the story of my friendship and love for Mary and of its tragic end, and of all the changes of my beliefs and purposes that have arisen out of that. I had meant it to be the story of my life, but how little of my life is in it! It gives, at most, certain acute points, certain salient aspects. I begin to realize for the first time how thin and suggestive and sketchy a thing any novel or biography must be. How we must simplify! How little can we convey the fullness of life, the glittering interests, the interweaving secondary aspects, the dawns and dreams and double refractions of experience! Even Mary, of whom I have labored to tell you, seems not so much expressed as hidden beneath these corrected sheets. She who was so abundantly living, who could love like a burst of sunshine and give herself as God gives the world, is she here at all in this pile of industrious inexpert writing?

358

THE ARRAIGNMENT

Life is so much fuller than any book can be. All this story can be read, I suppose, in a couple of hours or so, but I have been living and reflecting upon and reconsidering the substance of it for over forty years. I do not see how this book can give you any impression but that of a career all strained upon the frame of one tragic relationship, yet no life unless it is a very short young life can have that simplicity. Of all the many things I have found beautiful and wonderful, Mary was the most wonderful to me, she is in my existence like a sunlit lake seen among mountains, of all the edges by which life has wrought me she was the keenest. Nevertheless she was not all my life, nor the form of all my life. For a time after her death I could endure nothing of my home, I could not bear the presence of your mother or you, I hated the possibility of consolation, I went away into Italy, and it was only by an enormous effort that I could resume my interest in that scheme of work to which my life is given. But it is manifest I still live, I live and work and feel and share beauty. . . .

It seems to me more and more as I live longer, that most poetry and most literature and particularly the literature of the past is discordant with the vastness and variety, the reserves and resources and recuperations of life as we live it to-day. It is the expression of life under cruder and more rigid conditions than ours, lived by people who loved and hated more naïvely, aged sooner and died younger than we do. Solitary persons and single events dominated them as they do not dominate us. We range wider, last longer, and escape more and more from intensity towards understanding. And already this astounding blow begins to take its place among other events, as a thing strange and terrible indeed, but related to all the strangeness and mystery of life, part of the universal mysteries of despair and futility and death that have troubled my consciousness since childhood. For a time the death of Mary obscured her life for me, but now her living presence is more in my mind again. I begin to see that it is the reality of her existence and not the accidents of her end that matter most. It signifies less that she should have flung out of life when it seemed that her living could only have meant disaster to herself and to all she loved, than that all her life should have been hampered and restricted. Through all her life this brave and fine and beautiful being was for the most part of her possibilities, wasted in a splendid setting, magnificently wasted if you will, but wasted.

§ 2

It was that idea of waste that dominated my mind in a strange interview I had with Justin. For it became necessary for me to see Justin in order that we should stamp out the whispers against her that followed her death. He had made it seem an accidental death due to an overdose of the narcotic she employed, but he had not been able to obliterate altogether the beginnings of his divorce proceedings. There had been talk on the part of clerks and possible witnesses. But of all that I need not tell you here; what matters is that Justin and I could meet without hatred or violence. I met a Justin grey-haired and it seemed to me physically shrunken, more than ever slow-speaking, with his habit of attentive silences more marked and that dark scar spread beyond his brows.

We had come to our parting, we had done our business with an affectation of emotional aloofness, and then suddenly he gripped me by the arm. "Stratton," he said, "we two—— We killed her. We tore her to pieces between us. . . ."

I made no answer to this outbreak.

"We tore her to pieces," he repeated. "It's so damned silly. One gets angry—like an animal."

I became grotesquely anxious to assure him that, indeed, she and I had been, as they say, innocent throughout our last day together. "You were wrong in all that," I said. "She kept her faith with you. We never planned to meet and when we met——. If we had been brother and sister——. Indeed there was nothing."

"I suppose," he said, "I ought to be glad of that. But now it doesn't seem to matter very much. We killed her. . . . What does that matter to me now?"

§ 3

And it is upon this effect of sweet and beautiful possibilities, caught in the net of animal jealousies and thoughtless motives and ancient rigid institutions, that I would end this writing. In Mary, it seems to me, I found both womanhood and fellowship, I found what many have dreamt of, love and friendship freely given, and I could do nothing but clutch at her to make her my possession. I would not permit her to live except as a part of my life. I see her now and understand her better than when she was alive, I recall things that she said and wrote and it is clear to me, clearer perhaps than it ever was to her, that she, with her resentment at being in any sense property, her self-reliant thought, her independence of standard, was the very prototype of that sister-lover who must replace the seductive and abject womanhood, owned, mastered and deceiving, who waste the world to-day. And she was owned, she was mastered, she was forced into concealment. What alternative was there for her? What alternative is there for any woman? She might perhaps have kept her freedom by some ill-paid work and at the price of every other impulse in her swift and eager nature. She might have become one of those poor neuters, an independent woman. . . . Life was made impossible for her and she was forced to die, according to the fate of all untimely things. She was destroyed, not merely by the unconsidered, undisciplined passions of her husband and her lover, but by the vast tradition that sustains and enforces the subjugation of her sex. What I had from her, and what she was, is but a mere intimation of all that she and I might have made of each other and the world.

And perhaps in this story I have said enough for you to understand why Mary has identified herself with something world-wide, has added to herself a symbolical value, and why it is I find in the whole crowded spectacle of mankind, a quality that is also hers, a sense of fine things entangled and stifled and unable to free themselves from the ancient limiting jealousies which law and custom embody. For I know that a growing multitude of men and women outwear the ancient ways. The blood-stained organized jealousies of religious intolerance, the delusions of nationality and cult and race, that black hatred which simple people and young people and common people cherish against all that is not in the likeness

THE ARRAIGNMENT

of themselves, cease to be the undisputed ruling forces of our collective life. We want to emancipate our lives from this slavery and these stupidities, from dull hatreds and suspicion. The ripening mind of our race tires of these boorish and brutish and childish things. A spirit that is like hers, arises and increases in human affairs, a spirit that demands freedom and gracious living as our inheritance too long deferred, and I who loved her so blindly and narrowly now love her spirit with a dawning understanding.

I will not be content with that compromise of jealousies which is the established life of humanity to-day. I give myself, and if I can I will give you, to the destruction of jealousy and of the forms and shelters and instruments of jealousy, both in my own self and in the thought and laws and usage of the world.

THE END

33 95

3-10-11 2

Printed in the United States
88183LV00001B/103/A

9 780766 169845